EGGNOG MURDER

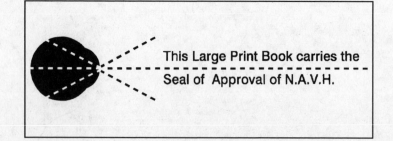

This Large Print Book carries the
Seal of Approval of N.A.V.H.

EGGNOG MURDER

LESLIE MEIER,
LEE HOLLIS
AND BARBARA ROSS

THORNDIKE PRESS
A part of Gale, Cengage Learning

Farmington Hills, Mich • San Francisco • New York • Waterville, Maine
Meriden, Conn • Mason, Ohio • Chicago

LIBRARY OF CONGRESS CATALOGING-IN-PUBLICATION DATA

Names: Meier, Leslie. Eggnog murder. | Hollis, Lee. Death by eggnog. | Ross, Barbara, 1953– Nogged off.
Title: Eggnog murder / by Leslie Meier, Lee Hollis and Barbara Ross.
Description: Waterville, Maine : Thorndike Press Large Print, 2016. | Series: Thorndike Press large print mystery
Identifiers: LCCN 2016037203| ISBN 9781410492784 (hardback) | ISBN 1410492788 (hardcover)
Subjects: LCSH: Detective and mystery stories, American. | Christmas stories, American. | Large type books. | BISAC: FICTION / Mystery & Detective / General.
Classification: LCC PS648.D4 E29 2016 | DDC 813/.087208—dc23
LC record available at https://lccn.loc.gov/2016037203

Published in 2016 by arrangement with Kensington Books, an imprint of Kensington Publishing Corp.

Printed in Mexico
1 2 3 4 5 6 7 20 19 18 17 16

CONTENTS

■ ■ ■ ■

EGGNOG MURDER

LESLIE MEIER

■ ■ ■ ■

CHAPTER ONE

" 'Beware of gifts from strangers,' that's what I told Wilf, when he found this bottle of eggnog on the back porch," said Phyllis, producing a distinctive old-fashioned milk bottle decorated with red and green ribbons and a sprig of faux holly from her red and green plaid tote bag and setting it on the reception counter in the *Pennysaver* office. The *Pennysaver,* formerly the *Courier and Advertiser,* was the weekly newspaper in the coastal town of Tinker's Cove, Maine.

"He said it wasn't from strangers, it's a welcome gift from this new club he's joined," she continued. Phyllis's official title was receptionist at the *Pennysaver,* but that only began to describe her duties, as she handled ads, subscriptions, billing, and the classifieds. Today was the Monday after Thanksgiving and the Christmas season had officially begun, so she had painted her fingernails in alternating shades of red and green polish and was wearing a sparkly sweater. She had long ago forgotten what color her hair actually was, but had dyed it a brighter shade of red than usual, also in honor of the holiday. Her cat's-eye reading glasses were decorated with candy cane stripes and were resting on her ample bosom, where they dangled from a rhinestone-encrusted chain. No one dared to ask Phyllis how old she was, but somewhere between fifty and sixty was a safe guess.

"What club is that?" asked Lucy Stone, who worked part time at the paper as a reporter and feature writer. She was already seated at her desk this Monday morning, tapping away on her computer keyboard. Lucy wore her dark hair in a short, easy-care cut and dressed in easy-care clothes, usually jeans and a sweater. In warm weather she wore running shoes, but now, since it was almost winter, she was wearing duck boots like just about everyone else in the little Maine town.

"The Real Beard Santa Club," replied Phyllis. "He was driving me crazy hanging around the house, now that he's retired from the postal service, but I can't say I'm very happy about his choice."

"I don't suppose growing a beard actually

keeps a person very busy," said Lucy, who was struggling to decipher the notes she'd scribbled when covering a Conservation Commission meeting. "Which is more likely?" she asked Phyllis. "Does the commission want to require that *dogs be leashed* in the conservation area or *days be limited*? The only word I'm sure of is *be.*"

"Probably both — I wouldn't put anything past that bunch of nincompoops," grumbled Phyllis, voicing the suspicion of the town's regulatory boards that was heard whenever two or more taxpayers were gathered together. "And like you said, growing a beard isn't really an occupation that keeps a person busy, though now that I think about it, Wilf does spend a lot of time in front of the bathroom mirror, admiring his facial growth. I told him it's like watching a pot to make it boil, admiring it in the mirror isn't going to make it grow any faster." She paused. "To tell the truth, I really don't like the beard. . . ."

"No?" asked Lucy, whose husband, Bill, had grown a beard when he gave up his Wall Street job to become a restoration carpenter in Maine, a move they'd made more than twenty years before. Once a lustrous brown, these days Bill's beard was lightly sprinkled with gray. "Why not?"

11

"Lots of reasons. It seems dirty. It's prickly when I kiss him. I miss seeing his chin. It makes him look old."

"Well, Santa's no spring chicken," said Lucy, reluctantly coming to the conclusion that she'd better call Dorcas Philpott, the chairwoman of the Conservation Commission. "And he's much fatter than Wilf. Is he going to try to gain weight so he'll have a belly that shakes when he laughs like a bowlful of jelly?" asked Lucy, paraphrasing the famous Christmas poem.

"Absolutely not," snapped Phyllis. "That was the deal. I'll put up with the beard but not a Santa-sized stomach." Her tone became very serious. "You know how they say belly fat increases your chances of dying young, and I'm not taking any chances. We got married late in life and I want to have as much time together as possible, so he's going to have to keep eating healthy. He says I've got him eating like a reindeer, what with all the baby carrots, but I'm not giving in. He'll have to wear padding, that's all there is to it."

"Is that okay with the Real Beard Santa Club?" asked Lucy, who was reaching for the phone. "They have to have real beards, but it's okay to have a fake stomach?"

"I presume so," said Phyllis, primly. "It's

not called the Real Belly Santa Club, now, is it?"

Lucy was suppressing a laugh when Dorcas Philpott answered the phone on the first ring. "Oh, Lucy, it's you," she said, with a distinct lack of enthusiasm when Lucy identified herself. "I was waiting for the oil man to call — my furnace went out. You know, for a while there at the meeting I thought you might be falling asleep."

"Oh, no, not at all," claimed Lucy, who had in fact struggled to stay awake during the evening meeting, which had not adjourned until after eleven o'clock. "But I do have a question about my notes. I can't seem to read my own handwriting."

"Well, I can't say I'm surprised, people nowadays hardly ever take pen to paper, they just poke at electronic screens. Do you know they don't even teach cursive writing anymore?" asked Dorcas, her voice trembling with indignation. "I was shocked when my granddaughter asked why my writing was so funny looking!"

"I didn't know that," admitted Lucy, fearing she wouldn't be able to keep Dorcas on track. "But about the meeting?"

"We should have a meeting with the school committee," declared Dorcas, jumping on the idea. "And let them know that

13

dropping penmanship instruction is simply not an option. They have a responsibility . . ."

"That's a good idea," said Lucy. "But about the concom meeting, didn't you make some new regulations for the conservation area?"

"They say it's because everyone uses computers these days, that nobody needs to have good penmanship, but I ask you: Can you write a proper thank-you note on a computer? And what about notes of condolence? Those absolutely must be on the very best plain white paper and written with great care. . . ."

"My late mother would most certainly agree with you," said Lucy, who had been most carefully instructed in the rules of formal correspondence, and thanks to an eighth-grade dance class she'd found excruciatingly awkward could also dance the waltz and the fox-trot, not to mention the cha-cha and Charleston. Times had changed, however, and she had found these skills were no longer appreciated or valued as they once were. "Now, are you changing the hours that the conservation area is open?"

"Where did you get an idea like that?" demanded Dorcas. "Next thing you'll be telling me we'll be requiring dogs to be leashed."

"I did wonder about that," admitted Lucy.

"I noticed you nodding off," said Dorcas. "Try coffee, that's what I do. I find a cup of coffee after dinner enables me to stay sharp in the evening, which is when I usually handle my correspondence — which I might add, I write by hand, with a fountain pen."

"I'll keep it in mind," said Lucy. "So no action was taken on either issue?"

"They were both tabled for a later meeting," admitted Dorcas. "But I will be expecting to see a story in the paper about the school committee's shortsighted and irresponsible decision to drop penmanship from the curriculum. . . ."

"I'll look into it and run it by Ted," said Lucy, ending the call just as the little bell on the door jangled, announcing Ted Stillings's arrival.

"What are you going to run by me?" asked Ted, bringing in a burst of cold air that made Phyllis, whose desk was by the door, shiver and pull the sides of her cardigan sweater together across her substantial chest. Ted was the chief reporter, editor, and publisher of the *Pennysaver,* which he owned. In other words, Ted was the boss.

"Hi, Ted," said Lucy, greeting him with a

15

smile. "I was talking to Dorcas Philpott. She says the school committee voted to drop penmanship from the curriculum and she's worried that the kids won't know how to write thank-you notes."

"That ship has sailed," declared Ted, hanging up his hat and coat. "Pam says she never gets thank-you notes from any of our ungrateful nieces and nephews, and not from Tim, either, even though our son was brought up to write them," said Ted, picking up the bottle of eggnog and examining it. "What's this?"

"It's eggnog, Phyllis brought it," said Lucy.

"It was given to Wilf as a welcome present from the Real Beard Santa Club. He's just joined and eggnog is the club's official drink," said Phyllis.

"Doesn't he want to drink it?" asked Ted. "Why is it here?"

"Wilf would love to drink it, but I won't let him," said Phyllis, who was reaching for the phone, which was ringing.

"Why can't Wilf drink his eggnog?" asked Ted.

"Because it's fattening," said Lucy, "and Phyllis made a deal that he can grow a real beard, even though she doesn't much like beards, but she doesn't want him to have a

16

Santa-sized stomach."

"Oh," said Ted, studying the bottle with hungry eyes. Hearing the jangle on the door, he turned, smiling as Corney Clark breezed in. "You're just in time, Corney. I'm thinking about cracking open this eggnog. Will you join me? It's officially Christmas, you know."

Corney stopped in her tracks, recoiling from the bottle. "I never touch the stuff. It might as well be poison!"

Ted looked crestfallen. "What do you mean? It's Christmas and eggnog is the traditional drink." He paused, thinking. "I've actually got a bottle of whiskey in my desk — journalistic tradition, you know? I could doctor it up. . . ."

"You're mad! Take the most fattening drink in the history of the world and add more calories?" Corney pulled off her knitted cap and shook out her blond hair, which she got cut and colored every six weeks at great expense in Portland. "And I might add that the sun is not anywhere near the yard-arm, much less over it!"

"I never thought you were a party pooper," grumbled Ted, replacing the bottle on the counter.

"I am certainly not a party pooper, I enjoy a good time as much as anyone. Why not serve the eggnog at the holiday stroll on Friday?" suggested Corney, remembering the errand that had brought her to the paper. She was the director of the Tinker's Cove Chamber of Commerce and her job required her to work closely with the *Pennysaver* staff to promote local events. "This year's stroll is going to be bigger and better than ever. We want to encourage people to shop here in town and support local businesses."

"Bigger and better's not saying much," said Phyllis. "Last year's stroll was pretty much a non-event. Wilf and I got all bundled up and attempted to finish up our Christmas shopping, but only a few places stayed open after six o'clock."

"That's true," said Lucy, with a nod. "Bill and I brought our grandson, Patrick, thinking he'd enjoy the horse-drawn sleigh ride. . . ."

"I know, I know," admitted Corney, pulling off her gloves and stuffing them in her designer handbag. "Ed Hemmings had to cancel because one of his horses lost a shoe and he couldn't get hold of the blacksmith. A lot of people were disappointed, which is why this year I'm determined to make it the best stroll ever. I've gotten commitments from every business on Main Street; they've

18

all agreed to stay open until nine and they're all going to offer refreshments and special promotions, raffles, giveaways, free gift wrapping, it's going to be great."

She paused for breath, then pointed a finger at Ted. "This is an opportunity for you, too, Ted. You can open your doors, put out eggnog and cookies, and offer a special reduced rate for new subscribers."

"Most everybody in town subscribes already," said Ted.

"Well, offer a special rate to folks to extend their subscriptions," said Corney, refusing to be deterred. "You know, the Chamber is a major advertiser, and that's why I'm here. The stroll will kick off the holiday shopping season — we only have three weekends this year because Christmas Eve is on a Saturday — and I want to go over the special insert with you and make sure it's got all the latest information . . ."

Ted scratched his chin thoughtfully. "There's still some ad space in the insert. I could run an announcement about the special offer," he said.

"And give the Chamber a break on the cost?" urged Corney, who didn't miss a trick.

Lucy bit her lip, wondering how Ted would react. She knew that these were

19

tough times for independent newspapers that faced competition from the Internet, rising costs, and ever-fewer readers.

"Why not?" said Ted with a nod of agreement. "It is Christmas after all."

"That's the spirit!" exclaimed Corney, pulling a couple of sheets of paper that were rather the worse for wear out of her tote and presenting them to Ted with a flourish. "This is going to be the most wonderful Christmas Tinker's Cove has ever seen!"

Ted ushered Corney into the morgue, which doubled as conference room, to put the final touches on the insert. Phyllis got up and put the eggnog in the office minifridge where they stashed their lunches and coffee creamer, and Lucy returned to her Conservation Commission notes, which remained as indecipherable as ever. She was about to raise the white flag and call the commission's secretary and beg for help when her cell phone beeped. A glance at the display revealed the caller was her oldest daughter, Elizabeth, calling from Paris where she worked at the tony Cavendish Hotel.

"Hi!" exclaimed Lucy, adding one of the phrases she remembered from high school French. *"Ça va?"*

"Très bien, merci, Maman," replied Eliza-

beth, automatically replying in French, but losing none of the efficient manner that had enabled her to leave the reception desk and cross the Cavendish's tastefully decorated lobby to her present post at the concierge's desk. She promptly switched to English. "Everything is fine, I just want to check some dates with you — I'm coming home for Christmas."

"That's wonderful!" exclaimed Lucy. "You're coming home for Christmas! When are you coming? How long can you stay?"

"That's what I want to discuss with you," said Elizabeth. Lucy could picture her, seated at an antique Louis XIV desk, thoughtfully fiddling with a pen and making careful notes. "I can get a seat on a flight December twenty-third, but it's expensive, but if I come two weeks earlier, on December ninth, it's much cheaper. I have a lot of vacation time due me, but I'm not sure about staying for such a long visit, especially since the house is already pretty full. . . ."

"Don't be silly!" declared Lucy, in a burst of motherly affection. She'd been thrilled when her son, Toby, who had been working on developing sustainable fisheries in Alaska, had announced he'd been sent to nearby Winchester College for a year to continue his graduate-level studies in genetic modification. Since their house on nearby Prudence Path was rented while they were in Alaska, Toby's little family had moved in with Lucy and Bill. "Toby and Molly are using the family room, so there's plenty of room upstairs. Patrick's little," she continued, referring to her adored five-year-old grandson, "he can sleep anywhere."

"Well, you know what they say about fish and company, that they stink after three days. . . ."

"You're not company, you're family!" said Lucy.

"Okay," said Elizabeth. "I'll order the tickets. I'll arrive in Boston on December ninth, at five forty-five PM. Can somebody pick me up at the airport? I looked into connecting flights to Rockland, but they're all sold out."

"That's a three-hour drive into rush hour on a Friday in Boston," said Lucy, a note of dismay in her voice. She'd been caught in Boston traffic a few too many times and knew that Friday evenings were the worst as the city's entire population seemed to be leaving for the weekend. "Couldn't you take the bus?"

"Mom!" protested Elizabeth. "I'm coming all the way from Paris and you want me to take the bus?"

"Of course not," said Lucy, relenting. "How about a limo? My treat?"

"I am really surprised, Mom. Don't you want to see me as soon as you can?"

"Of course I do," said Lucy, somewhat chastened. "I'll take the afternoon off to give myself plenty of time, and after I meet you we can get a bite to eat before attempting Route 1."

"Super!" exclaimed Elizabeth, pronouncing it "soup-air" in the French manner. *"A bientôt!"*

"A bientôt," replied Lucy, ending the call. She was saddened to realize she wasn't quite as enthusiastic about Elizabeth's homecoming as she had been at first. Maybe Elizabeth was on to something when she suggested a short visit would be preferable to a long one. Then she shook her head, remembering how much she loved her daughter and how eager she was to see her, and made up her mind to banish such thoughts. "I'm being a Grinch," she decided, taking a page from Corney's book and resolving to make this Christmas the best Stone Family Christmas ever, a Christmas when the entire family would be together.

CHAPTER TWO

After work, Lucy headed over to her friend Sue Finch's house for a late-afternoon meeting of the Hat and Mitten Fund. Lucy and Sue, along with their friends Rachel Goodman and Pam Stillings (who was married to Lucy's boss, Ted), had created the fund some years ago to provide warm winter clothing for the town's less fortunate children. The plan at first had been to simply collect outgrown parkas, boots, and snow pants, but they soon realized the need was much greater than they had imagined and began organizing fund-raisers so they could also provide school supplies as well as formula and diapers for babies. This year they were planning an ambitious holiday gala and raffle featuring a dinner dance and a visit from Santa.

It was already dark when she pulled up in front of Sue's house, which was a handsome Federalist style home located on a street filled with large houses built in the 1800s by prosperous merchants and sea captains, and she smiled to see that Sue and her husband, Sid, had already put up their outdoor Christmas decorations. Brass urns containing Christmas trees with lights and red bows were placed on either side of the front door, which also held a large wreath. All of the windows on the front of the house were illuminated by electric candles and were decorated with wreaths, and the branches of a Japanese maple on the front lawn were outlined with tiny twinkling lights.

She gave a couple of knocks on the door, then opened it and hallooed, which was the custom in a town where nobody bothered to lock their doors. She was greeted with the scent of cinnamon potpourri and a call to come on in to the kitchen.

She knew the way well and continued through the hall, past the staircase whose banister was wrapped in a pine garland, and pausing to take a peek at the enormous Christmas tree in the living room and the bowl of blooming amaryllis in the center of the dining room table. As usual, Sue had set up a smaller tree in her country French kitchen, decorated with cookie cutters and gingerbread men.

"Wow, Sue, you've certainly got the Christmas spirit," exclaimed Lucy, joining her friends at the antique wine-tasting table that was Sue's pride and joy. She plucked a cookie from the plate of holiday treats that Sue had set out for her friends — but wouldn't dream of eating herself — and took a bite. "This chocolate crinkle is fabulous."

"They did come out well," said Sue, tucking a lock of her carefully maintained black hair behind an ear with a beautifully manicured hand and causing the other three to share amused smiles. "I discovered you have to let the dough sit on the counter for ten minutes before you shape the cookies. It's like magic."

"And the decorations are beautiful," added Lucy. "I don't know how you do it."

"It's nothing, really," said Sue, with a shrug. "Sid and I just pull out stuff we've collected over the years."

"Oh, right," said Pam, who had been a college cheerleader and still wore her hair in a ponytail, "you must have been working on all this for weeks. I wonder, how long did it take Sid to wrap that tree with all those lights?"

"Not as long as you'd think, once Sid got the knack of it," insisted Sue, referring to her husband, who had a custom closet business. "But I did have to show him that wrapping was much nicer than just draping the lights so they're all droopy and weird." She paused. "I just hate that, don't you?"

Lucy thought of how she and Bill had struggled to hang what was undeniably a free-form pattern of Christmas lights last weekend and kept her peace. She had long ago given up comparing herself to Sue, who was, like Mary Poppins, "practically perfect in every way."

"I think it's wonderful that Sid and Sue get in the spirit of the holiday," said Rachel, who had majored in psychology in college and never got over it. She was married to Bob, a busy lawyer with a practice in town. "Holidays are a way of coming together as a community, they're very life-affirming."

"I think this is going to be a very special Christmas," said Lucy. "We're going to have the whole family, for the first time in years. Elizabeth's coming home . . . ."

"You must be thrilled!" enthused Pam. "Your baby girl is coming home!"

"She can tell us what they're wearing in Paris. . . ." said Sue.

"It is wonderful when adult children come home, but there can also be challenges," warned Rachel.

27

"We'll roll with the punches," vowed Lucy, thinking of the many times she'd been tempted to offer advice to her daughter-in-law, Molly, but had bitten her tongue, fearing that Molly would take it as criticism. "Meanwhile, let's get busy here. I've got to cook supper for a hungry family."

"Doesn't Molly help out?" asked Pam.

"She does, but she's into whole grains and veggies in a big way and Bill loves his spaghetti with meatballs," confessed Lucy, with a wry smile. "Like Rachel says, living with extended family is sometimes challenging."

"I bet it is," said Sue, flipping open a file folder and consulting the top sheet of paper. "But to get back on track, so far we've sold a hundred and forty-six tickets. . . ."

"Only fifty-four to go, that's great!" said Pam.

"Oh, I forgot, I sold twelve last week," said Rachel.

"Even better, that gets us to a hundred and fifty-eight sold, forty-two to go," said Sue, making a notation, and then putting down her pencil and adopting a serious expression. "But we do have a problem. Our Santa has canceled; he's going to have hip-replacement surgery."

"Oh, no," moaned Pam. "It won't be a

Christmas gala without Santa!"

"We'll just have to get someone else," said Rachel, with a shrug. "I suppose Bob could do it. . . ."

"Bob's really skinny and he doesn't have a beard," said Pam.

"He's awfully serious, which is great for a lawyer, and I love him, don't get me wrong, but he's not really a ho-ho-ho sort of guy," said Sue.

"He can wear a costume," insisted Rachel.

"I've got it," announced Lucy. "We can hire Wilf. He's actually growing a beard, he's a genuine member of the Real Beard Santa Club."

"Great," said Sue, crossing that item off her list. "Now, what about tablecloths? Red, green or white? I saw some plaid ones. . . ."

Driving to work the next morning, Lucy replayed the dinner table conversation from the previous night. Bill had been delighted to learn that his oldest daughter was coming home for Christmas; Elizabeth had enchanted him from the moment she was born, screaming her head off in protest. Toby and Molly were also pleased, and explained to Patrick that his aunt Elizabeth would be coming from faraway France in a jet plane. Her sisters, Sara and Zoe, however, hadn't been quite so enthusiastic.

"Does this mean I have to move back in with Zoe?" demanded Sara, with a scowl. There had been a natural rearrangement of the family's sleeping quarters after Toby and Elizabeth left home, and the two younger sisters who had shared a room now each had one of her own. Patrick was now occupying his father's old room, complete with original *Star Wars* posters, while Molly and Toby were using the family room sleep sofa, which offered more privacy than the close quarters upstairs in the old farmhouse.

"I'm not sharing with Sara," declared Zoe. "She's on her computer half the night doing research for her senior thesis." Sara was a senior at nearby Winchester College, where she was majoring in earth science.

"This thesis is my ticket to graduate school and I've got to have someplace to work," protested Sara. "It's bad enough listening to Little Miss Chatterbox here, yammering away to her friends all night." Zoe also attended Winchester, where she was a freshman, apparently majoring in being the most popular girl on campus.

"Well, there's more to college than being a grind," countered Zoe. "I'm establishing contacts for the rest of my life. It's called networking."

"Well, I don't think either of you has to move," said Bill. "Elizabeth can stay in Toby's old room with Patrick. We'll set up the rollaway cot for Patrick."

"I don't want a crib," protested Patrick, looking worried. "I'm a big boy now."

"A cot, sweetie, not a crib," said Molly. "It's the same size as your bed, but it folds up so you can put it out of the way when you're not sleeping."

"Okay," he agreed, sounding doubtful and pushing his meatball around on his plate, watched closely by the family's black Lab, Libby.

"Toby's room is full of Patrick's stuff," said Sara, referring to the ever-growing collection of toys provided by the little boy's indulgent grandparents.

"Not to mention Toby's old posters," said Zoe, giggling. "The décor is not *à la français,* for sure."

"We can organize the toys and take down the posters," said Lucy, "maybe even slap up some paint. That room could use it."

Now, as she drove the familiar route to work, Lucy was wondering when she and Bill would find the time to redecorate Toby's old room in the midst of the Christmas blitz of activity. Maybe they could get away with a quick clean-up and a new bedspread?

31

The *Pennysaver* office was empty when she arrived; she liked to get in early because she could get a lot done before the phones started ringing and people started dropping in. But this morning the phone was already ringing when she unlocked the door and turned on the lights.

"*Pennysaver,* this is Lucy," she said, grabbing the nearest phone, which happened to be on Phyllis's desk behind the reception counter.

"Uh, I want to submit an oh-oh-oh," began a woman, with a quavery voice.

It was a phenomenon Lucy was familiar with. "An obituary?" she replied, in a gentle, coaxing voice.

"That's right," responded the woman, in a somewhat firmer tone.

Lucy knew that certain words were minefields for the bereaved, and *obituary* was definitely one of them. "I'll be happy to take the information," she said, aware that maintaining a kind but businesslike tone seemed to help. "What is your name?"

"Nancy Fredericks. I live at 14 Winter Street here in town. Do you want my phone number?"

"Yes, please," said Lucy, who was writing it all down in the reporter's notebook she always carried and had pulled out of her purse.

"Can I pay with a credit card?" asked Nancy.

"That's not necessary. We don't charge, this is a community service," she said, careful to omit the word *obituary*.

"That's nice," said Nancy with a sniffle.

Lucy braced herself. Now came the hard part. "The name of the deceased," she asked, quickly adding, "and your relationship?"

There was a pause before Nancy finally spoke. "It was my sister, Holly. Holly Fredericks."

"I just need to check the spelling," said Lucy, who had found that the journalist's need for accuracy was also a useful technique for helping a grieving person to get past her emotional hurdles.

Nancy spelled out her sister's name, adding that she would have been forty-four, if she had lived until her birthday, which was Christmas Eve.

"That's awfully young," said Lucy, somewhat shocked, and straying from her usual script. "Do you want to give a cause?"

Now Nancy's voice was somewhat stronger, almost angry. "Well, I guess you could say complications from her condition, which was that she was completely paralyzed from the neck down. She was a vet, you know, she was in the first Iraq war, but medals and parades don't really matter much when you're flat on your back and have to be fed through a straw and you can't even clean yourself."

Lucy knew that due to medical advances many of the soldiers who were wounded in the Middle Eastern conflicts had survived, but often had to contend with missing limbs, paralysis, and posttraumatic stress. Hardest for some of these brave souls, she imagined, was having to rely on others for their care. "Were you her caregiver?" she asked.

"I was. I did the best I could," said Nancy, "but it wasn't enough. She got pneumonia, it's not unusual with paralysis, you know."

"I know," said Lucy. "In cases like this we usually put in 'complications from a long-term disability,' is that all right?"

Receiving Nancy's murmured assent, Lucy continued. "Do you want to tell me a little about her? You said she was in the Army, what prompted her to enlist?"

"It was back in 1990, she was looking for adventure." There was a pause, then Nancy added, "And, of course, she wanted to serve her country and when President Bush announced he was sending troops to fight Saddam she signed up."

"And where did she serve? What was her rank?"

"She was part of Operation Desert Storm, doing community work, you know, building schools and health clinics in Iraq." There was a long pause. "She liked working with the kids there, especially the girls. She'd give them magazines, they loved those celebrity magazines. *People* and *OK!* They were supposed to be building democracy, but we know that didn't really work out, did it?"

Lucy heard the anger in Nancy's voice and wanted to avoid a discussion about the nation's foreign policy, so she returned to the usual format. "Any special interests?"

"She loved dogs, she had a companion dog at first, Wolfie, but he got run over by a car."

"I'm sorry," said Lucy, thinking how upset she'd be if anything happened to her Libby. "Did she enjoy books? TV?"

"Oh, yes. She loved those *CSI* shows, and *Ellen,* of course. She watched a lot of TV."

"It's a godsend, when a person's ill," said Lucy, remembering watching Three Stooges shows with Toby when he was in the hospital with appendicitis.

"And she liked audiobooks, too," said

Nancy. "Those *Outlander* books, you know."

"Those are great," said Lucy. "What about survivors? Friends? Family?"

"There's just me," said Nancy, with a sniffle. "We were a small family and I'm all that's left."

Moving right along, Lucy asked about funeral arrangements. She was just finishing up, getting contact information for a local animal shelter, which Nancy had specified for donations in lieu of flowers, when the little bell on the door jangled and Ted came in.

"That's the Best Friends Forever No-Kill Shelter," repeated Lucy. "And if you'd like to drop off a photo, we can run it with the story, but we would need it before noon on Wednesday. That's tomorrow," she added, mindful that bereaved people often lost track of time.

"I'll see what I can find," promised Nancy.

"Thanks for your call," said Lucy, "I appreciate this opportunity to honor your sister."

Lucy replaced the handset in its holder and let out a big sigh. "An obit call is not the best way to start the day," she said, speaking to Ted, who was hanging his jacket on the coat stand.

"It never ceases to amaze me, but obits

are the most popular part of the paper. A lot of big papers are charging for them, they're real moneymakers. And I can't tell you how many people tell me that the obits are the first thing they turn to." He cracked a smile. "Just checking that they're not there, they say."

"This was a sad one. A vet, a young woman, only forty-four," said Lucy, who had moved to her own desk and was powering up her computer. "Came back from Desert Storm completely paralyzed."

"That's awful," said Ted, busying himself making a pot of coffee. "Desert Storm was in the early nineties, wasn't it?"

Lucy consulted Google. "1991. That was more than twenty-five years ago."

"And all this time, this poor wounded vet has been right here in Tinker's Cove and nobody knew," speculated Ted.

"It's shameful, isn't it? Maybe I could cover the funeral," suggested Lucy. "We haven't really done anything about local returning vets, have we?"

The coffee began to drip, filling the office with its warm aroma, and Ted sat down in his desk chair, crossing his arms across his chest and leaning back, propping one ankle on the other knee. "It's definitely overdue," he said in a decisive tone. "We could do a story, or even better, a series. . . ." He looked up as Phyllis bustled in, with an array of shopping bags and totes dangling from her arms. "Been shopping?" he asked.

"Early bird sale at the outlet mall," she replied. "Began at six AM."

"Looks like you did well," said Lucy, adding a sigh. "My day began with an obit."

"Better you than I," said Phyllis, stowing the bags beneath the reception counter.

"The deceased was only forty-four, a female vet," said Ted, who was definitely getting excited about his idea. "I'm thinking of running a series on disabled vets, and maybe even starting a campaign to raise money for the Honor the Heroes fund. What do you think?"

"With one of those thermometer charts?" asked Phyllis, who had hung her coat on the rack and was now checking the thermostat, something she did every morning.

"Don't touch it, it's at sixty-eight," ordered Ted.

"Feels chilly to me," said Phyllis, putting on the sparkly sweater she'd left hanging on the back of her desk chair. "And I don't like your idea about featuring disabled vets. . . ."

"Why not?" protested Lucy. "After all they've sacrificed for us . . ."

"Let me finish," Phyllis said, holding up

her hand with one finger raised. "I was going to say, before I was so rudely interrupted, that I don't think we should cover vets now, at Christmas. It's not very holidayish, but it would be a good way to start the New Year."

"I think she's right," said Ted. "But that leaves us without a feature. Any ideas?"

"Sure do," said Phyllis, a note of triumph in her voice. "How about the Real Beard Santa Club?"

"You can't get more Christmas than that," said Lucy.

"Okay," said Ted, starting up his computer. "But you've got to interview somebody beside Wilf. That could be a conflict of interest."

"I can get a list of contacts from Wilf," said Phyllis.

"I'm on it, boss," said Lucy, ashamed to admit she would rather shelve the issue of the disabled vets, at least until Christmas was over.

CHAPTER THREE

Lucy had no trouble at all getting an interview with Kris Kringle, the president of the Real Beard Santa Club. He invited her to come to the next meeting of the executive committee, which just happened to be taking place later that week, on Friday afternoon, at his home in Northville, which was some distance away.

"We're gearing up for the season, you see," he explained, adding that the meeting would take place at his home, North Pole Farm, in the nearby town of Christmas Point. As she drove the country roads to Christmas Point she wondered what North Pole Farm would be like, and tickled her imagination by creating a mini version of Santa's Village, the New Hampshire amusement park that she'd visited when the kids were small.

She wasn't totally surprised, therefore, when she saw the huge red sleigh displayed next to the driveway, but even she hadn't imagined the small herd of reindeer that were busy munching hay that had been scattered on the fenced front lawn. Several cars were parked in the large driveway, and she smiled to see the vanity license plates: H0-H0-H0, MR-CLAUS, and ELF-1. After parking alongside them she stepped onto the roomy porch of the log cabin–style home and rang the bell, which sounded like sleigh bells.

Kris Kringle, a bearded gentleman dressed in a red and green plaid shirt and red pants held up with suspenders, answered the door and ushered her into a pine-scented hallway, which was filled with several artificial Christmas trees. He apologized for that fact, explaining that otherwise they couldn't stay up all year-round. "Come on in and meet the others," he urged, leading her into a large room with a stone fireplace, where a number of Christmas stockings hung from the mantel, beneath a large painting of Rudolph, the red-nosed reindeer.

Lucy had expected to meet more Santas, but still found it somewhat surreal to walk into a room filled with jolly old elves. Each of the bearded gentlemen was wearing a complete Santa suit, right down to the sturdy black boots, and they greeted her

41

with a chorus of hearty ho-ho-hos.

"As you know, I'm Kris," said her host. "These fellas are Harold Jansen, Bill Flynn, and Jack Johanson. Harold is the vice president, Bill is secretary, and Jack —"

"Has the thankless job of treasurer," said Jack, finishing the introduction.

"Great to meet you all," said Lucy. "Thanks for letting me interview you for the newspaper, it's going to be a great holiday feature."

"Well, make yourself comfortable," urged Kris, taking her coat. "Can I get you some eggnog?" he asked, indicating a tray on the coffee table containing a vintage-style milk bottle just like the one Phyllis had brought to work, minus the ribbons and faux holly. "It's our own blend, we sell it at holiday fairs. . . ."

"It's very popular," said Bill.

"And we're thinking of licensing it to one of the big dairies, like Hood or Garelick," said Jack. "Kind of like Girl Scout cookies."

"I guess I'll have to try some," said Lucy, seating herself in one of the overstuffed chairs that filled the room and pulling her notebook out of her bag. "As it happens, our receptionist at the paper, Phyllis, is married to your newest member, Wilf Lundgren."

"Wilf's a great guy, we're glad to have him," said Bill.

"And his beard is coming along nicely," said Kris, presenting Lucy with a crystal punch cup full of creamy liquid.

Lucy took a sip and, finding it delicious, downed a big swallow. "That is amazing," she said, mentally adding up the calories she suspected the mixture must contain. "Heavy cream?" she asked. "Plenty of vanilla, a dash of nutmeg . . ."

"It's a secret recipe, but we don't skimp on the good stuff," said Harold, patting his stomach. It was a substantial tummy, and Harold wasn't the only one with a genuine Santa belly. Realizing that all four of the men looked to weigh at least 200 pounds apiece, Lucy decided that Phyllis was on to something when she refused to let Wilf drink his eggnog. She set down her half-empty cup, deciding it was time to get started on the interview. "I guess you get asked this all the time, but is Kris Kringle your real name?"

"You're right. I do get asked that all the time and it sure is my moniker. My dad was Kris Kringle and his dad before him, and so on. I figured there was no sense fighting destiny, so I've just gone with it and made it my profession."

"So there's money in being Kris Kringle?" asked Lucy.

"Sure is. I make appearances at malls and parties, business conferences, you name it. If I bring the reindeer, I charge extra." He paused. "In case you were wondering, I have a special permit to keep the reindeer. They're all rescue reindeer, unable to live in the wild, you see."

"How interesting," said Lucy, turning to the other bearded gentlemen. "Are you all professional Santas?"

"Not to the same extent as Kris," said Bill, "but I do Christmas parties."

"I've got a gig at the Maine Mall," said Jack.

"I'm a lawyer," confessed Harold, "but my grandkids get a big kick out of my Santa act."

"So the club members include hobbyists, part-time and full-time Santas?" asked Lucy.

"Right. But we all have real Santa-style beards."

Lucy couldn't help smiling, thinking of their real Santa-style tummies and Phyllis's fantastic invention of the Real Belly Santa Club. "So I assume you are mostly older gentlemen? And are there any women?"

"We have younger members, and some of them bleach their beards," said Kris. "But so far no bearded ladies."

"If one did come along, we'd have to admit her," said Harold, "otherwise we'd be discriminating. And we do have a special membership category for the Mrs. Santas."

"So what does membership entail?" asked Lucy.

"Well, we have a convention every July, Christmas in July it's called, where we get together with members from other chapters. We're nationwide, you know," said Kris, producing a thick photo album. He opened to a page picturing a number of chubby, bearded Santas in very large bright red swim trunks.

"It looks like you fellas have a lot of fun," said Lucy, amused.

"It's not all fun and games," said Jack. "We collect donated toys for underprivileged kids and we fund summer camp scholarships, too. That's why we're considering the eggnog deal. We could do a lot more good if we had more money."

"Well, I have to say I'm very impressed," said Lucy, closing her notebook. "Would you mind if I took some photos?"

"Not at all," said Kris, "and the reindeer love posing, too. Especially Prancer."

The Santas wouldn't let her leave without giving her an oversized peppermint stick, as well as a thick folder filled with information about the club. She hadn't had lunch, so she couldn't resist licking the peppermint stick as she made the long drive back to Tinker's Cove, and when a light snow began falling she thought it was truly beginning to feel a lot like Christmas.

The snow continued to fall and there was a light dusting covering the sidewalks and parked cars when she turned onto Main Street. The streetlights were lit, and there were twinkling white lights in the Christmas trees the Chamber had installed on every light pole, too. Many storekeepers were out, putting up the final touches on their holiday decorations, and there was a sense of happy bustle as folks got ready for the evening stroll. Noticing a truck with a cherry picker parked in front of the Community Church, Lucy drove to the end of Main Street and snapped a few photos of the fellows from Rob's Electric installing colored lights on the huge balsam fir that stood on the church lawn.

A wonderful spicy aroma greeted her when she arrived at the *Pennysaver* office, carefully stamping her feet on the mat to loosen the snow that had caked on her boots. It was the first time this season that she'd done this little dance, but, she thought to herself, certainly not the last.

"What are you cooking?" she asked, unwinding her long woolen scarf. "It smells divine."

"Mulled cider, I've got it in my Crock-Pot," said Phyllis.

After hanging up her coat, Lucy checked out the refreshment table, which Phyllis had covered with a vintage tablecloth printed with holly leaves and berries. The festively decorated bottle of eggnog was nestled into an ice bucket next to the Crock-Pot, along with a generous supply of small paper cups, and there was also a big platter filled with black and white cookies, as well as another with home-baked spritz snowflakes and Santa's thumbprints.

"Get it?" asked Phyllis. "Black and white cookies, just like the newspaper!"

"I get it," laughed Lucy. "And is it okay if I have one? I didn't get any lunch."

"Sure," said Phyllis, with a generous sweep of her hand. "I've got plenty. I didn't want to run short, though I doubt we'll get many takers. It's not like we're a store or anything and people can't do their Christmas shopping here."

"We do have gift certificates, I had them printed up specially," said Ted, emerging from the morgue. "How'd the interview

47

with the Santas go?" he asked, choosing a spritz cookie dusted with sparkling sugar and taking a bite.

"Great. I got good photos, and I also got a shot of the guys from Rob's Electric hanging lights on that big tree in front of the church."

"Great," said Ted, as the door opened and two members of the town's board of selectmen came in.

"Merry Christmas!" bellowed Joe Marzetti. Joe owned the local grocery store and was the longest-serving member of the board. "We just stopped by to let you know how much we appreciate your good work."

"Even when we disagree, the *Pennysaver* is an important community voice," said Franny Small, the newest member of the board, elected only last May.

"Thanks," said Ted, blushing. "It's great to know we're appreciated. . . ."

He was cut off by the entrance, en masse, of the entire Conservation Commission, including their chairman, Dorcas. Spotting her and wishing to avoid a discussion of penmanship, Lucy went to the door to welcome incoming members of the Budget Committee and the Board of Health. The little office was soon filled with a lively crowd, eager to discuss various town matters. Ted's recent editorial approving the selectmen's recent vote to equip rescue personnel with Narcan, a drug that can reverse the effects of a drug overdose, was a popular topic.

"Great piece, Ted," said Jim Kirwan, the chief of police. "We've only had it a couple of weeks and we've already used it five times."

"That many?" asked Lucy, who was genuinely shocked. She knew that the nation was coping with the opioid epidemic, but she hadn't realized the scope of the problem in her own backyard.

"That's just our town," replied Kirwan. "I know they've used it over in Gilead, too. Folks like to think this opioid epidemic is a big-city problem, but it's actually worse in rural areas."

"Well, I don't see why people can't simply say no," declared Dorcas, as she piled a small mountain of cookies on a paper plate. Dorcas's sweet tooth was well-known; she often brought baked goods or candy to con-com meetings, and sometimes even shared with the other members.

"That's the thing about addiction," said Chief Kirwan. "People get trapped and it's very difficult to get clean; there's precious little help for addicts who want to kick the habit. Even worse, their need is so over-whelming they sometimes turn to crime, stealing whatever they can in order to get money for drugs. It's really an illness, but we've criminalized it. . . ."

"People who take drugs make a decision to do so," said Dorcas, who had steadily munched her way through most of her cookies while the chief was talking.

"That's not always the case," said Ted, chiming in. "A lot of people get hooked on painkillers prescribed by a doctor. Maybe they had surgery, or an injury, and needed relief. My doctor prescribed oxycodone when I put my back out a couple of months ago."

"I find an aspirin pretty much takes care of any pain," sniffed Dorcas, surveying the refreshment table and refilling her plate. "People today have no self-control. Why, when I was a girl we didn't even know about heroin, or gay people, or any of this modern stuff. People led simple, wholesome lives and they weren't afraid of work. Baked beans on Saturday night, church on Sunday, lots of good fresh air and exercise, and we got along just fine without all these fancy gadgets. Why, my granddaughter hardly even speaks to me anymore, she just stares into that so-called smartphone of hers." She paused for breath, her eyes alighting on the bottle of eggnog. "I must say, I have worked up a bit of a thirst."

"Let me get you something," said Lucy, thinking it was not surprising, considering the number of cookies she'd eaten. "Would you like some mulled cider or eggnog?"

"Well, that's very sweet of you," said Dorcas, popping an entire Santa's thumbprint into her mouth and gulping it down. "I don't know about cider, I have a delicate system, and it's rather acidic, isn't it?"

"I don't think so," said Lucy. "I imagine there's some sugar in it, as well as the spices."

"I made it with cider from MacDonald's farm stand," said Phyllis.

"Dr. Oz is very down on sugar," said Dorcas. "Perhaps I'll try the eggnog. It would be safer, wouldn't it? What's eggnog made with? Milk and eggs, I suppose . . ."

"There's cream and a good deal of sugar in that eggnog," said Lucy, remembering the rich and creamy drink she'd enjoyed earlier that day.

"No, I don't think there's much sugar in eggnog," said Dorcas. "And there are certainly no nuts, I can't have nuts, you know. Allergies. But there are no nuts in eggnog."

"If you have an allergy I really do think

water would be safest," cautioned Lucy. "I happen to know that eggnog recipe is a closely guarded secret. You really shouldn't take chances with something like that."

"That's right," said Phyllis, who was refilling the cookie plates that Dorcas had pretty much emptied. "It was a gift, I didn't make it and I don't know what's in it."

"It does contain nutmeg, I can see the brown specks," said Lucy, who had picked up the bottle and was examining it, noticing the Real Beard Santa Club's logo on the bottle.

"I'm not allergic to nutmeg," laughed Dorcas, stuffing another cookie in her mouth. "Nutmeg is fine."

"Well, I wouldn't touch eggnog with a ten-foot pole," declared Sue, who had just dropped in and was helping herself to a scant tablespoonful of mulled cider. "Not only is it madly fattening, but it usually contains raw eggs, which I absolutely never eat."

"Salmonella," said Lucy, replacing the bottle in the ice bucket. "You have to be so careful when you handle raw chicken, too."

"Absolutely," agreed Phyllis. "I have a separate cutting board just for chicken."

"Well, that's exactly the sort of thing I've been talking about. All this constant information and making people fearful of eggs. First it was the cholesterol that was supposed to kill you if you ate more than two eggs a week. Then it was coffee. And now it's this salmonella. I bet they'll find out it's really good for us and promotes a healthy gut. Dr. Oz is very much in favor of healthy intestinal flora, you know! They say it can take up to four years to replace your beneficial bacteria after a single dose of antibiotics," declared Dorcas, spraying everyone with cookie crumbs. "I refuse to live in fear and I do love a good eggnog! There's only one way to find out if it's any good and that's to taste it!"

She plucked a paper cup from the stack on the table and held it out. "Fill it up, Phyllis!"

Phyllis untied the red and green ribbons that had been wrapped around the old-fashioned milk bottle, and carefully removed the fake holly that had been taped to the rim. "It's your funeral," she said, filling the cup with a generous pour.

Dorcas took a sip, which she sloshed in her mouth, rather like someone tasting a fine wine. "It's not like Mother's," she said, sounding a bit puzzled. "It's rather odd tasting, rather like diet soda."

"That's funny, I had some earlier and it

was delicious," said Lucy, ladling some of the eggnog into a paper cup. She took a sip and grimaced, finding it didn't taste at all like the Real Beard Santa Club's eggnog. "I think it's gone off," she said, tossing her unfinished cup into the trash bin and carrying the ice bucket containing the eggnog into the bathroom, where she set it on the floor, intending to discard it later.

When she returned, she noticed Dorcas was still holding her cup of eggnog. "I wouldn't drink that —" began Lucy, only to be interrupted by Dorcas.

"Waste not, want not, that's how I was brought up," said Dorcas, "and it is rather tasty when you get used to it. Bottoms up!" she declared, tilting the cup and drinking the contents in one gulp.

CHAPTER FOUR

Lucy shrugged, amazed by Dorcas's greed, and turned to Sue. "I'm glad you stopped by, I want to ask a favor. Would you mind sharing that fabulous boeuf bourguignon recipe of yours? The one you do in the Crock-Pot? I'd like to make it for Elizabeth, when she comes home."

"Sure, you can have the recipe, but I doubt it will impress Elizabeth," said Sue. "It doesn't have the subtlety of the true French dish."

"Well, it's got to be closer to French cuisine than my meatloaf," said Lucy, philosophically.

"Sure thing," said Sue, who was contemplating drinking the swallow of cider she was swirling in the paper cup. "And it will get you points for trying . . ." she said, leaving her sentence incomplete when Dorcas uttered a most unlady-like noise. Not quite a retch, or a gasp, and certainly not a cough, the guttural groan was a plea for help.

The newsroom was suddenly silent as everyone turned to see what was wrong, and the chief of police rushed to her side. Dorcas's face was bright red, her eyes were popping, and she was clutching her throat. Kirwan assumed she was choking and grabbed her around her ample waist to administer a Heimlich, but the maneuver didn't help. "Call the rescue squad," he yelled, as the horrified group saw Dorcas's face turn blue and she slipped to the floor where her body began to stiffen and thrash with a seizure.

It was a horrible sight to be sure seeing this respectable matron, who wrote thank-you notes by hand with a fountain pen and wouldn't dream of leaving the house with a hair out of place, lose all control of her body. Poor Dorcas was frothing at the mouth and a dark stain had appeared on her beige skirt. Lucy was ashamed of looking, but she couldn't turn away.

Ted was already on the phone. He'd made the call the moment he realized Dorcas was in trouble, and the ambulance siren could already be heard as the rescue squad covered the two-block distance on Main Street from the fire station to the *Pennysaver* office.

"Thank goodness they're so close," murmured Sue, grasping Lucy's hand.

Lucy squeezed her friend's hand in response, but she wasn't at all sure the rescuers were going to arrive in time. Dorcas had suddenly gone limp, lying splayed on the floor, and Chief Kirwan was administering CPR, but to no avail. "I can't get an airway!" he yelled, as the door flew open and the first EMT arrived, carrying a case of equipment.

Chief Kirwan hopped to his feet, allowing the EMTs to take over, and immediately began ordering everyone to give the rescuers room to work. "Step back, step back," he said, extending his arms and urging the gawkers to move away from the stricken woman. "Nothing to see here, nothing to see," he added, but while everyone was willing to move out of the way, nobody was interested in leaving.

Contrary to the chief's order, there was plenty to see, thought Lucy. She noticed how poor Dorcas's knee-high nylons cut cruelly into her chubby legs, creating rolls of fat around her knees, and the way her many rings seemed permanently affixed to her fingers, making it impossible to get past the puffed and stretched skin. The unconscious woman was lying flat on her back, with her legs spread wide and her skirt rucked up over her knees, while the EMTs worked frantically to save her life.

One was attempting an emergency tracheotomy, actually cutting into her throat to allow life-giving air to enter her lungs, bypassing her obstructed throat. The second was stripping off Dorcas's blouse and preparing to employ a portable defibrillator that would deliver an electric shock that would cause her heart to resume beating.

"Clear!" he shouted, and the first EMT stepped back. The electricity surged through Dorcas's body, which convulsed once again, but to no avail. A second attempt was made, but that also failed.

Lucy turned away, unable to watch any longer, and saw two uniformed cops coming through the door; she recognized her friend Sgt. Barney Culpepper and the chief's younger brother, Officer Todd Kirwan. The two conferred with the chief, and when they concluded their conversation she noticed a change in atmosphere. Officer Kirwan stationed himself in front of the door, preventing people from exiting or entering. Barney shepherded everyone into the morgue, where the newspaper's archives were kept, and where there was a large conference table and chairs. The room soon filled up, but it was very quiet as the gathered citizens maintained a respectful silence.

Lucy and Sue were among the last to enter and, since there were no seats left, found themselves standing by the doorway. From that vantage point Lucy could see that the EMTs had stopped working and were covering Dorcas with a blanket. She could clearly hear the EMT's report to the chief. "I'm no doctor, but my guess is anaphylactic shock," the EMT was telling the police chief. "It's a typical allergic reaction."

The chief responded, posing a question, speaking so softly that Lucy couldn't hear.

"Could be, I suppose," replied the EMT, sounding rather doubtful.

"Better safe than sorry," said Chief Kirwan, shaking hands with the two EMTs.

They set about collecting and packing their equipment while the chief had a quick word with his brother officer; then he entered the morgue and faced the crowd of shocked onlookers. "This appears to be a tragic accident. Mrs. Philpott seems to have died from an allergic reaction, but we need to be sure. I've ordered a call to the medical examiner and in the meantime Officer Culpepper and I will be collecting names and contact information. And," he added in a very serious tone, "no one is to leave this room or touch the refreshment table."

"What do you mean?" demanded Ted. "You think the refreshments were contaminated somehow?"

"Do you consider us all suspects?" asked Roger Wilcox, the chairman of the board of selectmen.

"I don't think anything yet," said the chief, "but I'm going to make darn sure."

Hearing this, Phyllis let out a huge sigh. "The eggnog, it was the eggnog. It had to be the eggnog, right? She collapsed right after she drank it." She looked at Lucy. "I warned her, didn't I?"

Lucy remembered Phyllis's exact words: *It's your funeral.* Best not to mention that, she thought, considering the circumstances. "Dorcas said she had a nut allergy and you said you didn't make the eggnog yourself and didn't know what was in it," said Lucy.

"What eggnog?" demanded Chief Kirwan, turning to Lucy. "I didn't see any eggnog on the refreshment table."

"I took it away, after I drank some. It tasted funny to me, but it didn't affect me. I don't think it could really be the eggnog," said Lucy, grappling with the notion that she had also drunk a possibly fatal brew.

"Where is it now?" asked the chief.

"After I tasted it I thought it had gone off or something so I took it away and put it in

60

the bathroom. Shall I get it?"

"No," said the chief, giving a nod to Officer Culpepper, who promptly left the morgue and quickly returned with the bottle of eggnog, still in the ice bucket.

"Let me get this straight," said the chief, taking the ice bucket and setting it on the table. "Only two people drank the eggnog, right? Lucy and Mrs. Philpott? Anybody else?"

Several people shook their heads.

"That's right," said Lucy, feeling as if the Grim Reaper was standing behind her, breathing down her neck. "Only me and Dorcas."

"And it came straight from this bottle? You didn't doctor it up or add anything?" asked the chief.

"Straight from the bottle," said Phyllis. "It was a gift, to Wilf, from the Real Beard Santa Club.

"I've had their eggnog," said Lucy. "This didn't taste anything like theirs, it tasted different."

"Someone must have reused the bottle and put their own mixture in it," said Sue, watching as the chief carried the ice bucket with the bottle outside, holding it as if it were a bomb that might explode.

With the chief gone, there was a slight

sense of relaxation in the morgue, and people began quiet conversations.

"It couldn't have gone bad because Lucy is okay," said Phyllis.

"I only had a sip," said Lucy. "She drank a whole cup."

"The EMT said it was probably an allergic reaction," said Ted.

"Mrs. Philpott said she was allergic to nuts. Eggnog is made from milk and cream and eggs, isn't it?" asked Phyllis.

"You can make eggnog with almond milk," said Sue, speaking up. "Or cashew milk, or even soy milk."

"You can?" asked Lucy.

"There's a recipe on the carton. It's all fake, it uses that nondairy dessert topping and lots of other stuff I never touch."

"Why did you have it then?" asked Lucy, who was puzzled.

"Almond milk is great," declared Sue, babbling from nervousness and upset. "I make smoothies with it. I sometimes have one for lunch. I throw in frozen blueberries and half a banana. Unsweetened almond milk's only got thirty calories and is full of calcium. It's really filling," said Sue.

"I bet it was made with almond milk," said Lucy, in a thoughtful tone of voice. "Dorcas did say it tasted like diet soda."

"Her last words," said Sue. "But she drank it anyway," said Sue, unable to stop talking. "You couldn't stop her. She was like a human trash compactor, she ate an entire plate of cookies. I saw her." Then, hearing Joe Marzetti clearing his throat, she realized how tactless she'd been, speaking so harshly of the dead woman, and suddenly blushed a furious red and started digging in her purse for a handkerchief.

"But if it's really almond milk, that makes it even worse!" moaned Phyllis. "What if Wilf drank it? He's allergic to nuts. It would've killed him!"

"It obviously should have been labeled. I don't know how anyone could be so reckless," said Lucy. "No one would think eggnog could be made with nuts."

"That's why I never touch the stuff!" declared Sue, still agitated. "It's dangerous. People use Grannie's recipe, which calls for a quart of heavy cream, and ladle out gobs of cholesterol, or pour in all their leftover booze, you know, those bottles with a half inch of liquor that are cluttering up their cabinets; they just throw it all in and give you alcohol poisoning. It's just too risky." She eyed the rather tired paper cup of mulled cider she was still holding and set it down on the table. "I don't think I want that," she said, narrowing her eyes.

"I don't blame you," said Lucy, who was looking around the room, wondering if the person who made the fatal eggnog was there, among them. At the far end of the conference table she saw several members of the board of selectmen, looking extremely shaken. Chairman Roger Wilcox was standing, he was retired Army and still maintained a ramrod-straight posture. Joe Marzetti was sitting with his head in his hands, shaking his head. As owner of the town's supermarket, he knew all about food safety.

Several members of the Board of Health were also there, no doubt reviewing the town's regulations for serving food to the public. Fritz Hollenbeck and Doris Baird, stalwarts of the Conservation Commission, looked stunned, clearly struggling to absorb the sudden death of their chairwoman.

But as she studied the faces of these earnest citizens, all of whom volunteered their time and energy to the community, she saw only expressions of concern and shock. No one looked guilty, and she really couldn't imagine any one of these educated and well-informed people concocting a possibly toxic brew. But it seemed that somebody had mixed up the eggnog and had delivered it to Wilf, presumably for his personal consumption. The question was twofold: Had that person known of Wilf's allergy, and had that person intended for the brew to kill him?

That last question was the stumbling point for Lucy: Who would want to kill Wilf? She knew him as the friendly, helpful mail carrier who had come to her rescue years ago, when she and Bill and baby Toby had first moved into their antique handyman's special on Red Top Road. It was winter, the house was freezing cold, and Wilf got the furnace going after it conked out. She knew that through the years he'd helped out many of the folks on his route, checking to make sure they were all right when their mail wasn't collected and calling for help when he found them in trouble.

Her thoughts were interrupted when Barney Culpepper approached, notebook in hand, to take down her information. It was merely a formality, they'd been friends ever since they found themselves serving together on the Cub Scout Pack Committee years ago, and Barney certainly knew who she was and where she lived. In fact, she thought, chances were he knew everyone in the room, and where they lived.

"Terrible thing, isn't it?" she said by way of greeting.

"Sure is," said Barney, who had removed his cap and tucked it underneath his arm, revealing his gray buzz cut. He was a big man, and his big belly made it necessary for him to frequently hike up his thick leather belt, which held his holster and other equipment. Lucy thought that if he were a dog he'd be a Saint Bernard, and his mournful expression this day amplified that impression. "Hell of a thing."

"Chief Kirwan is treating this like a crime," said Lucy.

"He's just playing it safe," said Barney, in a low voice. "The EMTs say it was an allergic reaction, and they're usually right." He looked over her shoulder, toward the door, and gave a nod. "But we'll know for sure. The ME's arrived."

Lucy turned to see a middle-aged woman, who was wearing white overalls, enter the office, escorted by the chief, who led her to Dorcas's blanketed body. She knelt down and removed the blanket, proceeding to examine Dorcas's face with her gloved hands. She lifted the dead woman's eyelids, then opened her mouth and peered inside. Those chores completed, she replaced the blanket and stood up, removing her gloves.

The police chief posed a question, in a voice too low for Lucy to hear, and got a shake of the head in response. Then the ME instructed the EMTs to load Dorcas's body on a stretcher, and it was wheeled out of the office.

There was a noticeable sense of relief once the body was gone, but people were still subdued and spoke in low voices. Most everyone was allowed to leave, but the chief asked Ted, Phyllis, and Lucy to stay.

"I believe you are allowed one phone call," said Sue, attempting a joke as she buttoned her coat.

"Ha-ha," said Lucy, who wasn't at all amused.

In the end, there wasn't much the *Pennysaver* staff members could tell the chief. Phyllis recounted how the decoratively wrapped bottle of eggnog had shown up on her doorstep, with Wilf's name on the card.

"Did you save the card?" asked Chief Kirwan. "Did it say who it was from?"

"Afraid not," said Phyllis. "It said it was from Santa, that's all. Wilf recently joined the Real Beard Santa Club and we figured it was a welcome present — eggnog is the club's official drink and the bottle has the club's logo. But I didn't want him to drink it because it's fattening. That's our deal: He can grow the beard but not the stomach. I was going to throw it out, but he said I

67

shouldn't waste it, I should take it to work. He used to work in the post office, you know, and the people there really appreciated free food. They were always hungry, especially the mail carriers."

"That's what everybody does these days, now that we're all on permanent diets," said Lucy. "You make a dessert and it's too big for your family, so you bring the rest in to work."

"How come nobody drank it?" asked the chief. "At the station, when there's goodies in the break room, word gets out and they don't last long."

"Ted wanted to drink it, but Corney came by and got us to agree to stay open for the stroll and we decided to save the eggnog and serve it with cookies," said Lucy.

"Which we did," said Ted.

"It seemed a good idea at the time," said Phyllis, dabbing her eyes with a tissue. "I should've just poured it down the drain."

"Hindsight is twenty-twenty," said Ted. "You couldn't have known."

"So you say you got it from this club, right? The Bearded Santas?"

"The Real Beard Santa Club," said Lucy, popping up and grabbing her notebook from her desk. "I have their info, I just interviewed them."

"Thanks," said the chief. "This just might be the break we need."

Lucy was exhausted by the time she got home, but she didn't sleep well, and she was distracted all weekend, unable to shake the horrible image of Dorcas's gruesome death. Even as she baked gingerbread cookies with Patrick, her mind was back in the *Pennysaver* office, seeing Dorcas's body convulsing on the worn linoleum floor. When she walked the dog, when she decorated the tree, when she wrote Christmas cards, she struggled to understand what sort of person would tamper with a bottle of eggnog. Had it been a simple mistake? Had the giver innocently thought that this was a better recipe? Or had it been done maliciously, on purpose, to kill Wilf?

That was the big question: Who would want to kill Wilf? He was a friendly, sociable guy, the sort of man who would grow a beard and join the Real Beard Santa Club. She thought of the other members of the club, the ones she'd interviewed, and she couldn't imagine Kris, Jack, Harold, or Bill harming anyone. Through the years she'd done lots of interviews for the *Pennysaver* and she believed she was a good judge of character, not easily fooled by an over-friendly smile or ingratiating attitude, and she hadn't sensed anything false about the Real Beard Santas.

That left Wilf's workplace, the post office. She knew that many of the workers there were vets, who got preference when jobs became available. She could see that this policy might cause resentment, some unsuccessful applicant might have resented vets like Wilf, but Wilf was now retired. There had been a time when there was a string of violent incidents committed by postal workers, it had even been dubbed "going postal," but nothing like that had ever happened in the little Tinker's Cove Post Office. Lucy knew everyone who worked there, and they were all nice people. Helpful people, who took the trouble to chat with lonesome folks, and who would bring the mail to your door if you hadn't been able to dig out your rural box after a snowstorm.

On Monday, when Lucy got to the *Pennysaver* office and opened her e-mail, she found one from Kris Kringle, marked "IMPORTANT" on the subject line. Opening the message, she learned he wanted her to call him, IMMEDIATELY. So she did.

"It wasn't us," said Kris as soon as he answered the phone. "The cops were here, questioning me, but I don't know anything about bad eggnog, and I sure don't want it to be in the paper. You had our eggnog — it's perfectly wholesome."

"Couldn't it have gone off? Spoiled?" asked Lucy. "It was in the same bottle as yours."

"I suppose it could spoil, if it was consumed after the clearly marked sell by date," admitted Kris. "But those bottles are everywhere. They're quite decorative and people save them. Anybody could have reused one. We stand behind our product, that's for sure, and furthermore, the club does not give eggnog to new members, we give them beard trimmers."

"Did you give Wilf a beard trimmer?" asked Lucy.

"Not yet. The beard has to be six inches long, it has to meet the members' approval. We take a vote and if it passes, then we give the beard trimmer. It's a special order, red, made just for us." He took a deep breath and his voice became very serious. "You know, we all think the world of Wilf. He's going to be a great addition to the Real Beard Santa Club."

"Thanks for telling me," said Lucy, "I really appreciate the heads-up."

"Well, I have the club's reputation to think of," said Kris. "We're Santas, we're good guys. We bring joy and Christmas cheer, that's what we do."

"The club's reputation is safe with me," said Lucy, ending the call. But as she reviewed her notes, she wondered if Wilf was safe, or if somebody wanted to kill him. Someone who would try again.

CHAPTER FIVE

The week flew by as tributes poured in from members of the various clubs and committees Dorcas had been involved with throughout her busy life in Tinker's Cove. Even though Dorcas wasn't particularly well-liked, and had never shied away from a fight, nobody wanted to say anything negative about her and so they went in the opposite direction, offering overblown and inflated praise.

"What a load of, um, hypocritical blather," said Ted, when he finished editing Lucy's front-page story about Dorcas's sudden death on Wednesday. Lucy had been working frantically all morning to meet the noon deadline and it was eleven-thirty when she got to the final item on her agenda, which was a call to the DA to ask about the autopsy results. Phil Aucoin had just become a father, and after accepting Lucy's congratulations confessed that he could use a little more sleep.

"Any word from the medical examiner?" asked Lucy.

"About what?" he asked, sounding puzzled.

Lucy smiled to herself, thinking that fatherhood had indeed fuddled the DA's mind. "Dorcas Philpott," she said.

"Oh, right. Yeah, that's a strange one. I've got a preliminary report right here, but we haven't got the toxicology results yet." There was a long pause, during which Lucy heard the sound of papers being shuffled. "Got it!" he finally announced. "Anaphylactic shock, most likely due to the ingestion of nut milk. Nut allergy, apparently, but this is unofficial, you know. She had a host of other physical problems: obesity, heart disease, liver didn't look too good, either."

"Will there be an investigation? Criminal charges?" asked Lucy.

"Unlikely," said Aucoin. "It would be quite a job to figure out who made the eggnog and even if by some miracle we got a confession, it seems to me it's more a matter of a labeling failure that had tragic consequences. Maybe I could get a charge of involuntary manslaughter, depending on the circumstances, but like I said, she had a number of physical problems that probably

74

contributed to the allergic reaction. Frankly, I've got more important matters to deal with. My calendar is full of drug-related crime; this opioid epidemic's really straining the justice system."

"But the eggnog killed Dorcas," said Lucy. "It could've killed anyone who has a nut allergy. And don't forget, it was sent to Wilf, who also has a nut allergy."

"Most likely nothing more than coincidence. It's not like it was laced with cyanide or something," said Aucoin. "To me, it's more like that church supper where the spinach salad turned out to be contaminated with *E. coli* and twelve people got sick. The poor woman who made it was mortified; she thought she'd made a healthful dish."

"Yeah, but so far nobody has admitted to making the eggnog," said Lucy, "and you'd have to live in a cave to avoid hearing about a nut allergy."

"You'd be surprised what people don't know," said Aucoin, with a sigh.

"So I guess we'll say Dorcas's death was an unfortunate accident?"

"Sounds about right," said Aucoin, ending the call.

Phyllis, who had been listening to Lucy's end of the conversation, erupted in angry disbelief. "That's crazy! Unfortunate accident! Where does he get a stupid idea like that?"

"He said Dorcas was in poor health and that contributed to her allergic reaction. Remember, I had some and it didn't kill me. It probably wouldn't have killed Wilf, either, since he's so hale and hearty," said Lucy. "Aucoin said it would be practically impossible to investigate, that they don't have the resources to discover who concocted the eggnog," said Lucy.

"I don't believe it, not for a minute," said Phyllis. "It's just a lame excuse for not doing anything. I'm really afraid that somebody has it out for Wilf. It's no secret that he has a nut allergy, everybody at the post office knew, and a lot of other people, too. Whoever sent him that eggnog wanted to kill him, that's why they made it with nut milk."

Lucy looked across the room, to the reception area where Phyllis sat at her desk behind the high counter that hid everything but her face. That face wore a worried expression that was at odds with Phyllis's brightly dyed hair and colorful cat's-eye reading glasses, today striped red and green and spattered with glitter.

"I think Aucoin's right and it was just a

tragic mistake," said Lucy. "Who would want to hurt Wilf?"

"Lucy's right," said Ted, who was hunched over his computer, struggling to format the front page. "Have you got anything on Dorcas's funeral?" he asked.

"Yup, there's a viewing at the funeral home on Thursday evening, and the service and burial will be Friday afternoon."

"It's gonna be big, Lucy. Can you cover it?"

"Sorry," said Lucy, "I've got to meet Elizabeth at the airport. Boston."

"I thought you hated driving to Boston," said Ted.

"Especially on a Friday afternoon," said Phyllis.

"Usually I do, but if it means getting out of Dorcas Philpott's funeral, it's a trade I'm willing to make."

On Friday afternoon, Boston traffic wasn't the problem, it was the huge traffic jam in Tinker's Cove for Dorcas Philpott's funeral that delayed the trip. It seemed to take a very long time for the long procession of cars with glowing headlights to clear before Bill and Lucy, along with Sara, Zoe, and Patrick, could even begin the trip from Maine to Boston. The girls had declared themselves eager to see their sister, while Molly and Toby had seized on the opportunity for some together time at home without Patrick and the rest of the family. As it happened, they reached the arrivals hall at Terminal E in Logan Airport just as the sliding doors opened and Elizabeth walked through.

Lucy could hardly believe this sophisticated young woman was the same daughter who had horrified as a high school student by chopping off her hair, wearing nothing but black clothes, and rimming her eyes in thick black eyeliner. Now Elizabeth was the very picture of French chic, dressed for travel in trim black slacks, a creamy cashmere sweater topped with a light wool camel-colored jacket, and carrying a roomy designer tote bag on one shoulder. She was sporting a colorful silk scarf, her dark hair was cut in a stylish bob, and she was wearing black ankle boots with a medium heel and was easily pulling a carry-on–sized suitcase with rollers. If she was wearing makeup you couldn't tell, except for the bright red lipstick she'd painted on her smile.

Lucy rushed forward to hug her, followed by Bill, Patrick, and the two girls, and they all made an excited circle around the prodigal daughter.

"Is this Patrick?" exclaimed Elizabeth, hugging her nephew. "You've grown so big!"

Patrick beamed, pleased by the attention.

"You look fabulous!" exclaimed Zoe.

"Tell us all about Paris!" urged Sara. "Tell us everything!"

"How was your flight?" asked Bill.

"Why don't you have a winter coat?" asked Lucy. "Did you forget how cold it is in Maine in December?"

"I didn't forget," replied Elizabeth, reaching into her tote bag and producing a small, shiny silk packet with a zipper. "Voilà!" she exclaimed, unzipping the packet, which immediately exploded into a full-length black down coat, with hood. "They're all the rage in Paris," she said. "You know how French women hate to be bundled up, they like to show off their tiny little size-zero bodies."

"Ooh, I have to have one of those coats," declared Sara.

"Me too, and I love your bag," said Zoe.

"A gift from a grateful guest," said Elizabeth, with a shrug. "I got him opera tickets."

Lucy eyed the scarf, which she suspected was Hermes, and wondered if it, too, was a gift from a grateful guest and what services Elizabeth had performed to deserve it. Not that her daughter would do anything immoral, at least she hoped not, but she worried that Elizabeth might be stepping onto a slippery slope by accepting such lavish gifts.

Noticing her mother's anxious expression, Elizabeth quickly added, "He wanted them as a special twenty-fifth anniversary surprise for his wife."

"The scarf is so pretty," said Lucy, holding the coat so Elizabeth could slip into it, and managing to add a motherly hug.

"I found it on the street, the wind had blown it against a fence," said Elizabeth. "Someone dropped it, I guess. Bad luck for them, *bonne chance* for me."

"I hope you washed it," said Lucy.

"Oh, Mom," moaned Elizabeth, rolling her eyes. "Haven't you heard? Silk is a natural antiseptic. It kills germs."

"I hadn't heard and now that I have I don't believe it," said Lucy, automatically grabbing Patrick's hand as they reached the crosswalk leading to the parking garage.

Once Elizabeth's bag was stowed and they were all seated and buckled in Lucy's new SUV and headed out of the garage, Bill suggested they stop for dinner at a roadside restaurant on the way to Maine.

Since the family rarely ate away from home, this idea was greeted with enthusiasm by Sara and Zoe. Patrick added his vote, declaring, "I'm really hungry."

"I've heard Olive Garden is very good," said Lucy.

"What about Ruby Tuesday?" suggested Sara.

"Or T.G.I. Friday's," volunteered Zoe.

"Those are all chains," said Elizabeth, as Bill inserted the prepaid ticket into the machine at the garage exit. "I'd really love some real New England food."

"There's the Lobster Pot," suggested Lucy. "But it's at the Maine border, that's at least an hour away."

"That's not real food, either," complained Elizabeth. "What about the diner? The one on Route 1?"

"That's quite a ways away," Lucy reminded her daughter. "And Patrick's hungry."

"But I love their pies, and the chowder," said Elizabeth. "And it's real food, cooked from scratch." She paused. "You know, when you've been in Paris a while, you really get to appreciate good food. Everything there is fresher. Somehow the salads are greener and the yogurt is richer, and the Parisians really take the time to cook things properly. They really value good food, even if it's only a bite of chocolate or a morsel of cheese."

Lucy was beginning to think Elizabeth's visit was going to be a lot more challenging than she'd thought when Bill spoke up.

"Well, if that's what you want, that's what you'll get," he said, deciding the matter as they zoomed down the slope into the Ted Williams Tunnel. "Lucy, haven't you got something Patrick can eat? A granola bar?"

Lucy dug a rather dented granola bar out of her purse for Patrick, but her own stomach was growling by the time they reached the diner, which was busy with Friday evening travelers. They had to wait a few minutes before one of the booths opened up and the table was cleared and wiped.

"I forgot about this disgusting wiping," said Elizabeth, with a disapproving sniff. "In French cafés they cover tables with sheets of paper and just pull off the dirty one. They wouldn't dream of using a dirty rag like they do here."

"Haven't you heard?" asked Lucy, sliding onto the faux leather seat. "Formica has natural antiseptic properties. Germs don't stand a chance."

"Ha-ha. Very funny, Mom," said Elizabeth. "There's nothing natural about Formica."

When the waitress delivered the menus she also announced that they were out of clam chowder but still had cream of tomato soup, and if they wanted pie they'd better let her know now because the apple and blueberry were gone, but there was still a slice of cherry and maybe some key lime.

Not exactly locally grown food, thought Lucy, who doubted even the blueberry and apple had been made with locally grown produce.

"Anyone for pie?" asked Bill, cocking his head toward Elizabeth.

"None for me," she said with a sigh, burying her face in the menu.

"I think we'll skip pie," said Bill. "Do you have beer or wine?"

"Afraid not," said the waitress, who was a tired-looking, large woman with tightly permed gray hair. "We have coffee, tea, and milk," she said. "Also tonic," she added, using the local word for soda pop.

"Diet Cokes all round?" asked Bill, receiving a horrified expression from Elizabeth.

"Just water for me," she quickly added. "Do you have Perrier?"

"Tap water," said the waitress. "Are you ready to order?" she asked in a rather impatient tone, noting down the beverages.

"Sure are," said Bill, requesting meat loaf. Sara and Zoe opted for mac and cheese, Patrick went for chicken fingers, and Lucy chose the cranberry pot roast. Elizabeth, however, couldn't seem to find anything on the menu that appealed.

"Can you tell me a bit about the broiled haddock?" she asked.

"Well, sure," said the waitress, with a sigh. "It's broiled."

"Is it a sustainable species?"

"That I don't know," said the waitress. "There doesn't seem to be a shortage, if that's what you mean."

"I'm just concerned that some species are overfished, which is not only bad for them but can alter the entire biosystem. . . ." said Elizabeth.

"Well, it's already been caught, it's not going to swim back into the ocean so you might as well eat it," said the waitress, growing impatient.

"True enough," said Elizabeth. "Does it come with a crumb topping?"

The waitress looked at her as if she was crazy. "Of course, made from Ritz Crackers."

"Can I have the haddock without the crumbs?" asked Elizabeth. "With just the tiniest bit of butter and lots of lemon?"

"Well, I never," said the waitress in a disapproving tone.

Lucy was growing a bit uncomfortable

with Elizabeth's behavior. She had asked particularly to eat at the diner, claiming she wanted traditional New England cooking, but was behaving as if she were in a four-star restaurant that provided *cuisine minceur* to size-zero French women who were concerned about the health of the oceans.

"I don't see the problem," said Bill, passing his menu to the waitress. "Just ask the cook to leave off the crumbs, okay? And please bring some crayons for my grandson."

"Whatever," said the waitress, collecting the rest of the menus and shuffling off, returning to present Patrick with a mini-pack containing four crayons. He immediately got busy, coloring in the Maine map on his paper placemat.

"Thanks, Dad," said Elizabeth, who was looking around the diner and taking in the handwritten signs advertising specials, the worn fixtures, and the equally tired-appearing patrons. "You know, I forgot how fat Americans have gotten," she whispered, as a very large man in a huge Carhartt jacket and work boots made his way past their table. "I suppose that explains why the cars are all so big," she continued, adding, "that guy would never fit in a FIAT."

Sara and Zoe thought that was very funny,

but Lucy had recognized Bob Landry, who was a hardworking volunteer at the town's food pantry. "You can't judge people on their appearance. Bob happens to be a very big-hearted, generous guy," she said, chiding them.

But as she sipped on her Diet Coke, she guessed that making snap judgments based on outward clues was probably part of Elizabeth's job at the upscale Cavendish Hotel. It would only make sense for the woman in the Chanel suit carrying a Hermes purse to get preferential treatment, since she would most likely be able to afford the best the hotel could offer.

A sudden wail came from a corner of the diner, where a young couple was seated with a three-year-old boy with rather long hair. "I won't!" the child was yelling.

The mother, a small woman wearing eyeglasses, was attempting to engage the child in conversation. "But, Hector," she was saying, "carrots help you see in the dark."

"That's right," the bearded, balding father added. "You'll have super sight, like an owl."

The child did not seem open to this line of reasoning, and jumped down from his booster seat and began running through the diner, making hooting owl noises.

"That would never happen in Paris," said Elizabeth, as the waitress arrived with a huge tray containing their orders. "I've been living there, you know."

"Honey, you're not in Paris anymore," she said, distributing the plates. "Bone appetite!"

When Monday morning rolled around, Lucy found herself positively eager to get to work. It had been a long weekend, negotiating conflicts between Elizabeth and her sisters, between Elizabeth and her brother, between Elizabeth and Molly, and even between Elizabeth and Libby the dog. Zoe had practically come to blows with Elizabeth when the older sister claimed the United States was entirely responsible for global warming, and Sara and Elizabeth had fought over the last yogurt in the fridge, which the triumphant Elizabeth declared wasn't nearly as good as French yogurt. Molly took offense when Elizabeth declared Americans spoiled their children, and refused to share a bedroom with her nephew, requiring the little boy to move in with his parents in the family room. She'd even attacked Toby's research, declaring genetically modified foods were unlawful in France, requiring him to defend genetic modification to preserve endangered species.

Even Libby had taken to sulking, retreating to her dog bed on the kitchen floor after Elizabeth kicked her off her favorite spot on the living room couch.

It was a great relief to Lucy to find the *Pennysaver* office empty, entirely free of squabbling voices. Lucy turned to her computer and started working on this week's second biggest story, a controversial proposal for pay-as-you-throw garbage collection at the town dump. She was about halfway through when she needed to check a quote about the projected savings for the town that appeared in last week's paper. She was flipping through the pages for the necessary story when her attention was caught by the obituary for Holly Fredericks and she noticed that the funeral was scheduled for that afternoon, when she would be on her way home.

Funerals were always popular in Tinker's Cove, as Lucy well knew from the traffic jam on Friday afternoon. Dorcas hadn't been particularly well liked, but almost everyone in town had turned out for the funeral and, perhaps more importantly, for the collation afterward. Lucy suspected that Holly's funeral would attract a similar crowd, even as she wondered why Nancy had chosen to delay the service for such a long time. Holly had died two weeks ago, and Lucy was ashamed to admit it had slipped her mind, and if she hadn't seen the obituary she would have missed the service. She believed attending and paying her respects was the least she could do for a woman who had made such a huge sacrifice for the country, and had suffered so terribly. She hesitated, remembering that she wasn't dressed appropriately and was wearing a bright red sweater over her jeans, but decided that her presence was more important than her appearance, and in any case she could keep her navy blue jacket zipped. Good thing she hadn't worn her orange and brown plaid coat, eager to avoid criticism from Elizabeth, who despised it and always let her know how unfashionable it was.

The funeral was in the Community Church, a classic white clapboard New England church with a tall steeple that housed the combined congregations of the Congregationalists, Methodists, and Baptists. The merger had become a difficult necessity when the various denominations could not support their separate churches due to shrinking congregations. The Community Church had been a huge success, however, and was currently benefiting from an upsurge in interest and was now offering two Sunday services.

Today, Lucy was shocked to see that interest was not in evidence and the white-painted pews with their red cushions were largely empty, except for a handful of people seated in the front pews. A closed coffin was resting in front of the altar, topped with a photograph of the young soldier whose body was lying beneath it. Most likely a photo taken at the end of boot camp, it showed a young woman who would have been attractive if she'd been smiling, but was instead wearing a very serious expression. There was no question of her health and vitality, however, as her eyes were clear and her skin glowed with youth.

How sad, thought Lucy, as the organist struck a few chords and they all rose to sing "Amazing Grace." There were too few people in the large church, and only one or two good voices, so the effort was rather pathetic. It was a relief to all when the final chord was played and they could sit down and hear the minister's welcome. Rev. Margery Harvey was new to the job, having assumed the post only a few months ago.

Rev. Marge, as she liked to be called, offered a prayer followed by a few words about the deceased woman. Admitting she hadn't known Holly well herself, she announced that her sister and caregiver, Nancy Fredericks, would offer a few remembrances.

Lucy listened as Nancy recounted how she and Holly used to play soldier when they were children, but only Holly went on to actually join the military. She told one anecdote after another, each one more moving than the last. When she recalled the time they'd been swimming together during a Cape Cod vacation and had been caught in a riptide Lucy found herself reaching for a tissue.

"There were lifeguards and they'd noticed us, they were coming into the water with big red surfboards, but I didn't think I could stay afloat long enough for them to reach us. I was ready to give up, I was actually sinking, the water was coming over my face, but Holly put her arms around me and held me up. 'Don't!' I told her. 'I'm pulling you down, you'll drown, too.'

"But she just kept kicking and holding me and she looked into my eyes, and said, 'Well, if you go down I'm going, too, because I don't want to live without my sister.'

"Now, of course," continued Nancy, "I will have to live without my best friend and the best Christmas present I ever got, my little sister, Holly."

Then the organist began playing the final hymn, "The Army Goes Rolling Along," and Lucy fought tears as she stood and joined in the rousing tune, which was sung as the casket was rolled down the aisle. When they reached the line "always fighting from the heart," she gave up and let the tears flow. She turned to follow the casket on its way to the church door when she noticed a familiar figure ducking out, not waiting for the minister to pronounce the final benediction.

Perhaps it was the tears that clouded her vision, thought Lucy, but she could have sworn that furtive figure was Wilf.

CHAPTER SIX

Driving home after the funeral Lucy thought about the unusually sparse attendance at Holly Fredericks's funeral. Tinker's Cove was a small town where everyone knew everybody else and the loss of one person affected everyone. Funerals were where the details of the deceased person's last days were thoroughly dissected in hushed voices, as well as his or her family ties, relationships with friends, neighbors, and suspected paramours, and the probable amount of the estate and thoughtful speculation about who would inherit it.

Holly's sister, Nancy, had done all the necessary preparation for a large crowd: She'd placed an obituary in the paper with the date and time of the service, she'd planned a church service complete with flowers and organist, and she'd hired a caterer who had set out a generous spread in the fellowship hall. Lucy had peeked in

93

and seen the platters piled high with sandwiches, the bowls of salad and pedestaled cake plates loaded with lemon bars and brownies, all the usual fare townsfolk expected. But judging from the number at the service, Nancy would be eating leftover sandwiches and dessert bars for a very long time.

It puzzled Lucy, and also disturbed her because of Holly's service in the military. She was a true hero and should have been honored at her passing, but instead was largely ignored by an ungrateful town. Of course, Lucy reminded herself, Holly had been a housebound invalid for many years and had most likely been forgotten by most townsfolk. It was a sad reflection on the power of the press, the *Pennysaver* in particular, but she also knew that most readers merely scanned the obituaries looking for names they recognized.

The more she thought about it, as she drove the familiar route home to Red Top Road, the more she felt she needed to do something. The nation's best and brightest young people were serving in the military in faraway, dangerous places where they faced combat injuries and even death. People living in safety here at home needed to be reminded, she decided, vowing to do whatever she could to bring the issue to the *Penny-saver*'s readers. She could start, she realized, with the Honor the Heroes story Ted had suggested.

Turning into the driveway, she noticed that Bill had strung icicle lights on the porch of their antique farmhouse, which along with the big wreath on the door gave it a festive, holiday air. The house looked lovely, and looking through the kitchen window she could see Bill and the girls, busy cooking supper and waiting for her to come home.

She was so fortunate, she thought, comparing her situation with Nancy's and feeling horribly guilty. She had a wonderful family, everyone was healthy, and while they certainly weren't rich they had everything they needed. There were disagreements and squabbles aplenty, that was true, but she never doubted for a moment that they all loved one another.

Parking the car in its usual spot in the driveway she pulled her cell phone out of her bag and called Ted. "I've been thinking," she began, "that I'd like to work on that Honor the Heroes story you wanted. I think it would be a good reminder about the meaning of Christmas."

"Okay," he replied. "What's your angle?"

"I thought I'd start with Holly Fredericks, the paralyzed Army vet who just died. . . ."

"Human interest, that's good, and I've got a big hole in the next issue."

"I'll try to set up an interview with Holly's sister, Nancy, tomorrow," said Lucy.

"Great, then you can take a look at the big picture, what's being done for vets and what more needs to be done. Maybe we'll even run it as a series over a few weeks." He paused. "Who knows? This is the sort of story that gets attention, maybe even an award."

Lucy smiled. She knew that Ted went to the Northeast Newspaper Association convention every year, hoping to win a prize and usually coming home empty-handed. Maybe this year would be different, she decided, climbing out of the car. Bill had opened the door and was standing in the doorway, welcoming her home to the warm, brightly lit house.

The next afternoon Lucy went straight to Nancy Fredericks's house, having called the night before and gotten a prompt invitation. Nancy apparently had a lot on her mind and was eager to share it.

Arriving at the address she had been given, Lucy was surprised to see that the

96

little ranch house was lavishly decorated for Christmas, with a huge, inflatable Santa on one side of the front lawn and an inflatable Rudolph on the other side.

Nancy had been waiting for her and opened the door before she could even knock.

"Come in, come in," she said in a high-pitched voice that revealed her nervousness. "Let me take your coat. Do you want coffee or tea? I have lots of sweets, left over from the funeral, you know. I've never been interviewed, I'm not sure what I'm supposed to do. Can I give you food, or is that against the rules?"

"I'd love some coffee and a bite of something," said Lucy, figuring it was the best way to calm her anxious subject. Lucy thought Nancy looked much older than her deceased sister's forty-four years, with dull, thin hair and pasty, pale skin. Her overlarge clothes hung on her thin frame, giving the impression that she had once been larger and more robust but had been worn down by the responsibility of caring for her sister.

"Do you want to sit here?" asked Nancy, indicating the cramped living room, which was dominated by a hospital bed. "This is where Holly lived, really. It was bigger and more comfortable than her bedroom."

Lucy looked at the room, noticing the details: the huge TV, the bedside table covered with medicine bottles, and the oxygen tank that stood next to the bed. The bed had taken the place where a couch would have been, but a recliner and a couple of easy chairs had been crowded into the room. Several garish paint-by-number pictures of flowers hung on the wall.

"Holly loved flowers," said Nancy. "I couldn't afford fresh ones so I bought these pictures at yard sales. She loved them."

"They're very cheerful," said Lucy, who was no art expert but knew what she liked, and didn't like the amateurish paintings. "Let's go in the kitchen, I think we'll be more comfortable there," she suggested, eager to escape the room where Holly had died.

"Good idea," said Nancy, leading the way down a narrow hallway to the back of the house. "I haven't had time to tidy up," she admitted, with a wave at the table, which was cluttered with piles of paper, and the limited counter space, which was filled with plastic containers of funeral leftovers. "Make yourself comfortable," she invited, filling the kettle with water.

Lucy sat down at the table and pulled a pen and notebook from her bag, then gave

Nancy an encouraging smile. Nancy began shuffling the papers in a futile attempt to clear the table, then sat down and buried her face in her hands. Lucy pulled a pack of tissues out of her purse and passed it to Nancy.

"I know this must be a very difficult time for you," she said. "Why don't we start with a little chat. What was Holly like as a child? You said you used to play soldiers as kids . . . ?"

Nancy wiped her eyes and blew her nose, then gave Lucy a wan smile. "That's true, but I was always wounded in battle and she was the Army nurse. Then when she got to high school she was better at sports than she was at the subjects; she had to repeat biology. She never had good grades, but she was a star athlete. All-state in field hockey, team captain of the basketball and soccer teams, she played everything really well. She was applying to colleges, but it looked as if she'd have to go to the community college, so she decided to enlist instead.

"Believe it or not, she loved boot camp. I mean, who loves boot camp? But for Holly it was like a walk in the park." She began flipping through the papers once again and produced a photo. "Here, this is Holly, with some of the others in her unit."

Lucy looked at the color photo, which pictured a group of healthy young women, wearing big smiles and camo.

"She loved it all," said Nancy, as the kettle shrieked and she got up to turn off the burner.

"The physical challenges, the guns, the long marches, it was all easy for her. She was one of the top graduates . . . ," she said, turning to Lucy. "Instant okay?"

"Fine with me," said Lucy, who had pulled a pen and notebook out of her bag and was writing it all down.

"Milk and sugar? I've got lemon bars, brownies, blondies, which do you want?"

"Black coffee and any and all," said Lucy, accepting a mug of coffee.

Nancy carried over one of the big plastic containers filled with baked goods, but stood holding it and staring at the over-loaded table. "Isn't this crazy?" she asked, with a nod at the overstuffed box. "I thought the whole town would come to Holly's funeral. I didn't rush it, I wanted to take the time to get it right, to plan every detail so it would be perfect for Holly."

"I think it was overshadowed by Dorcas Philpott's funeral," said Lucy in a gentle voice. "She was very active in town affairs."

"Never heard of her," said Nancy, with a

shrug, "but Holly and I didn't get out much."

"It was very odd," said Lucy. "She had an allergic reaction to some eggnog. It was fatal."

"How old was this woman?" asked Nancy. Her voice was unsteady and Lucy's heart went out to her, knowing how deeply she mourned for her sister.

"Seventy-four, I believe," said Lucy, shoving some of the papers to the side, creating a slight depression in the pile, and Nancy set down the plastic box.

"Thirty years older than Holly," she said, unsnapping the lid. "Holly should have lived to seventy, even eighty. It makes me mad and I feel so helpless," she admitted, smacking her fist against her thigh. "I'm lost. I used to have so much to do, taking care of Holly. But now she's gone, it's all over, and I don't know what to do with myself."

"Did you get any help from the VA? Or from any of the veterans' groups like Honor the Heroes or the VFW?"

"Nothing," said Nancy, shaking her head. "It was all on me."

Lucy felt a building sense of outrage that a veteran should be treated so callously by an ungrateful nation. "That's not right," she said. "Holly served her country."

"I know!" exclaimed Nancy, exhibiting some spirit. "But the VA, well, you have to wait a long time to get an appointment and then how was I going to get Holly there? It wasn't like she could just sit in the car. She was completely paralyzed, she couldn't even change channels on the remote. I had to do everything. Bathe her, change her diapers, feed her, manage her meds, get the visiting nurses and all, it was a full-time job."

Lucy looked at Nancy, noticing her rough, chapped hands and her badly cut hair, her baggy pants and shapeless sweatshirt. "Forgive me for asking," she began, "but how did you manage financially?"

"Good question," replied Nancy, with a tired smile. "Holly had disability, it wasn't much, and I'm divorced and get a bit of alimony. We both had some savings, but that's all gone now, so we have Medicaid, which was a blessing." She lifted her mug to her lips and took a sip. "It wasn't easy, that's for sure."

"I think we have to take better care of our veterans," said Lucy, studying the photo. "We take these wonderful young people and send them into harm's way and when they are injured we abandon them."

"Exactly," said Nancy, producing a small photo album. "Here, you can take this. See."

She opened the book to a photo of Nancy sitting in a jeep, along with a couple of young male soldiers. "This was in Iraq," she explained, pointing to the picture. "And here's Holly with a local woman and her baby, oh, this is her unit," she said, pointing to a posed photo, like a class picture, except that the neatly arranged subjects were all young people dressed in matching camouflage uniforms. Lucy turned the pages slowly, as Nancy provided a running commentary, describing the work Holly did in Iraq. "She loved the local people; she was setting up schools for the children and teaching the women about sanitation. That was the strategy, to improve their lives and teach them about democracy."

"These photos are great," said Lucy. "Can I use them to illustrate my story?"

"Sure," said Nancy, her eyes lighting up. "Maybe now Holly will get the recognition she deserves."

"She sure will, if I have anything to do with it," said Lucy, taking a bite of a lemon bar.

When she got into work on Wednesday, Lucy gave Ted and Phyllis the briefest of greetings and sat right down at her computer to begin writing, finding the story almost wrote itself. It was as if Holly was whispering in her ear, telling her how she was bringing democratic ideals to a former dictatorship. At boot camp she discovered strengths she didn't know she had, and was eager to deploy overseas, in a war zone. Once in Iraq she fought a new kind of war, one in which books and blackboards and vaccinations replaced guns and bombs. Deeply idealistic, her tour of duty came to an abrupt end. . . .

Here the voice went silent and Lucy realized she didn't know how Holly was wounded. Was it a roadside bomb, an IED? Was it a bullet from a sniper? A helicopter crash? Friendly fire? She didn't have a clue, so she reached for the phone to call Nancy, but her call went straight to an answering machine.

"How's that story coming?" asked Ted, causing her to check the clock. It was twenty to twelve, which meant the deadline was in twenty minutes.

"It's not a guideline, it's a deadline," said Phyllis, rolling her eyes and mocking one of Ted's favorite maxims. Ted didn't appreciate the joke.

"Damn right," he growled.

"I'm almost done," she said, biting her lip. What to do? She didn't have all the information she needed, and she couldn't reach her source. On the other hand, she had a great story, one of the best she had ever written. She could ask Ted to hold it, or she could gloss over the missing details of Holly's devastating injuries and go straight to the aftermath, when she returned home and was cared for by her sister.

The voice returned, answering the question for her. "After I was injured, my world became much smaller; it was one room in a small house in Tinker's Cove. There I was cared for by my sister, Nancy. Completely paralyzed, I spent my days and nights in a hospital bed, watching TV and looking at the paintings of flowers on the wall. Painted flowers because we couldn't afford real ones."

"Done!" exclaimed Lucy, hitting the send button as the big hand on the clock clicked into place on the twelve.

"How many inches?" asked Ted.

"Twenty," said Lucy.

"Perfect. And next week you're going to look at the various resources available for wounded vets, right?"

"Right," she replied, leaning back in her chair and stretching. It felt good, really good to write a meaty human interest story that dealt with real people and real problems rather than the usual routine accounts of town committee meetings and small-town trivia. "Do you need me?" she asked, feeling suddenly restless, buoyed by an emotional high.

"No, I've got everything I need," replied Ted, adding, "Good work, Lucy. Really good."

Ted rarely praised her work, so Lucy felt airborne as she left the office and began tackling a long list of Christmas errands. She was still replaying his words of praise when she finally headed home later that afternoon in her new SUV, not noticing the potholes and bumps in the road. This was the sort of story that made all the grunt work and repetition of day-to-day reporting worth doing. A story that would move people and might actually make a difference. Wouldn't it be wonderful, she thought to herself, if her story prompted people to rally and demand better treatment for disabled vets?

It was possible, she decided, picturing herself at the NNA dinner, receiving a standing ovation when she was presented with the award for Best Feature Story. A story, the emcee was saying, that began a movement and showed the valuable role community newspapers can play in today's media-saturated environment. . . .

Before she knew it, she was climbing the hill on Red Top Road and turning into her own driveway. Weird, she thought, as she parked the car, but she didn't actually remember the drive at all. Did she stop at the stop sign? She assumed so, she always did, but she had no memory of it. She'd been driving on automatic, lost in her daydream.

Enough, she scolded herself, time to get real. Christmas was coming and she had a long list of things to do. Approaching the back porch, she was surprised to see Molly standing there in an unbuttoned coat, smoking a rare cigarette. Libby, the dog, was sitting mournfully beside her, leaning her shoulders against Molly's thighs.

"What's up?" she asked, climbing the porch steps.

"Elizabeth and her buddy Renee have taken over the kitchen," she said, rolling her eyes. "I tried to start the pot roast, like you asked, but they kicked me out."

"So there's no supper?" asked Lucy.

"Elizabeth said I was making a big deal out of nothing, why couldn't we have a quick salad, or pasta with butter and cheese, which is what they do in Paris?" She stubbed out the cigarette in the flowerpot she was using as an ashtray. "I guess in Paris they don't have hungry husbands and fathers to feed who want meat and potatoes, not to mention little boys who are always hungry."

"I'll sort it out," said Lucy, opening the back door and stepping into the kitchen where she was assailed by the delicious smell of chocolate. Inside she found Elizabeth, along with Sara, Zoe, and neighbor Renee La Chance, all busy measuring ingredients and sifting flour and stirring batter.

"Hi, Mom," said Zoe, who had a smudge of flour on her nose, "we're making Yule logs."

Bûches de Noël," said Elizabeth. "They're traditional in France."

"They're going to be beautiful," said Renee, who was piping meringue in the shape of little mushrooms onto a cookie sheet covered with parchment paper.

"And yummy, too," said Sara, who was engaged in mixing cream and melted chocolate to make ganache icing.

"We're going to give them to the nursing home, for a special treat for the old folks," said Zoe.

"That's a wonderful idea," said Lucy, impressed with the girl's thoughtfulness. "Only problem is I need the kitchen to cook dinner. Your father's been working out in the cold all day and he needs a substantial meal."

"But we're icing and decorating these two and there are two more baking in the oven," said Elizabeth. "That's if we're going to have one for us and one for Renee and her mom."

"We've never had one, it's going to be a real treat," said Sara.

"That's right, Mom," said Zoe. "Don't we look like Santa's little helpers?"

It was true. The girls were all wearing holiday aprons and Santa hats, and the kitchen was festively decorated with sprigs of holly tucked behind the framed pictures, holiday-themed mugs replacing the usual blue and white ones on their hooks, and the wreath on the door. But the aspect of the scene that struck Lucy was the way that the girls were working together, filled with good fellowship and Christmas spirit.

"I guess we can order pizza," she said, hanging her jacket on the hook. "But in the future, I wish you'd check with me before commandeering the kitchen. Molly was quite upset because I asked her to start the pot roast."

"Molly needs to take a chill pill," said Sara, just as Molly opened the door.

She stepped in, followed by the dog, who

109

skulked across the floor toward her doggy bed, casting a wary glance in Elizabeth's direction. "What do you mean? Just because I want to help your mother, I'm some sort of control freak?"

"Well," snapped Elizabeth. "You have to admit you're rather rigid, especially when it comes to Patrick. It really doesn't matter if he has a bit of chocolate for a snack, for instance. In France all the children have *pain au chocolat* for their *goûter*."

"For your information, Elizabeth, we're not in France. We're in Maine, and I prefer for my child to have plenty of fruits and vegetables at regular mealtimes."

"Well, excuse me," countered Elizabeth, "but I thought it would be nice for him to have a little treat."

"Well, I'll thank you to remember that he's my child and I get to decide what he eats and when," said Molly.

"Okay, girls, that's enough," said Lucy, making a timeout sign with her hands. In her heart, she rather sided with Elizabeth, having had her own differences in the past with Molly concerning Patrick's diet. On the other hand, as a parent herself, she knew how strongly she'd wanted to make sure she was bringing the kids up right. She also knew that it hadn't been easy for Molly to give up running her own household and move in with her in-laws while Toby continued his research. "I think we can agree that Molly and Toby get to decide what's best for Patrick — they've certainly done a fabulous job so far."

"Thanks, Lucy," said Molly, wiping her eyes and disappearing into the family room.

"I know you had good intentions," said Lucy, speaking to the others, "but you have to remember that there are a lot of people in the house and if things are going to run smoothly we have to communicate. I was planning to have pot roast tonight, Molly was right, and I don't mind having pizza instead, but it's an unanticipated expense at a time when the budget is tight. . . ."

"I was only trying to do something nice," said Elizabeth, "for everybody."

"I know," said Lucy, giving her oldest daughter a hug, "that's the problem with good intentions. They don't always work out the way we hope."

Lucy got to work, filling the sink with suds, and as the water ran she thought of Nancy's sad kitchen, filled with leftovers from the funeral that so few people had bothered to attend. She hated to think of the grieving woman spending Christmas all by herself, in the house that was filled with reminders of her absent sister. It was too awful, she thought, thinking that it might be nice to invite Nancy for Christmas dinner. Or, she wondered, would it be a case of good intentions that went awry?

When she broached the subject the next day, at the usual Thursday morning breakfast with her friends at Jake's Donut Shack, her friends urged caution.

"I know it always seems like such a nice idea, to invite some poor lost soul for a holiday dinner, but you have to remember that there's a reason why these folks don't have any friends or family," said Sue, tucking a lock of glossy hair behind her ear with a freshly manicured hand. "It's like these homeless people everybody frets about — most of them are alcoholics or drug addicts and they don't want to sober up and get jobs and pay rent and take responsibility for themselves."

"Sue!" exclaimed Pam. "That's an awful thing to say. Sometimes circumstances get the better of people."

"Pam's right," said Lucy. "Nancy took care of her sister twenty-four/seven. She didn't have time to maintain friendships or a life of her own, it was a struggle for her to get through each day. Think back to what it was like when we were caring for our babies, that's what it was like with Holly, except she was a grown woman."

"Caregiving takes a huge toll on the caregiver, both physically and psychologically," said Rachel. "A lot of caregivers suffer from depression, as well as physical exhaustion. It's very important for them to have respite breaks from their responsibilities."

"So you think I should invite Nancy?" asked Lucy. "I'm a little worried that seeing our happy family celebration might make her feel worse."

"How can you be sure it's going to be so happy?" asked Sue, with a wry smile. "In my experience somebody always drinks too much, somebody's jealous that her sister got the American Girl doll she wanted, and the hundred-dollar prime rib is overcooked because Uncle Harold insisted on watching *It's a Wonderful Life* for the eighty millionth time."

"So true," said Rachel. "Last year Bob sulked all day because our son Richie didn't call on Christmas. He was busy excavating some site in Turkey and lost track of time, he finally remembered to call a couple of days later."

"Emotions do tend to run high on Christmas," said Lucy. "And the house is crowded. We've already had quite a few conflicts."

Pam scooped up the last of her yogurt and granola and set down her bowl with a thump. "Well, I never! What a bunch of Scrooges! Sure Christmas is messy and emotional and sometimes you drop the turkey, but it's still the one time of year when we forgive and forget our petty differences and take time to let the people in our lives know how much we love them." She paused a moment. "And we get presents!"

CHAPTER SEVEN

Pam had been right about the presents, which family members were busy squirreling away in various hiding places, but not about forgiving and forgetting. It began again Friday morning when the girls were clearing the breakfast table and Elizabeth claimed that one of her sisters had taken her best pair of Hanro tights, which had cost a small fortune but were worth it because they really lasted. Sara denied any knowledge of the tights, but Zoe admitted she had taken the tights, which were in a basket filled with clean laundry waiting to be folded, but hadn't thought they were anything special, mistaking them for her own No Nonsense tights.

"That's ridiculous!" scoffed Elizabeth, who was emptying the dishwasher of last night's dishes. "Anyone could see that they were really nice tights!"

"And I'm the one who's supposed to need

a chill pill," observed Molly, on her way to the cellar with a basket of dirty laundry. Her comment added fuel to the fire as Zoe thumped upstairs. She returned with the tights, tossing them at Elizabeth, who failed to catch them. They hit her in the face, which angered her.

"Don't throw them at me!" she yelled, grabbing a dish towel and whipping it across Zoe's face.

"Ouch!" yelled Zoe, grabbing Elizabeth by the shoulders and shaking her. "You think you're so special, coming home with your fancy French tights and acting like you're Marie Antoinette."

The scuffle excited Libby, who bounded from exile in her doggy bed and began barking at the combatants.

"Hey, hey," scolded Molly, attempting to step between the combatants.

"Well, you're acting like a big baby!" countered Elizabeth.

"Anyone can make a mistake," said Sara, attempting to make peace and shooing the dog out the kitchen door. "She gave them back."

"That's right," said Molly, taking Elizabeth by the arm.

"She didn't apologize!" said Elizabeth, reluctantly letting go of Zoe and speaking through clenched teeth.

"I'm sorry," muttered Zoe, rolling her eyes.

"You don't sound like you mean it," grumbled Elizabeth.

"That's enough," said Lucy, who had heard the squabble from upstairs but had hesitated to intervene, hoping the girls would work things out. When that didn't seem to be happening, she finally decided to put an end to it and came down the back stairs into the kitchen. "You girls are too big to be acting like this."

"Your mother's right," said Molly, wisely deciding to leave the scene and continuing on her way to the basement laundry.

"She started it," claimed Elizabeth, pointing at Zoe.

"It was a mistake, I said I was sorry," responded Zoe.

"What Zoe says is true," said Sara, taking Zoe's side and ganging up on Elizabeth.

Lucy had an overwhelming sense of déjà vu; she'd seen this scenario play out many times through the years. "You're too old for this nonsense," she said. "What happened to all that Christmas spirit you were displaying, when you were baking cakes to take to the old folks' home?"

"You're right, Mom," said Sara, in a

contrite tone.

"Let's wrap 'em up and deliver them," said Zoe.

"I'll drive," offered Elizabeth.

"I think I should drive," insisted Sara. "You haven't driven in a long time."

"That's exactly why I should drive," declared Elizabeth. "I need practice."

"I need practice, too," said Zoe. "I just got my license and I hardly ever get a chance to drive."

"No way," said Sara. "I want to make sure those cakes arrive in one piece. . . ."

"What do you mean? Like I can't drive as well as you?" demanded Elizabeth.

"You know you drive too fast," declared Zoe. "Mom even says so, don't you, Mom?"

That was the last thing Lucy heard as she ducked out the door, already late for work.

Lucy knew something was wrong the minute she walked into the *Pennysaver* office. For one thing, Phyllis didn't welcome her with her usual cheery greeting, but instead grimaced and hunched her shoulders, nodding her head in Ted's direction. Ted didn't greet her, either, but pointedly ignored her while he continued with a phone conversation. Lucy wasn't sure if she should take off her coat and get to work, or if she should keep it on because he was probably going to fire her and she would be leaving the job she loved for good. So she stood there, waiting for the phone call to end and the ax to fall.

It didn't take long. "About time you showed up," said Ted, slamming the phone down and turning to face her. "All hell's breaking loose and you're nowhere to be found."

"I was home, dealing with a family matter," said Lucy. "What's wrong?"

"Your story about Holly Fredericks is completely false, hardly a word of truth in the damn thing."

Lucy felt as if the earth beneath her feet had opened up and she was falling into a deep, dark hole. "What?"

"I just got off the phone with Eddie Culpepper, the town veterans' agent. He says there's no record that Holly suffered any injury while serving in Iraq and in fact" — he paused to glare at Lucy — "he says she was discharged after less than a year of active duty. Not a dishonorable discharge, he says, but not honorable, either. Just a general discharge, which means a sort of mutual agreement that things weren't working out."

"But she was paralyzed," said Lucy, trying

to make sense of this information.

"Nobody's arguing about that," said Ted, "it's just that she wasn't injured while serving as a soldier. And she wasn't even a very good soldier."

"But I swear her sister told me . . ."

"Check your notes," said Ted. "I hope she misled you, because otherwise I am going to have to print a correction that puts the blame squarely on you. Why didn't you check the facts?"

"I thought I was on solid ground," said Lucy, realizing she was instead on a very slippery slope. "And we were coming up on deadline . . ."

"I could have held the story," said Ted. "We could have avoided the firestorm that's coming. Besides Eddie I've already heard from the VA and the Fallen Heroes Fund, and I'm pretty sure we're going to hear from every relative and mere acquaintance of every genuine wounded veteran."

"I am so sorry, Ted," said Lucy, opening her notebook and rereading her notes, looking for Nancy's statement that her sister's paralysis was due to an injury sustained in Iraq. But even though she went through the scribbled pages numerous times she couldn't find the quote she needed. There was nothing for it but to call Nancy for clarification.

As soon as Lucy identified herself, Nancy began enthusiastically thanking her for the wonderful story about her sister. "You did a great job, you really captured Holly, and that story is going to make a big difference. It really shone a light on the problems that vets face —"

"Well, we have a problem," said Lucy, interrupting her. "It seems there was a misunderstanding. The town's veterans' agent says the military has no record that Holly was injured while on active duty, but when I spoke to you I think you said her paralysis was the result of a wartime injury."

"Oh, no, I never said that," replied Nancy, dashing Lucy's hopes of avoiding blame for the error.

"You definitely gave me that impression," said Lucy, fighting the urge to yell and struggling to maintain a civil tone. "You showed me all those photos of her in Iraq, now it seems she was only there for a few months before she was discharged from the Army. What really happened?"

"Holly did not get a fair shake from the Army, that's what happened. They promised all sorts of education and opportunities for foreign travel and she ended up in this horrible, dirty little village in Iraq. She was supposed to get this school up and running, but whenever she asked for supplies for the people in the village or tried to do things in a different way she'd get yelled at and told to stop trying to buck the system. She was one of the few women in her unit and was constantly sexually harassed by her fellow soldiers. After a while she couldn't take it and asked for a different posting, but instead they told her they would give her a discharge. She struggled on for a bit and then decided to quit."

Lucy bit her lip and sighed. "I wish you'd been more honest with me," she said. "That's an important story, too, that needs to be told."

"I was honest!" insisted Nancy. "I never said she was wounded in Iraq."

"Well, how did she get wounded?" demanded Lucy, losing patience.

"It was PTSD," said Nancy. "You know what that is? Posttraumatic stress disorder. It affects a lot of returning vets. They can't forget the horrors they saw, the friends they lost, and they have all sorts of mental troubles."

This time, Lucy was determined to get the facts. "I know what PTSD is," she said. "Was Holly actually diagnosed, by a mental health professional?"

"That's part of it, you know. She was embarrassed to ask for help. Holly kept insisting that she was all right, until all of a sudden . . . it was awful," replied Nancy, her voice breaking. "I found her hanging in the garage. At first I thought she was dead, but when I touched her she was warm so I cut her down and called the rescue squad. She was just barely alive, they said, a few more minutes and she would have died. Maybe that would have been better, but I didn't know that her spinal cord had been damaged. How could I know? I think she hated me for saving her."

Lucy let out a long sigh. Just when she thought things couldn't get worse, well, this was one of the saddest things she'd ever heard. Not only did Nancy have to shoulder the burden of caring for her paralyzed sister, but she'd had to deal with Holly's anger and resentment. And, of course, she would have been burdened with a huge sense of guilt.

"I am so sorry," said Lucy, "that must have been truly awful."

"It was," said Nancy, with a big sniff. "But I did the best I could for Holly. There was nobody else, just me."

Lucy had an uneasy feeling that once again Nancy was not telling her the whole story. "But why didn't you ask for help? Holly was a vet and there are lots of services available for vets with PTSD."

"They make it sound like they're ready to help when they're running TV ads for money, but believe me, it's a whole different story when you need help. These outfits are mostly in it for themselves, they're scams more interested in collecting donations than helping vets. Do you know how expensive TV advertising is? And mailings? That's where the money goes. All so a handful of executives can collect big paychecks. They help themselves, that's who they help."

"The VA is a government agency," said Lucy. "You could have gotten help from them, couldn't you?"

"The VA is a scandal, haven't you heard? Did you miss that story? About the long wait times, the incompetence, the red tape?"

Lucy was familiar with the story but had suspected it was overblown, driven largely by politics. "It would have been worth trying," she said.

"Like I had time for anything but taking care of Holly," scoffed Nancy. "Can you imagine what it was like, caring for someone twenty-four/seven?"

"No, I can't," admitted Lucy.

"Well, I hope you never find out!" exclaimed Nancy, ending the conversation.

"So?" demanded Ted, who had been listening.

"I'm screwed," admitted Lucy. "Holly hung herself but didn't finish the job. That's how she got paralyzed. Nancy claims she had PTSD, but it was never officially diagnosed."

"Lots of times it isn't," said Phyllis, who was making a fresh pot of coffee. "That doesn't mean it's not real. It's a big problem for returning vets. Some of those guys — and gals — have been on multiple tours of duty. They're under huge amounts of stress, and then they come home and there's a big sense of emptiness and loss. They're soldiers, though, they're supposed to be tough. They're not supposed to need help. It's hard for them to admit they're in trouble."

"That may be true," said Ted, looking stern as a judge delivering a long sentence, "but without an official diagnosis Lucy can't include PTSD in the correction."

"I know," agreed Lucy. "I'll simply say that due to a reportorial error it was mistakenly stated in a story in last week's issue that Holly Fredericks's paralysis was due to an injury suffered while on active duty in Iraq." She paused. "Do I need to say it was because of the suicide attempt?"

"We don't usually put that in obituaries," said Phyllis, arguing Lucy's case. "We just say 'unexpectedly.' It's kind of code, everybody knows that means suicide or a drug overdose."

"In this case I think we have to give the whole story," said Ted. "Lucy really milked the wounded vet angle. We've got to clear this up and give readers the truth."

"I agree," said Lucy, swallowing hard. She was eager to take her medicine, put her mistake behind her and move on.

"I'll get it right up on the Web site and we'll put it in a box on the front page next week," said Ted, giving her a serious look. "And from now on you'll check your facts, right, Lucy?"

"You betcha," said Lucy, relieved that she still had a job.

"You can't just ignore the PTSD part," said Phyllis, with a troubled expression. "It's real and I happen to know several families here in town that are dealing with it."

"I could do a separate story," said Lucy, eager to redeem herself. "Do you think I could interview some of these folks?"

"Like I said, these people are struggling, the last thing they want is publicity," said Phyllis, who was bent over double, reaching for the half-and-half in the mini-fridge.

"You could talk to Eddie Culpepper, though. He's right there on the front lines, he can tell you all you need to know about PTSD."

"Thanks," said Lucy, wondering why Phyllis felt so strongly about this particular issue. Then she remembered that Wilf was a vet, and she wondered if he'd struggled with PTSD when he returned from duty in Iraq. Was that why he was at Holly's funeral?

"Coffee's ready," said Phyllis, interrupting her thoughts.

Lucy glanced at Phyllis, noticing how her serious expression contrasted with the whimsical "Café Girl" design on her coffee mug, and almost asked the question that was on her mind. The words were just about to spill out when it occurred to her that if Wilf had struggled with PTSD it probably wasn't something that Phyllis wanted to share with the entire town.

"Thanks, Phyllis," she said, getting up to pour herself a cup. "And, Ted, thanks for not firing me."

Ted almost smiled. "Let's just say you're on probation."

"For how long?" asked Lucy, lifting the pot.

"Long," answered Ted, turning back to his computer.

Lucy drank the coffee while she struggled to get the right wording for the correction, though the two spoons of sugar she'd added to her cup didn't make the task any sweeter. Finally finished, she sent it to Ted for editing, then picked up her phone and called Eddie Culpepper. He was her friend police officer Barney Culpepper's son and had recently returned home to Tinker's Cove from a hitch in the Marines. He was studying for a degree in social work. When longtime veterans' agent George Keller retired, he was a natural choice for the job.

When he answered the phone Lucy quickly apologized for the erroneous story and told him the paper would run a correction. "It seems Holly tried to kill herself; her sister claims she had PTSD, but it wasn't actually diagnosed. I'd like to do a separate story, without mentioning Holly at all, about PTSD."

"But kind of implying that's what happened?" asked Eddie.

"We'll let the readers draw their own conclusions," said Lucy.

"I guess that's fair enough," said Eddie. "I'd sure like to get some attention for PTSD. I've got a ton of information here at the office."

"Why don't I come over?" suggested Lucy.

"How about one o'clock this afternoon?"

"Works for me," said Eddie.

When she arrived at Eddie's office, in the basement of the town hall, Lucy was struck by how much Eddie resembled his father. He was younger, of course, and didn't have Barney's beer belly, but he did have the same freckled face and reddish brush cut. Lucy's eye was caught by a photograph he'd hung over his desk, picturing himself in the full dress uniform of a Marine, and she commented on it.

"You made a very handsome Marine," she said.

"It's just to let the vets know that I served, that I'm one of them," he said, blushing.

"And you share their pain?" prompted Lucy, sitting down in one of the chairs for visitors and pulling her notebook and pen out of her bag.

"Sort of," admitted Eddie. "But the service was good for me. I was a pretty messed-up kid when I went in. I grew up in the Marines — and I'm taking advantage of the new GI bill and getting an education. Mostly I want to help other vets get the services they need and are entitled to. Sometimes it's burial in a military cemetery, sometimes it's help with taxes and finances, sometimes it's PTSD."

"What about PTSD? What services do you offer?"

"Mostly we have a support group here in town, a licensed therapist conducts it, and it gives the vets a chance to talk and learn they're not alone."

"How many come?"

"It varies. Sometimes fifteen or more."

"That many," said Lucy, who was surprised by the number. "I didn't know."

"It's kind of a hidden problem, which is why this story is a good thing." He started pulling brochures and pamphlets out of a desk drawer. "Like I said, I've got lots of information for you."

"Anyone I could interview? To put a face on the problem?" she asked in a coaxing tone.

"Absolutely not," he said, looking exactly like that stern-faced Marine in the photo.

CHAPTER EIGHT

Lucy had been so caught up in the PTSD story that she'd almost forgotten about Dorcas's death. An announcement from DA Phil Aucoin that he was holding a press conference on Friday morning to reveal the medical examiner's official findings was a grim reminder. Lucy didn't want to relive that awful evening and didn't want to go to the press conference, which was taking place so soon after her big goof, but knew she was in no position to protest.

"But, Ted, you get on much better with Aucoin than I do," she suggested, hoping Ted might take the bait. "He likes you."

"Sorry, but I've got better things to do. Pam wants me to help with decorations for the Hat and Mitten Fund gala." He gave her a look. "And I don't expect you to argue when I give you an assignment. It's not optional, Lucy."

"Sorry," she said quickly, eager to make

amends. "I just thought . . ."

"Do me a favor and don't think," said Ted in a curt tone.

Phyllis caught Lucy's eye and gave her a sympathetic smile, rolling her eyes at Ted's bossy attitude.

As Lucy gathered up her things to go to the press conference she reminded herself that Ted really was the boss at the paper, and he'd been more than fair to her by keeping her on. Most bosses would have fired an employee who made such a whopping big mistake, but Ted had kept her on. It was only fair, she supposed, that he was closely supervising her work. She would have to work hard to regain his trust if she wanted to return to the freewheeling days before she wrote the erroneous story, when she could pick and choose her stories.

The press conference took place in the basement meeting room of the Tinker's Cove town hall, and was sparsely attended. Besides herself there were only Pete Withers, who was a stringer for the *Portland Press Herald,* and Deb Hildreth, who wrote news copy for the local radio station. Both, of course, constantly checked the Web for breaking news and would certainly have seen the correction that Ted posted.

"I saw your correction, Lucy," said Pete,

"tough break."

"Yeah, it's easy to lose your objectivity when you're covering a heartbreaker like that," said Deb. "I bet that sister misled you."

"It was my own fault," said Lucy, with a big sigh. "I should have dug deeper, but I was working on deadline and didn't want to hold the story. I'm older and wiser now, believe me."

"It's a sad business," said Pete as Aucoin marched into the room, accompanied by Police Chief Jim Kirwan and the town's health inspector, Jennifer Santos.

The chief took the podium and noted the sparse attendance. "Thanks for coming," he said. "I have to admit I thought this might attract more interest, especially since it's Christmas and people are attending parties and eating foods prepared by others."

"None of the big papers have reporters anymore," said Pete. "They rely on locals like us."

"I'm pretty sure this story will get picked up," said Lucy, determined to get it right, straight from Aucoin's and Santos's mouths.

"Well, I'm supposed to introduce DA Phil Aucoin," said the chief, "but I think you all know who he is. Phil . . ."

Aucoin stood up and took the chief's place

at the podium, where he set down a pile of papers. "Thanks for coming. As the chief said, we think this is an important story to get out, especially at this time of year. The ME performed a thorough autopsy on the body of Dorcas Philpott, who collapsed and died during the Tinker's Cove Holiday Stroll on Friday, December second. Her conclusion was that the death occurred due to an extreme allergic reaction resulting in anaphylactic shock. Ms. Philpott had unknowingly ingested eggnog made from cashew milk, which produced the fatal reaction. Furthermore, the ME stated that it is unlikely that a prompt injection of epinephrine, say from an EpiPen, would have saved her because the reaction to the nut product was so fast and so severe." He paused. "Any questions?"

"It's been two weeks," said Pete. "What took so long?"

Aucoin nodded in agreement. "It was the toxicology; the samples had to be sent to the state crime lab. We asked them to give the tests top priority and they did; this was actually a fast turnaround." He waited for the reporters to finish their note-taking, then asked if there were any more questions. Getting no takers, he moved on to the next order of business, "And that brings me to our health inspector, Jennifer Santos, who will take it from here. Jennifer . . ."

Jennifer was a trim woman in her early thirties, who favored short hair, plaid shirts, and sturdy work boots. Lucy suspected that since she had to work in a male-dominated world she'd decided to dress like the boys, so contractors wouldn't notice they were taking orders from a girl when they needed approval for a new septic system.

"Thanks, Phil, for giving me this opportunity," she began. "Dorcas Philpott's death is very disturbing because it was entirely unnecessary and could have been prevented by proper food labeling. In my time as health inspector I've frequently had to deal with food poisoning, and it is almost always completely unintentional. Salad greens, for example, are sometimes tainted with *E. coli,* which persists even after the most thorough washing. Other instances that come to mind resulted from careless food handling, or ignorance, such as when stuffing is not adequately cooked. My department has worked very hard through the years to offer courses in proper food handling and I'm proud to say that since the courses were instituted we have reduced food poisoning incidents in the county by over ninety percent.

135

"Now, I have nothing against cashew milk, or soy milk, or any food, for that matter, but people need to be aware that they can cause allergic reactions in some people. It is imperative that dishes containing nut products, peanut butter, dairy products, and gluten be clearly labeled, so that people who are allergic can avoid them. We all know about the people who suffered terrible reactions from eating chili that contained peanut butter — who would ever think that chili would be made with peanut butter? It's these kinds of foods that contain unexpected allergens that are most dangerous.

"Now, don't get me wrong. Nut milk is a fine choice for people who are allergic to dairy products, but if it is included in a recipe that normally includes cow's milk, it must be labeled as such. That's all, thank you and please do your best to get the message out."

Jennifer stepped aside and the chief took the podium again. "Any questions?"

Lucy raised her hand.

"Oh, boy, here we go," said the chief. "I suppose you want to know if the eggnog could have been intentionally concocted to kill someone who had a nut allergy."

"Well, yeah," said Lucy.

"I suppose it could have," admitted the chief.

"But it would have taken a lot of rather personal information because whoever made the eggnog would have had to know that the intended victim had a nut allergy," said Aucoin.

"And there was always the risk that the eggnog would be passed along to someone else, or served to a group of people, which in fact happened. That cashew milk eggnog could have killed others, beside Dorcas Philpott," said Jennifer.

Lucy thought of the group of people at the *Pennysaver* office that evening, all innocently enjoying a festive holiday gathering, and thought that whoever made the cashew eggnog was either very careless or extremely coldhearted.

"The ME's official conclusion was accidental death," said Aucoin.

"So you won't be looking to charge someone with manslaughter?" asked Pete.

"No, and I hope you'll make this very clear to people. We really want to know who made the eggnog, and it's important that this person come forward, so we can make sure it doesn't happen again," said Jennifer.

"Whoever it is will not face charges, and we will maintain confidentiality, but we really want to talk to this person and explain the risks involved in preparing foods for other people," said Aucoin.

"Especially at this time of year, when people often give gifts of homemade food," added Jennifer.

"So, Jennifer, if you received a beautifully wrapped gift of food, say, Christmas cookies, would you eat it?" asked Deb.

"I'd sure think twice about it," she replied. "If I didn't know the sender, I would most certainly toss it in the trash."

That afternoon, Lucy was standing at the town pier, along with Patrick, waiting for the annual arrival of Santa by boat. This was a town tradition and made a great front-page photo for the *Pennysaver.* Quite a crowd of children and parents were gathered, bundled up against the chill wind that blew off the water and sent little puffy white clouds scooting across the blue sky. All eyes were fixed on the horizon, eagerly watching for the appearance of Santa's red boat, and this year it was little Adam Levitt who spotted it first.

"There's Santa, he's coming!" yelled Adam, jumping up and down and pointing at the approaching red lobster boat that was making its way across the cove.

Soon the boat was idling at the dock, and one of Santa's elves tied it fast, while Santa himself greeted the crowd with a wave and a hearty "Ho-ho-ho!" Lucy snapped several photos, recognizing Kris Kringle himself as Santa and noticing with surprise that Wilf was his helpful elf.

"Hi there," Lucy said, greeting him with a smile and taking in his elaborate costume, which included the traditional pointed cap, green jerkin, red-and-white-striped tights, and curly pointed shoes complete with jingle bells. His beard had filled in nicely, covering his chin with a froth of white curls.

"Hi, Lucy," he replied in a low voice. "How'm I doing? This is my first official gig. We start out as elves."

"It's nice to meet you, Mr. Elf," said Lucy. "This is my grandson, Patrick."

"Well, hello there, Patrick. Are you ready to meet Santa?"

Patrick didn't answer but carefully studied Wilf. "What's your name?"

For a moment Wilf was stumped, then came up with a reply. "Jingles. I'm Jingles the Elf, and I help Santa. In fact," he continued, "I've got to help him off the boat. See you later, and remember, you better be good!"

Lucy chuckled to herself as Wilf gave a

hand to Santa, helping him onto the dock and carrying his bag of toys. A makeshift throne of lobster pots awaited Santa, and he was soon seated, ready to meet his young admirers, who Wilf was arranging into an orderly line. As she waited with the crowd she wished she'd had more time to talk to him, wanting to get his thoughts about the fatal eggnog. Was he as worried as Phyllis? Or was she indulging in paranoid thoughts, making a big deal about a simple accident?

Then it was Patrick's turn, and Lucy was curious to hear what Patrick would say to Santa. She knew he was a bit shy and feared he might waffle at the last minute, perhaps even refusing to climb onto Santa's lap, but now that the big moment had come Patrick was handling the situation with youthful aplomb.

"Have you been a good boy?" asked Santa, as Wilf hoisted him onto Santa's lap.

"Pretty good," said Patrick, after giving the question some thought.

"And what do you want for Christmas?"

Lucy waited with bated breath for the little boy to reveal his heart's desire. What would it be? A computer game? Legos? A bike? A puppy?

Patrick didn't hesitate, he knew exactly what he wanted. "A guitar," he said. "A real one, not a toy."

Lucy's mouth dropped in surprise. She had no idea that Patrick wanted a guitar or was even interested in music.

"Well, we'll see what we can do, young man," said Santa, giving Patrick a tiny candy cane.

Wilf lifted him off Santa's lap and passed him to Lucy. "Merry Christmas!" he said, before turning to the next child.

As they made their way through the crowd, back to the car, they passed a table where PTA members were selling baked goods and hot cocoa. Lucy recognized her friend, Lydia Volpe, among the volunteers and stopped to chat.

"Hi, Lydia, how are you?"

"I'm fine, Lucy. Who's this?" she asked, indicating Patrick. Lydia was a retired kindergarten teacher and took a keen interest in her friends' grandchildren, who were often the offspring of her former students.

"My grandson, Patrick. He's Toby's little boy. The whole family is here from Alaska and staying with us while Toby does some graduate work at the university."

"Toby always was a bright one," said Lydia. "How about some nice hot cocoa, to warm you up? It's for a good cause, only a dollar a cup."

"Uh, I'm not . . ." she began, hesitating as a vision of Dorcas's thrashing body popped into her head.

"Please," said Patrick, tugging on her arm. "I'm cold."

"Well, I don't know . . ." she began, unwilling to disappoint Patrick but mindful of the health agent's warning to think twice before consuming foods made by others.

"It's perfectly good, Lucy," said Lydia. "I made it myself."

"Not an old family recipe, I hope," said Lucy, attempting a joke.

"Look, I know what happened to Dorcas and so does everybody else. We aren't selling anything today, which is a shame because a lot of folks worked hard to contribute delicious baked goods."

"It's true," said one of her companions, who had been rearranging the assorted cookies and cakes on the table. "And it's all perfectly good."

"I made the cocoa myself, and it's not an old family recipe. I added boiling hot water to a jumbo canister of store-brand cocoa mix I got at Marzetti's," said Lydia. "It's entirely artificial, far as I can tell."

"Well, then, it must be safe," said Lucy, opening her purse. "We'll take two. With marshmallows, please."

"And if people see that you don't drop dead," said Lydia, "maybe we'll sell some more."

"Which would make standing out here in the freezing cold worthwhile," added the companion, stamping her feet and rubbing her hands together.

Lucy took a sip of the hot liquid and smiled. "It's good, very good," she said. "What do you think, Patrick?"

"Mmmm," said Patrick, licking his upper lip, which was already sporting a cocoa mustache.

Lucy went straight to the office, after handing Patrick off to his mother, who was taking him Christmas shopping. Ted wasn't there, which was a big relief to Lucy. Ever since her big goof she hadn't felt comfortable with him; she knew she was on probation. Another mistake, she feared, would be her last.

"Ted's still out?" she asked Phyllis, who was hunched over her computer, working on the events listings.

"Yup," she replied. "I bet Pam's got a long 'honey do' list for him and those decorations for the gala tomorrow night are just the beginning."

"It's that time of year," said Lucy, setting

her bag down on her desk and unbuttoning her jacket.

"And Ted wants us to work Saturday. . . ."

"What?" asked Lucy, dismayed.

"He says it's mostly the end-of-year wrap-up and if we get a head start on it he can give us a longer Christmas break," explained Phyllis. "Is it a problem for you?"

"Kind of," admitted Lucy, who still had a long list of things to do before Christmas. Top of that list was the fact that she hadn't yet wrapped the presents she planned to send to Bill's parents in Florida, and was worried about getting the package off in time to arrive for the holiday. "Do you know the last day you can mail a Christmas package?"

"They say right up until the twenty-second, I think, but if I were you I wouldn't wait. The sooner the better."

"Maybe if I call home I can catch Elizabeth and she can wrap the stuff we're sending to Bill's folks," said Lucy, sitting down at her desk and shrugging out of her coat while reaching for the phone. The call went to voice mail, but when Lucy began leaving her message Elizabeth picked up.

"Were you screening calls?" asked Lucy, who was always worried for her girls' safety.

"No, Mom. And there are no Level Three

sex offenders lurking outside the house. I was in the shower," answered Elizabeth.

"Well, you can't be too careful," said Lucy, going on to explain the reason for the call. "So it would be terrific if you could wrap the package for Grandma and Grandpa in Florida and get it to the post office."

"No problem, Mom," said Elizabeth. "And if you want I'll pick up some groceries and make a real French supper, to make up for the pot roast fiasco."

"That would be lovely," said Lucy, who was surprised by her daughter's sudden helpfulness.

"De rien," said Elizabeth, ending the call.

Having dealt with that crisis, Lucy decided to put off writing up her account of Aucoin's press conference to take advantage of Ted's absence while she worked on the PTSD story. She didn't want Ted looking over her shoulder; she wanted to present it to him completely finished and perfect, like a Christmas present.

As she read through her notes she realized that while she had plenty of facts and figures, the story was going to be little more than a compilation of statistics. She needed to put a face on the problem and she knew that face had to belong to someone other than Holly Fredericks. She looked up from her computer, trying to think of someone she could talk to, just as Phyllis came over to her desk with a press release.

"This might be a little story for you — the Queen Victoria Inn is having a gingerbread house contest."

"A photo op, anyway. Thanks," she said, taking the announcement. "By the way, didn't you say you know some PTSD vets?"

Phyllis was quick to respond. "Why do you ask?"

"Well, Wilf is a vet . . ."

"Oh," she replied, letting out a big sigh. "I was afraid you thought Wilf . . ."

"Wilf?" asked Lucy, surprised at Phyllis's reaction. "He's the last person I'd think of when I think of PTSD."

"Well," admitted Phyllis, "he did have some trouble, years ago, when he first got back from Iraq."

"Do you think he'd talk about it with me?"

"For the paper? Are you crazy? He doesn't even want to talk about it with me! As far as he's concerned that was then and this is now and it's all over and done with." She paused, a troubled expression on her face. "But I don't think it's ever over. He's been having nightmares, tossing and turning. Something's definitely bothering him."

"That's too bad. Maybe if you ask him

146

about it . . ." began Lucy, as the little bell on the door jangled and Marty Jasek, the mail carrier who had taken Wilf's place, came bustling in. "Are you ladies working or gossiping?" he asked in a joking voice.

"This is community news," said Phyllis, puffing out her chest. "What's the difference? It's all the same thing."

"What have you got for us today?" asked Lucy.

"Not much today," he said, placing a small pile of envelopes on the reception counter and turning to go.

"Hold on," said Lucy, casting a glance in Phyllis's direction and reaching for her jacket. "I want to ask you about, um, dates. I have a package that needs to get to Florida by Christmas."

Marty had the answer ready. "Right up until two days before Christmas, if you ship pri—"

"Oh, I don't want to hold you up," said Lucy, buttoning her coat. "I'll walk with you. I could use some fresh air."

"Whatever you say," said Marty, looking puzzled as he held the door for her.

Once outside, Lucy got to the point. "Look, I don't want to give the wrong impression, I love everybody at the post office, but Phyllis is real worried about that

147

eggnog that was sent to Wilf. It was made with cashew milk and it could have killed him if he drank it. . . ."

"Wilf's allergic to nuts," said Marty, as they walked along the street.

"Did a lot of people at the post office know that?" asked Lucy.

"Yeah, he was pretty careful about what he ate." Marty had stopped in front of the next store, Dorothy's Gifts and Souvenirs, holding a handful of mail. "I've got to . . ."

"I'll wait," said Lucy, with a shiver.

Marty was back in a moment, and she continued her questioning. "I don't want to hold you up," she said, "so I'll get right to the point. Is there anyone at the post office who's had problems with Wilf?"

Marty stared at her, his mouth open in disbelief. "Are you kidding? Everybody likes Wilf. Everybody."

"That's good to know," said Lucy, not quite convinced. Maybe everyone at the post office liked Wilf, and so did the Real Beard Santas, but there were plenty of other folks in Tinker's Cove. After Phyllis's admission that *something* was bothering Wilf, Lucy wondered if she really meant that *someone* was bothering her husband. She only hoped it wasn't the same coldhearted and careless person who'd made the eggnog, a person who she was beginning to think had tried to kill him and might try again. "Thanks, Marty," she said, turning to go back to the office, eager to warm up.

As she hurried along she noticed Ted walking down the street from the opposite direction, and met him at the door. "How was the press conference?" he asked, opening the door and jangling the bell.

"The ME says Dorcas's death was an accident and Aucoin is not investigating further," she said, stepping inside.

"Good," said Ted, pausing at the reception desk and nodding. "Nice to know we won't be facing charges for poisoning our readers."

"Only their minds," quipped Phyllis, getting an evil look from Ted as he leafed through the pile of letters on the counter.

"She's on a roll," said Lucy, hoping Phyllis wouldn't question her about her odd behavior, chasing Marty Jasek down the street.

"What's this?" he asked, opening one of the envelopes. "A bill from the plumber?"

"Don't you remember?" asked Phyllis. "That leak in the bathroom?"

"Oh, yeah," he said. "But I need to go over our maintenance costs with you, for next year's budget. Have you got a minute?"

"Sure," said Phyllis, with a resigned sigh.

When she got home that night, Lucy was greeted with a delicious aroma emanating from the oven. Elizabeth was bustling about the kitchen, lifting pot lids and peeking inside, taking little tastes of whatever she was cooking as well as steady sips from a large glass of red wine.

"What are you cooking?" asked Lucy. "It smells delicious."

"Lapin," replied Elizabeth.

"It's rabbit, Mom," said Sara, sounding unhappy. "A nice little fuzzy bunny that never did anyone any harm."

"It's a classic French dish," said Elizabeth, refilling her glass. "Once you eat lapin you'll never think of rabbit the same way. They're delicious."

"I'll just have a peanut butter sandwich," said Sara, with a sniff.

"You'll be missing out on a rare treat," insisted Elizabeth. "Oh, and by the way, Mom, I mailed the package."

"Thanks," said Lucy, noticing that the bottle of wine that was sitting on the kitchen table was nearly empty. "Did you drink all this yourself?" she asked.

"Most of it's in with the fuzzy bunny," said Elizabeth, defending herself. "I've been cooking all afternoon." She paused. "And don't worry, I've got a second bottle for the table. This is the cooking bottle."

When they gathered at the dining room table, which Elizabeth had set with the good china and silver, Lucy had to bite her tongue. While there had been a lot of sound and fury in the kitchen as Elizabeth put the final touches on the meal, there wasn't much to show for it. The rabbit was rather small, and there was barely enough to serve seven adults and one growing boy. It was a good thing that Sara had stuck to her guns and made herself a sandwich, and Molly had fixed an organic hot dog for Patrick. Elizabeth had also cooked some tiny baby potatoes and carrots as sides, but the dinner plates were largely empty.

"Delicious," exclaimed Bill, polishing off his serving in three bites. "I'll have seconds."

"Me too," said Toby.

"There's salad, that's the second course," said Elizabeth. "That's how they do it in France. It's very good for the digestion."

"You mean there's no seconds?" asked Toby, incredulously.

"I guess I'll have my salad now," grumbled Bill.

"Uh, you need to wait until everyone's finished and I can clear the table and bring salad plates. And I have to dress the salad."

"I'll take ranch," said Bill, looking down at the plate that would have made him a member of the clean plate club. "And I don't need a new plate. This one's fine."

"Same here," said Toby.

"I made a vinaigrette dressing, for the whole salad," said Elizabeth. "In France, there's always a fresh plate for each course. So much nicer than jumbling all your food together."

"I hope you're going to do the dishes, then," said Zoe. "I know it's my turn, but it isn't fair if I have to wash a whole lot of extra plates."

"Don't forget the pots," said Sara. "I think she used every single one."

"Girls, Elizabeth made a special treat for us," said Lucy, ignoring the rumbling in her tummy, "and it's good to try new things."

"Is there dessert?" asked Bill, in a hopeful tone.

"Mais oui!" exclaimed Elizabeth. "I have a chocolate truffle for each of us." When this was greeted with silence, she added, "In France, they value quality over quantity. Fresh food, like this rabbit, and I found hydroponically grown salad greens. I got it all at this new organic store. Funny you don't know it, it's right opposite Marzetti's."

"I love that place," said Molly. "That's where I got Patrick's hot dogs, made from grass-fed beef with no artificial additives."

"The prices are astronomical there," said Lucy.

"But what would you rather have? That cheap ice cream from the IGA, made with carrageenan and who knows what, or a beautifully hand-crafted chocolate."

No one answered, although Bill allowed himself a large sigh, and Elizabeth got up to clear the table and prepare the salad.

"You get what you pay for," said Molly.

"I like ice cream," said Patrick, who had polished off his expensive hot dog wrapped in an equally expensive whole-grain bun and still looked hungry.

"There's always cereal and peanut butter and jelly, in case you need a snack," whispered Lucy, as Elizabeth returned with the salad.

CHAPTER NINE

As Ted had ordered, Lucy went into the office on Saturday morning, but she was less than enthusiastic. The flood of press releases announcing holiday events had dried up, all the usual town government committees had rescheduled their regular meetings due to the holiday, and at all the schools, teachers and students alike were counting the days until Christmas vacation. "There's absolutely nothing happening," said Lucy, sifting through the meager pile of mail.

"It's like this every year. Christmas starts the day after Halloween, but when you really get in the Christmas mood and want to watch a nice holiday movie on TV, you're out of luck," complained Phyllis.

"Nonsense," said Ted, just arriving and bristling with energy. "This is my favorite time of year," he declared. "Time for the annual review issue. Time to go through the year's news and give readers a recap. Phyllis, you can go through the real-estate sales, the legal ads, and don't forget the obits. I'll do sports, business, and the economy, which leaves everything else for you, Lucy: theater, arts, and town government."

"Righto," said Lucy, booting up her computer. Soon she was immersed in the highs and lows of the past year: the high school drama club's winning performance at the state theater competition, the contentious battle over new zoning regulations, and the feature story she'd written about an award-winning quilt maker. She had just about gotten through all her saved files when she accidentally opened the story about Holly Fredericks.

"Ted, are you recapping the news stories?" she asked, hoping she wouldn't have to revisit the biggest mistake of her career.

"I think we'll each do our own," said Ted. "You summarize the stories you covered and I'll do the same for mine."

Lucy groaned. "What should I do about the Holly Fredericks mess?"

Ted smiled. "Be brief, very brief." Then, after thinking for a minute, he said, "Skip it. Phyllis can just include it with her obits."

"Thanks," said Lucy, greatly relieved. She was about to close out the file when a photo caught her eye. It was the one Nancy had given her that showed Holly pictured with the other members of her unit in Iraq. One face, sporting a heavy five o'clock shadow, looked awfully familiar. She enlarged the photo with a few clicks of her mouse, zooming in on the face that looked a lot like Wilf, now that he had a beard.

"Hey, Phyllis," she called across the office, "will you take a look at this photo?"

"Sure," said Phyllis, getting up from her desk and looking over Lucy's shoulder at the picture of the unidentified soldier, whose face filled the computer screen. "Am I supposed to know this guy?"

"Doesn't he look like Wilf?" asked Lucy.

"Maybe," admitted Phyllis. "When was Desert Shield? Twenty-five or more years ago, right? That's quite a while ago, and I didn't know him then. We weren't exactly kids when we started dating."

"But people don't change all that much and now that he's got his beard, you notice his eyes more, and the way his nose is bent a little, like this guy in the photo."

"His cousin broke his nose when he was a kid," said Phyllis. "But since he grew his beard I've noticed that guys with Santa beards all look sort of alike. You know some guys shape their beards, so they're just around their mouths, or they have a soul patch or something distinctive like big lamb chop sideburns. But the Santa beard is just full and white and covers a lot of face."

"That's true," said Lucy, as Phyllis returned to her desk to answer the phone and was soon involved in taking a complicated classified ad.

Lucy's finger was on the delete button, but she hesitated, staring at the photo, and recalling the glimpse she got of Wilf at Holly's funeral. She remembered Wilf's courtship of Phyllis, and the way their faces lit up each day when he arrived with the mail, and how amused she had been to watch these mature lovers' flirtatious behavior. They had been like kids, despite their ample waistlines and sagging chins.

But, she realized, they had both done quite a lot of living before they became involved. Lucy knew that Phyllis had been married before, briefly, and didn't like to talk about it. Wilf had been in the military, but judging from Phyllis's reaction when she asked if she could interview him about PTSD, Lucy sensed he hadn't shared his wartime experiences with Phyllis. Probably not with anyone, for that matter.

But if the soldier in the photo really was Wilf, it meant that he had served with Holly in the same unit. Which explained why he attended her funeral. But why had he behaved so oddly, ducking out before the service was over and skipping the reception afterward? He had seemed, thought Lucy, like a man who was involved in an affair. But that, she reminded herself, was impossible since Holly was paralyzed.

Or was it? Maybe they had been lovers before, and maybe Wilf had continued to visit, even after he married Phyllis. Maybe he still carried a torch for the paralyzed woman despite the hopelessness of their situation — and didn't want his wife to know.

But that simply didn't seem like the Wilf she knew — he was crazy about Phyllis. Maybe, she thought, he'd been involved with Holly before he met Phyllis. Maybe he'd even jilted Holly in favor of Phyllis and felt guilty about it; that sense of guilt would certainly have grown when Holly became paralyzed.

Then an awful idea occurred to Lucy, an idea that made her feel absolutely sick to her stomach. "Phyllis, when did you and Wilf get married?" she asked.

"We'll be celebrating our sixth anniversary in May," she replied. "Why do you ask?"

"Just curious," answered Lucy. "What's the date?"

"May twelfth."

"That was my parents' anniversary," said Lucy.

"Funny coincidence," said Phyllis. "How long were they married?"

"Thirty-three years when my father died."

"I wonder if Wilf and I will have that long," mused Phyllis. "We weren't exactly spring chickens when we got married."

"I bet you'll make it," said Lucy, "people are living well into their eighties these days."

"I'm not counting on it," said Phyllis, "I'm just taking each day as it comes."

"That's probably the recipe for a long, happy life," said Lucy, who was already dialing the fire department's business line.

It was answered by Patsy Kirwan, a member of the Kirwan clan who dominated the town's police and fire departments. Her cousin, Todd, was chief of police, and several other members of the family were public safety workers. Patsy was a dispatcher and worked on weekends, when her husband was free to watch the kids.

"Hi, Patsy, this is Lucy Stone, at the *Pennysaver.*"

"Hi, Lucy, what can I do for you?" replied Patsy, sounding cautiously helpful. Lucy knew the police and fire departments had a bit of a love-hate relationship with the weekly paper. They loved getting positive coverage for saving lives and helping people, and hated any sort of criticism, such as Ted's recent editorial calling for more diversity in hiring.

"Well, I was wondering if you still have records of rescue calls made in the past? Say ten or twelve years ago?"

"Sure do," said Patsy.

"And this would be public information?"

"Sure is," said Patsy. "The rescue calls are funded by taxpayers, so we've got to be open about them. Are you interested in a particular date? I can get it for you in a minute, a few clicks on the computer."

Lucy glanced across the room, where Phyllis was hunched over her desk, applying address labels to renewal forms to be sent to subscribers.

"I think I'd better come over," said Lucy.

"Sure thing," said Patsy. "I'll be here 'til five."

Lucy didn't wait, she popped right up and grabbed her coat, telling Phyllis she'd be back in a minute, she had an errand that couldn't wait. Once out on the sidewalk she hurried across the street to the fire station, where she went straight to the chief's office.

"Wow, you didn't waste any time," said Patsy, greeting her.

"It's a sensitive matter," said Lucy. "I just wanted to know if the rescue squad was called to 14 Winter Street a few years ago, it would have been an attempted suicide."

"Do you have a name?"

"Holly Fredericks."

Patsy was right, it only took a few clicks of the mouse to recover the information Lucy was looking for. "Here it is, May twelfth, six years ago, Holly Fredericks was transported to the hospital with a suspected spinal cord injury."

"Thanks," said Lucy, who suddenly felt as if a terrible weight had fallen on her. Holly Fredericks had attempted suicide on the day Wilf married Phyllis.

CHAPTER TEN

When Lucy left the police station she was terribly upset, unsure what to do with the information she had just obtained. Tell Phyllis? That wasn't her place, not if Wilf hadn't told her about his relationship with Holly. Tell the police that she suspected Nancy had deliberately concocted the nut milk eggnog and delivered it to Wilf as revenge for her sister's death? She knew that Todd Kirwan would politely hear her out and then would patiently explain that mere suspicion was not enough to charge someone with a crime, the law required actual evidence. She was walking along, lost in thought, when she practically bumped into Wilf himself.

"I was just thinking about you," she said.

"Well, Lucy, I'm mighty flattered, but I am a married man," he joked, smiling broadly. With his new white beard he was the very picture of Santa himself.

"Not in that way, Wilf," said Lucy, unable

to resist smiling. She had always enjoyed Wilf's sense of humor, and his easygoing ways. "Listen, I just figured out about you and Holly. . . ."

"There was never any me and Holly," said Wilf, dropping the smile.

"She tried to kill herself on your wedding day," said Lucy.

"That's not on me," he said, quickly. "I never encouraged her, I did everything I could to *dis*courage her," he continued, emphasizing the *dis*. "She was crazy, she wouldn't take no for an answer. Said we were meant to be together, it was fate, it had to be, stuff like that."

"I believe you," said Lucy. "But I think you need to be wary of her sister, Nancy. I think she's out for revenge."

"Nancy? She's the sane one," said Wilf, raising his eyebrows in disbelief. "If there was ever a candidate for sainthood it's Nancy. You know she took care of Holly for years, even before the, uh, accident. She always looked out for her little sister."

"Well, I think she may have become a little unhinged now that Holly's gone," said Lucy. "I think she's the one who sent you the cashew milk eggnog."

"Now you're the one who's talking crazy," said Wilf, with a sharp nod. "Nancy would

163

never do anything like that. As a matter of fact, she saved my life when I had an allergy attack. She's allergic to bee stings herself and had an EpiPen, so she recognized the symptoms when I had a bad reaction. Oh, it was years ago now. I was delivering the mail, they were on my route, you know, and her neighbor gave me a Toll House cookie. Little did I know that it was packed with walnuts."

"But, Wilf, don't you see? That means she knows you're allergic to nuts, and she's the one who sent you the eggnog. Think about it: How many other people know?"

"Probably quite a few. I've never tried to keep it a secret." He scratched his beard. "Say, I've been practicing my ho-ho-hos for the gala tonight, want to hear?"

"Sure," said Lucy. It was obvious that Wilf only had one thing on his mind, and that was his debut performance as Santa at the Hat and Mitten Fund gala that night. She waited until he'd finished delivering a very impressive string of hearty ho-ho-hos and, after complimenting him on his effort, issued one last warning. "Watch your back, Wilf," she said, resigned to the fact that she'd done all she could. She'd warned Wilf about Nancy, now it was up to him to protect himself.

When Lucy returned to the *Pennysaver* office she discovered the CLOSED sign was hanging on the door. Considering Ted's earlier enthusiasm for working on Saturday she assumed Pam must have given him orders to report to the Community Church Hall to help out with last-minute preparations for the Hat and Mitten Club gala. Lucy had been involved early on, enlisting subscribers for the program and soliciting contributions for the raffle, so the only thing she had to think about was deciding what to wear. Since she had collected several gaudily decorated Christmas sweaters, bought at tag sales through the years, it was simply a matter of choosing the right one.

There was a bulky black cardigan with a sequin-trimmed Christmas tree, a red turtleneck with a pair of dancing elves sporting striped stockings and fuzzy pom-poms, and a green boat neck with a red suited Santa complete with shiny plastic belt and boots, as well as a silky beard. Which one should she wear, she wondered, as she turned into her driveway, where Sue's little mini Cooper was parked. What was Sue doing here, when she ought to be folding napkins for the gala?

"Surprise!" said Sue, greeting her when she entered the kitchen. She was sitting at the kitchen table, which was strewn with sewing supplies, stitching away on a piece of black clothing. Behind her the ironing board was set up and the iron was releasing puffs of steam.

"What on earth are you doing?" asked Lucy, who rarely touched either the iron or her sewing box.

"I'm turning up a skirt for Zoe," she said. "Elizabeth called and said it was an emergency."

"That's right, Mom," said Elizabeth, coming down the kitchen stairs with an armful of clothing. "When we started to get dressed for the gala we discovered nothing looked right, so Auntie Sue agreed to come and make a few alterations." She put the clothes she was holding down on the table and held up the scarf she'd been wearing when she arrived at the airport, now transformed into a halter top. "See? Isn't it gorgeous?"

Lucy had to admit the scrap of silk was lovely, but offered no protection from the cold. "You'll freeze in that!" she exclaimed, divesting herself of parka, hat, gloves, scarf, and boots.

"She's going to wear it with my tuxedo jacket," said Sue. "Layering is the key. She'll be warm when she's sitting at the table, eating, but she'll be able to shed the jacket for dancing."

"And what are Sara and Zoe wearing?" asked Lucy, fearing they would be togged out in similarly skimpy and revealing outfits.

"Don't worry about them, they're going to look lovely," said Sue, peering at Lucy over her half-glasses. "The question is, what are *you* planning to wear?"

"Well, I can't quite decide," admitted Lucy, taking a seat at the table. "I have three great sweaters. . . ."

"Oh, please, Mom, not those ugly Christmas sweaters," said Elizabeth, rolling her eyes.

"When will I get to wear them, if not at Christmas?" demanded Lucy. "They're perfect, warm and festive, too. The question is, which one? Christmas tree, elves, or Santa?"

"None!" said Sue and Elizabeth in chorus.

"Why not?" asked Lucy in a sulky tone. "I love those sweaters."

"They are, well, festive is one word I would use," said Sue, choosing her words carefully. "But I think you should save them for more intimate, family occasions. Say, Christmas morning, when opening presents, or for your traditional Christmas afternoon hike with the kids."

"That's right, Mom," said Elizabeth, catching Sue's drift. "They're really too special for an occasion like the gala. You'll be hopping up and down and fetching and carrying and you wouldn't want to spill gravy on Santa's fluffy beard, now would you?"

"You're not fooling me," said Lucy, pouting. "You think my Christmas sweaters are in bad taste, you think they're ugly."

"Face it," said Sue, looking her in the eye. "I'm only telling you because I'm your friend. They're atrocious, and we want to save you from yourself."

"Like an intervention, Mom," said Sara and Zoe, coming into the kitchen from the family room, where they had been listening. "It's for your own good."

"That's right," said Bill, joining the group from the dining room, where he had been hiding, waiting for Lucy's return. He was carrying a large silver box with the Carriage Trade logo tied with a huge red bow, which he placed on the table, in front of her. "Elizabeth and Sue helped me pick it out."

"It must have cost a fortune," objected Lucy, staring at the box, which she knew came from the town's fanciest and most expensive boutique.

"Think of it as an early Christmas present," he said.

"Aren't you going to open it?" demanded

Sara, speaking for them all. They were all eagerly anticipating her reaction when she saw the outfit.

"You shouldn't have. . . ." she said, unwrapping the bow and lifting the top, revealing a simple black dress tucked in multiple layers of tissue paper.

"It's just a classic . . ." she began, much relieved. She'd been terrified the gift would be some sort of lacy, beaded horror.

"Little black dress!" said Sue, finishing the sentence. "You can wear it for years."

"That's what the French women do," said Elizabeth. "Pearls for one look, add a jacket for another, or a scarf. Sometimes boots, sometimes pumps. It's endlessly versatile."

"It is lovely," admitted Lucy, noticing the designer label.

"Go try it on!" urged Zoe.

"Okay," she said, carrying the box upstairs to her room. There she set it on her bed and wiped away a tear or two; she'd never had such a nice dress. Of course, she realized, as she lifted it out of the paper, it was sleeveless and the fabric seemed very light, not nearly warm enough for a winter night in Maine.

She shivered a bit, pulling off her sweater and jeans, and slipped the dress over her head, amazed at how perfectly it fit. Studying her reflection in the full-length mirror that hung on the back of the door, she saw a stylish, sophisticated woman looking back at her. A woman she hardly recognized. Shrugging, she hurried back downstairs, where she was greeted with applause.

"Wow!" said Bill, with an approving grin.

"Very nice," said Sue.

"Way to go, Mom," said Sara.

"Cool," was Zoe's verdict.

"Magnifique!" declared Elizabeth.

Later, after Sue had left and the girls had disappeared into their rooms to dress for the evening, Lucy went back upstairs to put the final touches on her outfit. She pulled on a pair of sheer black pantyhose and her dressy black boots, and added her good pearl earrings and the lavaliere she'd inherited from her grandmother. She still wasn't comfortable about going sleeveless, however, and at the last minute tossed the black cardigan with the sequin-trimmed Christmas tree in her tote bag, along with her Christmas apron.

When the family arrived at the church hall, Lucy had to admit that Ted and Pam had done a great job with the decorations. The usually bare, utilitarian room had never looked so lovely, with lighted Christmas trees clustered in every corner, frothy swags of white tulle on the windows, and white LED candles twinkling on the tables dressed with red and green plaid cloths. Frankie LaChance, Renee's mom, was seated at the piano, playing classic tunes from the American Songbook, while revelers greeted each other, surveyed the offerings on the raffle table, and bought tickets.

Soon Rachel went to the podium and clinked a glass, silencing the room and welcoming everyone to the gala, thanking them for coming, and assuring everyone that the funds raised would go to the Hat and Mitten Fund, which provided warm clothing and school supplies for the town's less fortunate children. Then the high school students who had volunteered for the evening began serving the roast beef dinner, cooked by Chef Oscar from the Queen Victoria Inn, also a volunteer.

The high school kids were serving dessert when Santa Claus arrived, complete with jingle bells and a hearty ho-ho-ho, accompanied by Phyllis, dressed as Mrs. Santa Claus. Wilf did a great job, announcing the prize-winning raffle tickets and presenting the lucky winners with prizes ranging from gift certificates, to clothing provided by Country Cousins, to the grand prize of a weekend theater trip in Boston.

Lucy was sipping the last of her after-dinner coffee when a sudden draft, probably caused by somebody coming or going through the big double doors, made Lucy shiver. Now that the raffle was over, she realized that some people probably wouldn't want to stay for the dancing and those doors would be opening quite a lot. It was definitely time to put on her Christmas cardigan sweater, even if it meant taking a lot of teasing. She slipped away from the table and headed for the kitchen, where she'd left her tote bag. Only Chef Oscar was there, along with a couple of volunteer dishwashers.

"Have you seen a tote bag?" she was asking, when she heard a sudden burst of loud pops, like gunfire.

Her first reaction was disbelief and denial. This couldn't really be gunfire, it must be some holiday joke, she thought. Perhaps someone brought Christmas crackers to the gala, and people were popping them and pulling out the paper hats and trinkets they contained. Or maybe someone had foolishly brought fire crackers, thinking it would add some excitement to the party.

She had found her tote bag and was pulling out the sweater when she heard Chef Oscar say, "Shots, gunfire at the Community Church." He was standing by the double swinging doors, looking through one of the little windows, and speaking on his cell phone. He must be calling the police for help, she realized, and went to join him.

"Get back!" he hissed. "Run. Go out the back. Go!" he ordered, and the dishwashers fled, running out the door to the outside, leaving their coats and belongings behind. Lucy, somewhat confused and unwilling to leave her family, went to stand beside him and cautiously peeked through the window on the other door.

"I can't believe it," she whispered, frozen in place. The festively decorated hall was now filled with panicking people, some falling to the floor, others running for the doors, fleeing a lone assailant dressed all in black, complete with a terrorist-type balaclava hood, who was firing some sort of gun into the air.

Lucy was horrified; she felt her heart might stop at any moment. She'd read about terrorist attacks in Paris and Newtown and San Bernardino, but she'd never thought such a thing could happen here in Tinker's Cove, Maine. Chef Oscar was right, the expert advice was to run, and if you couldn't run, to hide, but most of the people at the gala were caught in the open, with no place to seek cover except under a table or behind a fake Christmas tree. She frantically searched for the table where she had been sitting moments before with her family, and saw that Bill and Toby were on the floor, crouched behind the table they'd knocked over as a shield and covering the girls' bodies with their own. Thank goodness they'd left Patrick home with a babysitter.

I can't bear this, she thought, clutching the sweater to her chest and turning away from the windowed door to the relative safety of the kitchen wall. One hand had flown instinctively to her mouth and she prayed for their safety, and for her own, when the shots suddenly ceased. The silence was terrifying, ominous. What was going on? She had to look, and bracing herself for a bloody scene of carnage, she returned to the window.

There was no blood, nothing but a roomful of terrified people, under the control of the single terrorist with a powerful assault rifle. Everyone who hadn't escaped was on the floor, arranged in awkward positions. Santa himself had ducked down and was crouching behind the podium. The floor was strewn with cloth napkins, high-heeled shoes that had been shed, purses that had been dropped, and chairs that had been knocked over. In the corners, the lights on the fake Christmas trees continued to twinkle, creating a surreal scene.

Lucy listened for the sound of approaching sirens that would signal help was on the way, but there was nothing but silence. Where were they? Why weren't the police on the way? Her family was in there, in deadly peril. She thought of Patrick: What would happen to him if they were all killed? "The shooting's stopped," the chef was saying, whispering into his phone. "There's only one shooter that I can see."

The black-clad terrorist stood in the center of the room, gun at the ready, coolly surveying the chaos. Then, spotting Santa, the shooter began advancing toward the podium, ordering Wilf to stand up.

The voice was high-pitched, feminine, and Lucy realized the shooter had to be Nancy Fredericks, and she was only after one victim: Wilf. "You killed Holly!" she said, her eyes glittering, as he clumsily got to his feet. "But I'm not going to kill you, you piece of scum. You deserve to die slowly, like she did. A single bullet in the spinal cord should do it. Then you'll be paralyzed like she was."

"Let's talk about this," said Wilf, his voice surprisingly strong as he raised his hands in a sign of surrender.

"Who the hell are you?" demanded Phyllis, stepping out from behind one of the Christmas trees, where she had gone for shelter. Lucy's heart skipped a beat. Phyllis's bravery actually took her breath away. "What exactly do you think you're doing?" screamed Phyllis, advancing toward Nancy like some furious superwoman, dressed in a plus-size Mrs. Santa outfit.

At the same time, Lucy noticed, Eddie Culpepper was advancing toward Nancy from behind, crawling commando-style across the floor.

"Hasn't there been enough pain?" asked Wilf, locking eyes with Nancy. "What will shooting me accomplish? You'll spend the rest of your life in jail!" His eyes wandered for a second, settling on Eddie who was just behind Nancy now and ready to spring to his feet. Nancy sensed her danger and suddenly whirled around, letting off a spurt of wild gunfire toward the ceiling. Ceiling tiles shattered and fell, looking bizarrely like clumps of snow, sliding off a roof.

Nancy quickly gained control of her weapon, holding fire and lowering the gun toward Eddie, when Lucy remembered the sweater in her hands. Nancy's back was toward the kitchen and Lucy realized this was her chance, maybe the only chance anyone would get to stop the killing. She charged through the swinging door and tossed the sweater like a lasso, sending it flying through the air. It seemed to float for a long time before it hit its target and fell on Nancy's head. Eddie grabbed her by the knees, bringing her down and knocking the gun from her hands.

Then, suddenly, cops and firemen were everywhere. Nancy was immediately handcuffed and taken away; the officers fanned through the room, helping people to their feet and checking their condition. Wilf and Phyllis clutched each other in an emotional embrace. Eddie was surrounded by friends and congratulated for his bravery. A few people needed care, including selectmen chairman Roger Wilcox, who appeared to have suffered a heart attack.

Bill wrapped his arms around Lucy and hugged her close, at the same time scolding her for her foolishness. "There was no need, the cops were outside," he said. "You should've stayed in the kitchen where you were safe."

"Wow, Mom, that was great," declared Zoe, as the family clustered together around Lucy and Bill.

"You're a hero!" announced Toby.

"So brave," said Molly.

"Cool under pressure," added Sara.

But it was Elizabeth who had the last word. *"Bien fait,"* she said. "Well done."

"But where's my sweater?" wondered Lucy, scanning the disordered room in search of it.

"I'm sure they'll keep it for evidence," said Sue, joining the family group and giving Lucy a hug.

"Will I get it back?" asked Lucy.

"I certainly hope not," said Sue. "That is one dangerous sweater."

By the time the deadline rolled around on Wednesday, just days before Christmas, Lucy found herself wishing for the news drought she'd complained about only days before.

"Good work, Lucy," said Ted, as he clicked send and e-mailed the formatted copy to the print shop, just as the bell in the Community Church steeple began tolling noon. "And right on deadline, too."

"I can't believe you had the presence of mind to take all those pictures," said Lucy, clicking through the dramatic images on her computer. Ted had gone to his car to fetch Pam's forgotten cell phone and had followed Nancy into the hall. He was in the vestibule when the shooting started and used the phone to take photos.

"Once a newsman, always a newsman," he said, leaning back in his wheeled desk chair and tenting his fingers. "This was the biggest story that ever happened in Tinker's Cove and I was determined to cover it."

"I can't believe you got her with that sweater," said Phyllis, looking over Lucy's shoulder at a photo of the airborne cardigan just before it landed on Nancy's head. "That was some brave move, you saved Wilf's life . . ." she broke off, choking up.

"I can't believe you, standing out there like that, chewing Nancy out," said Lucy.

"I honestly don't know what came over me," admitted Phyllis, staring at the image of herself in the Mrs. Santa outfit, arms akimbo, angrily challenging Nancy.

"You're a hero," said Lucy, plucking a tissue from the box on her desk and wiping her eyes. "You distracted Nancy long enough for Eddie to get close."

"You were both amazing," said Ted, offering a rare bit of praise. "And now we've got a humdinger of a story to follow in the New Year, what with the trial and all. Nancy's already confessed that she cooked up the eggnog that killed Dorcas."

"So now she'll face charges for Dorcas's

death, as well as attempting to kill Wilf," said Lucy.

"And Federal charges for terrorism," said Ted. "They'll throw the book at her."

"Now that it's over and nobody got shot, I feel kind of bad for her," said Lucy. "She was a devoted nurse to her sister. I think it was all too much for her and she cracked."

"That's what Wilf says," said Phyllis, reaching for her coat, "but I'm not quite so forgiving. I hope she goes to jail for a very long time."

Lucy thought how frightened she'd been in the church kitchen, terrified of losing her family, and understood why Phyllis felt the way she did. But she had interviewed Nancy, she had sat with her at her kitchen table, and she believed the stress of caring for Holly and then the pain of losing her had been more than Nancy could bear. "There's got to be a better way, there's got to be more help for caregivers and . . ."

"Crazy people?" suggested Ted.

"Yeah," said Lucy. "We don't have a functioning mental health system in this country, we just send them to jail."

"I don't care," said Phyllis. "I want that woman put away, period."

"Maybe something good will come of this in the end," said Ted, who had shut down his computer and was standing up, sliding his chair beneath the desk. "The trial will focus attention on mental health and gun control, too." He walked over to the thermostat and squinted at it, turning the dial. "I'm closing the office 'til Monday," he said, surprising Lucy and Phyllis, who had given up hope of the promised holiday break. "Have a merry Christmas."

"You too, Ted," said Phyllis, who had put on her coat and was ready to go.

"But I'll expect you both to be at your desks bright and early Monday morning," he added, flicking off the lights.

"With bells on," said Lucy, zipping her parka.

Bells were ringing from the steeple of the Community Church, and a light snow was falling late Christmas Eve as Lucy and Bill made their way home from the candlelight service.

"Penny for your thoughts," said Lucy, breaking the silence as they drove along the familiar route.

"I was just thinking of all the Christmases we've had together," said Bill. "Remember that first year in Tinker's Cove?"

"The year I found snow had blown into Toby's room and covered his pillow?"

"That's the one. Everything went wrong. The furnace died, the pipes froze, I was sure I'd made a big mistake quitting my job in New York and moving to Maine."

"Your folks sent a check, a huge check. . . ."

"Best Christmas present ever," laughed Bill. "What were you thinking?"

"I was wondering if we had enough cocktail sauce for the shrimp," said Lucy.

"That's my girl," said Bill, chuckling as he turned the car into the driveway. "Always the romantic."

They admired the Christmas lights and decorations as they walked arm in arm up the path to the house; inside they found Elizabeth putting finishing touches on the dining room table where candles glowed in silver holders. She'd set out the good china and cloth napkins, and placed the silver dessert forks facedown, to show off the hallmarks as they did in France.

"I thought we'd have the *Bûche de Noël* tonight, it's a French tradition," she said.

"What a lovely idea," said Lucy, quickly shedding her outdoor clothes as the family gathered at the table, where the elaborately decorated chocolate cake held center stage. She hurried to join them, pleased by this unexpected treat.

"Isn't this wonderful?" she asked, looking around at the faces of the people she loved most in the world. "We're all here, every one. This is a special Christmas."

"Let's hope we have many more," said Bill, carefully carrying a ceramic pitcher into the room from the kitchen.

"That's not eggnog, is it?" asked Lucy, suspiciously.

"Of course not," declared Elizabeth, with a big smile. "It's red wine. Delicious with chocolate."

"Because that's the way they do it in France!" they all chorused, breaking into joyful laughter.

EGGNOG CHIFFON PIE

1 prepared graham cracker crust
1 tablespoon unflavored gelatin
2 tablespoons cold water
3 egg yolks
1/4 cup sugar
1/4 teaspoon nutmeg
2/3 cup whipping cream, scalded
2 tablespoons dark rum
1 1/2 teaspoon vanilla extract
3 egg whites
1/4 cup sugar
1/2 cup whipping cream
2 tablespoons confectioners' sugar
2 tablespoons rum

Soften gelatin in water for five minutes.

Beat egg yolks, then add 1/4 cup sugar and nutmeg and mix well. Stir a small amount of hot cream into egg mixture, stir eggs into hot cream. Stir in softened gelatin until dissolved.

Add rum and vanilla. Chill for three hours.

Beat egg whites until soft peaks form. Add 1/4 cup sugar, beating until stiff peaks form. Fold into cold mixture, then spread in crust. Freeze for eight hours. Move to refrigerator two hours before serving time.

Beat whipping cream until soft peaks

form, add confectioners' sugar and rum, then beat well. Spread over pie. Add a dusting of nutmeg if desired.

KILLER EGGNOG

12 eggs, separated
1 pound confectioners' sugar
1 quart milk
1 quart whipping cream
4 cups bourbon
2 cups light rum
2 cups brandy
Nutmeg, to taste

Beat egg yolks with confectioners' sugar in large bowl. Beat in milk, then add cream; blend well.

Stir in bourbon, rum, and brandy.

Beat egg whites until stiff peaks form, slip on top of eggnog in punch bowl. Dust with nutmeg if desired.

Dear Reader,

Through the years, as I've written more than twenty Lucy Stone mysteries, the Stone family has become very dear to me. You might even say these fictional characters have become part of my own family!

The series began when Lucy and Bill were young parents, struggling to establish themselves in the small Maine town of Tinker's Cove after moving from New York City. Bill gave up a lucrative job on Wall Street to realize his dream of being a restoration carpenter — a plan that involved moving the family into a ramshackle antique farmhouse.

Life in Tinker's Cove has not been as tranquil as Lucy and Bill expected. In fact, through her job as a reporter for the local newspaper Lucy has discovered that many things are not quite what they seem in this picture-perfect New England town. Her investigations into local news stories have led her to uncover numerous crimes, including murder.

I hope you enjoyed reading *Eggnog Murder* and that you will seek out other Lucy Stone Mysteries. The series traces Lucy's path from young mother to investigative reporter and sleuth. You'll meet Toby as a Little League player and Cub Scout, Elizabeth before she becomes a Parisian sophisticate, Sara as an awkward middle-schooler, and Zoe as a baby. As an armchair detective you can join Lucy in her adventures, and take part in the life of my favorite fictional family.

Wishing you a joyous holiday,
Leslie Meier

■ ■ ■ ■

Death by Eggnog: A Hayley Powell Food & Cocktails Mystery

LEE HOLLIS

■ ■ ■ ■

CHAPTER ONE

Hayley wasn't sure she had heard right. She looked up from her desktop computer to see *Island Times* crime reporter Bruce Linney staring at her and waiting for an answer.

"I'm sorry, Bruce, did you just ask me out on a date?"

"What? No! Of course not!" he said, running a shaky hand through his wavy brown hair nervously. "Is that what you thought?"

"It sure sounded like you were asking me out on a date," Hayley said, swiveling her office chair around to face him head-on and folding her arms.

It was going to be fun watching him squirm out of this one.

"I just . . . I mean, I was curious to know . . . if you were going to this year's Restaurant Association Christmas Dinner . . ." Bruce stammered, red-faced, scooting over to the coffeepot to pour himself another cup just so he had something to do.

"You know I'm going. I go every year and cover it for the paper."

"Yes, right. That's your job. Of course I know that."

"And that's when you asked me if I would like to go to the dinner with you," Hayley said, smiling, though slightly weirded out by the prospect of a date with Bruce Linney. Just a few months ago they couldn't even stand being in the same room with one another. Then they teamed up to investigate a baffling murder case and discovered to their surprise that they actually worked well together.

"Okay. I'll give you that. But you completely misread my intentions!"

"Did I?"

"Yes! I know you've been single for quite some time now that you're no longer seeing the vet. . . ."

"How do you know that?"

"Well, I just assumed . . . You mean you're not? You've been seeing someone?"

"Well, no. But how dare you think I spend my Saturday nights all alone with my pets and eating a plate of homemade peanut butter oatmeal cookies and watching some cheesy Hallmark Channel show with Andie MacDowell playing a small-town judge?"

Which was exactly how she spent last

Saturday night.

But did Bruce really have to know that?

"Okay, I won't think that," Bruce said. "Though I have to give you credit for painting such a remarkably detailed picture of your hypothetical Saturday night at home."

"You were asking me out, Bruce," Hayley said, unfolding her arms and turning back to her computer. She had a lot of work to finish before quitting time.

"No, I wasn't! I just thought because you cover the dinner for the *Times* you usually get comped two tickets, and I wondered, if you weren't taking one of your friends . . ."

"So this is all a ploy to get yourself a free meal?"

"Not just one meal. Every restaurant in town is going to be there," Bruce said, smacking his lips. "Mexican, Italian, Thai, Lebanese . . . It'll be like a trip around the world!"

The Restaurant Association Christmas Dinner was an annual event where every holiday season all the restaurants in Bar Harbor open during the winter months catered their signature dishes to the year-round residents who paid a fee to attend. All the proceeds went to a local charity that bought Christmas presents for needy families.

"So what do you say?" Bruce asked, a sweet smile on his face.

"For your information, the Association always gives me two complimentary tickets, but I always buy my own because the dinner is for such a good cause."

"You mean you'll give me both tickets so I can bring a date?"

"No! Buy your own ticket, Bruce! For the love of God, it's for charity!"

"What the hell is going on out here?" Sal Moretti bellowed as he barreled out from his office. "You two are like one of those Hepburn and Tracy romantic comedies my wife binge watches on Turner Classic Movies!"

"Believe me, Sal, there's nothing romantic about Bruce being too cheap to buy a disadvantaged child a toy for Christmas this year!"

"Fine. Point taken, Hayley. Forget I said anything," Bruce snarled, slamming down his coffee cup and heading for the back bullpen.

Sal grabbed him by the arm as he tried to pass. "I can't go to print until I get your column, Bruce."

"You'll have it, Sal. Before the end of business today. I promise."

"It was due last night. What's the holdup?"

Bruce sighed and rubbed his eyes with his thumb and forefinger. "I'm having a little trouble coming up with something to write about."

"Again?" Sal asked, scratching his belly before glancing over at Hayley with a raised eyebrow.

Hayley shrugged.

The exchange was not lost on Bruce, who quickly became defensive. "It's just a quiet time of year. Nothing much happens around the holidays. It'll pick up at New Year's, especially with all those DUIs the cops will be handing out!"

"Maybe we need to revisit cutting your column down to once or twice a week instead of every day," Sal said off-handedly before quickly changing the subject. "Do we have any snacks around? The ball and chain has me on a new low-carb diet! Can you believe that? During the holidays! Merry Christmas!"

"I think we may have some leftover Halloween candy in the supply closet," Hayley said.

Hayley had never seen a man with Sal's heft move with such agility. He was gone in a flash. She turned to Bruce, whose face was a ghostly white.

"I can't afford to lose any columns," he

stuttered. "You know that means he'll cut my salary after the first of the year. I can't afford that!"

"Don't worry, Bruce. It'll work itself out."

"I need a dead body to turn up and fast!"

Hayley's jaw dropped open.

It took a second for Bruce to notice.

"I'm kidding. It's not like I want somebody to die, but if a body does turn up, it would be nice if it was under suspicious circumstances. . . ."

Hayley watched him backpedal.

He wasn't very convincing.

"I mean, I'll settle for a cottage break-in or a car theft. Something less serious. Although a murder investigation would give me weeks of material. . . ."

Hayley had heard enough. She focused on the classified ads for tomorrow's edition displayed on her computer screen and tuned out Bruce's rambling voice.

Little did she know, nor Bruce for that matter, that his wish was about to come true.

In a way nobody in town would ever have expected.

CHAPTER TWO

When Hayley walked through the back door into her kitchen after driving home from work, she was stunned to see her daughter, Gemma, tossing a salad while a familiar mouthwatering smell wafted out from the oven.

"Is that — ?"

"Turkey meatloaf. Pretty much the only thing I can make." Gemma laughed as she set the salad aside and crossed to give her mother a hug. "I nixed the twice-baked potato because your glucose number was up at your last physical so we're cutting down on carbs while I'm home. You're going to have to settle for a side salad."

"I love you," Hayley said, squeezing her daughter tight, not wanting to let go. It had been a tough adjustment after Gemma left for college. Hayley missed not having her around. So she was thrilled when Gemma called from the University of Maine at

Orono where she was studying Animal and Veterinary Sciences and told her she was going to spend the month of December living at home while completing a work study program at Dr. Aaron Palmer's vet practice in Bar Harbor.

"Mom?"

"Yes?"

"Mom, I love you, too, but I can't breathe."

Hayley suddenly realized she was still hugging her daughter.

She finally let go and Gemma jokingly gasped for air.

"I'm sorry. I just love having you home. Especially with your brother visiting your father in Iowa for the holidays."

"By the way, he called me today, and I hate to be the bearer of bad news, but I think he may have a little crush on Dad's girlfriend."

"Oh, dear God, no! Becky?"

"He couldn't stop talking about how pretty she looked in her tight red sweater with nine tiny little reindeer embroidered across her mountain of a chest, and how sweet she was to bake him homemade chocolate chip cookies while they watched a James Bond marathon on Spike TV, and how she let him help her brew her family's apple cider recipe that she shares with no one, but she showed him and only him because she trusts him. The entire conversation was Becky, Becky, Becky!"

"Well, to be fair, he is closer to her in age than his father is! They obviously have more in common."

Gemma giggled and carried the wooden bowl of salad to the dining room and set it down on the table. "Mom, go relax in the living room and I'll bring you a glass of wine."

This whole Gemma waiting on her hand and foot thing was starting to feel suspicious. But Hayley wanted to give her the benefit of the doubt.

She took her coat off, hung it on the rack, and sauntered into the living room where she stopped dead in her tracks. The white pine tree Hayley had bought from the tree farm just outside town stood tall and proud in the corner of her living room. But when she left this morning for work it was naked with no ornaments, lights, or tinsel. Now it was a majestic, brightly lit, fully decorated Christmas tree. There were even a few small wrapped presents underneath it. All of Hayley's holiday figurines she had collected over the years were carefully placed around the living room. Her dog, Leroy, was in one corner gnawing on a meat bone. Her cat, Blueberry, was stretched out in another corner, exhausted from having torn open catnip sewn inside a mouse made of felt.

She heard Gemma pad into the room behind her. She spun around to see her holding out a glass of wine, a sweet smile on her face. "Here you go. Oh, I almost forgot. I followed one of your recipes and made some blue cheese and pecan stuffed dates as an appetizer. Let me go get them and you can have some with your wine!"

She turned to run out, but Hayley reached out and grabbed her arm. "Hold it right there, missy."

Gemma slowly turned toward her mother, a sheepish grin on her face. "What?"

"The turkey meatloaf I could buy. Decorating the tree I could almost buy. But presents for the pets and stuffed dates? You're up to something! What is it?"

"Mom, I've missed you while I've been away at college, and so while I'm home I want to show my appreciation by making things a little easier on you. I knew you dreaded decorating the tree, especially since Dr. Aaron was here to help you the last couple of years."

Dr. Aaron Palmer.

The handsome vet she had been casually

seeing for the last eighteen months, who broke it off with her last spring. They hadn't spoken in months. She spotted him at the Shop 'n Save in November, buying a turkey during the Thanksgiving rush, but she veered her cart down the spice aisle to avoid having to say hello. They had promised to remain friends, but it was awkward, and quite honestly, it still hurt a little. Ever since Gemma came home and began working in his office, Hayley believed a reunion was inevitable, but so far she had managed to avoid one.

Hayley snapped back to reality.

Her daughter was trying to change the subject.

She was fast becoming an expert.

Just like her mother.

"What do you want, Gemma?"

"Mother, I am insulted you would even think — !"

"Gemma!"

"I want to go skiing with some friends for Christmas."

"What?"

"I know it's awful and we decided I would spend Christmas here with you and I really want to, but . . ."

"But . . ."

"But there's this really cool bunch of

premed students I'm in this study group with, and they've rented a cabin in Sugarloaf for the week during Christmas, and they invited me to go along, and of course I said no because I told them I had already promised to spend the holidays with my dear mother who is all alone because my brother is in Iowa and her boyfriend dumped her last spring and she has no one . . ."

"Can we just cut to the chase, please? I'm about to kill myself," Hayley said, gulping down the glass of wine.

"Well, today I got a call from one of them, his name is Pierre, and he's so cute and sweet and he's from Montreal, so he's got the French thing going for him, and, well, he practically begged me to change my mind, and you know I'm a sucker for a French accent. . . ."

"You told him you'd go."

"Yes, I'm sorry. It just came out and then he sounded so excited I was going and I didn't have the heart to change my mind again so I just sort of hung up. But I can call him back, if you really don't want me to go. . . ."

Hayley knew she had to let Gemma go.

She couldn't be one of those mothers who held on to her kids for dear life, not wanting them to grow up, live their lives, enjoy new experiences. And since her daughter was legally an adult, she would just ignore the fact that it was a handsome French Canadian with a seductive accent that convinced her to ditch her mother for Christmas for hot toddies and God only knows what else by the fireplace at some remote cabin in the snow-covered mountains.

"Have fun. I'll be fine."

"Really? Are you sure?"

"Yes, I'm sure. There are plenty of people I can spend Christmas Day with . . . like your Uncle Randy and Sergio, or Mona and her family, or Liddy and Sonny! I have endless possibilities!"

"Thank you, Mom! I love you!" Gemma said, enveloping her mother into another quick hug before releasing her and running back into the kitchen. "I have to check on the meatloaf."

She had already told Randy and Sergio, as well as Mona and Liddy, not to include her in any of their plans because she was going to have some much-needed quality time with her only daughter. But it might not be too late to snag a last-minute invite to one of their gatherings. Or she could just spend the day munching on fruit cake and watching Christmas movies and cuddling with Leroy and Blueberry, who were so disinterested at the moment they didn't even know she was in the room.

As her buddy Mona often liked to say around the holidays, "Merry friggin' Christmas!"

CHAPTER THREE

Mona pounded her fist on the bar at Drinks Like A Fish, the local watering hole owned by Hayley's brother, Randy. Her face was a deep red, her large brown eyes about to pop out of their sockets. With her other hand, she desperately grabbed at her throat and opened her mouth to speak, but she could only manage a cough and some sputtering.

Randy, who was behind the bar, had already sprung into action. He grabbed a glass, scooped up the beverage nozzle, filled it with water, and then quickly handed the glass to Mona. She gratefully gulped it down until the glass was empty. Then she slammed it down on the bar as she caught her breath.

"What are trying to do, kill me?" she gasped.

"Too spicy?" Randy asked.

"Too spicy? That's putting it mildly," Mona said, pushing the plate of chicken wings across the bar away from her. "Hand me a towel to clean my hands. I'm afraid if I lick the sauce off I'll go into cardiac arrest."

"Once again you're being way overdramatic, Mona," Liddy said, sitting on the stool next to her and taking a big bite out of one of the wings.

A dab of sauce was left on her right cheek.

Hayley, who was on the other side of Mona, grabbed a napkin off the bar and dutifully wiped the sauce off of Liddy.

"I can't believe you can eat those wings and not feel a thing," Hayley said.

"I grew up eating jalapeño peppers out of the jar. I love spicy food," Liddy said before grabbing another wing off the plate. "Aren't you going to try one, Hayley?"

"I'm not sure I have the courage," Hayley said, eyeing the wings warily.

"Come on. I just saw on the news that eating spicy food makes you live longer," Randy said.

"I don't see how!" Mona barked. "My life just flashed before my eyes! I thought I was a total goner!"

Randy filled up another glass of water and placed it in front of Hayley. "Here. Just in case."

"Don't do it, Hayley!" Mona cautioned.

"Learn from my mistake!"

But Hayley could see in her brother's eyes that he wanted his sister's unvarnished opinion, so she picked one up between two fingers and bit a generous piece of chicken off the wing bone. She chewed it for a few seconds before she felt her tongue burning. Mona was right. These were fiery hot! But also zesty and delicious. She tore off another piece of chicken until only the bone was left in her hand.

"Are you friggin' kidding me?" Mona wailed. "You like them?"

"Some of us have more of a varied culinary palate rather than your usual diet of franks and beans, followed by a Twinkie," Liddy said, rolling her eyes.

"Randy, they're amazing," Hayley said, taking a sip of water to wash the wing down.

"I use Frank's Red Hot sauce, but my secret ingredient is a pinch of ghost pepper powder."

"I'm not surprised it's called ghost pepper," Mona snarled. "I'm going to be haunted by those wings for days."

"How about a Bud Light on the house if you stop trashing my wings, Mona?" Randy asked, reaching into the cooler and pulling out a bottle, which he then waved tantalizingly in front of Mona's face.

"Deal. I guess those wings aren't half-bad if your stomach's strong enough," Mona said, grabbing the beer out of Randy's hand before he even had the chance to pop the cap off. "I'm just too delicate."

"Delicate is not a word I would ever associate with you, Mona," Liddy said.

"Oh, lay off me, will you, Liddy? I'm in no condition to fight back. I'm in a weakened state from those wings. . . ." Mona said, her voice trailing off as Randy appeared with the bottle opener but waited for her to finish her sentence before opening her free beer.

She got the hint. "Because those wings just knocked me over, they were so tasty."

Satisfied, Randy opened the bottle of beer and Mona happily chugged it down.

"So you're going to serve these wings at the Restaurant Association Dinner?" Hayley asked, perusing the plate and choosing another wing to eat.

"Yeah, you think it's too bold of a choice? I mean, most of the restaurants serve food that's right down the middle, not too exotic, not too spicy, because a majority of the attendees are old and set in their ways and are meat and potatoes kinds of people. But I really want to stand out and make an impression since I only recently started serving food in the bar."

"Oh, those wings will stand out all right," Mona said, chuckling. Her eye caught Randy glaring at her. "Because, you know, they're just so damn good."

Randy reached in the cooler and gave her another beer, which Mona accepted with a big grin.

"That'll be four dollars, Mona."

The grin swiftly faded and she reached into the pocket of her jeans for some dollar bills.

"I think you'll be the hit of the Restaurant Association Dinner and that's just my honest opinion as your favorite sister. Completely unbiased," Hayley said, grabbing more napkins to wipe off the wing sauce covering her face as she chowed down.

"So you promise you'll write something nice in your column?"

"If the batch of chicken wings you prepare for the dinner is anywhere near as good as these, it'll be a rave review," Hayley said.

The ghost pepper had finally gotten to Hayley as she chomped on the last wing from the plate. Her throat burned, her mouth felt like it was on fire, and she began coughing.

"Or an obituary," Mona snickered.

CHAPTER FOUR

"Do you mind? I am trying to enjoy a nice dinner with my husband!" the woman seated at a corner table screeched loud enough for the other patrons to turn their heads and see what all the commotion was about.

Hayley and Randy both stopped eating, their forks in midair, and swiveled around to get a good look at Fannie Clark-Van Dam, bristling in her seat, eyes blazing, waving a fork stabbed with a beef and portabella mushroom ravioli at a hunched-back elderly woman with white pulled-back hair who hovered over her table at Mama Di-Matteo's on Kennebec Place in town.

Hayley and Randy had just come by the restaurant for a quick, quiet dinner of slow-roasted garlic with hunks of bread and the owner's delectable Mussels Marinara seafood pasta dish.

The service was quick, but the dinner was

anything but quiet.

The elderly woman refused to budge. She snatched the fork out of Fannie's hand and hurled it down on the table. "You can eat when I'm through talking to you!"

There were scattered gasps throughout the dining room including a very loud one from Fannie herself. Fannie's dining companion, her husband, Dutch Van Dam, just sat motionless in his wheelchair opposite his wife, a blank expression on his face.

"Is that . . . ?" Randy asked, straining to get a good look at the old woman accosting the Van Dams at their table, whose back was to them.

"Agatha Farnsworth," Hayley nodded.

Agatha Farnsworth was the local librarian who had worked at the Jesup Memorial Library since the 1960s and, in Hayley's opinion, was an ill-tempered, nasty old woman who could frighten children, not to mention their parents, with just a sideways glance.

There was no love lost between her and Hayley. Agatha relished torturing Hayley for talking too much ever since she was a young girl checking out Nancy Drew mysteries from the library. Hayley despised her, as did her own kids, who also faced Agatha's wrath mostly for the crime of being

Hayley's spawn.

In fact, pretty much everyone in town couldn't stand Agatha Farnsworth.

And now it appeared her enemies list was growing.

Fannie Clark-Van Dam slowly picked her fork up off the tablecloth and placed it on the edge of her plate. She seethed, trying to remain composed, but having a tough time of it. "I'm going to ask you politely one more time, Agatha, to let us get back to our dinner. We can discuss your issue tomorrow over the phone."

Fannie glanced over at her husband, who wasn't even paying attention. He just stared down at the gorgonzola steak on his plate while chewing a small piece in his mouth with a blank look on his face. Poor Dutch Van Dam had suffered a debilitating stroke several months back and had not been the same since. He had been confined to a wheelchair and had lost the power of speech. It was a devastating blow for his wife, Fannie, who strutted around town, the proud wife of a wealthy businessman. She was a local girl from meager means who struck pay dirt one summer after meeting the dashing out-of-towner with rich family connections. He was her meal ticket and once she got her hooks in him, there was no turning back. She became the grand dame of Bar Harbor, dining out at the most expensive restaurants, flaunting her new-found money. People wondered what Dutch saw in the ambitious spoiled girl. She was attractive enough, but far from a trophy wife. She lacked a sparkling personality and often just left people cold. Perhaps she was, in Randy's words, "a tiger in the sack."

Nobody would ever know for sure.

But despite his questionable taste in women, Dutch was a stand-up, solid guy who would always lend a helping hand to those in need, at least whenever his wife wasn't around to put a stop to it. She was despised and ridiculed. He was beloved and admired. But now, it appeared he was a shell of his former self, a near vegetable, unable to communicate, left in the care of his flighty, self-absorbed wife. Hayley had heard a few locals commenting that poor Dutch Van Dam, left to the mercy of the shrill, annoying Fannie, had a fate far worse than death.

And tonight, the poor guy couldn't even eat his gorgonzola steak in peace.

"I'm done calling you. I've left four messages this week and you refuse to call me back. This needs to be settled right now," Agatha said in a raised voice.

Eric, the restaurant owner and resident chef, hustled out of the kitchen at the behest of his jittery hostess who had no idea what to do, and casually strolled over to the table. "Is everything all right?"

"No, everything's not all right, Eric. This woman is trying to kill me!" Agatha shrieked.

A hush fell over the dining room.

"How, Agatha? How is Mrs. Van Dam trying to kill you?"

"She wants to poison me!"

"Oh, please! That's preposterous!" Fannie scoffed as she finished off the ravioli on her fork. "By the way, the raviolis are delicious tonight, Eric."

"Thank you," Eric said with a smile. "And how's the steak, Dutch?"

Dutch ignored him. He was busy concentrating on his chewing, staring straight ahead. A piece of gorgonzola fell out of his mouth and dropped onto his cream-colored sweater and he used his fingers to try to pick it up, but it was a slow process because he couldn't quite get ahold of the stray piece of cheese buried in the fabric. But it gave him something to focus on other than the two bickering women in front of him.

"The fact of the matter is, Eric, that Agatha and I both serve on the committee for the Restaurant Association Dinner, and we are having a small disagreement because I am going to bring my family's Christmas eggnog recipe that dates back generations. . . ."

"And I've asked her to make something else because I'm allergic to dairy," Agatha said, crossing her arms, waiting for Eric to see the severity of Fannie's offense.

"Well, why don't you just not drink it?" Eric asked, foolishly under the impression he had solved the problem.

Agatha glared at him. "If someone were deathly allergic to smoke, would you suggest they just not breathe?"

"No, but that's not really the same thing. . . ." Eric mumbled like a chastised schoolboy who was being picked on by the teacher unfairly.

"I want all dairy banned from the Restaurant Association Dinner out of respect to those with dietary issues like myself!" Agatha screamed.

"And I think that is wholly unreasonable!" Fannie scoffed.

"What do you think, Eric?" Agatha said, eyes narrowing, challenging him to try to disagree with her one more time.

"I think . . . I think I smell something burning in the kitchen," Eric said, spinning around and retreating, no longer concerned with the disturbance in his dining room.

"Agatha, I'm sorry about your condition, but I think it's grossly unfair that everyone else at the dinner has to pay for it. I will make sure all the food and drinks are clearly marked so you don't eat or drink anything with dairy in it. That's the best I can do. And if that's not good enough, then you can always stay home," Fannie said in a haughty superior voice that made the hair on the back of Agatha's neck stand on end. If there was one thing Agatha hated more than anything else it was someone acting high and mighty. It rankled her to the core.

She picked up a glass of water in front of Dutch and hurled it in Fannie's face and then stormed out of the restaurant.

There was utter silence in the dining room as Fannie picked up her napkin and dabbed at her wet face. Then she set it back down and continued eating as if nothing had happened.

Hayley stared at Dutch. There seemed to be a slight, almost imperceptible smile forming on his lips. As if he enjoyed watching his wife get drenched. But then as quick as it came, it was gone again. At least there was some movement in his facial muscles. The physical therapy was at least working just a bit.

Randy twirled some linguini around his fork, and said, "So Team Agatha or Team Fannie?"

"Team Fannie. Without a doubt," Hayley said as she and most of the other diners went back to eating their meals.

"Because you've hated Agatha since you were a kid?"

"No, because I love eggnog and now all I can think about is having some of Fannie's age-old recipe at that dinner."

ISLAND FOOD & COCKTAILS

BY HAYLEY POWELL

Last night after work, I swung by my brother Randy's bar to refuel and recharge by having some of his delicious and addicting ghost pepper chicken wings. I had barely taken my seat on the stool in front of him when he placed my usual drink of choice, a Jack and Coke, in front of me, and said, "Dish and don't leave out any details!"

Sadly I knew exactly what he was talking about. There had been a "little incident" the previous weekend that I had hoped would be swept under the carpet by now but no such luck. Unfortunately for me, with all the tourists long gone for the season and the cold, boring winter months upon us, there wasn't a whole lot to talk about in town so this was definitely news.

It had all started out innocently enough. Macy's Clothing Boutique was having its early winter sale, so I decided to take advantage of the deep discounts and pick up a new outfit for the upcoming Restaurant Association Christmas Dinner on Saturday morning. My friends Liddy and Mona offered to tag along on the condition we stop at Jordan's for their lip-smacking blueberry pancakes afterward.

When we showed up at the store it was clear most of the women on the island had the same idea as us. It was a madhouse outside with what seemed like hundreds of hysterical women pushing and shoving to get near the door, which still had the CLOSED sign in the window, which was unusual since the store supposedly opened at 10:00 AM and it was already 10:15.

Finally at 10:20 a car came to a screeching halt in front of the store. The passenger door flew open and owner Debbie Macy stumbled out, appearing as if she had just come out of a wind tunnel, her hair wild and loose, her dress wrinkled, looking nothing like her usually coiffed and perfectly put-together self. As she fumbled for a key to open the store, a hush fell over the crowd and there was a lot of mumbling about Debbie's haggard appearance. As she passed by me, she growled, "Spicy Night Cocktail!"

I knew instantly what had happened. Debbie was a big fan of my brother's Spicy Night Cocktail and enjoyed treating herself every Friday night after closing up the shop to celebrate the end of another long work-week. If Debbie had a really bad week, she would have two or three. She must have had a horrible week!

Once Debbie unlocked the door, she was nearly mowed down by the horde of women racing to check out the sales. I was about to suggest to Mona and Liddy that we come back later, but Liddy was already inside elbowing her way to a table of cashmere sweaters that were marked down. Mona and I shrugged and tried making our way through the swarm of overeager shoppers to join her.

After what seemed like hours in the over-crowded boutique, my head pounding from all the yelling and screaming and my arms tired from all the pushing and shoving, I just wanted out of there.

But then, like a beacon of light shining down from the heavens illuminating a gift from God, I saw the most beautiful, perfect dress on the mannequin right in the front window.

How had I not seen it?

How had the mob of excited women missed it?

I yelled for Liddy and Mona, and pointed at the dress, and the three of us charged like bulls toward the store window display.

Unfortunately our sudden movement alerted about a half-dozen women, who raised their heads and saw us running and then spied that perfect dress. Within seconds, there was a stampede.

Liddy managed to reach the window first, leaping into the air, wrapping her arms around the mannequin as she crashed with it to the floor.

Mona kept the others at bay like the defense at a Patriots game, flinging women left and right. I climbed over the pile of women and began trying to help Mona push the women back so we could get the mannequin to the checkout counter, but it was too late. The massive wall of women broke through, and Liddy, the mannequin, and I all tumbled back into the display window with such force, the mannequin's head broke the pane of glass.

By now poor Debbie Macy looked paler by the minute and not from her hangover, as she stood atop the counter screeching and waving her arms trying to get the situation under control. Finally, left with no choice, Debbie called 911 to report a riot in her boutique.

In hindsight, perhaps Debbie should not have used the word *riot* as every available police car (all three) came with sirens blaring and the police officers (all three), Chief Sergio and his loyal deputies, Earl and Donnie, jumped out of their cars, dressed in full riot gear. I didn't even know the Bar Harbor Police Department owned riot gear.

Chief Sergio pushed his way through the crowd and just shook his head, not surprised to find me, Mona, and Liddy in the thick of all the craziness.

Well, you can read more of the details that I left out in Friday's upcoming Police Beat column in the *Island Times.*

But one thing I will tell you is . . . I got the dress!

RANDY'S SPICY NIGHT COCKTAIL

Honey Syrup Ingredients
2 ounces honey
1 ounce very hot water

Mix together in small glass and set aside.

Other Spicy Night Cocktail Ingredients
1 slice fresh jalapeño about 1 inch thick (for
  less heat, remove the seeds)
2 ounces of your favorite tequila
1 ounce fresh lemon juice
1 ounce honey syrup

In a cocktail shaker, muddle your jalapeño
slice. Add your tequila, fresh lemon juice,
honey syrup, and ice. Shake and pour into a
chilled glass. Garnish with a jalapeño slice
and lemon wedge if desired.

RANDY'S GHOST PEPPER APPETIZER WINGS

Ingredients

2 pounds chicken wings
1 tablespoon baking soda
1 tablespoon garlic powder
1 tablespoon Italian seasoning
1 teaspoon (or more if you dare) ghost pepper powder
1 teaspoon salt

Rinse and pat your wings dry.

Place wings in a large bowl and season with your baking soda, garlic powder, Italian seasoning, and ghost pepper. Stir to coat all of the wings.

Place chicken wings in a deep fryer set at 350 to 375 degrees and fry for about eight minutes until golden brown and crispy. If you are at home and don't have a deep fryer you can bake in a preheated oven on 375 degrees for forty-five to sixty minutes until golden brown and crispy.

Put your wings on a paper towel–lined platter and blot grease.

Now it's time to prepare your sauce.

Wing Sauce Ingredients

2 tablespoons butter

1/2 cup of your favorite hot sauce (Randy uses Frank's)

1/2 cup blue cheese dressing

In a saucepan over medium heat melt the butter, then add the hot sauce and blue cheese dressing. Stir and remove from heat. Toss and coat the wings in the sauce and serve.

CHAPTER FIVE

Hayley browsed the Mystery and Crime section of the Jesup Memorial Library looking to add to her reading pile since it was abundantly clear she was going to have a lot of free time during the holidays now that Gemma was going off on her own fun-filled ski vacation with some college pals.

Hayley tried not to think of the suave French Canadian stud who had made such an impression on her young daughter, and what intentions he might have once he got her up in the mountains away from her overprotective mother.

All of the book titles she perused seemed to just add to her anxiety.

Fatal Affair.

Love Is Murder.

And one to really raise her blood pressure, *Death, Snow and Mistletoe.*

"Have you read the new Leslie Meier? It's a real page-turner."

Hayley turned to see Missy Donovan, the library's second-in-command after Agatha Farnsworth. Missy was in her early fifties, with short red hair and freckles, a sweet face, and unassuming demeanor. She was wearing a green sweater with a white snowman on the front and a long brown skirt and snow boots. Missy had been with the library for over fifteen years, hoping one day to take over, but like a pesky virus, Agatha was still lingering, fighting any effort to eradicate her.

"Oh, yes. I read it the minute it came out," Hayley said. "I'm thinking of rereading all of Agatha Christie's books in alphabetical order."

"Well, I hope you have a lot of free time to read them," Missy said, chuckling.

"That's not an issue, I'm afraid."

"Well, let's see. You would assume *The A.B.C. Murders* would be the first book, but actually I believe numbers come before letters, so why don't you start with *4:50 from Paddington*," Missy said, removing a weathered paperback off the shelf from the Mystery Authors A–L section and handing it to Hayley.

"Oh, this is a good one," Hayley said, skimming through the book.

"I used to love Agatha Christie," Missy sighed.

"Used to?" Hayley asked, puzzled, until it dawned on her that the most successful mystery author of all time shared the same name as Missy's bullheaded and impossible boss Agatha Farnsworth.

"Every time I pick up one of her books, I just see the name Agatha and I break out into a sweat and have an anxiety attack and I have to put it back," Missy said, shaking her head.

Poor Missy. She was a very nice lady. And everyone knew visiting the library would be a much more enjoyable experience with her in charge. But Agatha wasn't going anywhere anytime soon. She was already north of eighty and hadn't even suffered a cold in all that time. So Missy's fate for the time being was to endure the torture of her cantankerous bitter old boss until that day came when she finally kicked the bucket.

And though Missy would never admit it because she was a God-fearing, churchgoing woman, deep down she prayed that day would come sooner rather than later.

"Missy! There you are! Where have you been hiding? I thought you had left and gone on vacation!" Agatha barked as she marched up behind her in a snit.

"Speak of the devil," Hayley said, putting a slight emphasis on the word *devil.*

Missy fixed a smile on her face and turned around to face her overbearing boss. "I'm right here, Agatha. How can I help you?"

"I noticed the book return bin is almost full. Those books are not going to put themselves back on the shelves. So instead of standing around gossiping I suggest you get back to work," Agatha said, her judgmental gaze moving from Missy to Hayley.

Hayley's stomach was suddenly in knots from nerves.

It was as if she was twelve years old again, clutching her hardcover copy of her first Nancy Drew novel, *The Secret of the Old Clock,* getting chewed out once again by Agatha for talking too loudly in the library.

"I should've known Hayley would somehow be involved in your slacking off," Agatha spit out.

Hayley was ready to tell the old bat off.

But she didn't want to get Missy into any more trouble, so she held her tongue.

"When I last checked ten minutes ago, the return bin was only half full so I was going to leave it until after lunch."

"Are you saying I'm lying?"

"No, that's not what I was implying at all. . . ."

"Because I just checked it and it looked full to me. Should we go over there and take a peek?"

"No, I'll go empty it right now," Missy said.

"I also just came from the bathroom and the toilet paper is nearly out," Agatha said in a hushed whisper.

"That's impossible. I put a fresh roll on the dispenser first thing this morning," Missy said, her voice cracking under the pressure.

"Well, then we can just assume it's been a very busy morning here at the library because we're almost out!"

"Okay, Agatha, I'll take care of it right away," Missy said, scooting off down the stairs to the basement where the restroom was located.

Agatha noticed Hayley just standing there, dumbfounded by her obnoxious behavior. "What are you looking at?"

Hayley shook her head. "Nothing."

She glanced at the paperback cover with Agatha Christie's name emblazoned on the cover.

"You know what? On second thought, I just don't think I'm in the mood for Agatha Christie," Hayley said, putting the book back on the shelf. "Ever again."

"Suit yourself," Agatha shrugged.

Suddenly the sound of singing children echoed through the library.

It was a rendition of "Rudolph the Red-Nosed Reindeer."

Agatha's eyes widened.

Her mouth dropped open.

She was about to blow a gasket.

The third-grade class from Conners Elementary School had filed into the lobby of the library to perform Christmas carols. They looked adorable in their embroidered winter hats, heavy coats, and tiny snow boots.

Everyone stopped their reading and researching and browsing and looked up and smiled as the children sang their adorable little hearts out.

Except for Agatha Farnsworth.

She pushed past Hayley and marched over to the gaggle of children. Hayley noticed Agatha was dragging a long piece of toilet paper behind her that was lodged in the back of her skirt.

She had to stifle herself from bursting out laughing.

Agatha glared at the kids. "Stop that! There is no singing in the library! You need to leave this minute!"

The children didn't know what to do.

So they kept singing.

" 'Then one foggy Christmas Eve, Santa came to say: Rudolph with your nose so bright, won't you guide my sleigh tonight?' "

"Are you deaf? I said stop singing! Now!"

The children's voices faded out and they looked at each other, confused. The reception they had received at most places in town was probably far more welcoming and gracious.

Their teacher, Crystal Shannon, a very attractive woman in her mid-thirties, smartly dressed with a very kind and loving demeanor, showed none of that when dealing with Agatha. She was ticked off this grouchy old Grinch was attacking her students and she reacted as a Mama Bear protecting her cubs.

"Agatha, stop yelling at my kids! If you have a problem, then you deal with me!"

Hayley stood there, watching like everyone else, and silently cheered Crystal on. She desperately wanted to scream, "You go, girl!"

But she already had a permanent spot in Agatha Farnsworth's doghouse.

"This is a library, not a Christmas concert! I find it mind-boggling that you drag these munchkins around town forcing them to perform like street beggars. Half of them can't even carry a note. And I see you hiding in the back, Bobby Higgins! I know it was you who stole that Dr. Seuss book during Reading Time last month!"

Bobby Higgins's eyes welled up with tears as he shook his head.

"Agatha, I'm warning you, stop picking on my kids!"

"I'm surprised you even have the gall to show up here, Crystal," Agatha said, walking behind the desk and rummaging through some papers.

"What do you mean?"

Agatha found a slip of paper and handed it to her.

Crystal unfolded it and stared at what was written. "Ninety-five dollars and sixty-two cents?"

"That's the amount you owe for the overdue book you have yet to return!"

"I called the library months ago and told you I lost the book and offered to reimburse you for the cost, but you never got back to me!"

"Well, you didn't talk to me. You must have talked to Missy. It's not my fault she's incompetent. Until you pay your fine and the cost of the book, your library privileges are revoked."

"I'm not paying a hundred dollars for a

James Patterson paperback!"

"The fine is actually forty-six dollars, but I calculated interest in order to deter a lack of responsibility when it comes to borrowing books from the library in the future."

"Come on, kids, let's go," Crystal said, her face flushed and on the verge of tears.

A few of the children noticed the toilet paper dangling behind Agatha and they tittered and giggled as Crystal herded them out.

"What's so funny?"

Hayley actually took pity on her.

She looked ridiculous with that toilet paper hanging out the back of her skirt so she stepped closer to Agatha and said in a soft voice, "Actually, you should know —"

"Before you start in on me, Hayley Powell, I have something to say to you. I heard through the grapevine that your brother, you know, the fruit cookie . . ."

"You mean gay, Agatha."

"Well, it's come to my attention that he's bringing some kind of exotic, weird dish to the Restaurant Association Dinner."

"I wouldn't call chicken wings exotic."

"Well, rumor has it they're spicy, and I think that's just disrespectful to those of us with weak stomachs."

First the eggnog.

Now the chicken wings.

Was there any kind of food that could win Agatha's seal of approval?

"They're very popular at his bar, Agatha, and even if you don't appreciate them, I'm sure a lot of people at the dinner will."

"I don't see why it is so difficult for people to adhere to my wishes! I'm just trying to make the event accessible to everyone, not just a few! Is that so wrong? I'm seventy-two years old . . ."

Eighty-two, but why correct her? It would just lead to more yelling.

"And I've had a lot of life experience and I know when people listen to me things run smoothly. And when they don't there are all kinds of problems. Like the bake sale we had at the library a few years ago. Do you remember that, Hayley?"

How could she forget?

She was feuding with a rival cooking columnist and it led to a rather over-the-top food fight. But in the end they made their fund-raising goal because people enjoyed the floor show of all the women hurling frosted cupcakes and chocolate brownies at one another. The event was a success, but Agatha was apoplectic that it happened in the library on her watch.

She had personally held Hayley responsible for the entire debacle and had never let her forget it.

"If you hadn't tried to outshine Karen Applebaum, may she rest in peace, and brought the dessert I asked you to, none of that appalling mess would have happened. It was all your fault. So I would think after that disaster you would be a bit more open-minded and listen to what I have to say."

Hayley nodded, seething.

She wished she had a cupcake in her hand at that moment to mash into Agatha's face. But she didn't, so she settled for just dreaming about it.

"Now, what is it you wanted to tell me?" Agatha asked, folding her arms and picking a piece of lint off her drab gray sweater.

"Nothing. It's not important."

"Good," Agatha said, turning back around and walking away, the long trail of toilet paper dragging behind her.

The snickering and giggles she heard as she crossed behind the desk infuriated her, but for the life of her she couldn't figure out what everyone found so funny.

CHAPTER SIX

Bar Harbor's annual Restaurant Association Dinner was shaping up to be yet another resounding success as locals packed the Masonic Hall where all the participating restaurants had set up tables to display their various dishes. Hayley was gleefully working her way through the appetizer section and had stopped to chat with the owner of Café This Way, named for its out-of-the-way location off the main drag and its sign set up on busy Mount Desert Street with a finger pointing toward the gravel path leading to the restaurant and the name Café This Way.

Hayley picked up one of their signature appetizers, Fried Brussels Sprouts with bacon, pumpkin seeds, and sriracha honey glaze, and popped it into her mouth. She closed her eyes, let the flavors explode in her mouth, and found herself actually moaning. She made a big scene of moving on to the next table but found herself circling back to snatch up another brussels sprout. The owner smiled knowingly and allowed Hayley to indulge on the off chance she might mention them in her next column.

Liddy hustled up to Hayley chewing on a bruschetta with mushroom confit and goat cheese from Mache Bistro. "Did you see Agatha over there? She's having a major meltdown!"

Hayley glanced over to see Agatha pacing back and forth, steaming, her mouth going a mile a minute as she railed about something to a couple of her underlings including the beleaguered Missy Donovan, who looked whipped and exhausted only twenty minutes into the event.

"What's got her goat this time?" Hayley asked, keeping her eyes on Liddy as she casually dropped her hand and swiped another brussels sprout off the plate behind her hoping the Café This Way owner wouldn't notice. Crystal Shannon, who was about to try one of the brussels sprouts, did notice and giggled.

"Fannie's not here yet. She was supposed to bring the eggnog and people have been asking for it. Agatha's convinced she's purposely trying to ruin the Restaurant Association Dinner so Agatha will be ousted from the committee," Liddy said, perusing the food choices at the surrounding tables.

"Well, Agatha should just calm down because she just walked through the door," Hayley said, watching as Fannie, looking harried, rushed in carrying two pitchers of eggnog, one in each hand.

Liddy was utterly uninterested. "Look, Poor Boy's just put out their blueberry pie!"

She was gone in a flash.

Hayley hurried over and took one of the pitchers of eggnog from Fannie. "Here, let me help you, Fannie."

"Thank you so much, Hayley. I'm so sorry I'm late."

Agatha marched over with her dowdy gray dress and sour face and glared at Fannie. "So nice of you to make it, Fannie."

"I had car trouble, okay, Agatha? I don't need one of your lectures on tardiness."

"Maybe if you drove an American-made car and not one of those fancy unreliable foreign ones that take jobs away from hardworking fellow Americans, you just might get places on time," Agatha barked, itching for a fight.

"I'm not doing this with you, Agatha. I'm in no mood to argue, so back off," Fannie said, her fingers tightening so hard around the handle of the pitcher of eggnog her knuckles turned white. "And just so we are all on the same page, and there are no more little dustups about food allergies, I brought two pitchers of my eggnog. Hayley is holding the one marked 'Dairy' and I am holding the one marked 'Non-Dairy' so there should be no confusion. The 'Non-Dairy' eggnog is made with soy milk. Okay, Agatha?"

Agatha shrugged her shoulders and walked away, unimpressed. "Makes no difference to me. I don't even like eggnog."

Fannie watched her go and shook her head and then headed to the beverage table and set her pitcher down. Hayley followed behind her and put hers down next to Fannie's, turning both around to face out so the labels were visible to anyone who might pour themselves a glass in the plastic cups stacked at the end of the table.

"Dutch is still in the car. I have to go unload his wheelchair from the trunk and wheel him on in. He hasn't eaten since lunch and is already grouchy," she said, scooting out the door.

The next twenty minutes were absolute heaven.

Hayley wandered from table to table sampling the buttery popovers from the Jordan Pond House, sipping the Blueberry Ale from the Atlantic Brewing Company, and gobbling down the pan-seared crab cakes from Havana. It was a smorgasbord of flavors.

Randy appeared behind Hayley with a chicken wing nestled in a small white napkin. "I saved you one. They're going fast. Why haven't you been by my table?"

Hayley turned around and smiled. "Because I know I can have anything I want anytime I want at your place for free since I'm your loving sister. The rest of these places I have to pay, so I'm taking advantage while I can."

"Well, at least try it and tell me what you think," Randy said, holding out the chicken wing on the napkin.

She took the wing lathered in barbecue sauce from Randy and chomped down on it. Within seconds, the spices seemed to be burning through her throat and she was coughing.

"Too much?" Randy asked.

Hayley shook her head. "No, I love spicy. I just need to find some water. Fast," she said, racing to the other end of the beverage table to fill a paper cup with water from the large plastic bottle.

Randy followed her.

She drank the entire cup of water in one swig.

"Those are the red-hot wings. I prepared another batch that's milder. I put a red flag on the plate to warn people which plate was spicy," Randy said, turning to point at the wings on the Drinks Like A Fish table located on the far side of the room. "That's odd."

"What?" Hayley said, clearing her throat and folding the remainder of the wing into the napkin before tossing it in the trash bin next to her. This one was too hot even for her.

"My red flag. It's gone."

"What do you mean?"

Hayley glanced over at the Drinks Like A Fish table, and sure enough, there were two plates of wings, neither one marked with a red flag.

Randy flagged down one of the waitresses he hired to work the event and make sure his food got circulated. "Amber, did you remove the red flag from the plate of spicy chicken wings?"

Amber was a buxom redhead who was squeezed into a tight red sweater and even tighter black leather pants but wearing a white apron over the slinky ensemble to give her a slight air of modesty. She pursed her bright ruby red lips. "Red flag? I didn't see a red flag."

"But I took extra care to make sure it was on the plate when I set the wings out," Randy said, his voice raised, suddenly concerned.

"I'm sorry, Randy, I swear I didn't see it when I picked up the plate," Amber said, her brow furrowed, worried she might be blamed for this unexpected crisis.

"You mean you've already served the wings?"

"Yes, I just finished taking them around the room a second ago. I was going to take the ones left from the first batch around again in a few minutes."

"Did anybody eat them yet?"

"Well, I don't know. I'm sure . . ."

"I have an extra flag here in my pocket. I better go and put it on the plate before somebody —"

The sound of wheezing and coughing suddenly cut Randy off.

The other guests at the dinner hadn't really noticed yet, but Hayley and Randy quickly scanned the crowd until their eyes settled on Agatha Farnsworth only a few feet from Randy's table, gasping, one hand on her throat while the other clutched a half-eaten chicken wing.

Her face was turning beet red.

She stumbled as she heaved and coughed.

The rest of the people in the room finally heard what was happening and the whole room fell silent.

Hayley sprang into action.

She quickly filled the paper cup in her hand with water from the bottle and dashed over to Agatha.

But Fannie got to her first and handed her a plastic cup of eggnog.

"Here, Agatha, drink this. It's the non-dairy one," Fannie said, placing the cup to her lips.

Agatha gratefully gulped down the eggnog, and for a moment, she stopped coughing and even smiled slightly to let everyone know she was feeling a bit better. But then it started all over again. This time more violently. She broke out into hives and her whole body shook. Fannie screamed.

Hayley was already on her cell phone calling 911 as she yelled, "Is there a doctor in the house?"

Nobody stepped forward.

Everyone was in a state of shock.

Agatha's whole face and throat were swelling.

She took one more gasp of air and then couldn't breathe or speak.

She just waved her arms frantically.

Hayley suddenly remembered a movie she saw once where someone saved a victim who was having an allergy attack at the last minute by taking a steak knife and stabbing it through the throat into the windpipe to open an airway so the victim could breathe. But she wasn't a doctor and she had no idea exactly where to make the incision. Since no one else was doing anything she had to at least attempt to perform an emergency tracheostomy.

She searched around for a steak knife. There had to be one around. This was a Restaurant Association Dinner. Every dining establishment in town was here.

But it was too late.

Agatha Farnsworth stopped moving and flopped over to the floor.

She was dead.

Island Food & Cocktails

BY HAYLEY POWELL

Jordan's Restaurant in Bar Harbor is famously known by locals and tourists alike for their delicious wild Maine blueberry pancakes and blueberry muffins. But when the summer season comes to an end and the tourists have all departed for home, there is another special treat at Jordan's available only during the holiday season that just us year-round residents of Bar Harbor know about. Kelton, the cook, always serves his delicious Eggnog Muffins and equally mouthwatering homemade Eggnog Milkshakes. It's a holiday tradition Kelton started quite a few years ago when old man Taylor and his wife, Betty, were in the business of making their own homemade eggnog every Christmas season and selling it at a table just outside the Shop 'n Save starting the day after Thanksgiving until right after the New Year. As a young boy, Kelton couldn't get enough of their tasty creamy holiday beverage and so he incorporated eggnog into his muffins and shakes, and voilà, a new holiday tradition was born and boy, do the year-round residents of Bar Harbor just love it!

So on Saturday morning, the night after the Restaurant Association Dinner, Mona, Liddy, and I found ourselves standing in a long line outside Jordan's waiting for an open booth. I hadn't seen the place so busy in December since that unfortunate incident with old man Taylor and his wife some years back. There's nothing like an unexpected scandal to bring out all the locals to a popular breakfast spot on a bitterly cold winter morning so they can rehash the infamous events of the prior evening.

I remember it as if it was yesterday. Old man Taylor had always been a bit rough around the edges and was quite the bad boy in his day while the quiet, demure Betty was very prim and proper. They made a very odd couple, but somehow they made it work. In fact, I heard they just celebrated their fortieth wedding anniversary.

Anyway, Betty attended church faithfully every Sunday. That was one thing she could never persuade her husband to do. He was afraid the walls would collapse if he dared set foot in a house of God. So old man Taylor would load Betty up in his old Ford pickup truck and drive her into town and drop her off at the Congregational Church every Sunday like clockwork; then he would leave to go play cards all day with some of his old cronies leaving Betty to catch a ride home with a friend after the service.

In the winter, Betty would bring jugs of her homemade eggnog to share at the church social hour in the parlor after the service and old man Taylor would bring jugs of the eggnog to share at his card game.

It was one early December Sunday just like any other when old man Taylor pulled into the church parking lot to drop off Betty, when he ran into an old friend and they began chatting while Betty tried to gather all of her jugs of eggnog with no help from her husband. Luckily, Edie Staples, the reverend's wife, happened by and helped Betty carry all the jugs into the church. Betty yelled a good-bye to her husband, who was still engrossed in his conversation with his old buddy and gave her a half-hearted wave, and so she and Edie headed into the church to drop off the eggnog before the service.

After the service, like every Sunday, the congregation streamed into the church parlor to indulge in muffin treats, hot coffee, and Betty's famous eggnog. After a while a few people who were not partaking in the coffee and eggnog began to notice that the volume of the crowd was beginning to grow quite loud and there was lots of laughter and boisterous hollering back and forth amongst the people in the parlor. Suddenly loud organ music began playing and the rambunctious crowd filed into the church to discover Ethel Swan, the church organist, banging out a medley from her favorite Broadway musical *Hello, Dolly!* at top volume. The happy churchgoers sang along, cackling and screaming as they messed up the lyrics. Red Stewart, a gruff, manly local lobsterman who usually never cracked a smile, even jumped up onto the pews and belted out the title tune as if he was channeling Carol Channing! Pretty soon everyone was hooting and hollering and dancing and singing!

Finally, a passerby, who was shaken by the noise of the loud and rowdy crowd inside and then spotted Doris Cook in the church window jumping up and down and swinging her prized fake fur coat over her head, decided to call Reverend Staples to find out why they were holding a Saturday night barn dance inside the church! When she couldn't reach Reverend Staples, she called the police.

When the officers arrived at the church, they stopped short in the doorway, mouths agape, watching Reverend Staples leading a conga line right down the middle aisle of the church!

Finally, after much persuading and coercing, the police managed to evacuate the unruly and frenzied churchgoers and get some order. After a quick investigation, the police discovered that old man Taylor hadn't been completely honest with his wife about the eggnog he served at his card games. He spiked his jugs with rum. Unfortunately, those were the jugs Edie Staples helped Betty carry into the church. The police spent the next four hours driving most of the parishioners home since they were all over the legal alcohol limit to operate a motor vehicle.

Betty was so humiliated and furious with her husband that she packed her bags and moved down to Boca Raton, Florida, to live with her daughter. But after a while, her poor husband missed her so much he sold the house in Bar Harbor and showed up in Boca begging for her forgiveness. She took him back and I hear Betty's now quite a fan of her husband's rum-infused eggnog.

I later heard after that scandalous church

social hour Reverend Staples's wife, Edie, insisted only coffee and tea be served after the service.

But I think we all know what's better than plain old coffee? Yes, Eggnog Milkshakes! And as a bonus treat, with Kelton's permission, I'm also going to share with you the recipe for his awesome Eggnog Muffins!

EGGNOG MILKSHAKE

Ingredients

1 cup vanilla ice cream

1 cup eggnog

1 teaspoon fresh nutmeg (or if using pre-ground 1/2 teaspoon)

Place all of your ingredients in a blender and blend together. Pour into a tall glass and enjoy! If you prefer your drink a little thinner, just add more eggnog until you have your desired consistency. For an adult eggnog milkshake, add a splash or two of your favorite rum or whiskey!

KELTON'S EGGNOG MUFFINS

Ingredients
3 cups all-purpose flour
1/2 cup sugar
3 teaspoons baking powder
1/2 teaspoon salt
1 egg
1 3/4 cups eggnog
1/2 cup vegetable oil
1/2 cup raisins (optional)
1/2 cup chopped pecans (optional)

In a large bowl combine the first five ingredients. In a separate bowl combine your eggnog and oil, then stir it into the dry ingredients just until moistened. If using the raisins and nuts, fold them softly into the mixture.

Spray or use paper liners in a muffin tin and fill each cup two-thirds full. Bake in a preheated oven for twenty to twenty-five minutes or until a toothpick comes out clean. Cool for five minutes and then remove muffins to a wire rack to finish cooling.

CHAPTER SEVEN

When Randy's police chief husband, Sergio, finally arrived at Hayley's house close to midnight, Hayley and Randy had already polished off a bottle of Chardonnay and Randy was singularly focused on screwing out the cork from a second bottle with a wine opener. The stress of Agatha Farnsworth's violent and disturbing death in front of half the town, not to mention every restaurant owner in Bar Harbor, had taken its toll, and the one surefire way to calm their nerves was to split a bottle of wine.

Or two.

Hayley's pets, her dog, Leroy, and her cat, Blueberry, sat obediently in separate corners of the kitchen, at full attention, hoping Hayley and Randy might get the munchies at some point, which would undoubtedly lead them to drop a few crumbs on the floor where both animals would be ready to pounce on them before the other.

After a few hours of questioning by Sergio and several of his officers, most of the guests and participants at the Restaurant Association Dinner were allowed to go home. Hayley and Randy were two of the last to leave because they chose to hang back and see what, if any, information Sergio's preliminary investigation would yield. Unfortunately as they inched closer to the body, which was now under a white tablecloth, stained with Randy's signature barbecue sauce, used to cover the corpse until the paramedics could wheel Agatha out on a gurney, they had a tough time eavesdropping because Sergio was huddling with a couple of his officers and speaking in a very low voice.

When Sergio noticed them, he politely asked them to leave the building and meet him back at Hayley's house where he would pick Randy up and take him home when he was done.

The one inescapable trait both brother and sister shared was their natural nosiness and incessant need to know all the details of a brewing scandal. And the fact that Agatha Farnsworth was so upset and so worried about Fannie Clark-Van Dam's eggnog, potentially poisonous to anyone with a dairy allergy, in the days before the annual dinner and was now possibly dead because of it meant this was going to be one whopper of a story.

If indeed that's how she died.

Hayley and Randy were hastily ushered out of the Masonic Hall by Officer Earl, one of Sergio's deputies, and they drove back to Hayley's house to wait with bated breath for Sergio to arrive and fill them in on what exactly happened.

It took a couple of hours of waiting and drinking, but he was finally here.

"The coroner won't say for certain until he completes his autopsy, but he is fairly confident Agatha died from anaphylaxis brought on by her severe allergy to dairy."

Hayley stared at Sergio in a state of shock.

Sergio noticed and raised an eyebrow. "What?"

"It's just that you always mix up the easiest words because English is your second language, and you actually pronounced anaphylaxis correctly," Hayley said, shaking her head.

"Don't pediatrician me, Hayley."

Hayley and Randy exchanged a look.

"It's patronize, honey," Randy said softly.

"See? It's amazing he got anaphylaxis right," Hayley said before sipping her wine.

Sergio glowered at Hayley for a moment

and then turned to Randy. "Are you ready to go home?"

Randy guzzled the rest of his wine and set the glass down on the kitchen counter. "I can't believe it. This is all my fault."

"Your fault? What are you talking about?" Hayley asked.

"If I hadn't brought my ghost pepper chicken wings, this never would have happened. She never would have taken a bite of one and started choking and then she never would have drank the eggnog that caused her to go into shock," Randy said, eyes welling up, completely consumed with guilt.

"Agatha knew your wings were spicy, Randy. You are not responsible for the fact she ate one," Hayley said, putting a comforting arm around his shoulder.

"But that's just it. She didn't know. When I arrived at the dinner, I went straight up to Agatha and told her that I made a batch of my chicken wings specially for her. I said the ghost pepper wings would have a red flag with a picture of a little chili pepper on the plate to warn everyone they were spicy and the mild ones would be on an unmarked plate. But right before we heard her start choking I looked over and there was no flag on either plate. I swear the flag was there when I set the wings out on the table. I was so careful. I didn't want anyone to eat something that disagreed with them. I can't imagine what happened to that flag."

"Maybe someone just knocked the flag off the plate accidentally while reaching for one of the wings," Sergio said.

"I don't think so. I searched everywhere. On the table, under the table, on the floor. For the life of me, I couldn't find it. Somebody must have taken it on purpose and pocketed it," Randy said.

"Or maybe a little kid passed by and saw the flag and decided he wanted it," Hayley said.

"In any event, I'm responsible," Randy said, burying his face in his hands. "I killed Agatha Farnsworth."

Even if it was Randy's fault, Hayley knew nobody in town would vilify him for it. There wasn't a soul in town who was going to miss Agatha Farnsworth. But that wasn't a point Hayley needed to make at this particular time. She just hugged her brother, trying to console him.

Sergio stepped closer to Randy and gently placed his hand on the back of his husband's neck. "You had nothing to do with this, babe. It wasn't your wings that killed Agatha. It was the eggnog. And at this point, I am inclined to believe Fannie Clark-Van

Dam served Agatha that eggnog made with dairy on purpose."

"Oh, Sergio, I don't know . . ."

"Everyone I interviewed at that dinner told me Fannie despised Agatha," Sergio said, checking his pocket notepad and nodding as he scrolled the pages. "Every single one."

"Well, yes, Agatha and Fannie had their differences. But Agatha had differences with just about everybody in town."

"Not everybody in town personally handed the eggnog to Agatha to drink," Sergio said, stuffing his notepad in his breast pocket and folding his arms. "The eggnog she knew would cause an allergic reaction."

"But, Sergio, the eggnog Fannie handed Agatha was clearly marked 'Non-Dairy.' It was obvious she double-checked before she gave it to her," Hayley said, unwilling to buy the flighty but relatively harmless Fannie as a murder suspect.

"Maybe that's what she wanted you to see. She could have switched the labels at the last minute to throw suspicion off herself."

Randy, who was hunched over the kitchen sink, rubbing his eyes and in a state of panic and despair, stood upright. "You know, Sergio could be right. It does make sense. Come on, we saw that altercation at Mama

DiMatteo's the other night. They really had it out for each other."

"I'm not convinced," Hayley said as she walked to the cupboard to grab a dog treat for Leroy, who was now at her feet, begging with his eyes for something, anything he could eat even though he had only licked his bowl clean of Kibble 'n Bits a mere hour ago. "Frankly, I don't think Fannie's bright enough to carry out some kind of murder plot."

"Well, the fact remains, Fannie either accidentally mislabeled the two pitchers of eggnog or her actions were more allocated," Sergio said, scratching the stubble on his face.

"Allocated?" Randy asked, at a loss.

"You know, deliberate," Sergio said louder.

"I think he means calculated. Her actions were more calculated," Hayley offered, trying to be helpful.

"Yes, that's what I said."

"But there's just one problem with that theory, Sergio. If Fannie planned on serving Agatha the wrong eggnog, if she had malice in her heart and wanted her dead, and planned on doing her in at the Restaurant Association Dinner, then how did she know Agatha would eat the spicy chicken wing? How could she have planned that?"

"Maybe she was the one who removed the flag at the last minute and then pushed Agatha into tasting one of my wings!" Randy announced, proud he was able to add to the conversation.

"But Fannie was clear across the room far away from Agatha. It was only after she started choking and gasping for air that Fannie raced over with the pitcher of eggnog. Besides that, Agatha would never do anything Fannie suggested. Especially eat something Fannie recommended," Hayley said.

Sergio wrestled with the facts in his mind, not quite ready to give up Fannie as his number one suspect.

"For once, I'm not ready to go chasing down a murderer," Hayley said. "Because if you ask me, I think it was all just a horrible accident."

Randy and Sergio exchanged surprised looks.

This was a first.

But in Hayley's mind, this time there was no murder.

And soon she would discover she was 100 percent without a doubt dead wrong.

CHAPTER EIGHT

When Hayley walked up on the front porch of the late-nineteenth-century Victorian-style Van Dam house nestled on a hilltop clearing surrounded by woods off Eagle Lake Road on the way out of town, she hesitated to knock on the door because of all the yelling coming from inside. It was Fannie and she did not sound happy. Hayley pressed her ear to the door and strained to hear what Fannie was screaming at the top of her lungs, but a stiff wind and some chirping birds in the trees near the side of the house made it virtually impossible. Finally giving up, she sighed and rapped her fist on the door.

The yelling stopped suddenly and all was quiet for a few moments before the door opened a crack and Fannie poked her head out.

She looked relieved at the sight of Hayley. "Oh, Hayley, it's you."

"Is this a bad time?"

"Good gosh no. I'm glad you're here. Please, come in."

Fannie opened the door wide enough for Hayley to enter.

Hayley was shocked at the sight of the house. On the outside it looked grand and pristine, but on the inside it was as if a category five hurricane had swept through.

Papers strewn everywhere.

Dust balls on the floor.

Scraps of food on the floor.

It was downright disgusting.

"I hope you'll excuse the mess," Fannie said, suddenly self-conscious. We've been without a housekeeper for about a month now and I haven't had time to do it since looking after Dutch is a full-time job these days."

"It looks fine," Hayley lied.

"I'm just trying to get Dutch to eat his breakfast. I'll be done in a minute," Fannie said, wiping sweat from her brow as she marched into the kitchen. Hayley quietly followed and nearly gasped at the piles of dirty dishes in the sink and Dutch Van Dam, his hunched-over body in his wheelchair, parked at a breakfast nook. There was jam from a half-eaten English muffin all over his face and a fork had been awkwardly placed in his bony fingers. Although his face was a frozen mask from the massive stroke he had suffered, it was still obvious he was angry and pouting.

Fannie took the fork out of his hand and stabbed at some scrambled egg left on his plate. "One more bite. Do it for me, okay, Dutch?"

Fannie raised the fork to Dutch's crooked mouth, and he managed to turn his head slightly away from her, his eyes wide with rage. "Come on, Dutch, don't fight me. Just finish your breakfast and then you can go watch the game."

Dutch had no intention of cooperating.

"He's perfectly capable of feeding himself. He's just being obstinate," Fannie sighed.

Dutch let loose with some angry grunts and snorts like a wild horse cornered in the barn determined not to be broken.

Fannie tried forcing the forkful of eggs past his lips, but he fought and struggled mightily; then he lifted a glass of milk in his right hand and hurled it at Fannie's face. It splashed her in the eyes and she yelped, nearly bursting into tears as the white milk dripped down her face.

"I give up," Fannie said, sighing. She reached for a dish towel off the counter and patted her face until the milk was gone, and then quietly wheeled Dutch into the living room where she set him up in front of the flat-screen television mounted on the wall and turned on a football game. Then she joined Hayley back in the kitchen.

"I'm at my wit's end. I can't take much more of this," Fannie said, pouring herself a cup of coffee. "Would you like some?"

"No, thank you," Hayley said, not trusting that any of the coffee mugs had been washed since the last time they had been used.

"My life has become a living hell ever since Dutch had his stroke. I've been running ragged picking up his prescriptions, making sure he eats, getting him to his physical therapy sessions."

"Are there any signs of improvement?"

Fannie shook her head. "Not really. He's stubborn and bitter and refusing to try. The doctors say if he doesn't make an effort soon, there's little hope he'll ever get better."

She suddenly burst into tears. Hayley crossed the kitchen and put a comforting arm around Fannie's shoulder. "Hang in there. You just have to have a little faith."

"He's already chased off three in-home caregivers. Two older women and a nice young Filipino man. They really tried to work with him, but he never gave them a chance. After a week or so, they quit. All three of them. And that left just me to get him up in the morning, get him dressed, and try to get him to work his facial muscles, his leg muscles, his arm muscles. He has such a long road ahead of him and I want to help, but he treats me like I'm the enemy. It's a constant battle of wills. Last night I swear he soiled his pants just to spite me. I looked at his face when I was cleaning him and it was as if he was sneering at me. It's just horrible, Hayley."

"Dutch was such a strong man. It must be agony to be bound to a wheelchair, unable to speak or take care of himself."

"I know that. I tell myself that every day when I wake up to face another day. But that doesn't make it any easier."

"I understand."

"And now to add to all this I'm going through, Chief Alvares thinks I purposely killed Agatha Farnsworth with my eggnog."

"He's looking at everyone. He's just focused on you right now because you're the one who served her the eggnog that caused the allergic reaction."

"You know, last night I had a dream that he came here and arrested me and I was carted off to jail and then convicted of first-degree murder and sent to a state prison and had to wear one of those unflattering orange jumpsuits like on that Netflix show."

"*Orange Is the New Black,*" Hayley said.

"Yes, that's the one. With all the lesbians. And you know something, Hayley? I was happy there. I didn't ever want to leave because it got me out of this house and away from Dutch."

"Fannie, you don't mean that."

"I love Dutch. I always have. From the day we met and he swept me off my feet and made me feel like Princess Grace."

"Princess Grace died in a car crash."

"Yes, I know. I dream about that too. Dying in a car crash and finally finding some peace."

"Is Dutch really that bad?"

As if on cue, the volume of the football game grew louder and louder until it was deafening and Hayley couldn't even hear herself talk.

"Dutch, turn it down!" Fannie screamed.

The volume just kept getting louder and louder until it was at its maximum.

"If I was going to murder anyone, it would be Dutch!" Fannie shrieked before waving at Hayley to follow her out the back door. Outside, they stepped into a small garden that was now bare, sporting just a few twigs because of the cold weather.

"This is my escape. My garden. Where I putter around and get my hands dirty and grow tomatoes in the summer and it's just wonderful. A little bit of solitude when I need it. But now it's winter and everything's dead and I have nothing."

Hayley was worried about Fannie's dour state of mind.

Dutch had really driven her to a point of despair.

Fannie stared off into the woods for a few seconds, lost in thought, and Hayley chose to remain silent and let her work through her thoughts. Then she spun around and faced Hayley.

"Hayley, believe me when I tell you, I took great care labeling those pitchers of eggnog. I made sure they were securely taped to the sides right in my kitchen before I even left for the Restaurant Association Dinner because I didn't want to forget when I got there. The last thing I wanted was for something like this to happen. Agatha and I had our differences, but I certainly didn't want to see her dead."

Hayley believed her.

The poor woman was distraught about the state of her life.

The last thing on her mind was carrying out some vendetta against a cranky old nuisance like Agatha Farnsworth.

"That's why I asked you to stop by today. I want to hire you."

"Hire me? To look after Dutch?"

"No, to prove my innocence."

"But, Fannie, I'm not a private investigator."

"You're as close to one as this town's got. And I trust you. You have a sense of justice, an empathy I admire, and I know if anyone can clear my name, it's you."

"Fannie, it's such a busy time of year . . ."

Although with the kids gone and her relationship with Aaron history, there really wasn't a whole lot on her calendar during this holiday season.

"Christmas comes and goes, Hayley, this is my life we're talking about! I don't want to spend the rest of it in prison! And if things keep going the way they've been going, that's a very real possibility. I'll pay you whatever you want. If Dutch is still good for one thing, it's a padded bank account."

"I can't take your money, Fannie."

"Hayley, I'm begging you. Please, do this for me."

"I'll look into it. But free of charge. As a friend."

Fannie's tight, worried face finally melted into a warm smile. She hugged Hayley and didn't want to let go. "Thank you. Thank you."

CHAPTER NINE

Hayley's first stop during her lunch hour was the Bar Harbor Hospital. Amber Harding, who served Agatha that fateful ghost pepper chicken wing, only waitressed part time to make some extra cash. Her other job was as a candy striper at the hospital. She was trying to save enough money to enroll in nursing school, which was her true passion.

The receptionist told Hayley that Amber was in the middle of a shift on the third floor so she took the elevator up and found Nurse Tilly, a chatty, perky girl who was friends with Hayley, at the nurses' station.

"Hayley, what are you doing here? Nobody's sick, are they? I mean medically speaking. I know you have a couple of crazies like Sal Moretti and Bruce Linney, who are sick in the head!" Tilly squealed erupting in guffaws at her own joke.

"Everyone's fine, Tilly. I'm just here to

talk to Amber Harding."

Tilly's smile instantly faded and her whole body went stiff. "I see. What do you want with that one?"

That one?

"I just wanted to ask her a couple of questions, that's all. Nothing important. Is she busy?"

"She's never busy. She just traipses around here in her tight sweaters and long legs like she's on *America's Top Model,* trying to get all the male patients' heart rates up. That's not how a legitimate nurse acts while on duty," Tilly said, buttoning up her own pink sweater over her white uniform to make the point that she was nothing like that two-bit floozy. "But then again, she's not a real nurse. She's just a candy striper."

The few times Hayley had actually spoken to Amber, she found her sweet and delightful. But she was also gorgeous with a rocking body, so it was obvious the rather dowdy and insecure Nurse Tilly found her to be obnoxious and an obvious threat.

Nurse Tilly was on a roll. "And that singsongy high-pitched voice of hers . . . like she's just sucked on a whole tank of helium drives me nuts! Every time I hear it I want to plug up my ears! I've begged the administrator to get rid of her, but he told me the patients like her, she has a nice energy, she's got a good heart. How would he know? I'm sure she's got him wrapped around her cute little finger too! I heard rumors his marriage was on the rocks, maybe she's the reason!"

Hayley just stood there, unsure what to do as Tilly spiraled, completely forgetting Hayley was even there. She just sat in her chair, seething, muttering to herself.

Hayley cleared her throat to try to redirect her attention.

Tilly snapped out of her own thoughts and turned and offered her signature perky smile. "I'm sorry, what were we talking about?"

"Could you tell me where to find Amber?"

"Down the hall. I think she's tending to that old coot Francis Sweet in room 332."

"Thank you."

Tilly opened a file folder and pretended to be studying a patient's test results, but it was clear she was still obsessing over Amber.

Hayley walked down the hall until she reached room 332 where she stopped short in the doorway at the sight of Amber, bent over, her perfectly round Kardashian butt in the air, as Francis Sweet, an eighty-six-year-old scrawny little man in a powder blue hospital gown, leered at her from his bed.

"Did you find it yet?" Francis said, reaching out to pinch her left butt cheek.

"It's under the dresser. How on earth did it get all the way back here?"

Hayley decided to intervene. "How are you today, Francis?"

Francis jumped at the sound of Hayley's voice and quickly withdrew his hand, using it to scratch behind his ear. "Hayley! What brings you here?"

Amber stood upright, a TV remote in her hand, and placed it on the plastic table next to Francis's bed. "I swear you lose this on purpose just so I have to look for it every day when I bring you your orange juice to take with your meds."

"I've loved staring at the moon ever since I was a little boy," he said, winking.

"Francis, you're incorrigible," Amber said, laughing.

"Actually he's as horny as a hound dog," Hayley said, smiling.

"Guilty as charged, ladies," Francis said, pretending to reach out for the remote but missing it by a mile and going in to touch Amber's left breast. She saw the move coming and managed to step back before he made contact.

"Well, I'll leave you two alone so you can visit," Amber said, starting to leave.

"Actually I'm here to see you," Hayley said. "Do you have a minute?"

"Sure. Francis, don't forget to take your meds. I'll be back to check on you in a little bit and we'll watch Ellen DeGeneres."

"You like Ellen DeGeneres, Francis?" Hayley asked.

"No, I can't stand her. All that dancing around. Gives me a headache. But Amber likes her and I like to make my girl happy so it's an activity we can share together."

"He only says he doesn't like Ellen because he knows she is impervious to his charms and he doesn't stand a chance. Can you try to behave yourself while I talk to Hayley, Francis?"

"If you give me a kiss," he said, smirking. "On the lips."

"You wish."

Amber stepped out into the hallway with Hayley, who barely had a chance to open her mouth before Amber's eyes were welling up with tears.

"I know why you're here. It's about poor Agatha Farnsworth. I've heard people talking. They think I served her that chicken wing on purpose. I know Agatha could be challenging, but I never had a bad word to say about her. She never gave me any grief."

Probably because Amber had never set

foot in the library to read a book.

Amber may not have been the brightest bulb in the chandelier, but she was going to devote her life to taking care of people as a nurse and that was a noble goal.

"No one thinks that . . ."

"Tilly does. She hates me and she wants to turn everybody against me!"

"When you served Agatha that chicken wing, are you absolutely sure it wasn't marked with a red flag?"

"I swear. Agatha was crystal clear about her weak stomach and her food restrictions. If I had seen a flag with a chili pepper on it, I never would have allowed her to take one! That's the God's honest truth, Hayley!"

"Did you see her eat it?"

"No, she took one but didn't eat it right away. She was focused on a stuffed mushroom. She had piled about four of them on her plate and was working her way through them. She was saving the chicken wing for later. Poor Agatha. I should have asked which plate was the spicy wings and which one was the mild wings. I just assumed they were both the same since they weren't marked! Oh, Lord! This senseless tragedy is all my fault!"

She fell into Hayley's arms and sobbed. Hayley patted her back softly and whispered to her that it was all going to be all right. Suddenly Hayley felt a presence behind her. Someone tugged on her coat. While still holding Amber in her arms, Hayley cranked her head around to see Francis out of bed, a look of concern on his face.

"Here, allow me," he said, pushing Hayley out of the way and wrapping his arms around the crying girl, who was so distraught she had no clue what was happening.

"There, there, child, Francis is here. You just hold on to me and I'll make everything better."

Amber sobbed for a few more seconds and then stopped. She raised her head off Francis's shoulder. "What's happening down there?"

"What do you mean?"

Amber tried wriggling out of his grasp. "Down there!"

"Oh, don't you worry about that. It's called Viagra!" Francis said, beaming from ear to ear.

Amber reeled back, horrified, and pushed him away.

Nurse Tilly rounded the corner, and bellowed, "Francis Sweet, get back in your bed right now or I'll reassign Amber to the second floor."

That was a threat Francis had no intention of testing.

He immediately hightailed it back inside his room, his sagging butt visible through the back of his flimsy hospital gown.

Tilly eyed Amber disapprovingly. "We have other patients on this floor with needs besides Francis Sweet, Amber. So please attend to them as well."

"Yes, Tilly. Sorry. I'll go make my rounds now."

"You do that."

Tilly flashed Hayley a knowing look as if to say, "See what I have to put up with?" But Hayley wasn't about to indulge her. She just turned and headed back to the bank of elevators.

Randy was certain he had placed the flag on the plate of spicy wings. And Amber was certain there was no flag when she picked it up and began serving them. So someone had to have intentionally removed the flag knowing Agatha would react to the intense spiciness if she ate one of the wings. And did that same person switch the labels on the eggnog pitchers, knowing if Agatha drank from the one made with dairy she would suffer a fatal anaphylactic shock? Whatever the exact circumstances, one thing was becoming abundantly clear in

Hayley's mind.

Someone had murdered Agatha Farnsworth.

CHAPTER TEN

Hayley struggled to balance a box full of paperback novels as she carefully maneuvered her way over an icy patch and gingerly made her way up the snowy paved pathway that led to the library. Luckily when she finally reached the front door, two grade-school kids came charging out with knitted scarves wrapped around their necks and knapsacks embroidered with Superman and The Flash on their backs, giggling over a private joke, nearly knocking Hayley over. After they were past her, she managed to slip inside before the door slammed shut on her.

She clomped her boots on the mat to free them of excess snow and then headed to the main desk. She had loaded the box the night before with all the cheap well-worn novels she had collected at yard sales and book drives over the past few years. Hayley was a voracious reader, a connoisseur of the old trashy, fast-paced classics from the masters like Sidney Sheldon and Jackie Collins. Plots rich with glamorous lifestyles and international intrigue were always a welcome escape from the bitter cold winter months where one particularly brutal snowstorm could knock out power for days, leaving her with nothing to do but sit in front of her fireplace, wrapped in a blanket, sipping hot herbal tea and imagining herself immersed in all the power, love, sex, lust, and crime just like her favorite character Lucky Santangelo, Collins's most popular character.

She went through so many during the barren months of January and February, they were piling up in her basement, so she decided to donate the lot to the library for their Christmas Charity Drive. Yes, she was aware that most people were donating children's books and toys for needy children, and Hayley had certainly given her fair share of board games and illustrated books and action figures from her kids' stash, but what about the mothers of needy children? Didn't they deserve a little consideration during the holidays? She knew they probably yearned for some kind of an escape from the harsh realities of life sometimes. A trashy page-turner could be just the right antidote to a bad case of the winter blues. It had sure done the trick with her.

Hayley set the box down on the desk. There was nobody around. It was rather strange not seeing Agatha Farnsworth in her bulky drab sweaters and dull plain skirts and knee-high panty hose skulking about the library barking orders at her staff and insulting the patrons with her prickly judgmental comments. The library would never be the same now that Missy Donovan had been promoted to take her place. She was certain with Missy now at the helm the library would finally feel more like a happy community center rather than a cell block on Rikers Island.

She was dead wrong.

"Whitney, I don't want to hear your pathetic excuses! I was very clear in my note that Mrs. Turner had reserved the hardback copy of the new Nora Roberts book. She is always the first on the list every time one comes in. You've been here long enough to know that!" Missy barked.

A young woman in her late twenties, very demure and soft-spoken, was nodding and quivering, a bundle of nerves. "I . . . I thought we had two copies. That's the only reason I let Tammy Downing check it out this morning."

Missy gestured to a stern-looking elderly woman with thick glasses and white hair pulled back in a bun, and practically drowning in an oversized fur coat, whose arms were folded tightly to illustrate her indignation.

"I'm so sorry, Mrs. Turner . . ." Whitney wailed, on the verge of tears. "You can always access our e-book library."

"I don't know how," Mrs. Turner sniped, stomping her foot.

"I would be happy to show you," Whitney cried, desperate to contain the situation, but fearing it was spiraling out of her control.

"I don't trust computers! I want to hold the book in my hand! Is that so wrong?" Mrs. Turner whined, turning to Missy for support.

"Now you've upset her. I think you should take your coffee break now, Whitney, and let me handle this," Missy said, pursing her lips tightly.

Whitney dashed down the stairs, fighting the urge to burst into tears.

Missy smiled and patted Mrs. Turner on the back. "She's young. She doesn't understand that some of us are old school and have no use for all these new technologies."

"Damn right," Mrs. Turner spit out before

huffily marching out of the library.

Missy turned to Hayley, who was standing there, mouth agape at Missy's unexpected power trip. "How can I help you, Hayley?"

"I . . . I'm here to donate some books for the charity drive," Hayley stammered, not quite sure why Missy was making her so nervous.

Maybe it was because Missy was suddenly channeling the ghastly personality of her old mentor and boss.

Missy nodded, stepping behind the main desk and dragging the box over in front of her. She picked up a handful of paperbacks and perused the titles. "A little advanced for a ten-year-old, wouldn't you say?"

"Oh, no, those aren't meant for the children," Hayley laughed. "I thought the parents could use a little entertainment."

"And you consider these entertaining?" Missy sniffed.

"Well, I enjoyed them. . . ."

"Junk food for the brain. It's like giving your kid a bag of Skittles as opposed to a healthier option like a carrot. Zero nutritional value."

"Like I said, these books aren't meant for children. . . ."

"I would hope we would want to encourage parents to read a work that's more high-minded and has a modicum of literary merit. . . ."

"You know, Missy, when I'm at home trying to pay the interest on my maxed-out credit cards and making sure my kids get a hot meal and hoping the furnace doesn't die before spring, I'm less interested in high-minded and literary, I just want to read a good, dirty, sleazy pot boiler. Sue me!"

Missy recoiled, speechless, crinkling her nose and deciding she had no more time or desire to engage with Hayley.

Crystal Shannon suddenly appeared, fresh-faced and rosy-cheeked, dressed in a white winter jacket and matching hat. She flashed a smile at Hayley and Missy and set a massive hardcover book down on the desk. "Merry Christmas, Missy. Hayley. I'd like to check this out, please."

Missy stared at her and then picked up the book and looked at the cover.

"It's the new Eleanor Roosevelt biography. I hear it's wonderful," Crystal said, smiling.

"I'm afraid I can't let you have this book," Missy said.

"Why? Not high-minded enough?" Hayley asked, realizing she had just said that out loud and shrinking.

Missy flashed her an irritated look and then spun back around to Crystal. "Not until you square up your late fees."

"My . . . My late fees? Missy, I just assumed now that Agatha was . . . gone from the library, those fees would be waived . . ." Crystal whispered, glancing around and not wanting to make a scene.

"Why would they be waived?" Missy hissed.

"Because they were unfair and unreasonable!" Crystal said, her back arched, ready to do battle.

"Unfair? I'll tell you what's unfair. Running this library on an insufficient budget, trying to keep the lights on so people like you can waltz in here and have free access to all of these stories and knowledge that line our shelves. What's unfair is watching our funds get slashed every year and having to have bake sales just to pay our heating bill in the winter. What's unfair is someone like you who shirks responsibility and thinks you are above the rules expecting a pass when it's convenient. Well, I am sorry to tell you, Crystal, that will not be happening under my watch. Do you hear me? I worked too many years here to watch this place go under because of people like you who try to take advantage!"

Some school kids in the reading room were getting a little out of control laughing and running around, and Missy took off like a shot to quiet them.

Crystal was in a state of shock.

This was not the Missy Donovan they expected to emerge as the head librarian.

"She did it," Crystal said softly.

"Did what?" Hayley asked.

"She somehow offed that evil troll Agatha Farnsworth!"

"Missy? That's crazy . . ."

"Is it? Look at her. That's the true Missy. A spiteful, power-hungry bitch on wheels! The other Missy, the one who worked for Agatha, the sweet and helpful assistant, I'm guessing that was all just an act."

"Maybe she's just under a lot of pressure since taking over. . . ." Hayley offered, not quite willing to believe Crystal's theory.

After all, the library was a far cry from the cutthroat boardrooms on Wall Street.

"Trust me on this, Hayley. She was at the Restaurant Association Dinner. And she's always been very good at fading into the background. She's been doing it most of her life. And those kind of people have the advantage of not being noticed. And people you don't notice can get away with just about anything."

And with that, Crystal glanced around to make sure Missy was nowhere in the vicinity and then picked up the heavy Eleanor Roosevelt biography, stuffed it inside her jacket, and marched out of the library.

Hayley watched her go, pondering the possibility of Missy Donovan as a cold-blooded killer.

It was just too bizarre, too out of the realm of reality.

But then again, Crystal was right about one thing. Hayley barely remembered seeing Missy at the dinner. She obviously kept a low profile. Was it possible for her to construct the perfect murder when no one was looking?

Did Missy Donovan covet the role of head librarian a bit too much?

CHAPTER ELEVEN

Hayley had never heard so many Portuguese swear words in her life, but they came pouring out of Sergio's mouth fast and furious as he struggled to jam the seven-foot spruce tree he had picked up at the local Christmas tree farm outside of town just that day into a tree stand.

Hayley and Randy came down the stairs from the attic, both carrying boxes of garland and swag to decorate the tree and set them down on the coffee table. Sergio and Randy's sprawling oceanfront home was already decked out for the holidays with Frosty the Snowman throw pillows, an elf-shaped wreath on the front door, and a Santa's sleigh packed with presents parked on the front lawn. A fire crackled in the fireplace. The hearth was dotted with Christmas cards and colored lights. Decorating the tree was the only thing left to be done.

If Sergio could manage to get the unwieldy tree to stand upright.

"You need a bigger tree stand," Randy said, before turning to Hayley. "I tell him every year, but he never listens."

"It will fit. I measured the tree before I paid for it," Sergio barked, bent over, his face drenched with sweat.

Randy shook his head. "I tell him not to go overboard and buy the biggest one they have, but he does anyway. I guess when it comes to Christmas trees, size really does matter."

Hayley chuckled as Randy steered her toward the kitchen. "Let's give him some time alone. He says he feels too much pressure when I stand here watching him."

"Because you always tell me I'm doing it wrong!" Sergio yelled back at him, huffing and puffing, shaking the base of the tree so hard it began shedding needles.

"Well, if you would just buy a bigger stand . . ." Randy said.

More curse words in Portuguese.

Or at least they sounded like curse words.

Hayley only knew how to say thank you in Portuguese.

Obrigado.

Randy crossed to the refrigerator in the kitchen, picked up a pitcher of eggnog, and poured some in two glasses.

"Oh, I don't know if I ever want to drink eggnog again after what happened at the Restaurant Association Dinner," Hayley said.

Randy sprinkled some nutmeg on top and handed one to Hayley. "You will definitely want to drink my eggnog. I included a special ingredient."

Bourbon.

Randy's favorite.

How could she say no?

She took a generous sip and it slid down so smoothly, the extra kick giving her a warm feeling all over.

This was how you were meant to enjoy the holidays.

They spent the next hour and a half holed up in the kitchen baking sugar cookies with Randy's wide assortment of holiday Christmas cookie cutters and frosting them with icing all while finishing off Randy's delicious and potent eggnog.

Finally, after devouring half the batch of Christmas cookies, they wandered back into the living room and stopped dead in their tracks. The magnificent Christmas tree stood erect and proud, strung with lights and garland and all the ornaments from the boxes, a beautiful glowing star on top. Sergio stood next to it, his arms folded, a big smile on his face.

"You just need to learn to trust me," Sergio said.

"Sergio, it's gorgeous!" Hayley said.

Randy nodded in agreement. "I didn't think you were going to manage it this year, but I was wrong."

"What was that?" Sergio said, playfully cupping a hand to his ear.

"I said I was wrong," Randy sighed.

"He rarely admits when he's wrong so I'd like to take a minute to enjoy it, if you don't mind."

"All right, all right. You deserve some eggnog for a job well done," Randy said, turning to head back into the kitchen.

"Uh, Randy, we drank it all," Hayley said.

"Oh, that's right. How about some hard cider?"

"I was looking forward to eggnog," Sergio said, disappointed.

"Well, we ran out. What can I do to make it up to you?"

"Say it one more time."

"I was wrong."

"Cider's fine."

Randy disappeared back into the kitchen while Hayley watched Sergio proudly admiring his handiwork.

"It really is a lovely tree, Sergio," she said.

"Obrigado," Sergio said, smiling, knowing that was the only word from his native tongue she understood.

"Are you going to be able to take some time off for the holidays?" she asked, brushing a few sugar cookie crumbs off her bulky brown sweater.

"I hope so. I am planning to make one arrest tomorrow and then hopefully things will quiet down and I can spend some time at home."

"Who are you arresting?"

"Fannie Clark-Van Dam."

"For the murder of Agatha Farnsworth?"

"Yes."

"I've been meaning to bring this up, but I hate making you talk about work when you're home . . ."

"And off the watch."

"Excuse me?"

"Off the watch."

"I'm sorry, Sergio, you're not making any sense."

"Off the watch. Off the watch. I'm not working."

"Oh, you mean off the clock!"

"Yes, that's what I said!"

"Not really, but let's move on. I think you might want to consider Missy Donovan as a

293

suspect."

"The librarian?"

"Yes, before Agatha drank the eggnog that killed her, Missy was very mousy and subservient, but then after Agatha died, she became a completely different person like a split personality. What if the shy, unassuming Missy was just an act? What if she was actually cold and calculating all along and wanted Agatha out of the way so she could finally take over as head librarian?"

"That sounds ridiculous, Hayley. No one would go to so much trouble just to become a boring head librarian," Sergio said, chuckling.

"But it was all she really had to look forward to and Agatha just kept hanging on year after year, torturing her and making her life miserable. Maybe she just finally snapped and couldn't take it anymore."

Sergio mulled this theory over in his head for a few seconds but then said, "No, I am not buying it. Besides, I already have enough to arrest Fannie."

"You do?"

"I interviewed the waitress at the Restaurant Association Dinner today."

"Amber Harding?"

"Yes, she recalled seeing Fannie putting the labels on the two pitchers of eggnog right before they were served at the dinner."

"She did?"

"Yes, according to Amber, Fannie taped one with 'Dairy' and one with 'Non-Dairy' and then quickly walked away only to come back and pick up the Non-Dairy pitcher when Agatha started choking, which was actually full of dairy."

Hayley was surprised by this news.

Especially since Amber never shared this information with her when she went to talk to her at the hospital.

"When I questioned Fannie, she told me she had carefully placed the labels on the pitchers of eggnog at home before she even left for the dinner," Sergio said. "So that means one of two things. She's either lying or she switched the labels at the last minute in order to purposefully give the wrong one to Agatha to cause the adverse reaction. That's at least enough to make an arrest."

"What about a third possibility? Amber Harding could be the one lying," Hayley said.

"For what reason? She has no motive to lie. She has no connection to Agatha Farnsworth or Fannie Clark-Van Dam for that matter."

Sergio was right.

But why all of a sudden had Amber Harding remembered that very important detail?

A detail that would incriminate Fannie and lead to her arrest?

Hayley noticed a lone wool, cheeky Santa mouse ornament lying in the box that Sergio had not seen. She scooped it up and walked over to the tree. "You forgot an ornament, Sergio. Allow me to do the honors."

She carefully hooked the ornament to the branch near the bottom of the tree and stood back to inspect it. "Perfect."

Randy came in from the kitchen with a mug of cider for Sergio, and screamed, "Hayley, look out!"

She just had time to look up and see the star on top of the tree teetering from side to side as the tree toppled over and Hayley was buried in an avalanche of branches, bulbs, tinsel, garlands, and lights.

The only thing she heard was Randy yelling, "I told you we needed a bigger tree stand!"

CHAPTER TWELVE

Hayley stared at the small toothpick flag with a picture of a hot chili pepper on it in her hand. She then looked up at the smug face of Nurse Tilly, who was sitting behind the reception desk at the Bar Harbor Hospital. When Tilly called Hayley earlier that morning and breathlessly told her she had to speak with her immediately, and that it was an emergency, she had no idea she was about to be given such a vital clue. It had been worth taking an extra early coffee break at the *Island Times* newspaper and rushing over to see her.

"Tilly, where did you find this?"

"In the pocket of my apron," Tilly said, pausing for dramatic effect before leaning in close to Hayley, and whispering, "The one I lent to Amber Harding the night of Agatha Farnsworth's murder!"

"Why did she need to borrow your apron?"

"Well, that day, just before her shift was over, I found Amber upset because an unruly child in the sick ward had thrown apple sauce all over her candy striper apron. She was going straight to the Restaurant Association Dinner to work as a waitress and pick up some extra cash and had been planning to wear that apron. But she couldn't serve the guests wearing a stained garment and she was desperate. So I very kindly offered to lend her mine. You know me, Hayley, always there with a helping hand."

"You're an angel, Tilly."

"Yes, I don't know why more people don't see that. Anyway, I had just picked it up at the dry cleaners that morning so it was all fresh and pressed and it looked very nice on Amber even though it was a little tight across her chest because, well, you know, she's a bit more full-bodied up there."

"I've noticed."

"You and every man in town," Tilly sneered.

"When did you find the flag in the pocket?"

"This morning. Amber returned the apron the very next day, and I took it home and forgot about it. Only last night did I bother emptying the pockets because I was going to drop it off at the dry cleaners again this morning on my way to work. And that's when the flag with the chili pepper on it turned up. I remember reading Bruce Linney's column the other day about what happened to Agatha at the Restaurant Association Dinner and he mentioned that the chicken wings that caused her to start choking were supposed to be labeled with this same flag. Which made me put two and two together. You're not the only amateur sleuth in town, Hayley. I watch a lot of those old detective shows on TV. I can be pretty clever when I want to be."

"Of course you can, Tilly," Hayley said, humoring her.

She turned the flag over in her fingers, her mind racing.

So Amber intentionally removed the flag from the ghost pepper chicken wings. She distinctly remembered Amber telling her that she never saw the flag on the plate.

But Amber also knew there was a picture of a chili pepper on the flag.

How did she even know that if she hadn't ever seen the flag?

Which could only mean she did see the flag and she was the one who removed it in order to fool Agatha into eating the spicy wing.

But why?

Why would Amber Harding want to kill Agatha Farnsworth?

Was she somehow in cahoots with Fannie Clark-Van Dam, who served the wrongly labeled eggnog that ultimately killed Agatha?

Was it a one-two punch?

One served the wings that caused Agatha to choke and need something to drink.

The other served the eggnog that would cause her to go into anaphylactic shock and drop over dead.

But what could either gain by knocking off an eighty-year-old woman?

None of it made any sense.

"What could Amber possibly have had against Agatha?" Hayley found herself saying out loud.

"Beats me," Tilly said. "She's never had much use for women. Only men. She's always finding a way to just take care of the male patients. The females could be ringing their buzzers for hours and she'd never show up, but a man? If a man needs something, she's in his room like a shot, prancing around with her boobs out to impress him, fluffing his pillows and spoon-feeding him his chocolate pudding! It's disgraceful!"

Hayley was truly stumped.

If Agatha was murdered, it was now clear two people had to be working together.

But Amber and Fannie?

They barely knew each other.

What connection could they possibly have to each other?

"Tilly, did Amber ever mention knowing Fannie Clark-Van Dam?"

"They would exchange a few words here and there when Fannie was here visiting her husband after his stroke, but they were hardly friends. But Fannie's the one I feel sorry for. That poor woman. First Amber tries to steal her husband and now Fannie's taking the fall for Amber's crime!"

"Wait. What did you say?"

"I also heard the police suspect Fannie of deliberately poisoning Agatha Farnsworth, and, well, that's just a bunch of bull pucky now we've cracked the case and know it's really Amber!"

"No, Tilly. Back up a bit further. What did you mean when you said Amber tried to steal Fannie's husband?"

"Oh, that. Like I said, Amber has always found a way to look after the men on her ward, and boy did she go after Dutch Van Dam when he was here recovering from his stroke. She signed up for extra shifts just so

301

she could spend time with him. Those two were inseparable. She would read to him at night, she'd make sure he was the first to get served his breakfast on the whole floor. She even smuggled in his favorite cigars and let him smell them even though he wasn't allowed to smoke them. He was besotted."

"How did you know? I mean, Dutch suffered a massive stroke. He can't even speak."

"Trust me. He didn't have to talk to show everybody how smitten he was with Amber. Let's just say, those hospital gowns can't hide everything when a man shows his attraction to a woman. It was disgusting! Do you know how embarrassing it is to pretend not to notice such a thing?"

"I imagine it's quite hard."

"It sure was. Oh, you mean hard to pretend! Yes, it was!" Tilly said, trying to compose herself.

The facts were slowly coming into focus.

But Hayley still had plenty of unanswered questions.

And although he was horribly debilitated by a stroke and unable to speak and was still on a long, challenging road to recovery, she knew her answers were with Dutch Van Dam.

CHAPTER THIRTEEN

Hayley rang the bell on the front porch of the Van Dam house, but no one came to answer the door. She noticed Fannie's car was gone so presumably she wasn't home.

But she wasn't there to see Fannie Clark-Van Dam.

She wanted to speak with Dutch.

She rang the doorbell again and waited another minute before circling around the side of the house and peeking through the windows to see if Dutch was home. The house was high on the hill outside of town so when she reached the large bay window in the back she had a magnificent view of the town and harbor and the deep blue ocean spreading out as far as the eye could see.

She peered inside the house through the window and on a large flat-screen television hung on the wall over the stone fireplace she saw the New England Patriots winning

a football game over the Green Bay Pack-
ers.

Hayley was shocked to see Dutch's wheelchair parked near the kitchen.

It was empty.

Where was he?

Had Fannie moved him before leaving to
run errands?

That's when she noticed him stretched
out on the couch watching the game. He
was chugging a beer and scooping up hand-
fuls of pretzels and stuffing them into his
mouth.

Then, suddenly there was a roar from the
television as the Patriots scored a touch-
down. Dutch Van Dam jumped up off the
couch and did a little victory dance, whoop-
ing and hollering.

Hayley's mouth dropped open in shock as
she watched the spectacle. Dutch wasn't
incapacitated at all. In fact, he was dancing
with the energy of a man half his age, pump-
ing his fist high into the air while crushing
the now-empty beer can with his other
hand.

It was all an act.

He may have suffered a stroke.

But he had made a full recovery.

And it was now clear in Hayley's mind
why he carried on the charade of being a

helpless invalid.

Hayley took a deep breath and then resolutely marched around to the back door that led into the kitchen and pounded on it loudly with her fist.

She tried the knob.

The door was unlocked.

It creaked open and she poked her head inside.

"Fannie, are you home? Fannie? It's Hayley Powell. I just dropped by to say hello."

It was quiet.

The television was now off.

Hayley entered the house, walked through the kitchen to the large living room to find Dutch back in his wheelchair, his face contorted into that of the disabled stroke victim.

"Dutch! I didn't know you were home. Sorry to barge in uninvited but I was looking for Fannie."

Dutch narrowed his eyes, grunting an unintelligible reply.

He was certainly not happy to see Hayley.

And there were worry lines on his forehead, probably over the fact that he had just nearly been caught.

"Did Fannie leave you here all by your lonesome to fend for yourself?"

Dutch nodded his head slightly, playing the sad, pathetic victim role to the hilt.

"It's so stuffy in here. Have you been out today? It's beautiful. How about I take you for a stroll? Would you like that?"

Dutch shook his head, groaning, trying to make it clear he had no desire to leave the house, but Hayley was already wrapping a red scarf around his neck.

"It's a bit nippy and we don't want you catching cold," she said, pulling the scarf so tight around his neck he choked and sputtered.

"Now let's see," Hayley said, glancing around the room and spotting a blanket draped over the couch. "That one looks nice."

Hayley grabbed the blanket and covered Dutch with it. He protested with grunts and moans, but Hayley ignored him. She wheeled him over to the front door, opened it, and pushed him outside.

Dutch was now panicking, slapping his hands on the side of his wheelchair, eyes wide with anger and fear, mouth open as desperate guttural sounds came out.

"Oh, calm down, Dutch, the fresh air will do you good," Hayley said, pushing the wheelchair roughly down the wooden porch steps and across the gravel driveway leading from the house to the street.

Just east of the house, Hayley spotted a small hill that led up to another overlook with a breathtaking view of Acadia National Park. She pushed the wheelchair toward the snowy slope that led up to the overlook as Dutch struggled to lift himself out of the chair, but Hayley firmly pushed him back down and kept her hand clasped on his bony shoulder to keep him in place, all the while using her body weight to push the wheelchair up the hill.

"Relax, Dutch, we'll be up there in just a minute and then we can sit and take in the picture-perfect scenery. How does that sound?"

Dutch wailed like a baby, rocking his body back and forth, trying to communicate to her that he wanted to go back to the house.

Hayley was impressed with his acting skills.

"Would you like me to tell you a story? Would you like that, Dutch?"

Dutch violently shook his head from side to side.

Hayley stopped a moment and tightened his scarf. She yanked it so hard Dutch gagged and wheezed, his breathing constricted.

"You'll like this one, Dutch. It's a love

story. About two people who met and fell hopelessly in love. Oh, it was so romantic. He was a patient who was hospitalized with a very serious stroke and she was the devoted candy striper who nursed him back to health. But like all love stories, there was a conflict. You see, the man was already married to a loud-mouthed domineering wife and she was never going to divorce him without a bitter battle because he was worth a lot of money. But he was miserable in his marriage and now he was in love with a girl young enough to be his granddaughter. While lying in the hospital recovering, the man imagined all sorts of ways he could try and get rid of his wife. Even murder. But if he killed her, he would immediately be a suspect because the grieving husband is always the first one the police take a close look at and he couldn't have that. He couldn't risk being exposed and going to prison. No, he had to find another way."

They reached the top of the hill and Hayley stopped. Dutch was now slumped over in his chair, eyes downcast, listening.

"So snuffing out the wife wasn't an option. He had to come up with another plan. And then it hit him. What if it was the wife who committed the murder? She would be sent away for at least twenty years and she'd finally be out of his hair and unable to touch his fortune. So a plot was hatched. He picked out a potential victim. A hateful, terrible old woman who no one would miss if she was gone. A spiteful old hag, who as luck would have it, was publicly feuding with his wife. Everyone knew the woman was allergic to dairy and had a weak stomach. So what if the man's love-struck paramour, the candy striper, was willing to do anything to be with the love of her life and got a job as a waitress at a dinner the old woman was attending. And what if she secretly pocketed a toothpick flag with a red chili pepper on it off a plate of ghost pepper chicken wings and served one to the victim, who had no idea that what she was eating was extremely spicy, and what if she moved all the water bottles clear across the room while helping to set up for the dinner so there were no other beverages nearby? Then, when the woman began choking and gasping and turning red, his wife, who was close by with her pitcher of eggnog, would rush in to save the day because even though she despised the old woman, he knew she would never just stand there and watch her die."

Hayley noticed Dutch's fingers gripping the sides of the wheelchair, his knuckles turning white, his whole body tense.

"But the wife had no idea her husband had recovered from his stroke and was only pretending to be an invalid. He could easily switch the labels and not be suspected because everyone just assumed the poor man was confined to a wheelchair and barely able to move. So when she picked up the pitcher of eggnog marked 'Non-Dairy' she hardly suspected it was the wrong one because she had placed the labels on the pitchers herself before she even left for the dinner. The old woman's allergy did the rest. She died on the spot and everyone in that room had witnessed the wife serve her the mislabeled eggnog. Of course the wife would say it was an accident and go on about how she had carefully labeled the pitchers herself. Maybe the police would believe her or maybe they wouldn't. But then the man's lover stepped forward and admitted she saw the wife fiddling with the labels before she served the old woman the fatal eggnog. Why wouldn't they believe her? She had no connection to anyone. She was just an innocent waitress serving the food. Her testimony would ultimately seal the deal. The wife would be arrested and tried for murder."

Dutch twisted his body in his chair and

scowled. "You nosy bitch . . ."

He reached out with his hands to grab Hayley by the neck and throttle her, but she was too fast for him. She forcefully shoved the wheelchair forward and down the hill just as Fannie pulled up to the house in her car.

"Your wife's home! Why don't you go say hello?"

She watched as the wheelchair bounced down the snowy hill, Dutch holding on for dear life, screaming all the way.

Fannie jumped out of her car and screamed at the top of her lungs. "Oh, my God! Dutch!"

The wheelchair tipped over halfway down the hill and Dutch was ejected like a pilot from a downed fighter jet plunging to earth and rolled the rest of the way until he hit the bottom, landing facedown in a pile of muddy slush.

Fannie scurried over to her husband and bent down. "Dutch, honey, are you all right?"

Sirens approached from the distance.

Dutch raised his head and listened for a moment; then, jumping to his feet and bulldozing past his wife, he made a run for the woods.

The police cruiser screeched to a stop and

Sergio hopped out, a surprised look on his face. "Is that . . . ?"

Dutch almost made it to the thicket of trees before tripping over himself and falling down in the snow.

By now Hayley had made it down the hill and was at Fannie's side while Sergio jogged after Dutch, a pair of handcuffs in his hand.

Fannie gazed at her husband now lying on the ground, stupefied. "I . . . I don't understand . . ."

Hayley put a comforting hand on Fannie's shoulder. "Dutch recovered from his stroke some time ago, Fannie."

"Why would he pretend to still be . . . ?"

"It was all a plot to set you up for Agatha's murder. He and his lover Amber Harding wanted you out of the way so they could be together."

"Amber . . . the candy striper at the hospital?" Fannie gasped.

"Yes, I'm guessing once you went away to rot in prison, he could hire Amber as his private nurse since he would need someone to look after him and care for him. They could finally be together, and then, once he faked his miraculous recovery, maybe six months or a year from now, no one in town would question the sweet fairy tale about the rich man who fell in love with the woman who nursed him back to health."

Sergio hauled a muttering Dutch to his feet, slapped handcuffs on his wrist, and led him back to the cruiser where Hayley and Fannie waited.

Fannie stepped in front of Dutch, her eyes pleading.

"Tell me they're wrong, Dutch. Tell me you didn't do this."

Dutch said nothing.

He just glared at her.

And Fannie Clark-Van Dam then reared back and punched her husband right in the face.

Hayley would have applauded the move if blood spurting from Dutch's broken nose hadn't landed on her brand-new Christmas sweater.

CHAPTER FOURTEEN

The arrest of Dutch Van Dam and his young lover Amber Harding for the murder of Agatha Farnsworth was all anybody was talking about in town. Even now on Christmas Eve the buzz was at a fever pitch, and everywhere she went Hayley had to hear about it. In her mind, the whole sad chapter was over. It was time to move on and focus on spending time with family and friends — or in her case, a good book, some baked treats, and a yummy cocktail — and snuggling with her dog and cat, Leroy and Blueberry, at home on the couch.

Hayley swung by the library to check out some new saucy, salacious books for the week between Christmas and New Year's. The idea of escaping into the sordid, complicated lives of the rich and famous, whose troubles dwarfed her own, was the perfect cure for her holiday blues.

Good old-fashioned trash.

She found three that looked like fast, compelling reads and carried them over to the checkout counter where Missy Donovan was waiting for her.

Hayley took a deep breath, braced herself, and set them down for Missy to inspect, steeling herself for another confrontation about her taste in reading material.

But Missy just smiled brightly, and said, "Merry Christmas, Hayley."

"Merry Christmas," Hayley said warily.

Missy lifted one particularly prurient sounding title, perused it, and then she raised her eyes to meet Hayley's, leaning in and whispering, "I hear this is a really good one! Very steamy!"

And then she giggled before getting serious again and handing the books to her mild-mannered and beleaguered assistant Whitney. "Here, Whitney, why don't you help Hayley with these and then you can take your break."

"My break?" Whitney asked incredulously. "But I'm not due for another hour."

"It's Christmas. Let's not be so strict about the rules. There's some special Christmas punch left in the fridge from the holiday party last night, so knock yourself out," Missy said, winking at Whitney. "I won't tell if you don't."

Whitney nodded and her shoulders re-laxed a bit, no doubt for the first time since she started this job.

Hayley had heard Missy was deeply af-fected by the fact that Agatha's sudden death was not an accident, that it had been an orchestrated murder plot. She was shaken at her core probably because she had many times fantasized about doing the deed herself when she was home at night after an exhausting day of Agatha's relentless nag-ging and tormenting. As venomous and vindictive as Agatha could be, no one deserved to die before their time at the behest of someone else. And now, as Hayley saw it, Missy was making amends by not following in the footsteps of her former boss. Missy had a good heart and she was not going to allow power to corrupt it.

"By the way, Hayley, I spoke to some of the parents from the toy drive for needy children and those books you donated were greatly appreciated."

"Thank you, Missy."

Whitney finished checking out the books for Hayley and handed them to her and then trotted off to the break room to get tipsy on the leftover punch.

Hayley turned to leave and ran into Fannie Clark-Van Dam, who was behind her with a stack of celebrity biographies she was planning on devouring during the holidays since she no longer had to sweat over caring for her husband.

"Hayley! I've been meaning to call you! It's been such a whirlwind since Dutch's arrest and all the newspaper interviews I've had to give! It's been exhausting!"

"I can only imagine," Hayley said.

She had heard through the grapevine Fannie was on a self-promoting publicity tour since Dutch's case garnered so much high-profile attention and everyone wanted to talk to the wronged wife, and she was lapping it up, even making noises about writing a book on the whole wretched affair. Hayley believed by next Christmas she would be checking out Fannie's best-seller from the library.

"I'm calling you tomorrow to schedule a dinner. You saved my life. And I owe you big time. Oh, and I want to talk to you about us going on a Caribbean cruise in February. My treat! I went to St. Thomas with my college girlfriends a few years back and it was amazing and I would just love to experience it again with my best friend!"

Best friend?

Did she just say best friend?

One disturbing offshoot of Hayley exposing Dutch and Amber's shenanigans was obviously Fannie's undying gratitude. And how she planned on repaying her.

"I have so many plans for the two of us! We're going to have so much fun running around together. Like those two funny ladies from *Absolutely Fabulous*! Drinking and carousing and causing all sorts of trouble!"

Hayley was speechless.

She never was a big fan of Fannie to begin with, she found her rather annoying in fact, and now they were going to be bosom buddies.

Fannie grabbed Hayley in a tight hug, crushing her library books against her chest, and squeezed hard. "Love you, girl. I wish we could hang out on New Year's, but I have a *Today Show* interview in early January and I need to drop a few pounds, so I'm going to a spa in Palm Springs. *The Today Show*, can you believe it? Apparently having the last name Van Dam gets you on a couch next to Matt Lauer! How crazy is that? Ciao!"

And she was off like a shot.

This was good.

She was busy.

It would give Hayley some time to figure out how to get out of spending any time with Fannie Clark-Van Dam.

Hayley left the library and drove home to her house.

She was surprised to see the Christmas tree lights on in the window.

She was sure she had unplugged them before she left for work that morning.

She got out of the car and carried her books inside through the back door.

In the kitchen, there was a ham baking in the oven.

Potatoes and a veggie medley on the stove.

An open bottle of wine breathing on the counter.

Assorted treats on paper plates wrapped in plastic.

She set the books down on the kitchen table and headed down the hall to the living room and turned right, spotting a few more presents under the tree than had been there that morning. Kelly Clarkson was softly singing "Underneath the Tree" on a music channel on TV. Leroy was in the recliner, his tail wagging expectantly, while Blueberry slept soundly, totally uninterested.

She bent down, picking up one present and inspecting the tag.

To Mom, Love Dustin.

She heard some rustling upstairs.

Her heart skipped a beat.

She smiled.

They had come home.

Hayley raced up the stairs where Gemma and Dustin rushed out of their rooms to greet her.

"Merry Christmas, Mom!" they said in unison.

"What . . . What are you doing here? I thought . . ."

"I can go skiing with friends anytime," Gemma said, hugging her mother.

"And I asked Dad to fly me home early as my Christmas present," Dustin said, laughing.

She grabbed her kids and held them tight, trying hard not to sob with joy.

They would never let her live down such a lame emotional outburst.

But one thing was certain.

It was the best Christmas present she could ever have hoped for.

ISLAND FOOD & COCKTAILS
BY HAYLEY POWELL

Whew! What a busy Christmas season this year has been! So much shopping to do and holiday parties to attend! There was little free time left on the calendar. But of course no one in town could possibly think to turn down the new head librarian Missy Donovan's invitation to join her at the Jesup Memorial Library for a remembrance celebration of our recently deceased past library matriarch Agatha Farnsworth, whom many of you have known for her tireless dedication to the library for over half a century! As I'm sure you read in the *Island Times*, Agatha recently retired and moved on to the Ledgelawn cemetery for a little peace and quiet. She has certainly earned the rest.

When we arrived at the library, we were treated to pizza and wings that were provided by Little Anthony's on Cottage Street and to some fabulous adults-only potent eggnog punch and some tasty homemade eggnog cookies made by Missy Donovan herself! It was one of the quietest celebrations I ever attended. No one dared to speak, or if they did, they whispered so softly none of the other attendees could hear what they were saying. Everyone feared that if they got too loud Agatha would rise from the grave as a ghostly apparition and yell at them to keep their voices down!

In a last-ditch attempt to get everyone more comfortable, Missy Donovan finally stood up and proposed a toast to the late great Agatha Farnsworth. She told a story about when she first started working at the library and had only been on the job a few days when Agatha discovered two twelve-year-old boys in the downstairs bathroom sneaking cigarettes. After lecturing them for almost two hours on library etiquette and the dangers of smoking, she told the boys she was going to call the police and have them thrown in jail because that is exactly where they were heading if they kept up their bad behavior.

The poor boys cried and begged her to call their parents instead so they could confess and face punishment at home. Anything to escape Agatha's wrath!

This funny little story opened the floodgates, and people began sharing their stories of their various run-ins with Agatha and pretty soon everyone was reminiscing and laughing and joking about how Agatha lived and breathed the library and took her job way too seriously. Mona even stood up on a table and did a dead-on impersonation of Agatha on a typical tirade that brought the house down.

I was wiping away tears from laughing so hard when an older gentleman appeared out of the crowd and said he would like to speak about Agatha. He was probably in his mid-sixties, attractive, well groomed, and had on a fancy Brooks Brothers suit.

Then he began to tell his story and the room suddenly fell silent.

He told us his parents had been killed in a tragic car accident in Bangor when he was just a week old. He was in the car but survived and was placed with his elderly grandmother. Agatha had been a friend of the couple and immediately drove to Bangor to check on the poor orphaned baby boy. Well, she became so smitten with him that she wanted to adopt him as her own. Unfortunately his grandmother wouldn't and couldn't part with the baby in her grief even though she was getting on in years.

Agatha was devastated, but she completely understood and recognized the challenges that would have come if she had taken the baby home. How would she explain a new-born baby to the doubting minds in town? People saw things differently back then. And her being so young, working at the library full time, and not a boyfriend in sight, she sadly accepted that the boy was better off with his grandmother.

But that didn't stop Agatha from driving the hour or so to Bangor and visiting him every single weekend after that. She never missed one. She took him to museums, parks, and movies. She enthusiastically fed his love of reading by bringing boxes and boxes of books she checked out of the library for him. She quickly became his second mother, best friend, and confidante.

When his grandmother passed away during his senior year of high school, Agatha stepped in and arranged for him to attend a very fine college in Boston and she even paid for it all out of her own pocket as she had already been doing for all of his needs for eighteen years, since raising the boy was a financial struggle for his grandmother.

After college he attended graduate school, also funded by Agatha, and received a Master's in Business Economics, and through it all she was by his side every moment that he needed her, proudly sharing in his successes and picking him up when he failed.

In short, he had had a very nice life, a successful business career, a lovely wife and two happy children who he also shared with Agatha, and they all adored her.

He said he was sad she never married and had a family of her own, but she always told him she was married to her job and devoted to him and his family and they loved her very much, and that was more than she could have ever hoped for in her life. She was blessed and contented.

He told us he just wanted everyone in Bar Harbor to know that there was another side of Agatha and he felt he owed it to her to let us all know.

He then thanked us for listening, turned around, and as he walked out the door, he placed an envelope on the small table next to the front desk, and then he was gone.

I looked around and there wasn't a dry eye in the house.

Everyone just stared at each other in quiet amazement.

Missy wandered over and opened the envelope out of curiosity and let out a deafening shriek! Her hand was shaking as she clutched the envelope and after a bit of stuttering she managed to get out that the gentleman had left a check for $50,000 to the library to be used at the library's discretion in Agatha's name.

We gave a final heartfelt toast to the only librarian most of us had ever known in our whole lives and everyone left that night still thinking about the Agatha Farnsworth she managed to keep hidden from pretty much everyone she knew. I guess it's true there are always two sides to every story.

With the holiday season finally winding down I'd like to share two more eggnog recipes to hold us over until next year. I have a feeling Agatha won't mind. In fact, I'm pretty sure she just might be smiling down on us.

Merry Christmas to everyone!

MISSY'S EGGNOG PUNCH

Ingredients
2 quarts eggnog
1/2 gallon your favorite vanilla ice cream
1 1/2 cups bourbon
1 can spray whipped cream
Ground nutmeg

In a punch bowl combine your eggnog and bourbon until well blended. Add scoops of the softened ice cream and blend in. Ladle into glasses, spray some whipped cream on top, and then add a sprinkle of nutmeg on top of the cream. Cheers!

MISSY'S EGGNOG COOKIES

Ingredients
3 cups yellow cake mix
6 tablespoons melted unsalted butter
2 large egg yolks
2 tablespoons eggnog
1/2 teaspoon ground nutmeg

In a bowl mix all of your ingredients together until blended. Do not overmix. Divide your dough into six balls and place on a baking sheet lined with parchment paper. Bake in a preheated oven at 350 degrees for nine to ten minutes. Remove from oven and cool for two minutes, then place on a wire cooling rack and cool completely. When cooled you can frost them.

Frosting
2/3 cup powdered sugar
2 to 3 tablespoons eggnog
Ground nutmeg for sprinkling

In a bowl whisk powdered sugar and eggnog together until you have a frosting consistency. You can use more powdered sugar and eggnog to achieve this. Frost your cooled cookies and sprinkle with a bit of nutmeg. Serve and enjoy!

Dear Readers,

We hope you've enjoyed *Death by Eggnog,* starring our intrepid crime-solving heroine Hayley Powell. If this is the first time you've met Hayley and would like to learn more about how she got her start as a food and cocktails columnist at the *Island Times* newspaper in Bar Harbor, Maine, and launched her secondary career as an amateur sleuth, you can always pick up a paperback copy or download to your favorite reading device her first hairraising adventure, *Death of a Kitchen Diva.* There are, as with all of the Hayley Powell books, a host of mouthwatering recipes included.

And since there is nothing better than curling up next to a crackling fire and reading a good book during the holidays, why not enjoy all the other titles in the series guaranteed to keep your brain guessing and your stomach growling?

There is *Death of a Country Fried Redneck,* featuring a recipe collection of down-home southern delicacies, *Death of a Coupon Clipper* with meals on a budget, *Death of a Chocoholic* designed for anyone with a sweet tooth, *Death of a Christmas Caterer* with a variety of holiday treats, *Death of a Cupcake Queen,* which focuses on scrumptious sugary desserts, *Death of a Bacon Heiress,* full of tasty dishes featuring, you guessed it, the key ingredient bacon, and last but not least, *Death of a Pumpkin Carver,* highlighting some delicious pumpkin-laced recipes.

We wish you and your family a happy and safe holiday full of good cheer!

Best wishes,
Lee Hollis

■ ■ ■ ■

NOGGED OFF

BARBARA ROSS

■ ■ ■ ■

CHAPTER ONE

I breezed onto the Acela at South Station in Boston and took a seat in first class. From my road warrior days working in venture capital, I had enough Amtrak points to take a train to the moon and back, should such a trip be offered, and I was determined to burn as many as possible before they expired. This was the last time I'd be making the trek to New York City for a good long time.

I snuggled into the comfy seat and closed my eyes. It had already been a long day. I'd left my apartment in Busman's Harbor, Maine, at four in the morning so my boyfriend, Chris, could drop me at the train station in Portland in time to catch the five-twenty. If all went according to plan, I'd be at Penn Station in Manhattan by lunchtime and at my apartment in Tribeca not long after that. Then, using the key I still had, with the permission of my subtenant, I'd take the few personal items I wanted from my soon-to-be-former apartment to UPS for shipping and be on my way back to Maine by early evening. Down and back in one day. If everything went perfectly, maybe I'd even have time to do a little Christmas shopping and drink in the glory of Manhattan during the holidays.

The young woman I'd sublet to, Imogen Geinkes, was not only taking over my lease when it was up on January 1, she had also agreed to buy most of my furniture. In addition, I'd soon be getting a check from the building management company refunding my security deposit, a little boost to the coffers that couldn't come too soon. The change in my life from my Manhattan job in the financial industry to managing my family's struggling clambake business in Maine had meant a considerable change in my finances as well.

Down and back in one day. I couldn't believe how perfectly the plan had come together.

I jiggled my key in the lock of my old apartment on North Moore Street. Manuel, the quasi-security guard, quasi-doorman, had made me sign in at the front desk, but he'd let me go straight up without calling ahead.

Whether it was because he remembered me, or because Imogen had told him about our arrangement, I didn't know. The lock had always been a little reluctant, and I was relieved when at last the tumblers turned and the door to the apartment swung open.

I stepped into the dark living room. One of the best things about the apartment was its view across the Hudson, and I was surprised Imogen kept the blinds closed. I turned on the lights and stepped into the kitchen area. I wasn't planning on taking much, just some dishes, three oil paintings that had been my grandfather's, and, the real reason for the trip, my books.

I piled my dishes on the breakfast bar. I needed to get my stuff together to calculate how many boxes to buy on my first visit to the shipping store. That's when I heard it.

Sniff.

"Hello?" I called. I waited, counting to ten. No response. I shrugged and reached for the dinner plates. I loved the apartment, but I had to admit it was entirely possible the sniff had traveled through the paper-thin walls from one of the adjoining units.

Sniff.

"Hello?" I said again. The sniff was louder that time, and seemed to come from close by. The bedroom door was closed. I started toward it. "Imogen?"

On my way through the living room, it happened again. *Sniff.* Right next to me. "Imogen!" She sat, hidden in a large, upholstered armchair that had been my grandfather's.

"Julia?"

"Imogen. I thought you were at work."

"I'm supposed to be." A solitary tear squeezed from the corner of her eye and tracked down her cheek.

Ho, boy. What is this about? I knelt beside the chair. "What's happened?" The water-works turned on full force. I waited while she pulled herself together.

Imogen worked at a small advertising firm on Hudson Street, an easy walk from the apartment. I'd spoken with her boss-to-be when I'd checked her references before subletting to her. He'd said she was a new hire, but he expected great things. That had only been nine months ago. What had gone wrong?

"There . . . there . . . there was a holiday party," Imogen stuttered out.

Oh no. She was twenty-two, eight years younger than me, and the same age I'd been when I'd arrived in New York. People can be awfully foolish at that age. I dreaded what might come next.

"It was just a little gathering. At the office, on Friday night."

I counted backward. Today was Wednesday. Only three workdays later. Perhaps the damage, whatever it was, could still be undone.

"They asked each of us to bring something. For the celebration." Imogen broke down and sobbed again. I moved to the matching chair opposite, waiting for the rest of the story.

"My mama makes a killer eggnog," Imogen said. "It's the best. At home, in Buckhead, Atlanta, we have an open house every year on New Year's Day. People rave about Mama's eggnog. So I made it. But, Julia, something was wrong with the eggs. I food-poisoned every one of my coworkers and their guests!"

"Oh my gosh!" I'd been expecting a tale of disaster, but not exactly this one.

"People were throwing up, and worse, Julia, much worse. We all ended up in the ER with salmonella poisoning."

"Were you fired?"

In the deep chair, Imogen shook her head. "No, but I can't go back there. I just can't. Once you've been in an emergency room, hooked up to an IV, being rehydrated, next to your boss and your boss's boss . . ." The tears returned. "I can never see any of those people again."

"So, you've quit?" No severance, no unemployment compensation. I braced myself for what was coming next.

"Uh-huh." Imogen nodded, tears sliding down her cheeks. "So I won't be able to take the apartment."

CHAPTER TWO

Even though I'd seen it coming, the news felt like a blow. *Drat! The best-laid plans . . .*

If I had any hope of getting my security deposit back, I had to get the apartment cleared out. Pronto. I was in New York on a Wednesday because I had it off from work at the restaurant I ran with my boyfriend, Chris, during the winter. I pulled up the calendar on my phone and saw nothing but a solid block of work and holiday obligations running until New Year's Day. I had to act.

I supposed I could donate most of the furniture to charity, but it was too late in the day to arrange for a pickup. I could follow the time-honored New York tradition of "donating" it to the passing crowd by leaving it on the sidewalk. But whatever I did, no one would take my mattress and box spring, or the upholstered furniture, due to the pervasive fear of bedbugs.

I looked around the apartment. So much of the furniture had come from my mother's father, who had spent the long years of his widowerhood in an apartment on Riverside Drive. He'd died shortly after I arrived in the city, and it had seemed to everyone the perfect solution for me to take most of his furniture. The pieces were old and unfashionable, but I was getting my MBA and hardly in a position to argue. Looking at it now, the overstuffed couch, the straightbacked chair where Imogen sat huddled, its twin where I sat across from her, the mahogany bed and bureau in the bedroom, I wondered how much of the furniture my mother had grown up with. Was she sentimentally attached to any of it? We had a bunch of photos of her at several ages sitting on that sofa.

My mother lived in closer communion with her family's past than most people. Morrow Island, where we ran the Snowden Family Clambake in the summer, had been in her family for five generations. But by the time she'd come along, the money was long gone and the family dispersed. Mom had some heirloom china and crystal in our dining room back in Busman's Harbor, but not much else.

It was one thing to sell my grandfather's

possessions to Imogen, who could genuinely use them. It was another to abandon them. I couldn't do that. I was going to have to cart it all back to Busman's Harbor.

While I worked my way toward this conclusion, I tried to ignore the steady snuffling from Imogen. But, of course, that was impossible.

"Do you have a place to stay while you look for another job?" She'd been new to the city when I'd sublet to her, but perhaps since then, she'd made a good friend, the kind who would offer a couch to crash on.

"No," Imogen wailed. "I could have gone to my boyfriend's, but we just broke up."

Her nose was red, eyes swollen. Something that looked suspiciously like snot covered her upper lip. She was smaller than me, and at five-two, I'm considered short. Scrunched in my grandfather's armchair, her feet didn't quite touch the floor. Her long hair was pulled back in a high ponytail. A few dark brown hairs had escaped and curled around her face in a way that would have been charming had they not been soaked in tears. Her skin was pale, her big eyes brown and, at that moment, wet. To go with her little-girl size, she had a little-girl voice. High-pitched and breathy.

She looked impossibly young. We hadn't

met when I'd sublet the apartment. She was still in Atlanta, and I'd done my due diligence over the phone, interviewing her, her landlord, and her current and future employers. She'd had an internship in Atlanta, but her job in New York was her first real post-college employment. The age gap between her fresh-out-of-college twenty-two and my almost thirty-one felt like an eternity.

"Are you going home to Georgia for the holidays?" Christmas and New Year's would make a Swiss cheese of the next two weeks. No corporate hiring would get done. Imogen might as well go home to Atlanta and come back after the first. When no answer came but sniffles, I prodded, "When do you leave?" I'd have to leave enough furniture to crutch her over until her departure, whenever that was. I had an old card table and chairs stashed in the hall closet along with an air mattress. She could put them on the street when she left the apartment for good.

My inquiries about her Christmas plans brought on a new set of wails. "I met my ex-boyfriend Wade online, on a matchmaking site. He was the best, the dreamiest, the nicest man I've ever known. He came to Atlanta for ten days and it was heaven. We were so in love. He lived here in New York, so when my internship in Atlanta ended, I moved up. But my parents said we hadn't known each other long enough for me to make such big life decisions. We had a huge fight. My parents and I have never gotten over it."

"Really?" My apartment wasn't cheap. It had taken me years of living with room-mates and working to get a place of my own. Imogen had paid her rent right on time every month. I'd assumed she was getting some help from home. If her parents were subsidizing her living expenses, how mad could they be?

"Imogen, I'm sure they'll understand. You've just had some bad luck." *And bad eggs.* "Besides, your boyfriend — Wade was it? — is gone now. They'll forgive and forget."

"But that's it." She punched her tiny fist into the arm of the chair. "I am not going home with my tail between my legs." She stuck out her jaw.

"That's great," I said. "But you realize, you can't stay here. At least not after New Year's Eve. Have you made any good girl-friends since you moved to New York?"

"Not really. None of the women at work are friendly. For some reason, they don't like me."

You mean, before you poisoned them?

Imogen burst into energetic tears once again.

The great thing about New York City is that, for a price, you can get pretty much anything you want or need at any hour of the day or night. In my case, that included a yellow rental truck and two big guys, Julio and Mike, to load it. I found the guys on Craigslist. Julio said they were just finishing another job and could be at my place by 8:00 PM. That gave me six hours to pack up everything and clean the apartment. More than enough time. Besides, I wasn't in a position to argue.

By the time I was done with the calls, Imogen was done crying, at least for the moment. She wandered into the kitchen area and got a glass of ice water.

"Where will you take the furniture?" she asked.

"Home, to Busman's Harbor, Maine."

"That sounds wonderful. Do you have a town green with a Christmas tree and a skating pond?" She rattled off the features of a Currier and Ives print.

"Yes," I admitted.

"And do you have presents under the tree

and dinner with family and friends?"

"Er, yes." Where was this going?

"And will you have a white Christmas?"

"No way to know. There wasn't any snow on the ground when I left this morning, but we've got a week until the big day." I answered in a "just the facts, ma'am" tone I hoped would discourage the question I feared was coming next.

"I have a great idea!" Imogen exclaimed, as if the thought had just occurred to her that second. "Why don't I come home in the truck with you for the holidays? I've always wanted to see a real New England Christmas. And that way we can clean out the apartment together today."

I began to understand her parents' concern about her impulsivity. On the other hand, what she was proposing wasn't completely crazy. If she left with me, I'd be the last person in the apartment and could make sure it was cleaned up to my specifications and ensure I'd get my security deposit back.

Besides, my family had a long history of taking in strays for holidays. Foreign students at my boarding school for Thanksgiving. Itinerant sternmen who worked on Grandpa Snowden's lobster boat for Easter. My mom would be fine with me bringing

Imogen home. Besides, I didn't think she'd last the whole week in Maine until Christmas. Once she was over the shock of the whole mess — food-poisoning her colleagues, quitting her job, breaking up with her boyfriend, and ending up in a little harbor town in Maine where she didn't know a soul — I figured she'd get homesick and be on a plane to Atlanta ASAP.

"Okay," I said. "You can come. I have to leave now to pick up the truck. You pack your stuff and start cleaning. I'll buy boxes at the truck rental place and be back as fast as I can."

During the cab ride over to the truck place, I called my mom and then Chris. Mom, the product of generations of good breeding, was as gracious about the unanticipated holiday guest as I'd expected she would be.

Chris was more skeptical. "Julia, you just met this person."

"I know, but I checked her out before I sublet to her. She's a perfectly nice person." Somehow, his doubts made me all the more certain.

He, apparently, wasn't opposed enough to argue. "Safe travels. See you tonight," he said. "Love you."

"Love you, too."

When I'd lived in Manhattan, I didn't have a car. I'd driven my late father's pickup down a few times to facilitate apartment-to-apartment moves, so I had some experience with city driving. But not in a big yellow rental truck. I called Imogen before I pulled out of the lot. "Can you go downstairs and wait for me in the loading zone? I may need someone to flag me in. Thanks."

I inched my way off the West Side Highway and made the terrifying trip around the block to one-way North Moore. It was rush hour and pedestrians crowded the sidewalk. Sitting high up in the truck cab, I was able to make out the tiny figure of Imogen Geinkes. She hadn't bothered to put on a jacket and stood huddled by the side of the street. I blew my horn to get her attention. She straightened up and waved me into the generously sized loading zone in front of the building.

"Thanks," I said, climbing out of the cab.

"No problem."

I went around to the back to get the boxes. Imogen followed, shivering like an overexcited toy poodle. "Don't you have a coat?" I tried not to sound like her mother.

"No." Her voice quavered and I worried she'd start sobbing again. "When we went to the ER after the thing with the eggnog, I left my coat back at the office." There was that defiant chin again. "I am never going back there."

"You can't visit Maine in December without a coat," I answered. "So we'll have to solve that problem."

Julio and Mike showed up just as we finished spit-shining the apartment. I had managed to corral all my stuff and lovingly packed my boxes of books, the things I had really come for. They included a small collection of vintage children's novels that had belonged to the women in my family down through the years. There were early editions of *Black Beauty, Anne of Green Gables, The Wonderful Wizard of Oz, Little Women,* and more, each with the names of all the women in my mother's family who had owned them on the inside cover. Ellen Morrow, the grandmother I had never met, Jacqueline Fields, my mother, and finally my name, Julia Snowden, written in a schoolgirl scrawl. I'd been so proud to put my name in those books.

Since Imogen didn't have a coat, I stood on the sidewalk and guarded my possessions while Julio and Mike made their way up and down the freight elevator with each load of stuff. First came my grandfather's furniture, then my modern desk and its rolling pedestal chair. Then came the boxes — dishes, pots and pans, my books, the three boxes containing my grandfather's oil paintings, and finally Imogen's giant suitcase and an overnight case.

When I'd first come out of the building, I'd spotted a dirty white car parked down the block with a man in it. I don't know why I noticed it. There was nothing particular about the car, just another anonymous white older Toyota Camry. The man sat in the driver's seat, a Yankees baseball cap on his head, staring into the street. What was he doing there? He stayed the whole hour it took to load the truck. The Toyota's engine wasn't running. He must be getting cold.

But then, the city was a complicated place. Eight million inhabitants meant eight million possible explanations. Perhaps the man was waiting for a buddy to come home after work. Or, in a city where street parking was hard to come by, maybe he was saving the spot for a friend who was even now racing in his direction. I shook my head and dismissed my concerns.

"That's it," Julio said. I handed him cash, his required legal tender, along with a generous tip for him and Mike, for adding my emergency to their already long day. I sent Imogen, bundled in a light jacket over a sweatshirt, to the deli around the corner for sandwiches, drinks, and snacks, while I did one last sweep and made sure the apartment was spotless. Then I closed the door and locked it one last time.

A wave of nostalgia swept over me. I'd worked hard to get that apartment. I'd been proud of my big-city accomplishments. The last thing I ever expected was to be home in Busman's Harbor. My life had taken a big left turn, but I was happy. Running my family's clambake in the summer and now my restaurant in the off-season was fulfilling. I was surrounded by family and I was in love. But you always wondered about the road not traveled. It was part of being human.

I opened the back of the truck, which was tightly packed with the remnants of my old life. Julio and Mike had done a good job. I threw my bulky coat into the back. I didn't want it in the heated cab. Imogen returned, clutching a giant grocery bag. I pulled down the big back door of the truck, which shut with a satisfying clang, and affixed the padlock the rental company had been happy to sell me. We were off.

CHAPTER THREE

It was nine-thirty before we got free of the city traffic. Imogen was in and out of the bag of snacks, consuming chips, popcorn, cookies, and soda.

"I have a super-fast metabolism," she explained. "I have to eat constantly just to maintain my body weight."

Staring straight ahead at the road, I rolled my eyes. No wonder she hadn't made any female friends at her office. That kind of remark was likely to get you shunned in the dog-eat-dog looks competition of New York. Or anywhere else, for that matter.

I'd hoped to make good time, but unfortunately, along with her birdlike metabolism, Imogen had a bird-sized bladder. We stopped twice before we got out of Connecticut.

In the darkened cab, Imogen chatted about her life, and about her boyfriend. A *lot* about her boyfriend, Wade Cadwallader.

"He was so sweet. The nicest guy. But then he wasn't. But then he was again. But then he wasn't. At all. When I first moved up, he took me everywhere in New York. He grew up in the city and wanted to share it — the museums, the shows, Central Park in the spring. It was all so beautiful and amazing."

I nodded to show I understood. I, too, had been seduced by New York, though I wondered just how much Imogen had been seduced by the city and how much by Wade Cadwallader.

"But then, this fall, Wade got so moody. Sometimes he would be the charming gentleman I know he is deep down, but other times he was cranky and snarky. Instead of taking me out, we'd sit in my apartment, your apartment, that is, and watch sports on TV, all night long. Nothing I said was right, nothing I cooked tasted good. He drove me crazy."

I nodded again. An old story, really. A person tries hard in the beginning of a relationship, but then gets comfortable and lets his or her natural jerkiness come out. I'd heard this sad tale from countless roommates and coworkers before.

"I'd be ready to call it quits," Imogen continued, "but then he'd show up the next night and take me out dancing, like nothing had happened. Honestly, it made my head spin."

"Was he having problems at work, or something else that could have affected his mood?"

In the light of the dash, I saw Imogen shrug. "Not that he told me. I never really understood his job. It was something at a big financial company."

Hundreds of thousands of New Yorkers do "something at a big financial company," much of it highly technical and difficult for others to comprehend. As we used to say when I worked in venture capital, "If your mom understands your job, you don't have a very good one."

"So a real Dr. Jekyll and Mr. Hyde," I said.

"Who?"

"Never mind."

We rolled along silently for several miles, Imogen eating continuously. At least she was no longer crying.

"What about you?" she asked. "How did you meet your boyfriend?"

"In middle school."

"And you dated all that time, with him in Maine and you in New York?" Imogen was no doubt rethinking her whole moving-to-be-with-a-guy-you've-spent-ten-days-with strategy.

I laughed. "We dated none of that time. I had an enormous crush on him, but I was in seventh grade and he was a junior, the quarterback on the football team with a cheerleader girlfriend. After eighth grade, I went away to boarding school and never talked to him again until I moved back to Busman's Harbor last March." I looked into my mirror and pulled out to pass a particularly slow-moving car. "My crush came roaring back as soon as I saw him. We got to be friends, and later I found out he liked me, too."

Imogen's brow wrinkled. "But if you didn't move back to Maine to be with your boyfriend, why did you?"

"To help run my family's clambake business."

It was the tiniest sliver of the truth. The previous March, when I'd heeded my sister's panicked plea to return to Maine to save the Snowden Family Clambake from foreclosure, I'd gone home feeling nothing but dread. What if I didn't succeed? What if my mother lost her house and the private island where we held our clambakes? What if my sister and her husband lost their livelihoods? But working against more obstacles than I could ever have foreseen, we'd succeeded.

At the end of the tourist season, I'd

intended to go right back to New York, but it hadn't worked out that way. I'd never expected to call Busman's Harbor home again, but, to my complete surprise, I'd found I loved living near my mother, my sister, and my wonderful almost ten-year-old niece. I'd even learned to work with my pain-in-the-rear brother-in-law. And, completely unexpectedly, I'd fallen in love — with my middle-school crush, Chris Durand.

"And now you live with your boyfriend?" Imogen asked.

Another complicated question. "Not officially, but he stays over most nights. I only have a studio apartment, so you'll be staying at my mom's house."

Imogen chewed on that for a few moments. "Thank you," she said into the darkness, "and thanks to your mom."

Between my conservative driving of the unfamiliar vehicle and Imogen's frequent bathroom breaks, it was 2:00 AM by the time we rolled over the Piscataqua River Bridge into Maine and almost 3:00 before I took us off the exit at Freeport.

"Are we there yet?" Imogen's squeaky voice made her sound like a petulant child.

"We have an hour left," I said, "but we're making a stop." A short time later, I pulled into the parking lot at L.L.Bean. "This is where everyone in Maine goes to buy a winter coat at three in the morning," I explained. "Open twenty-four hours a day, seven days a week, then, now, and always."

When I climbed out of the cab, the cold air hit me like a punch in the chest. The temperature had dropped steadily as we'd made our way north. "You go on in. I want to get my coat." I pointed to the building where she'd find the women's clothing section, though watching her tiny figure scurry away, I wondered if she should be headed to the girl's department.

I stood on the truck's bumper, turned the combination dial on the padlock, rolled the big door partway up, and pulled out my black down coat. I was pleased to see the load hadn't shifted at all. Julio and Mike had done good work. I shut the door and replaced the padlock, twisting it to obscure the combination. As I jumped down from the truck, something caught my eye — a dirty white Toyota Camry.

There were about a half-dozen cars in the customer parking lot at that hour. The Toyota was in the row behind my truck, off a little to the left. Even in the dim light of the parking lot, I could see the front New York State plate.

Zipping up my coat, I walked toward the car. It was empty. I circled around it, questioning my memory and my sanity. *No way it's the same one.* It was a common brand, a common color. A streetlight threw enough illumination that I could see inside. A folded newspaper sat on the backseat; a pair of black gloves lay on the dash on the passenger side. Absolutely nothing extraordinary. Until I saw the Yankee cap sitting in the driver's seat.

I turned toward the entrance and hurried inside.

Inside the building, I looked warily for the Toyota's driver. Could it possibly be the same car? Neither New York plates nor Yankees caps were rare in Maine, particularly around the holidays. And if he were here, how would I even recognize him without the baseball cap? I shook off my misgivings and let Leon Leonwood Bean's wonderful store win me over.

I slowed down and meandered, taking it all in, the colorful clothes and the holiday decorations. Christmas at L.L.Bean was a family tradition. During my childhood, my father's sister had laid claim to Thanksgiving, so that day was spent in the relaxing atmosphere of her antique house, sur-

rounded by cousins, aunts, and uncles —
the fishermen, lobstermen, shipbuilders,
and teachers who populated my late father's
family. Christmas was left to my mother's
father, a quiet, socially awkward professor
of philosophy, who never gave much of an
indication he was interested in my sister,
Livvie, and me, or in our mother, for that
matter.

It had always been a glum little Christmas,
just the five of us in Grandfather's Riverside
Drive apartment. The saving grace was, we
always stopped on the way down to New
York at L.L.Bean, where we were allowed
to pick out our own presents. My mother
had lost her mother when she was five and
never got into making the kind of fuss over
Christmas that other moms did. I was much
older before I realized this ritual of choosing our own gifts was odd and other kids'
presents came wrapped up under the tree.
Christmas might be devoid of magic — our
grandfather always seemed surprised to find
it was the day and unfailingly presented Livvie and me with twenty-dollar bills — but
our dreams always came true on Christmas
Eve at L.L.Bean.

I wandered through the warm building
into the women's department upstairs and
found Imogen trying on sweaters. "Look

what I got!" Beside her was a pile of long silk underwear, tights, plaid wool shirts, lined jeans, flannel pajamas, a green corduroy skirt, a red Christmas sweater with reindeer on it, a quilted bathrobe, and an enormous bright pink down coat.

"Um, Imogen, it's not really my place to say, but didn't you just lose your job?"

"I'll put it on the old plastic," she said, waving her card under my nose.

I tried one more time. "You know you have to pay that off eventually."

"My dad pays it. Help me carry this stuff. I want to stop in the shoe department for warm slippers and winter boots before we check out."

I helped her gather the clothes, swaying a little when I bent over. Being awake for twenty-two hours had caught up to me. "Let's get a move on," I urged. "You're not going to the Arctic, just an hour farther up Route 1. And my mother's house is heated." I stared at the packages of long underwear. How long was she planning to stay?

"I want to be prepared." Imogen tried on boots and slippers and made her final choices. At the checkout counter, she whipped out her credit card and dragged it through the swiper with the wrist snap of someone who'd had a lot of practice.

In the parking lot, I opened the back of the truck once more to stow the purchases. Imogen gazed into the dark interior. "I loved living with this furniture," she sighed. "You're doing the right thing bringing it home."

Before we pulled out of the lot, I made a point to notice — the dirty white car was still there, but this time it was occupied, the silhouette of a man wearing a baseball cap inside.

"So, all the moodiness, is that why you broke up with Wade?" I knew I risked bringing on the waterworks again with this question, but he was the only person I could think of who might have a reason to follow us to Freeport.

"It was the night of the eggnog." There was a quiver in Imogen's voice. "He came to the party, but I could tell he didn't want to be there. He ignored me from the moment he arrived. Then, suddenly, everyone was throwing up. Never in my life had I ever needed my boyfriend's support more than that night, but when I looked for him, he was gone. He'd slipped out during the commotion. Can you imagine?"

"That's awful." I could see how it had been the final straw.

"I called and texted him to phone me. Finally I sent a text, breaking us up."

"How'd he take it?"

"At first, he texted back like he didn't know what I was talking about. Why was I so upset, he kept asking. I was so mad, I ignored him. Then, he couldn't stop apologizing. He called and called, filled up my voice mail, begging me to take him back. But I'd had enough by that point. If it was the first time he'd been a jerk, I might have forgiven him, but it wasn't." She sighed. "I love that man," she said dreamily. Then the steel returned to her little voice. "And I hate that man."

"Was he ever overly possessive? Or violent?"

Imogen was horrified. "No, no, no. Nothing like that. Sometimes he was devoted, and sometimes he acted like I wasn't even there. That's all."

"What kind of car does Wade drive?"

Imogen laughed. "He doesn't have a car, silly. He lives in Manhattan."

Her words reassured me, but I kept careful watch as we rode along. At that hour, Route 1 was deserted. If anyone had followed us, I would have seen him. Probably my overeager imagination, I told myself. It couldn't have been the same car.

We didn't see a single car as we drove down the peninsula into Busman's Harbor. The town was still, not a light burning in a window. In seven hours, we'd gone from The City That Never Sleeps to The Town That Takes Its Rest Very Seriously.

I pulled the big truck just far enough into my mother's driveway to be sure I'd cleared the sidewalk. I wanted to accomplish the final piece of the journey without waking the whole neighborhood. I opened the back of the truck and we pulled out Imogen's Bean shopping bags and overnight case. "We can bring your big suitcase in tomorrow," I whispered. Before I closed and locked the door, I looked around at the truck's shadowy contents, the outline of my grandfather's sofa and bureau, the boxes that held the paintings. I had done the right thing. My mother would be so pleased I'd brought it all to Maine.

I led Imogen into the always unlocked house and up the stairs. I put her in the pink princess room Mom had decorated for my niece, Page. Imogen was so tired; I thought despite the two new nightgowns, she might fall into bed in her clothes. Back down in the kitchen, I left a note for Mom saying Imogen had arrived and thanking her. I left the keys to the truck next to the note, in case Mom had to get out of the driveway in the morning. Then I crept out the back door. Except for a nap on the train, I'd been up for twenty-four hours. I was eager to get home.

The air was bracing, cold and dry, the stars bright overhead. I stared up at them as I made the short walk to my apartment over Gus's restaurant. That was a sight you'd never see in the city. Everything had its trade-offs.

Le Roi, my Maine coon cat, greeted me at the top of the stairs. Maine coons have lots of doglike traits and welcoming me home was one of Le Roi's. "Hello, boy. Finally here." I swept my hand down his big, muscular body as an acknowledgment of his efforts.

Ten minutes later, I was in my warm bed, Chris breathing rhythmically at my side.

CHAPTER FOUR

I slept in the next morning, but eventually the sounds and smells coming from the restaurant downstairs wafted into the apartment and seduced me awake. I patted the bed next to me, hoping for Chris, but my hand hit a tangle of sheets and duvet. No doubt, he was long gone. I checked my phone. A text from him — **CALL WHEN UNLOAD TRUCK**. I snuggled in the warm sheets for an extra moment, appreciating my life and the helpful man in it, so unlike the odious Wade Cadwallader, who had bailed on Imogen in her hour of need.

I pulled on jeans, a Snowden Family Clambake T-shirt, and a flannel shirt over a top; then I put on thick socks and work boots. My landlord, Gus, spotted me as I came down the stairs and stopped cooking long enough to raise a hand. "Need a cup?"

"Rain check. Got to get to Mom's." I fast-walked over the hill to Mom's house, screeching to a halt as I reached the top.

There was no big yellow truck in the driveway.

Darn. Mom obviously had to move it. She was supposed to have the day off, but since her promotion to assistant manager at Linens and Pantries over in Topsham, she often got called in for emergencies. The holiday season sometimes seemed like one long emergency.

I looked around the street. No truck parked on either side. I ran to the side of the house. No truck pulled farther down the driveway. By then, I was worried.

I burst through the back door. "Halloo!"

"In here!" Mom's voice traveled from the living room. That was odd. The formal front rooms of our Victorian house were rarely used. I pushed through the swinging kitchen door into the front hall and stopped in my tracks. Christmas had exploded all over our house.

Mom turned from the mantelpiece where she was arranging a row of smiling snowmen. "Hello, dear. Imogen is helping me decorate."

"Truck?" I croaked.

"What, dear?" Mom inclined her head, puzzled. I wondered if smoke was coming out of my ears.

"Where's the truck?" I repeated. "The big yellow truck Imogen and I drove up in last night."

"Is it missing?"

Oh, boy. "Believe me, if it was here, it would be visible."

"Oh no." Imogen came out from behind the Christmas tree, a string of colored lights in her hands. She was dressed in the green corduroy skirt, green tights, and the red Christmas sweater with the reindeer I'd spotted in her Bean's haul from the night before. The whole outfit was much too young for her and looked like something a child would wear. A child with a sadistic mother.

I ran back into the kitchen. The truck keys weren't on the table where I'd left them. My note to Mom was there, obviously opened and read, but no keys. My stomach clenched.

I pulled my phone out of my bag and found the non-emergency number for the police station. It was already in my contacts.

My childhood friend Jamie Dawes showed up five minutes later to take the report. He was the newest full-time member of Busman's Harbor's seven-person police force.

He still lived in his parents' house right next door.

"When's the last time you saw the truck?" he asked. We sat at the kitchen table, while Jamie filled out a form on a clipboard he'd brought from his cruiser.

"Four-fifteen-ish."

"In the morning?"

"Yeah."

He raised a dark blond eyebrow at me.

"Long story," I said.

"I think you'd better tell it."

I gave him the fastest version I could of Imogen's decision not to take my apartment and our late-night trip to the harbor.

"You locked the truck?"

"Of course," I protested. *I'm not an idiot.*

"Where're the keys?

"They're gone. I left them here on the table in case Mom had to move the truck."

"Was the house locked?" As he asked this, Jamie stood and took a long stride toward the back door to examine it, presumably for signs of forced entry.

"Uhmm . . ." Back in the spring and summer, when I'd been living with her, the door had been a matter of some contention between Mom and me. I was forever locking up, a New York habit not easily lost. She was forever coming home and finding herself locked out. Finally, I'd given in. Her house, her rules, even overnight.

Jamie gave me a form to list the contents of the truck. He told me to bring it to the station, where he'd give me all the paperwork I'd need for dealing with the rental company.

I walked him out to the front porch. As he started down the steps, I put a hand out to stop him. I didn't want Mom and Imogen to hear what I was about to say.

"It's probably nothing," I began.

"Tell me anyway." I'd been pulled by circumstances into working with the police on a few cases since I'd been home. Jamie was one of the officers who always gave credit when credit was due. Unlike some others.

"There was a car, a dirty white Toyota Camry with New York plates. It was parked on the street in the city when we loaded the truck, and then I thought I saw it again in Freeport when we stopped at Bean's."

"You're sure it was the same car?"

"No."

"Do you remember the license number? Did you write it down or take a photo with your phone?"

"No." Though that probably would have been smart. On the other hand, I'd had no idea the truck would be stolen.

"Can you describe the person in the car?"

"It was a man. Thin face. Pale. Twenties, I think. Wearing a Yankees baseball cap."

"Do you think he saw you loading the truck and followed you? You mentioned some antiques."

The only things I could think of were my grandfather's paintings. You could tell they were artwork from the shape of their boxes. But that was ridiculous. Compared to the kind of art you'd find in New York, the paintings were small potatoes. Not worth the effort of following us all the way to Maine. "No, I don't think so."

"Then what do you think happened?"

I hesitated. "Please, don't take this for any more than it's worth. It was my crazy imagination, trying to figure out why someone would follow us. It probably wasn't even the same car."

He looked at me directly, putting on his serious cop face. "Out with it."

"Imogen just came out of a bad breakup. Her ex sounds like a jerk. I thought he might be following her."

"Do you have a name for this guy?"

"Wade Cadwallader."

"Phone number? Photo?"

"No, but I can get them."

"I'll do it." He took a step back toward the house.

"Let me. If you ask her, it'll just freak her out. I don't want to upset her over some sleep-deprived idea I had in the L.L.Bean parking lot at three in the morning."

He turned, considering what I'd said. "Okay. Call me as soon as she gives them to you."

"Of course."

I turned back inside to finish the paperwork and make a no doubt unpleasant phone call to the rental company. What a mess.

I was grumbling over the police inventory form when I heard the unmistakable clang and wheeze of my younger sister Livvie's ancient minivan pulling into the drive. The kitchen door burst open and Livvie breezed in, a statuesque, auburn-haired beauty in her seventh month of pregnancy. "What are you doing here?" she asked.

"Good morning to you, too."

"Sorry. You startled me. I thought you were in New York."

"That was yesterday." I brought her up to speed on the whole chain of events, starting with Imogen's mishap with the eggnog and ending with the stolen truck.

"Geez."

"I haven't even told Mom that all Grand-dad's furniture was in the truck. She seems to have forgotten about it."

"Can you hold off telling her for a while? She has the day off work and I'm here to help her decorate the house for Christmas. I want it to be a fun day."

"Um, sure, but she got a head start on you."

"What?" Livvie strode through the swinging door and stopped dead in the front hall. I followed behind. "You started without me?"

Mom couldn't have missed the hurt in Livvie's voice. "There's so much more to do this year! I thought I'd get going and Imogen was eager to help." She introduced Imogen, who turned from decorating the Christmas tree, holding an ornament of a bird in a gilded cage that had belonged to Grandmother Snowden. I heard Livvie's teeth grate. Imogen smiled at Livvie, but it didn't look like a nice-to-meet-you smile to me, more like the triumphant cat-who-swallowed-the-canary variety. Like the bratty younger sister we'd never had. And never wanted.

Mom was right about one thing, there certainly was "a lot more to do." When we were growing up, my mother, so unaware of or indifferent to Christmas rituals, had not been one for decorations. When Livvie reached her early teens, she had orchestrated the tree trimming and stocking hanging. Later, decorating the house became a tradition that maintained our delicate family balance during the year of my father's cancer and following his death. It helped enormously that Livvie and her husband, Sonny, had a daughter, Page, who, as a little one, had gaped wide-eyed at the tree with all the love and awe you could hope for. Livvie's pregnancy at eighteen had been treated like a tragedy at first, but in many ways Page had saved us as a family. Page and Livvie.

Livvie stared into the living room, taking in the piles of stuffed Christmas penguins, poinsettia-covered linens, and ceramic houses with candlelight glowing from their windows. "What is all this?"

"I used my employee discount at Linens and Pantries to spruce things up," Mom answered. "I thought we were due for a refreshing. I even got new stockings for all of us."

"New stockings!" Livvie swiveled her pregnant self to look where my mother pointed. Laid out on the couch were six stockings printed on their tops with my mother's name, JACQUELINE, and then JULIA, LIVVIE, SONNY, PAGE, and CHRIS.

"Chris!" I squeaked. When I'd asked if he planned to travel to Florida to spend the holidays with his family, Chris had replied simply, "I'd rather be with you," neatly sidestepping the topic of his parents, as he always did. But we weren't engaged, or even officially living together, and I wasn't sure how he'd react to having a stocking with his name on it hanging from our hearth.

Livvie stared daggers at the new stockings. I didn't blame her. We were both sentimentally attached to the old ones, which we'd bought with our allowances at a Christmas craft fair — misshapen cut felt personalized with drizzly glitter. They'd started as a mess and hadn't worn well. Sonny's and Page's had been added later and were mismatched. And the one that said DAD had been put away.

"C'mon," Mom urged. "We don't have all day. Santa arrives in the harbor at five."

Livvie hesitated, then smiled bravely. "Of course," she said. "Let's get going."

"Imogen, can I borrow you for a minute?" I asked. "You need to list the items in your big suitcase on the form for the police inventory." I'd been amazed at how lightly she'd lived in my apartment, and how quickly she'd cleaned her stuff out.

"Sure." She followed me into the kitchen. I figured that would give Livvie some time to regain her equilibrium.

"Officer Dawes needs a photo of your ex-boyfriend and his phone number," I told her after she'd sat down.

Her big brown eyes opened wide. "Why on earth would he need that?"

I kept my voice calm and even. "Think about it, Imogen. You just had a bad breakup. You said Wade didn't take it well. Who else would have followed us here and stolen the truck?"

"Followed us!"

I immediately regretted mentioning "followed." I wasn't prepared to share my suspicions about the dirty white Toyota.

"Show me a photo of Wade," I asked.

Imogen held her phone out in front of me, scrolling through the photos. There was Wade Christmas shopping in Union Square, skating at Rockefeller Center, drinking cappuccino at Eataly. Sometimes the two of them posed together, no doubt having asked some hapless tourist to snap the shot. Imogen glowed. Wade sometimes smiled and sometimes glowered. He had a thin face and fair features. And in several of the photos, especially the most recent ones, he wore a Yankees cap.

CHAPTER FIVE

As I walked the forms over to Busman's Harbor's ugly, brick fire-department-town-offices-police complex, I snuck a peek at Imogen's inventory list. Just clothes and toiletries. I was relieved she hadn't packed any jewelry or other valuables in her big suitcase.

Jamie told me he'd driven his cruiser around town looking for the truck, on the off chance it had been stolen by joy riders who'd ditched it at the first opportunity. Improbable as that scenario was, I felt the air go out of me when he said he hadn't spotted it.

He must have noticed the slump to my shoulders. "Don't worry, Julia. Your stuff will turn up. We'll let all the pawn shops in the area know, and the art galleries that deal in old paintings."

"And antique bookshops," I reminded him. I was depressed about all the stuff, but most of all my precious books. The thought of losing that direct link to my mother's family brought tears to my eyes.

"Easy," Jamie said, patting my shoulder. "It's going to be okay."

On my way back home from the police station, I called Chris.

"Hey, beautiful. Time to unload the truck?"

"Not exactly." I filled him in on the events of the morning.

"Wow. I'm sorry. How's the houseguest taking it?"

"Better than I expected. She didn't lose much beyond clothes and shampoo."

"So she's settling in at your mom's?"

"Mom's doing great with her, but somehow Imogen has managed to annoy Livvie."

"Livvie?" Chris's baritone rose in surprise. Livvie was the most easygoing person on the planet.

"Don't ask. Where are you?"

"Just leaving the Daniels' house." One of Chris's many jobs, an extension of his landscaping business, was taking care of people's summer homes over the winter. A few of the families he worked for returned to Busman's Harbor for the holidays. Chris had turned up the Daniels' heat, tested their hot water, plugged in their refrigerators, and generally made sure everything was ship-shape for when they arrived.

"Okay, see you later. Love you."

"Love you, too."

In my absence, Livvie and Imogen appeared to have made peace and were happily involved in decorating the dining room.

"Where should these go?" Livvie held up a box of dancing wooden elves. She rolled her eyes at me, but I could tell it was in a better humor.

We broke for lunch, tomato soup and grilled cheese, gathering around the kitchen table. "This is exactly the way I imagined Maine would be," Imogen said with a happy sigh. "Do you think we'll have a white Christmas?"

"You never know," Mom answered, though there was no snow in the forecast.

"You imagined Maine would be a place where the truck containing all your worldly possessions would get stolen?" Livvie asked.

"Well, maybe not that part," Imogen admitted. "But it wasn't all my worldly possessions. I didn't bring everything to New York. I still have lots of stuff at home in Georgia."

"Speaking of home," Mom said, "have you called your parents? Even if you're not ready to tell the whole story about the breakup and the eggnog, at least let them know where you are." Imogen must have bent Mom's ear with her tale of woe as they worked.

"Maybe," Imogen answered. "Soon. But I want them to see I can go where I want, when I want. That I'm a grownup."

My mother practically bit through her tongue on that one.

Livvie looked over at the digital clock on the stove. "Gotta run if I'm going to pick up Page at school and get back to the pier in time for Santa."

"Oooh, Santa!" Imogen squealed. "Can I come, too?"

At five o'clock, the five of us — Mom, Imogen, Page, Livvie, and I — made our way to the town pier. The air was cold and crisp, and for once, there was no wind off the harbor. The high school band, augmented as always by as many year-round resident band alumni as they could find, played a merry round of holiday tunes. The Y choir led us all in song, hoping their strong voices would keep us more or less in tune, in tempo, and on the right verse. They were only moderately successful.

Every boat in the harbor was ablaze with Christmas lights outlining its rigging or cabin. Soon they would form the little flotilla and would escort the Coast Guard boat with Santa and Mrs. Claus aboard into the harbor.

Mom, Imogen, Livvie, and I smiled at one another and bounced up and down to the music to keep warm. The only sourpuss was Page. Ten was an awkward age, particularly for her. Sonny and Livvie knew the jig was up re: Santa Claus, but Page still claimed to believe. Maybe she thought there'd be fewer presents. Or as the only child in the family, she felt responsible for carrying the myth and ensuring the rest of us had a joyous Christmas. Whatever the reason, to the family, Page still professed a belief in the man with the beard.

But she wasn't an idiot. She wasn't going to admit she knew the truth to her parents, and she wasn't going to pretend she believed with her friends around. She slouched at the back of the crowd, stone-faced, neither with family nor friends. I kept looking back to check on her. She had her mother's height and her father's flaming red hair, features that already promised to make her a stunner of an adult, but with adolescence closing in, her best features only embarrassed her. Poor kid.

The lighted boats motored to the mouth

of the harbor, then circled back. Little voices cried, "I see him, I see him!" Most American children believed Santa arrived on a sleigh with flying reindeer, but children raised in Maine harbor communities knew better. Santa arrived on a boat. Always had, always would.

The Coast Guard boat drew nearer and nearer. In the glow of the Christmas lights, I could see the young corpsman in the red suit on the deck, along with a female colleague in a Mrs. Claus costume. Many of the others on the deck were dressed as elves. Most of them would get some sort of leave over the holidays, but a crew would have to stay on duty. The Coast Guard participated in this event as a thank you to the town, but the town also used it to thank the Coast Guard. They made the lives of everyone in our seafaring community safer. A rousing cheer went up as the boat pulled up to the pier, from the children and adults alike.

I'd been so concerned about my conflicted niece, I hadn't noticed that Imogen had worked her way to the front of the crowd. She was so tiny, she barely stood out among the children, and the bright pink puffy coat she'd bought at Bean's added to her camouflage.

"Santa! Santa!" she called. "Over here!" It

was dead low tide, and the gangway up to the pier was angled steeply, not an easy climb for even a young Santa with a sack full of presents.

As he started up, the crowd of children surged forward. I spotted Imogen in the lead. *Imogen?* Surely she knew enough to make way for the little kids. But Imogen burst through the line and ran down the plank toward Santa. "It's just the way I imagined it!" she cried. But she was unprepared for how steep the plank was. She lost control as momentum propelled her forward. She ran straight into Santa, knocking him hard in the chest and he flew — shocked face, arms pinwheeling, and bagful of presents flying up in the air — into the cold harbor water. Only the quick reflexes of the Coast Guardsman next to him kept Imogen from tumbling in after.

"Noooh!" a little boy wailed.

CHAPTER SIX

Santa was rescued quickly. He had hit the water right in front of a Coast Guard vessel, after all. He was led below decks, presumably to dry off. The sack of gifts still floated in the water. Fortunately, it was a decoy, a bag of wrapped but empty boxes. The real gifts were already at the library, as always.

The little boy had started a cavalcade of whines and sniffles. Santa was supposed to lead the crowd off the pier, across the town common, and into the library, where hot chocolate was served and every child who wanted to got to sit on his lap. He listened carefully while each one handed him their list and he asked if they'd been naughty or nice. Then he gave each of them a gift, an inexpensive token intended to tide them over until the big day. Livvie and I had sat on that lap, as had Chris and Sonny, Jamie and Page.

Fortunately, the Coast Guard had selected

a very self-possessed Mrs. Claus.

"Come with me, children," she said as she walked up the gangway. "We'll go to the library, and you'll give me your lists so I can give them to Santa." She grabbed two little hands and marched toward the town common.

A cheer went up and the crowd followed her. The children were comforted; the grown-ups relieved.

I found Imogen standing off to the side, apologizing profusely to the young Coast Guardsman who had grabbed her before she went over. "Imogen, he gets it," I said. "C'mon. I'll take you back to Mom's house."

At the corner of Main and Main, where the only street in and out of town curved back around and crossed itself. Jamie, bundled up in his police overcoat, caught my eye and burst out laughing.

"I don't think that's allowed when you're on duty," I grumbled as we passed. Great guffaws followed us all the way down the street.

Back at the house, Imogen rallied impressively. "What happens next?" she asked.

"In a while, after Santa's done at the library, he and the crowd move to the gym at the Coast Guard station for the Festival of Trees."

Imogen blew her nose. "Okay, let's do that."

"Are you sure?" I wasn't sure Imogen should be seen in public again so soon. And I wasn't sure I wanted to be seen with her.

She squared her shoulders. "I came to experience Christmas in Maine. Let's experience it."

My chest tightened with worry, but I couldn't help but be inspired by her determination and lack of embarrassment. "Okay," I said. "We'll go."

"My goodness, what is this magical world?" Imogen looked around the interior of the Coast Guard gym, mouth open. In the huge room stood row after row of Christmas trees, each magnificently and uniquely decorated.

"Every business and social organization on the peninsula donates a decorated tree," I said. "People view them over the next two days and then on Saturday, there's an auction. Our restaurant did one. Come and see."

I led her through the rows of balsams and Scotch pines. I knew many people had cut their own to save the cost of purchasing a tree. In Busman's Harbor, even those who didn't have a lot gave to those who had less.

I found the tree Chris and I had decorated with Gus and Mrs. Gus. The lights were white; the ornaments — little rolling pins and wire whisks, griddles and frying pans — were supplemented by bright red bows.

"It's gorgeous!" Imogen exclaimed. "People buy these and put them in their homes? Then why did your mom decorate a tree at your house?"

"It's customary to donate the tree you buy back to the organizers. They give the trees to the hospital and several nursing homes and other places where people need cheering up. And then Family Services finds homes for the rest of them with families who wouldn't otherwise have a tree."

"You buy one of these beautiful trees and then give it away?" Imogen seemed genuinely amazed by our act of small-town charity. It was pretty cool to see the rituals of your hometown, things that were so familiar they were like wallpaper, through the eyes of a stranger.

Santa was there, looking exactly like the faux fur on his red suit had been dipped in saltwater and then blown with a hair dryer. His beard looked more sea monster than jolly old elf, but the children didn't seem to care. The Y chorus and high school band had reassembled and started up, jumping enthusiastically into "Boogie Woogie Christmas."

"Oooh!" Imogen exclaimed and rushed the stage. Given her already demonstrated penchant for mayhem, I followed right behind. "I love this!" Imogen tapped her toes, then gyrated enthusiastically. I noticed that with every step, she backed up a little.

"Imogen, I don't think it's really a dancing occasion."

"Hello, beautiful." Chris came up behind me and bent to give me a quick smooch on the cheek. "What have I missed?"

"Let's see. Santa ended up in the harbor."

His eyebrows flew up. "Imogen." I answered his unspoken question. "Anyway, let me introduce you." I turned, just in time to see Imogen dance her way backward into the tree in the front corner of the gym. She whirled around, a look of horror on her face, just in time to see the tree wobble and then go down, straight into the two trees behind it, which in turn fell into the four behind that. Then, like dominoes or a perfect strike at the bowling alley, trees were falling everywhere, with the crash of branches, the tinkle of shattering ornaments, and the gasps of the crowd.

When it was over, all the trees lay on their

sides. Everyone stared at Imogen, who blushed bright red, and said, "Oops."

CHAPTER SEVEN

The crowd began righting the trees, replacing the unbroken ornaments on branches and sweeping up the rest. Fortunately, the damage didn't appear to be as extensive as it could have been. Many trees, like ours, had unbreakable ornaments. Parents removed their children — already traumatized by seeing Santa flailing away in the harbor — as quickly as possible, so they could go home to bed and forget the whole ordeal.

Imogen helped clean up, apologizing constantly. "I'm so sorry. I didn't know. I didn't see. I loved the music so much." Finally, I sent her back to Mom's with Livvie, Page, and Sonny, because I could tell she was close to breaking down.

Chris and I stayed through to the end and then walked home. The air was cold and as dry as ocean air ever gets. The lights in the windows of the shops — Gleason's Hardware, Walker's Art Supplies, Gordon's

Jewelry — twinkled at us as we walked along Main Street. It wasn't Rockefeller Plaza, or Macy's windows, but it was beautiful and where I belonged.

In the warmth of the apartment we shed our coats, hats, scarves, and gloves. "You never exactly explained what she's doing here," Chris said.

"Bad boyfriend," I answered, the tersest summary I could think of. I wanted to forget the whole horrible day.

"But doesn't she have a job?" he probed.

"Bad eggs."

"Yeah, I get that about the boyfriend, but what about the job?"

I sighed. "Not bad egg. Bad eggzz." She poisoned her whole office with salmonella-laden eggnog."

"You're kidding!"

"I wish I was. Frankly, after spending slightly more than twenty-four hours with her, I've never seen someone attract trouble like she does. I think she's a jinx."

Chris laughed, green eyes crinkling at the corners, and my heart melted. We'd been together for six months and I still felt the same physical pull I had from the beginning.

"I mean it. Think about it," I said. "The eggnog. The truck. Santa and the Christmas trees. In less than a week. And I can prove she's a jinx."

I rooted through the files in my desk. It took me less than a minute to find it. "Aha!" I brandished the sublease Imogen had signed back in March. "It's been bugging me all day. I knew her name was unusual, but I couldn't remember how. Look." I pointed to the signature line.

"Imogen Mary Ann Geinkes," Chris read. "What are you saying? Her parents jinxed her first with that ridiculous name?"

"Imogen Mary Ann Geinkes." I repeated slowly. "I. M. A. Geinkes. I'm a jinx!"

Chris laughed, throwing his head back. His full-body laugh was one of the traits that made me love him so. "That is insane," he gasped.

"Insane that they gave her that name or insane what I think it means?"

"Insane," he confirmed, collapsing on the couch. "Come here."

I moved forward to be enveloped in his strong arms.

CHAPTER EIGHT

In the morning, I booked it over to Mom's as soon as I was dressed. I didn't believe in jinxes, or that it was dangerous to have Imogen staying there. Not really. But still, I jogged over the harbor hill to Mom's out of an abundance of caution.

I pushed the kitchen door open and was hit by the most delicious smell. Christmas cookies! Today must be the day! Dozens of unbaked hazelnut wreathes sat on cookie sheets on the table waiting to be decorated. My nose told me some were already in the oven. At the kitchen island, rolling out the dough was — Imogen.

"Mom?"

My mother looked up from the task of cutting the red and green sugared pineapple that would turn into bows on the hazelnut wreaths. "Hello, Julia."

"What are you doing?"

"Goodness, what does it look like we're doing?"

I shrugged out of my coat and hung it on a peg in the back hall. "No, I mean why are you doing it without Livvie?" Christmas cookies were Livvie's thing. She had learned to bake them at my grandmother Snowden's side. Livvie was the one who wrote down the recipes, preserving them for the whole family. She always planned and ran "cookie day," starting work with Mom in the morning and adding Page as a helper after school. Livvie was the family baker. Cookie day was Livvie's.

"Imogen was here and eager to help out. Your sister's seven months pregnant. I have to go to work later. What's the problem?"

What, indeed? It was all perfectly logical. I put some of the tiny pineapple chunks Mom had cut on a saucer and sat down to begin decorating. Even though you only put three little pieces on each cookie prior to baking (a red one in the center and two green ones on either side of it forming the "bow"), it is the worst job in the whole cookie-making extravaganza. The pieces stuck to one another and to your fingers, and to any implement, like tweezers, you tried to use to place them. The job required the manual dexterity of a cardsharp and the patience of a saint.

I had two cookie sheets in the oven and was cursing quietly over a third when Livvie's minivan rattled into the drive. *Uh-oh.* She was at the point in her pregnancy when her belly preceded her into the room. Which was a good thing, because I was sure Baby Ramsey was in a better mood than Livvie.

"What's going on here?" She stood in the doorway, eyes wide with surprise. No, shock.

Mom ran through her now-practiced explanation, her work schedule, Imogen's eagerness, and Livvie's condition. Livvie blinked a few times. "But I always make the cookies," she said in a hurt tone I hadn't heard since she was a little girl.

"And so you shall," my mother said, pulling out a kitchen chair. "Come help your sister decorate."

"Decorate?"

Livvie decorating. It was like Michelangelo being told to clean a paint-by-numbers artist's brushes. Like Serena Williams being asked to be a ball girl for a weekend warrior. It was . . . unimaginable.

"I've finished rolling out the hazelnut cookies," Imogen said. "I call them filberts, by the way, not hazelnuts. Now I'll start making the dough for the chocolate-covered toffee cookies." She pulled the index card with the recipe on it closer so she could read it. The index card Livvie had created.

While she studied the card, Imogen's hand snaked across the kitchen island, picked up one of the hazelnut wreaths cooling on a white cloth, and popped the cookie into her mouth.

Livvie's head snapped in Imogen's direction. I may have actually gasped. It was understood by everyone involved in cookie day that the cookies were not to be casually eaten. They were for friends and neighbors, the open house at Page's school, her swim team holiday party. Throughout cookie day, any burned or broken cookies were carefully collected to be shared among the helpers when the day's baking was done. And not before.

Imogen reached for another. "Excuse me —" I started, but Mom waved me off.

"Imogen has to eat continuously just to maintain her body weight," Mom explained.

"Crazy-fast metabolism," Imogen added.

Livvie put her hands over her swollen belly. Her amber eyes flared. I thought flames might shoot out of them. Imogen, apparently oblivious, began noisily creaming butter in the food processor.

"Isn't Imogen such a help?" my mother shouted.

"She's like the daughter you never had," Livvie muttered, tone murderous, though her words were mercifully drowned out by the food processor.

Somehow, we stumbled through — Livvie seething, Imogen and my mother happily working, me waiting for the whole thing to blow. At a little after noon, the landline rang.

Mom answered. "Hello." As she listened to the caller on the other end, her eyes opened wide. "What! No, no, no. Officer, there's been a mistake."

I stared at her, heart thumping, while the person on the other end spoke.

"Officer, I assure you, she's fine. She's a grown woman and she's right here." Mom gave me the phone, hands shaking. "It's someone from the county sheriff's department. He thought you'd been carjacked!"

I took the phone from her and she sank into a kitchen chair.

"Officer, this is Julia Snowden."

"Sheriff Donohue, Lincoln County. You don't know how grateful I am to hear your voice. I'm standing on a dirt road in Woolwich. There are clothes scattered all around. I found children's books with your name in them. Given the size of the clothes and the nature of the books, I had thought something awful had happened to a child."

"No, Sheriff. Nothing quite that awful, but the clothes and books are from a rental truck that was stolen from my mother's driveway yesterday morning. You don't see the truck anywhere around there, do you?" On the kitchen table, my cell phone buzzed. Chris. I let it go to voice mail, concentrating as the sheriff talked.

"I don't see a truck, but I'm pretty far out on a point. Nothing around me but woods and water. With the leaves down, there's a little visibility, but not a lot. I'll contact the Busman's Harbor PD and tell them I've got a lead on your theft. Can you come out here and identify your stuff?"

My cell phone buzzed. Chris, again. Now I was worried. I hurried through the rest of the conversation. "Sure, Sheriff. Tell me where you are. We'll come right along." I wrote down the directions as he reeled them off, then hung up the phone. "Imogen, the sheriff found —"

Tires screeched in the drive. A vehicle door slammed. Footsteps pounded up the back steps. The door flew open. Chris, wild-eyed, crossed the room and enfolded me in his arms. "Thank God," he said. "Gus called me and said Bud Barbour heard on his scanner you'd been carjacked."

I leaned into his embrace. "Not exactly."

■ ■ ■ ■

Imogen, Chris, and I piled into his pickup
and went to meet the sheriff. The directions
he gave us were about a half hour away, up
our peninsula to Route 1 South and then
down the next point. We turned off the main
road onto a side road, then sped past a dirt
road. Chris cursed and reversed.

"Our stuff's not going anywhere," I
pointed out.

He made a low guttural acknowledgment.
I could tell he was still working out the fear
and adrenaline from Gus's phone call.

Less than half a mile down the dirt road,
a pleasant-looking, mildly rotund man in a
sheriff's uniform waved us down.

"Sheriff Donohue." He shook our hands
in the order we descended from the truck.
"Let's take a look." He led us into a small
clearing not far from the road. Through the
trees, sun glinted off dark blue water.

"Oh my gosh!" Imogene's hand flew to
her mouth.

I stepped back, too, unprepared for how
violent and violating the scene felt. Imogen's
big black suitcase had been slit open, probably with some kind of knife or box cutter.
Her clothes were scattered around, tossed

on the ground, caught on low branches. Nearby, my books had been pulled from the boxes and tossed. Chris put an arm out to steady me.

"Gave me quite a turn when I saw it myself," Sheriff Donohue said. Between the diminutive size of Imogen's clothing and the juvenile nature of my books, I could understand why the scene would have scared the sheriff when he discovered it. "Are these yours?" he asked.

"The books are mine." I picked *Little Women* gingerly off the ground to look for my grandmother's name, my mother's, and my own, but I'd known the signatures would be there the instant I spotted the books.

"These are my clothes." Imogen's high-pitched, excited voice was suddenly subdued.

"Is there anything missing?"

"Can we move things while we look?" I asked.

Sheriff Donohue nodded. "I've got plenty of photos."

I could tell by the way the books were treated the thief hadn't been interested in them. It took me little time to be certain they were all there. Thank goodness it hadn't rained and the dirt on the ground was frozen.

Imogen spent more time picking through her clothes, including her underwear. Chris and Sheriff Donohue withdrew to the side of the road to have a pro forma conversation about the New England Patriots in order to give her some privacy.

"I think everything that was in my suitcase is here." Imogen stepped back onto the road.

"Is this all you found?" I asked. "Nothing else nearby?"

Sheriff Donohue pulled out his phone. "Busman's Harbor PD sent me an inventory. Looks like the rest is furniture and household goods. I had a look around when I first got here, but I wanted to stay with the scene. Officers Howland and Dawes are on their way from Busman's to help out."

"Mind if we have a look around?"

"Suit yourselves."

Chris nodded curtly. "Will do."

We set off down the road, which was really more like a double track. The day was crisp and dry and we were all warmly dressed. It would have made a nice walk in the woods in another set of circumstances. Around a bend, we came upon an old camp, the fall leaves piled on its sagging porch roof. It was the first dwelling we'd seen on the road.

A crow cawed overhead.

"Do we keep going?" Imogen asked, peering around the next bend, which seemed to go deeper into the woods.

"Why not?" Chris stepped ahead confidently.

For a brief moment, it felt like we were surrounded completely by trees, but then the vista opened up. Not far ahead, the road turned out of sight. We all trotted a little faster.

"Look!" Chris, with the advantage of height, pointed toward a nearby boulder. "On the other side."

By then we were running. I got there first. My grandfather's furniture sat in a semicircle, surrounded by kitchen items and other flotsam. It looked like the three bears had been playing house in the woods. Even the boxes with the paintings in them were there, propped up against the couch. Not a very discerning thief, to have left the most valuable items.

"Is that everything?" Chris asked.

"I think so. Except the truck," I answered.

"That's probably what they were after."

"I guess." I shook my head to clear my brain and get a new perspective on the stuff. As I did, I caught a flash of something off to my right. Something big and yellow. "The truck!" I moved toward it, careful to check my footing on the rough terrain.

The rental truck was at the end of the point, front wheels in the water, like someone had driven it as far as it would go. Whoever it was must have gotten wet when they climbed out of the cab. I shivered involuntarily, feeling the December cold radiating off the bay. The back of the truck was on land, its wheels balanced on a small stone beach.

Chris tried his mobile. "No signal. I'll go for Donohue. You and Imogen stay here."

Chris had just started up the road when a Busman's Harbor cruiser bumped down it. The doors swung open and Jamie and his partner, Officer Howland, climbed out of the front. Sheriff Donohue emerged from the back.

"Well, look at what you found," Howland called.

The three officers walked around the truck. "Think we can drive it out of there?" Donohue asked.

Jamie shook his head. "Nope, we're going to need a tow truck."

"Down this road?" Donohue grimaced.

" 'Fraid so." Jamie squared his shoulders. "Is all your stuff in that pile back there?"

I nodded, squinting into the low winter

sun. "I think so, but I can't be sure."

"Well, let's open 'er up and see what we got."

My padlock, needless to say, was gone. Jamie donned latex gloves, climbed up on the tailgate, and rolled up the door.

There was a moment of stunned silence, followed by the sounds of Imogen shrieking.

Sitting in my desk chair, the one I had completely forgotten about, his hands duct-taped to the arms, his legs to the pedestal foot, was the man in the Yankees ball cap. His head was down, so I couldn't see his face, but there was no mistaking the bib of blood on his shirt. His throat had been cut and he was very, very dead.

"Wade! Wade! Wade! Wade!" Imogen fell on all fours to the dirt.

Jamie pulled the truck door shut so fast, it shuddered. He jumped off the tailgate. "Get back!" he ordered.

Chris and I took two steps back, propping up Imogen between us. Her jinxiness, which Chris and I had laughed about the night before, didn't seem funny anymore.

CHAPTER NINE

The three officers sprang into action. Donohue got on the radio, calling the state police for backup. Howland retrieved tape from the trunk of his cruiser and marked the crime scene. Jamie corralled Imogen, Chris, and me.

"You knew the victim?" he asked Imogen.

"He was my boyfriend, Wade Cadwallader. My ex-boyfriend." She took a deep breath.

"Are you sure?" It was a reasonable question. The victim's head had been down and we'd only seen the body for a second.

"Yes," Imogen whispered. "I'm sure." I was sure, too, that it was the man I had seen in the baseball cap outside my apartment building in Manhattan.

"State police patrol will be here in ten minutes." Officer Howland stowed the radio. "Forty-five minutes for a detective."

In Maine, only the Portland and Bangor

police departments were big enough to have their own homicide detectives. The rest of the state was served by two State Police Major Crimes Units. I knew the detectives from the northern district, Lieutenant Jerry Binder and Sergeant Tom Flynn, from previous cases. I strongly hoped Chris and I, and most important, Imogen, would be delivered into Jerry Binder's capable hands.

Jamie looked at Imogen, who stared, white-faced, at the back of the yellow truck. "Why don't you sit in the back of the cruiser?" he suggested. "Julia, you can sit with her."

I'd much rather have heard what the cops were saying to one another, but Imogen needed comforting. I nodded to Chris, who nodded back, receiving my message, "Keep your ears open," though there was no need to convince him to stay out of the back of that car with the weeping Imogen. He was probably happy to be anywhere else.

Forty minutes later, there were two state police cruisers and an evidence van crammed along the little road when another state police official car pulled into view. I was still in the back of Jamie and Howland's cruiser, holding Imogen's hand and saying the most inane, probably unhelpful things. I had never been so happy to see a state police car.

The driver's side door opened and Sergeant Tom Flynn climbed out, hitching his not-even-slightly sagging trousers around his fighting-trim waist. He removed his sunglasses and looked around, scowling as he spotted Chris, who'd been a suspect in a previous investigation. Neither had gotten over their disapproval of the other.

As Flynn approached Jamie, I waited for Lieutenant Binder to get out of the car. And waited. From my angle, I didn't have a view inside the state police vehicle. Flynn and Jamie marched off toward the truck, presumably to look at the body, and I waited. Finally, I had to conclude Lieutenant Binder wasn't in the vehicle. Perhaps he was coming separately.

The back of the cruiser was cramped. I longed to get out, get some air, and find out what was going on. The last forty-eight hours had been a whirlwind from the moment I put my key in the lock at North Moore Street. I struggled to put the pieces together. If Wade had followed us to Busman's Harbor, had someone else followed him? And killed him? Which one of them had stolen the truck, and why had either one of them wanted it? None of it made sense.

Twenty minutes later, Flynn was back. His dark glasses were on, even though the sun was low in the sky, barely peeking through the trees.

"Hullo, Sergeant," I said when he opened the cruiser door. "This is Imogen Geinkes. Where is Lieutenant Binder?"

"Vacation," Flynn growled. "Perhaps you've heard, it's almost Christmas."

Great.

"Ms. Geinkes, I understand you think you can identify our victim. I'd like to ask a few questions. Please step out of the vehicle."

I slid across the seat, following Imogen out of the car. As I stood, facing Flynn, I said, "Can I come along? Imogen's quite upset and me being there will reassure her."

"Yes, please," Imogen said in her little-girl voice, putting a hand on my arm.

Flynn drew his brows together above the sunglasses. He wasn't that much older than me, but with his ex-military bearing, he could be quite intimidating. "No, thank you, Miss Snowden. I can handle it. If you would please stay here."

He led Imogen off to a quiet spot. *Drat.* Lieutenant Binder would have seen the wisdom of letting me be present for the initial conversation with Imogen. Binder understood that though I wasn't a professional, sometimes I was useful. Flynn had always disapproved of my involvement in their cases. Sometimes I felt as if he disapproved of me, period.

Less than fifteen minutes later, Flynn walked a teary-eyed Imogen back to the cruiser. She climbed in as he went off to talk to Chris.

"How did it go?"

"Terrible. He kept asking questions that made it sound like somehow this was my fault. Like, did I ask Wade to come to Maine? Did Wade know I was here? Did I give him the keys to the truck? Julia, I swear, I would never help him steal your truck. Why would I do that?"

Why, indeed. "I'm sure you didn't." I patted her curly hair in what I hoped was a reassuring manner. "What else did Sergeant Flynn ask?"

"He wanted to know about Wade's family because he has to make a death notification. I'm just an ex-girlfriend, so I don't count." Her chin quivered.

"Could you help him out?"

"That's the thing. I know Wade's mom died when he was young, and his dad was never in the picture. I never met any family." She broke down.

I'd managed to get poor Imogen calmed down by the next time Flynn opened the cruiser door. "Ms. Snowden? Would you step out?"

"I hope you're happy," I said once I was out of the car. "You've got her completely hysterical."

He gave me a squinty-eyed look that clearly communicated his feelings about my naïveté. "I have to question everyone as quickly as possible. I'm sure she wants her ex-boyfriend's murder solved. Now, what is your role in all of this? I understand you brought Ms. Geinkes to Maine."

His slow, careful questions led me through the whole story. How I met Imogen. How she happened to be a guest at my mother's house. The theft of the truck. The discovery of it. By the time I finished, I was breathless.

Flynn had taken his sunglasses off. The sun was sinking rapidly. Soon it would be twilight. "Anything else I should know?"

"Yes." I squared my shoulders. "I think I know how Mr. Cadwallader got here. That is, how he came to be in Maine." Flynn put on his listening face, flat, devoid of emotion or judgment, so I continued. "He followed us. When we were in front of my apartment loading the truck, I noticed him sitting in a dirty white Toyota parked down the street. I didn't know who he was, of course, but he had on that Yankees cap. And then I saw the car again the same night in Freeport, when we stopped at L.L.Bean."

"You saw him twice? Did you ask Ms. Geinkes about him?"

"I didn't say anything to Imogen about it directly. I wasn't sure he was following us. I wasn't even sure it was the same car both times. Camrys are a dime a dozen. And, of course, I didn't know he was Wade Cadwallader."

"And now you're sure it was the same person?"

I hesitated. "I can't be absolutely. But if I were you, I'd be looking for a white Toyota Camry with New York plates. It must be somewhere near my mom's house if Wade ditched it in order to steal the truck."

"You think that's what happened? He stole the truck? Did you see him in Busman's Harbor?"

"No," I admitted. "I didn't see any vehicles on the road down our peninsula. But I can't think about two people following us. It's too creepy to imagine one."

"But, there must be at least one other

person involved," Flynn pointed out. "The killer."

We'd walked on a path through the woods away from the scene until we'd dead-ended at a rocky shore. Flynn looked around. "Whatever happened out here," he said, "I doubt we have any witnesses."

We both spotted it at the same moment. A cabin on the opposite shore, about a hundred yards away. Improbably for the place and the season, smoke curled from its chimney and a light glowed in the front window.

"Maybe we just got lucky," I said.

Mercifully, Flynn let us all go before the medical examiner's van was loaded. He personally directed the cruisers to move so Chris could pull the pickup out. It was just past four-thirty and fully dark, the shortest day of the year, when we reached the hard-top road and rolled toward Route 1. We hadn't seen a single vehicle along the unlit road.

We were crammed into the pickup's front and only seat, three across. I turned to Imogen. "Chris and I have to go to work. In fact, we're late. My mom is at her job. I don't want to leave you by yourself."

"Can I come to the restaurant with y'all?

If you're pressed for time, let me help. I really don't want to be alone."

In the reflection of the dashboard light, I saw Chris furrow his brow. Given the eggnog debacle, I doubted he wanted Imogen's help in the kitchen. But he didn't object aloud, so it was settled. We got back to Busman's Harbor a little after five, less than one short hour before our restaurant, Gus's Too, opened for dinner.

We were busy, too busy, in the restaurant that night. As soon as we got there, I set Imogen to chopping vegetables for the salad station and fruit for the bar. Livvie appeared with the desserts — apple tarts and delicate meringues to be served with mixed berries. She must have channeled her hard feelings about the Christmas cookie situation into over-the-top baking for the restaurant. Lucky us. Lucky customers.

"Sonny and I will be here for dinner. Page is at a sleepover. Got to take advantage of this time while we've got it." Livvie placed both hands on her belly, underscoring the countdown until my new niece or nephew arrived. As she did, she caught sight of Imogen working behind the bar. "Don't tell me she's here, too."

I had never seen Livvie react so poorly to any person. "She's had a bad day," I whispered. "Come outside." I gave Livvie the rundown of what had happened from the time we all took off to meet the sheriff until we left the scene.

Even Livvie softened. "The poor thing."

"I know. So I'm keeping her here. I can't leave her at Mom's by herself."

Livvie gave me a quick hug. "Roger that. See you later."

We kept Imogen busy the whole night, bussing tables, running the dishwasher, swiping credit cards, and making change. The truth was, it was great to have the help. In all the craziness of the day, I'd forgotten that it was "Gentleman's Night" in Busman's Harbor.

Gentleman's Night started as a traditional Friday evening when the shops stayed open late, and the men went out to buy a Christmas gift for their beloved. It originated back when men only bought that one gift and their wives took care of everyone else. In the twenty-first century, it had evolved into an evening out for whole families with one added feature, every shop still offered free gift wrapping, one of the original features of Gentleman's Night. Apparently, gift wrapping was a skill gentlemen were not expected to have.

This year was the first Christmas season

Gus's Too had been open, and we hadn't foreseen that Gentleman's Night might include something new — going out to dinner afterward. Imogen stayed the whole time. All night long, no trays were dropped, no dishes broken, and no one clutched his stomach and dashed for the restroom. Perhaps the jinx thing was overstated. Or not true at all.

After everyone else left, Livvie and Sonny, Imogen, Chris, and I gathered around the bar for a well-earned beer. Finally, exhausted from the emotion and activity of the day, Imogen turned back to the subject that must never have left her mind.

"Wade was such a good boyfriend," she sighed.

"Not always," I pointed out. "You broke up with him because he was moody and mean." I didn't want to speak ill of the dead, but it was important for her to have some perspective on Wade Cadwallader's character, particularly as she dealt with Sergeant Flynn.

"That's true," she admitted. "Some days he was wonderful, and other days just awful. Selfish, inconsiderate, neglectful. Sometimes even in the same day. I remember when he got that Yankees cap. That was the first time he was mean to me.

"He took me to a game at Yankee Stadium. We had a wonderful time. It was a beautiful summer night, and Wade was just so sweet, jumping up and down to get me a hot dog or a beer." Her smile disappeared and her voice grew quieter. "But then he got a text on his phone. He excused himself to go make a call. He was gone for a whole inning, and when he came back he was wearing that stupid hat.

"And after that, he was horrible. He buried himself in the game stats, paying more attention to the program book than he did to me. He made us leave before it was over. On the subway home he stared at his phone, and then, in midtown, he jumped off the train without saying good-bye. He'd always seen me home before. Always. I sat on the subway, wondering what had happened. When I asked him about it on our next date, he apologized profusely and swore it would never happen again. But then it did. More and more often. Until, like I told you, I had to break it off."

"You need to tell Sergeant Flynn about this," I said. "He needs a true picture of Wade's behavior in the months before his . . . his death." I stuttered, censoring the M word. It seemed unnecessarily cruel.

The evening broke up. Sonny and Livvie

took Imogen back to Mom's house and Chris and I trudged up the stairs to my apartment. What a day. And what new surprises would the morning bring?

Chapter Ten

In the morning, as usual, I awakened to the happy sounds and smells of breakfast being served downstairs at Gus's. "Pancakes!" I whooped, shaking Chris. "Must have pancakes."

Le Roi looked up lazily from the folds of the duvet. "Go on, you crazy kid," his yellow eyes seemed to say. "I'll stay here where it's warm."

Showered and dressed, Chris and I climbed down the stairs into Gus's busy front room. Everyone sitting at the counter, and everyone in the dining room just beyond it, was wearing pajamas.

"Why did we get dressed?" Chris asked from behind me.

The Busman's Harbor Pajama Party. Like Gentleman's Night, it was another long tradition, and one that I usually loved. The town shops opened at 6:00 AM, had huge sales, and everyone shopped in their pajamas. Really. At some stores, you got an extra discount if you came in your pajamas. At others, it was a progressive thing, the deepest discount at six o'clock, slightly less at seven, and so on, until prices returned to normal at ten. It was kind of genius. The shops, many of which would close down for the season at the end of the weekend, got one more chance to unload their merchandise. Local people got to shop for the holidays at tourist-focused stores they usually couldn't afford. People came in from out of town, so the B & Bs got one last gasp of business for the season. Families treated it like a happy, relaxed time together, capping the morning off with breakfast out at Gus's.

Chris and I avoided the line for tables by grabbing two seats at the counter. Gus, running his tail off, just as we had the night before, served up two heaping plates of blueberry pancakes with real maple syrup. I looked around the room, full of laughing people, buoyed by the dent they'd put in their holiday shopping. "I'm so happy I'm home," I said.

"I'm happy you're home, too." Chris grazed my cheek with his lips.

After breakfast, I made my way to Mom's house. The day was sunny and cold, like the one before. Still no snow, but like Imogen, I was beginning to wish for it.

I found Sonny out front, on a ladder, cursing loudly as he strung lights along the evergreen bushes that surrounded the high front porch.

"What the heck?" Mom had never decorated outdoors except for a simple Maine-made wreath on the front door.

"I know, right?" Sonny responded. "I came over to drop off Livvie and Page. They're inside finishing the cookie baking. Then your mother cornered me. More decorations from her discount at Linens and Pantries, this time for the outside."

Sonny's bright red hair was covered by a ski cap. He was so big, with his broad shoulders, bull neck, and barrel chest, he looked like he might topple the ladder. We'd had our differences over the year. Our attempt to run the Snowden Family Clambake together had been like two people trying to drive the same car, each tugging the steering wheel in the opposite direction. But we'd done a lot of sorting out since the summer, and in the process learned much about each other. It was Christmas and I was feeling good will toward men, even brothers-in-law. "Let me check on Imogen," I called up to him, "then I'll come help."

Inside, the air smelled of pecans and sugar. The front parlor looked beautiful in all its finery. Mom's Christmas spirit was infecting me. Just because we'd never decorated like this before, didn't mean we shouldn't start now. We still had time to make a world of memories for Page and the new baby.

My sister's pecan puffs were lined up like soldiers on the kitchen table, cooling.

"Ouch. Ouch. Ouch." Page took the latest batch off the hot cookie sheet, rolled them in confectioners' sugar, and lined them up with the others.

Livvie and Imogen chatted at the kitchen island and rolled the dough into walnut-sized balls with their hands. There was no tension between the two of them. The scope of Imogen's tragedy had brought out the best in Livvie.

It was such a happy scene, I almost turned around without saying anything and went back outside to help Sonny, but I hung around for a moment, inhaling the smells. Lots of families made these cookies and called them by different names, from Russian teacakes to Mexican wedding cakes to nut puffs. Livvie's, however, were the best in the entire world. The most flavorful, the best textured, the most perfect, bite-sized —

The front door swung open. Sonny stuck his head in. "Julia! Imogen! Sergeant Flynn's here for you. Wants to see you both at the station."

Imogen and I walked silently down the hill with Flynn to the ugly brick fire-department-town-offices-police complex.

"Good news, Ms. Geinkes," Flynn finally said when we were almost there. "We found our victim's next of kin. His brother."

Imogen halted where she stood. "Brother? Wade never mentioned a brother. Does he live far away? California? Outside the U.S.?"

Flynn shook his head. "New York City. With help from local law enforcement there, we reached him. He's on his way here."

Imogen looked like she'd been slapped. "A brother? In New York City? How come I never met him?"

Flynn cleared his throat. "Maybe we'll get some answers when he arrives."

In his typical, by-the-book fashion, Flynn talked to us separately. I squirmed on the hard bench across from the civilian dispatcher while Imogen went into the multi-purpose room that Flynn used as his office when he was in town. Half an hour later, she emerged, eyes and nose red from crying, and he called, "Snowden!"

My witness statement from the day before had been typed up. We walked through it and I made a few corrections, which I initialed. Then I signed it and figured we were done.

"By the way," Flynn said, "we got a corroborating witness on your dirty white car. A Mrs. Hitchens, who lives on the point opposite the site where they found your books, saw both the yellow rental truck and the white Toyota parked there at dawn on Thursday. She figured it was some sort of illegal dump site and planned to take her rowboat over to investigate. But before she got to it, she spotted Sheriff Donohue's vehicle and figured he was on top of it. She couldn't see where the truck ended up from her vantage point."

I gave him the tiniest of smiles. "Glad I could be helpful."

"There's CCTV in Bean's parking lot. They got him, too." Flynn laid in front of me a glossy still from a video camera. Eerily, it captured the front corner of the rental truck's cab. I was turned toward Imogen's seat. It looked like I was barking some sort of order at her — reminding her to fasten her seat belt or something like that. Behind me, looking ghostly in black and white, was the face of the dead man, sitting bolt upright in the Toyota's driver's seat, Yankee ball cap on his head.

"Is that the man you saw?"

My heart pounded. I breathed slowly, consciously pushing out air. "Yes, and I saw him in New York City, parked down the block."

"You're sure."

"Absolutely." There was no mistaking him. "And that's the car."

"Thanks. This helps us confirm the timeline of where he was in the hours before he was killed."

"Always happy to help. As you know." Silence from Flynn, so I asked, "By the way, when you said law enforcement in New York helped you find Wade's brother, was that an example of polite interstate cooperation, or was Wade Cadwallader known to them?" Over the last couple of days, I'd definitely developed my doubts about Imogen's boyfriend. Not only the moodiness she described, but the whole setup — the online dating, the appeal to come to New York. The fact that he'd never introduced her to his family. In the past twenty-four hours, my assessment of his behavior had moved from odd to suspect. I assumed Imogen's parents were well-off, and perhaps she was, too. My apartment wasn't cheap. Now I wondered if she had been the great love of Cadwallader's life, or his target. Whatever the scam was, I hoped she'd broken off the relationship before she'd given him any money.

Flynn allowed himself a hint of a smile, but said nothing.

He walked me to the door. Imogen jumped off the wooden bench the moment it opened. She was anxious to get out of there.

"Will you be staying in town?" Flynn asked her as we pushed open the glass doors to the outside.

"Yes," she called. "Indefinitely."

Wait, what? Indefinitely?

Before I could ask her what she meant, a dark blue Audi drove into the parking lot. The driver pulled into a space across from us, threw open the door, and stepped confidently out of the car. As soon as he stood, Imogen stopped, frozen.

"Wade!" she cried out. And fainted dead away.

CHAPTER ELEVEN

I managed to catch her before she hit the sidewalk. The man, who looked very much like the Wade Cadwallader I'd just identified in the photo from the L.L.Bean parking lot, exactly like him in fact, rushed toward us.

"Oh, my God, Imogen! What's wrong with her?" His even features puckered with concern.

"She thought you were dead."

"Oh, my God!" he repeated, getting it. Together we moved her to the bench in the waiting area. The dispatcher had already called over to the fire department and two big firemen dashed into the room, elbowing Wade and me out of the way.

"What's her name?" the younger of the two demanded, taking her pulse.

Cadwallader seemed paralyzed, eyes bulging.

"Imogen," I told them. "Imogen Geinkes."

"Imogen. Imogen!" the fireman repeated. "Are you with me?"

Imogen's eyes fluttered open. She turned her head wildly, stopping when Wade came into view.

He rushed to her side. "I'm here."

The door to the multipurpose room flew open and Flynn appeared.

"Identical twins!" I shouted at him. "You might have told her. She's gone for twenty-four hours thinking her boyfriend is dead. Look at that poor girl!"

I pointed dramatically at Imogen, who was, at that moment, looking anything but distressed. In fact, she and Wade looked like they were trying to remove each other's tonsils. With their tongues.

"She seems okay." The firemen burst out laughing as they walked away.

"Eww, yuck!" More than two hours later, Imogen and Wade were making out again, though they'd moved their location to my mother's living room couch, much to Page's disgust. "Get a room," she muttered.

I'd brought Imogen back to the house with me. Wade had arrived over an hour later, after his meeting with Sergeant Flynn. Imogen introduced him to my mother.

Wade took Mom's hand and stared deeply

into her eyes. "Mrs. Snowden, thank you for taking Imogen in."

"Call me Jacqueline, please. I'm so sorry about your brother. A twin. It must be difficult."

Wade's voice was low and serious. "He was a dangerous man. He's been in and out of prison since he's been an adult. Trouble all his life." He turned toward Imogen. "That's why I never introduced you. I didn't want you to know him."

"Still," Mom persisted, "he was your brother." Wade hadn't let go of Mom's hand. He had a conman's smooth moves. My misgivings about him, formed from Imogen's descriptions of his behavior, before I'd even met him, solidified.

"Believe me, I tried to have a relationship with my brother. But he was incapable of caring about anyone but himself. He took every opportunity he could to blame me for the illegal things he did, to throw me under the bus. The only way I could live my life was to separate myself from him. My only living relation."

"You poor thing!" Imogen cried.

Finally, Wade dropped Mom's hand. "Jacqueline, is there a place in the harbor where I can stay through the holiday?"

There was. There were lots of places. But

before I could get the words out of my mouth, Mom said, "Don't be silly, Wade. You'll stay here."

When Mom took off for work, the make-out session on the couch resumed, and I took refuge in the kitchen.

"What the heck?" Livvie asked as she put her amazing butter cookies into a tin.

"Crazy," I confirmed.

"I cannot imagine what that poor girl has gone through in the last twenty-four hours."

"Me neither," I had to admit. Wade, on the other hand, didn't seem disturbed or regretful at the loss of his twin. In fairness, though, as he said, he'd worked hard to distance himself.

"This has been one weird day," Page remarked. "I think it's been the weirdest day ever."

I went to work. Chris was already deep in prep when I arrived.

"How was your day?" he called.

"You wouldn't believe me if I told you."

He put his knife down. "Try me."

By the time I finished my story, his mouth was open and his eyes wide. It really was preposterous. Identical twins. A good twin and a bad twin. It was mythological.

That evening we had another good night

at the restaurant. Imogen and Wade arrived around seven, clearly intent on having a date night. As I plated Wade's salad, Chris leaned into my prep area. "So those two are definitely back together."

"Yup. It's on."

"I thought he was a moody louse."

I stared at their booth. "Apparently he's been forgiven."

I delivered their starters, scallops wrapped in bacon for her, salad for him. "Thank you, Julia," Imogen said as I backed away to give them their privacy.

While they ate, I went about my work, but I did look over to check on them from time to time. I noticed that Wade held his fork in his left hand. Not British-style, but tines upward. His grip was awkward, the way some left-handed children's were, though most southpaws, in my experience, looked more natural and comfortable by adulthood.

Flynn wandered in at close to nine. Obviously off duty, he sat at the bar and ordered a Sam Adams.

"I'm surprised to see you here." I pushed the bottle toward him.

He picked it up and took a swig. "Why? You're the only restaurant open for dinner in the off-season."

"How flattering."

I handed him a menu and went off to take a dessert order. Profiteroles with vanilla ice cream and fudge sauce or orange-juice cake. Livvie was outdoing herself. What would we do in the weeks or months she'd need to take off after the baby was born?

By the time I served Flynn his entrée, the crowd had thinned considerably and I lingered at the bar. He and I watched as Wade politely held Imogen's new coat. Laughing and waving good-bye, they left through the front door.

"You never answered my question," I reminded him.

"Which question?"

"About whether it was just extraordinary interstate cooperation that found Wade Cadwallader so quickly, or whether he was already known to the New York City police."

Flynn gazed thoughtfully at the door they'd just left through. "You have your doubts about him?"

I noticed he hadn't answered my question. "Yes."

Flynn, in a mellower mood than this morning, leaned back on his barstool. "It's a sad story, like so many I have to read. Wade and Wayne Cadwallader. The twins' father is unknown. Their mother was young, and who knows, maybe she could have handled one kid, but twins? She voluntarily surrendered them into the foster system the first time when they were six months old. After that, it was a patchwork. Sometimes she had custody, sometimes she didn't. Sometimes they were placed together in a foster home. Other times they were separated. She finally died of bad luck and bad life choices when they were twelve."

So far, everything that Wade had told Imogen was true. His father had never been in the picture and his mother was dead. He'd left out a lot, but he hadn't lied.

"From twelve on it gets interesting," Flynn continued. "They started out placed together, but Wayne was removed from the home after less than a year and sent to a group home."

"What does that mean?"

"We don't know, officially. Wayne's juvenile record is sealed, but it's clear he was a troubled kid. He had multiple arrests as an adult, starting with burglary and moving on to armed robbery and assault."

"Wade told Imogen he had to separate himself because his brother tried to frame him for his criminal activity."

"I believe it. Wayne's file reads like a classic psychopath's. Both brothers were math whizzes in school. Genius level. Wayne eventually went to work as a moneyman for the Russian mob."

"A moneyman for the mob? Sounds like the kind of job that could get a person murdered."

Flynn nodded. "Exactly. Moneymen rarely retire. The NYPD and the feds are working sources trying to find out if there's any chatter around about missing money, rivalries, and so on."

"And Wade?" I asked.

"Wade graduated from high school, went to college, and got a master's degree. He has an actuarial job with a big insurance company. He's really made something of his life. Your friend is involved with the right Cadwallader."

I hesitated, not sure if I should say anything. I had no proof, just a suspicion. Finally, I spilled it. "That's just it. I'm not sure she is involved with the right Cadwallader."

Flynn's smooth brow furrowed. "I don't understand."

Across the room behind the lunch counter, Chris had finished cooking for the evening. There was still a ton of cleanup to do, but he wandered over and joined me behind the bar.

I cleared my throat. "I think, without knowing, Imogen was dating both Wade and Wayne." The two of them stared at me, so I continued with my theory. "Imogen described a guy who was nearly the perfect man when they met online and continued that way through the spring and summer in New York. Then he turned moody. Sometimes he was his lovable self, other times he was withdrawn, curt, barely aware she was alive."

Chris shook his head. "So you think sometimes one turned up for a date, and sometimes the other one? Wouldn't she know? They looked alike, but it seems to me a girlfriend would know."

"I think in normal circumstances, she would have known. But I think Wayne impersonated his brother in order to deliberately fool her."

"Why would he do that?" Flynn folded his arms across his chest. I could tell he was skeptical, but not completely dismissive.

"I suspect Imogen's parents are quite wealthy. She may even have money of her own. Perhaps Wayne found out his twin had got himself a good thing and decided to horn in on it. To marry her under false pretenses. If he'd gone through with it, something quite awful might have happened to Imogen not long afterward."

Chris rested his dimpled chin in his hand. "But how would that even work? She'd certainly notice she was getting calls and texts from two different numbers."

"Lots of people have two phone numbers," I responded. "They carry a work phone and a personal phone, or they have a cell and a landline. Wayne would have found a way to explain it."

"But if he was trying to charm her into marrying him, why did he act like a jerk?" Chris asked.

"I think he was quite charming most of the time he was with her, but since it was, fundamentally, an act, he couldn't keep it up. Sometimes his real character asserted itself. Like when her office holiday party descended into chaos because of the tainted eggnog. He bailed and left her to face the consequences when she needed his support the most. That's when she broke it off."

"Wow." Chris leaned against the back bar. "That's quite a theory."

In that moment, the penny dropped. "Wait a minute. What if . . . what if the impersonation is still going on? What if that's Wayne with Imogen right now?" That would explain the terrible feeling I'd had about Imogen's boyfriend almost from the moment I'd met him. I turned to Flynn. "What if the man you said is a classic psychopath is at my mom's house this very minute?"

Flynn had listened to Chris and me talk without saying a word. He wouldn't give me the satisfaction of saying I might be onto something, but he pulled out his wallet and threw some money on the bar. "Excuse me," he said. "I've got to make some calls."

CHAPTER TWELVE

I spent an uneasy night. Early in the morning, giving up on sleep, I crept out of bed and spent some time on the web reading about identical twins, a subject I hadn't thought about since my college Intro to Psychology class. What I learned was that Flynn wasn't going to be able to tell who was staying at Mom's house via DNA. Wade's and Wayne's would be identical. Fingerprints were a better bet, since they were shaped by both genes and environment. Even subtle interactions with other things in the womb — amniotic fluid, the cord or placenta, even the other twin — could alter them. The Cadwallader brothers' fingerprints would be quite similar, but not completely identical. Given his extensive criminal history, Wayne's fingerprints had to be on file. All Flynn had to do was check the fingerprints on the body and the fingerprints on file, and we'd have an answer. That is, if he believed my Shakespearean theory of twins switching identities enough to make the effort.

While I was at it, I also looked up "psychopath." Flynn had called Wayne Cadwallader a psychopath a couple of times. I expected to read about an antisocial loser, someone who couldn't form attachments and whose self-centeredness made trouble for others. That described the "moody guy" who had shown up occasionally for a date with Imogen, the one I assumed was Wayne masquerading as his brother. But evidently, that was a description of a sociopath. Though definitions of psychopaths differed, I ran across one in an article in a 2014 issue of *Psychology Today* titled "How to Tell a Psychopath from a Sociopath," that made my blood run cold.

"Psychopaths, though unable to form emotional attachments or feel empathy with others, often have disarming or even charming personalities. Psychopaths are highly manipulative and can easily gain people's trust. They learn to mimic emotions, despite their inability to feel them, and can appear normal to others."

So I wouldn't know. I wouldn't be able to

spot if that guy staying at my mother's house was a psychopath at all. I shuddered, remembering the oily charm he'd used to get Mom to invite him to stay at her house.

The article went on to say that sociopaths were "hot." Unable to feel emotions themselves, they sought stimulation by generating drama in their families and upsets with their neighbors. They often ended up alone. Psychopaths, on the other hand, were described as "cold." Cold, calculating, and manipulative. Which was what reading about them made me feel. Cold. Like there was a cold pit of fear in my stomach.

Le Roi jumped into my lap and began to purr. He had an unerring instinct for knowing if anyone he cared about was in distress. He was like a heavy lap robe that could maintain its own body temperature. As I stroked his long fur, my heart rate returned to normal.

Finally, as a last thought, I read up on salmonella poisoning and its symptoms. There was something about the way Imogen had described the events the evening of her office party that felt wrong to me, though I couldn't put my finger on what it was.

After I finished on the web, I dressed quickly and kissed a sleeping Chris on the cheek. Le Roi protested me leaving, but I told him I had to go.

Outside, the sky was gray and the air had that pregnant feel that signals snow. Maybe Imogen would get her wish for a white Christmas after all. I doubted that would make up for finding her boyfriend dead, then getting him back, and then, worst-case scenario, if my hunch was correct, finding out he was dead yet again and his psycho twin was impersonating him. But it would be something.

When I opened Mom's back door, Imogen, Wade, and Mom were in the kitchen, eating scrambled eggs and bacon.

"Look what Wade made!" My mother was delighted.

"There's plenty," Imogen said. "Please join us."

"Thanks." I picked a piece of wheat toast off a plate and slathered it with blueberry jam. "What's the plan for today?" I asked, in a tone that tried for a casual, and not at all obsessive, interest in their plans.

"I have to work." Mom glanced at her watch. "In fact, I have to leave. Thank you so much, Wade, for a delicious breakfast."

"Wade and I are going Christmas shopping," Imogen answered. "We'll cover the little shops in town and then maybe drive back down to Freeport. Want to come?"

"Thanks, I'll pass. I'm headed over to see Sergeant Flynn."

Imogen was immediately wary. "Why do you need to see him again?"

"The murder hasn't been solved. No one's been arrested."

"Julia's helped the police with several cases," Mom bragged as she pulled on her gloves. She'd never grasped the finer point that though Lieutenant Binder valued me, Sergeant Flynn was skeptical about my contributions.

"Wayne was a bad man," Imogen protested. "There were probably lots of people after him."

"For sure," Wade added.

"I'm going upstairs to change," Imogen announced. "I'll be ready to go in twenty."

Mom went out the back door, so I was left alone with Wade. It was the first time I'd really gotten to study him. He was short statured, maybe five or six inches taller than Imogen. His pale blond hair was worn in a buzz cut. Blond brows and blond lashes framed pale blue eyes. He shoveled the scrambled eggs into his mouth using his left hand with that awkward grip.

"So you and Imogen are back together?"

He shrugged. "Yup."

"It's a shame you ever broke up in the first place. If it hadn't been for the whole fiasco with the eggnog, maybe it wouldn't have happened."

"Maybe."

A man of few words. He turned on the charm for Imogen and Mom, but he didn't bother with me. Perhaps because he didn't want anything from me.

I excused myself to go upstairs. He grunted noncommittally, not looking up from his eggs.

On the landing, I heard a door open and soft footsteps in the hall. I hurried to confront Imogen.

"Julia," she said.

"I want to talk. I'm worried about you. You and Wade are all lovey-dovey now, but you told me on the way up here he was a terrible boyfriend. Moody, self-centered. What's changed?" I wouldn't tell her I believed she'd been dating, and possibly sleeping with, two men until I was positive.

"He has changed. Ever since he's been in Maine, he's been super. Besides, when I saw Wayne in the truck, and I thought it was Wade . . ."

She let the sentence drift and I felt a pang. The poor kid had been through it lately. I changed the subject. "Imogen, when you were at the emergency room with your colleagues, did a doctor or a nurse, any medical professional at all, tell you that you all had salmonella poisoning?"

"I don't remember," she admitted. "Everyone who drank the eggnog got sick, and everyone who didn't, didn't. They all said it was the eggs. All my coworkers were staring at me."

Her voice was tight with upset. I moved to my next topic. "Let me ask you this — were there ever times when you told Wade something, and the very next time you saw him, he didn't remember it?"

That brought a smile to her lips. "Of course, silly. He's a guy. That happens with Mama and Daddy all the time. Mama gets so aggravated at Daddy. It's comical." She glanced toward the bathroom door. "Can you excuse me?"

"Sure. By the way, is Wade right-handed or left-handed?"

"Left-handed," she answered instantly. "Why would you even ask me that? Now, please excuse me."

I waited until I heard the shower running and snuck into my niece's room. Imogen's clothes were laid out on the neatly made bed. It seemed funny that Page had outgrown the princess decor, yet it suited

Imogen perfectly.

I slid her phone off the bedside table. If her contact list had two different numbers for Wade, it might help prove my theory Wayne had been impersonating his twin. But Imogen's phone asked for a thumbprint in order to open. *Drat.* I put it back where I found it and slunk out of the room.

CHAPTER THIRTEEN

Sergeant Flynn was on the phone when I arrived at police headquarters, but he waved me to a seat across the folding table from him. I waited, impatiently, while he wrapped up the call. "Ms. Snowden, what brings you here?"

"I want to know if that man in my house is Wayne or Wade Cadwallader, and I want to know it now."

"Whoa. What's the hurry?" The corners of his mouth turned upward, one of the few times in our association I'd seen him smile. I wondered if he was laughing at me.

"I need to know if I'm responsible for a stone-cold psychopath staying at my mother's house. If Imogen was dating both of them, then she can't tell the difference. None of the rest of us has ever met either of them before. Wayne's prints must be on file. You need to test them against the corpse."

Flynn held up a hand. "Already done. As

it happens, we have both Wade's and Wayne's fingerprints available, from a couple of times Wayne tricked the NYPD into arresting his brother. It always got straightened out, but Wade was booked a few times."

"Fantastic. I assume if that guy at Mom's house wasn't Wade, you already would have been over to arrest him."

"It's not so simple. The differences between twins' fingerprints are usually very subtle. It's not something I could notice, or anyone in the ME's office. I've had to send them off to the FBI. They have more sophisticated equipment and a trained specialist who can read the results."

"A specialist in differentiating twins' fingerprints?"

"His most famous case involved murderous identical triplets."

My head spun with the possibilities. The situation we were in was tricky enough. "When will we know?"

"The results will take time."

"How much time?"

"Not clear. A couple of weeks."

"What?"

"The FBI guy is an expert, Julia. He's in high demand. And, in case you haven't noticed, it's the holidays."

"I can't have a psychopath living in my mom's house for a couple of weeks. You must put some credence to my theory that Wayne sometimes impersonated Wade or you wouldn't be checking the corpse's identity."

He spread his fingers out on the desk. "Out of an abundance of caution. To make sure the identity of the body is correct. Nothing more. We'll know in two weeks."

"I hear you," I said. "Just do me, and yourself, two favors. One, find out whether Wayne Cadwallader was left-handed or right-handed. Would that be in his criminal record?"

Flynn blinked. "I don't think so. I'll check. Why?"

"A hunch. If you can't get the information from law enforcement, is there a way to look at the twins' school records, or something else that would tell us?"

He made a note. "Maybe. Why?"

"I noticed last night that whoever it is at my mom's house eats left-handed, but his grip is awkward, like he's pretending to be a lefty. I asked Imogen about it. She confirmed her boyfriend is left-handed."

Flynn sighed. "Julia, remember the twins were bounced from foster home to foster home from a very young age. Maybe no one

ever showed them how to hold a fork.
Besides, if one is left-handed, wouldn't the
other be, too?"

"I did some reading about twins on the
web this morning. I think Wade and Wayne
were mirror-image twins."

"Which are?"

"Identical twins who are opposite-sided,
like a person looking in a mirror. They'll
part their hair on opposite sides, one is
right-handed, the other left-handed, and so
on. I think that's what the Cadwalladers are.
Their hair is cut too short to tell about the
parts, but I believe whoever is at my house
is eating with his left hand, even though it
isn't natural."

"Mirror image twins, eh?" Flynn put
down his pen and closed his notebook.
"Sounds rare."

"It is, but it does happen."

Flynn held up a hand. "Okay. Okay. I'll
find out. But, Julia, I've been doing this
detective thing for a while now, and I've
learned the simpler explanations are usually
the right ones. The guy at your mom's house
is most probably Wade, law-abiding actuary,
just as he claims."

"Do you have a 'simpler explanation' that
fits this case?"

"I told you Wayne was a moneyman for

the Russian mob. The Organized Crime Task Force in New York has picked up some chatter. It seems there may or may not be some missing money. Whatever the case, bad men are looking for Wayne Cadwallader. Very bad men."

"When will you know something?"

"Soon."

"Let's hope," I said. What a relief that would be. If Wayne was really Wayne, and out-of-town mobsters had killed him, the rest of us could go on to live happily ever after. Well, maybe not Imogen. I still didn't like that guy at my mom's house, even if he was Wade. But prying Imogen away from the real Wade was a simpler problem that could be dealt with later, and was really none of my business, anyway.

"One more thing," I said. "You should also check on emergency room admissions at NYU Hospital on Friday night, December fourteenth. A whole group of people from Imogen's office came in, allegedly with food poisoning. She thinks it was salmonella, but I'd like to know the real diagnosis. The symptoms seem a little off to me. It's true, salmonella can make you really sick, but from the way Imogen described it, this was too fast-acting and uniform across the group. Her colleagues assumed it was salmonella because everyone who got sick had drunk the eggnog and everyone is wary of raw eggs nowadays, but I'd like to know what the doctors there actually diagnosed. If my theory is right, that Wayne was her date that night, pretending to be Wade, and your theory is right, that bad people were after Wayne, I wonder if he knew it and thought the poisoning was an attempt on his life. That would explain why he slunk off before the EMTs arrived."

"The bad guys would have to be pretty motivated to poison a whole group of people for one target."

"They'd have to be pretty motivated to follow a truck four hundred miles to Busman's Harbor, Maine, too."

As soon as I left Flynn, I went in search of Imogen and Cadwallader, whichever one he was. I found them shopping at Gordon's Jewelry on the corner of Main and Main.

"Look, Julia!" Imogen held out her left hand with a diamond the size of a dime on the ring finger. "Look what Wade just bought me! We're engaged!"

"My gosh. That's gorgeous. Let me see it in the light." I hustled her over to the other side of the store. "What are you doing?" I whispered. "You broke up with him less than a week ago."

"I know," she sighed. "But I told you, since he's been back, he's been wonderful." Her eyes took on a dreamy, faraway look. "We'll get married in the same church my parents were married in and I'll wear my mama's dress. The church will be filled with magnolias and all my family will be there. My parents will see I was right about Wade. He wasn't a fling. I was right about everything."

I wanted to shake her. "You've been back together less than twenty-four hours. How do you know 'moody guy' isn't coming back?"

She dug the heel of her new L.L.Bean boot into the wooden floor. "Julia, don't tell me what to do. You're just like my parents."

Across the room, Cadwallader studied the earrings beneath the glass countertop. There was no way around it. This latest turn of events meant I had to tell her what I believed. I kept my voice to a low hiss. "Imogen, I think you've been dating both Wade and Wayne. That's why your boyfriend's personality seemed so changeable. Because he is . . . was two different people."

I expected a stunned look of dawning comprehension. Instead, the defiant chin jutted out. "Don't be ridiculous. Why would you believe that? Do you really think I don't know my own boyfriend?"

It was now or never. I stared down at her. "Not only do I think you dated both of them, I think you don't know who you're with right now. You don't know which one you've agreed to marry."

"Well, I never." She turned around and called across the room to Cadwallader. "We're leaving." Turning back to me, she spat, "Julia, I'll thank you to stay out of my business." She and Cadwallader made for the door. "Why does everyone in the world try to tell me what to do?" she whined to him. Then, staring back at me, she said, "You're just like my parents. We're getting out of here." She gave the door a good slam behind her.

"Sorry, Mr. Gordon," I said to the owner after they left.

"Don't apologize for them," he answered. "That was an expensive ring I just sold. Funny that they put it on her credit card instead of his, but I guess it takes all kinds to make the world nowadays. She said her daddy would pay for it."

CHAPTER FOURTEEN

I was at the restaurant helping Chris prep the ingredients for Italian wedding soup when Livvie arrived with the evening's desserts: pineapple upside-down cake and chocolate mousse.

"Where's your little buddy?" she asked, looking around the restaurant for Imogen.

"I don't think she'll be shadowing me anymore. She's hanging out with Cadwallader full-time. They're engaged."

Livvie cast her eyes heavenward. "Let me guess. Mom's throwing her a big church wedding followed by a reception with live music and a five-course meal."

"Will you get over that? You were five months pregnant at the time you got married and you said — no, you insisted — that you wanted only immediate family. Anyway, in addition to being otherwise occupied with her fiancé, Imogen's kind of done with me. We had a fight." As fast as I could, I gave her the rundown on my suspicions about the twins and the ensuing argument with Imogen. "Besides," I finished, "Mom doesn't even know about all this. She's been at work all day, thank goodness."

"Can we hope at least Imogen has packed her bags and gone back to New York with Wade, or whoever he is?" Livvie asked.

"If Imogen hasn't left already, I'm going to ask her to go. Or at least tell Cadwallader he has to go, which will cause Imogen to leave, too, I'm certain. But I hope it won't come to that. I hope, like you say, they're already gone."

Livvie started toward the door. "Good luck, whatever happens. Stay strong."

"I will."

The restaurant opened its doors at six o'clock and Chris and I settled in for what looked like a routine Sunday evening. Flynn arrived at seven and took a seat at the bar.

"What can I get you to drink?"

"Cola. Thanks."

"Still on duty?"

"I have some paperwork to finish up before I knock off for the evening." He inclined his head toward the booth Imogen and Cadwallader had occupied the night before. "Lovebirds not here tonight?"

"No, and I don't think they will be. Did

you find out anything new today?"

"Well, much as it pains me to tell you this, I found out you were right. Wade and Wayne Cadwallader were mirror-image twins."

I filled a glass with ice and cola and put it on the bar in front of him. "Who was who?"

"Wayne was right-handed. Wade, left. And the guy hanging out with Imogen, you said he's left-handed?"

"*Engaged* to Imogen," I corrected. I filled him in on the scene at Gordon's. Flynn raised his eyebrows. "He appears to be left-handed," I continued, "but I swear he's faking it to fool Imogen."

Flynn's squint showed his skepticism. "Something else turned up —"

"Excuse me," I said. While we'd been talking, a young couple had wandered in and shed their coats and scarves. They looked around impatiently for someone to show them to a table. "Right back," I said to Flynn, and rushed away.

I got the newcomers settled and ran back to the bar with their drink orders. "So what was the other thing you learned?" I asked Flynn.

He didn't answer because we were distracted when the street door opened and in walked Imogen, followed by Cadwallader . . . and Mom! I dashed to meet them as they hung up their coats. "Mom, what are you doing here?"

"Well, hello to you, too, Julia," Mom said. "Wade and Imogen stopped by Linens and Pantries on their way back from Freeport and invited me to dinner."

"We wanted to buy your mom a thank-you dinner for putting us up," Cadwallader said.

I showed them to a crescent-shaped booth along the dining room wall. Imogen slid along the banquette to the middle while Mom and Cadwallader sat on the outer ends, facing each other.

I passed out menus. "Can I get you something to drink?"

"Can you hang on while we order?" Cadwallader dove for his menu. "Imogen has such a fast metabolism, she has to eat continuously just to —"

"I've heard." I cut him off using a tone of voice no service worker should ever employ. I cast a nervous look over my shoulder and saw that the couple that had come in earlier had put down their menus and waited to order. But I figured the faster I got Imogen and Cadwallader fed, the faster I could separate them from Mom and serve them their walking papers. "Sure," I said. "What'll you have?"

They each picked a different entrée off our limited and ever-changing menu. Mom went with pollock, a white fish that was plentiful and fresh in December. Chris prepared it lightly breaded in cornmeal, fried and served with an avocado salsa. Imogen went with chicken Française, while Cadwallader chose our rarely offered Delmonico steak. For starters, Mom selected the clam chowder, Imogen the oysters, and Cadwallader a salad.

"And to drink?"

"Champagne!" Imogen piped up. "We're celebrating!" The others nodded their assent, so I rushed off to take the other couple's order.

When I got back to the prep area, Chris inclined his head toward the booth where my mother sat with Cadwallader and Imogen. He knew their presence had to be driving me crazy. I rolled my eyes back at him and returned to the bar. "Do you see that?" I banged my hand on the bar to get Flynn's attention. "They have my mom with them."

Flynn squinted, looking through the archway into the dining room. "She doesn't appear to be a hostage. She seems more like an adult who has voluntarily come to a dining establishment for the purpose of having a meal."

"Very funny, but I need to know if I'm responsible for a psychopath sleeping under my mother's roof."

I grabbed a bottle of champagne from the small refrigerator under the bar. Though it wasn't something we usually offered, we'd purchased a couple of reasonably priced cases in preparation for the upcoming holidays. I took two steps before I turned back to Flynn. "Look," I said, "this is about my mom. Can you at least call the finger-print guy and get him to rush the results so we know for sure who we're dealing with?"

"That's what I wanted to tell you before you rushed off. I've already made the call. Analysis will be back the day after Christmas."

"The day after Christmas!"

Flynn's voice was low. "I understand your concerns. I really do. But it's Sunday evening. Tomorrow is Christmas Eve. Then Christmas Day. You have to be realistic."

I came back to the bar and stood next to Flynn's stool. "What if it's worse?"

"Worse than what?"

"Worse than being responsible for putting a psychopath in my mother's house. What if he's the murderer?"

Flynn stared back at me impassively. I'd expected more of a reaction to my brilliant deduction.

"Think about it," I urged. "Imogen is rich. Wayne sees his brother's got a good thing there. He decides to make the charade permanent. He kills his brother and takes his place. He's got Imogen. He's out of reach of the Russian mob, because as far as they're concerned, he's dead. All his problems are solved."

"And what, Wayne the high school dropout takes his brother's job in the actuarial department in an insurance company permanently?"

"Didn't you say they were both math geniuses? Or maybe he tells Imogen he's quit the job for some reason. I don't know, but I think it all fits." I looked straight into Flynn's eyes. "Was the killer right-handed or left-handed?"

Flynn sighed. "Right-handed. Stood behind the victim as he did the deed. The killer had to be pretty strong."

"Right-handed!" I said. "That proves it. That man is Wayne, pretending to be Wade, and he had the motivation to kill his own brother."

Flynn broke into a broad grin. "What would you like me to do, Julia? 'Your honor,' he imitated himself, talking to a judge. 'I'd like a warrant for the arrest of Wayne

Cadwallader.' "

Flynn also played the part of the judge. " 'What is your evidence, Detective?' "

" 'A witness reports he has terrible table manners.' "

" 'Well, if you say so.' " Flynn continued as the judge. " 'I don't normally issue arrest warrants for men whose bodies are lying in the morgue, but in this case —' "

"Stop," I said. "Enough. I get it. We can't prove he's Wayne."

I stalked off with the champagne and an ice bucket. On my way into the dining room I stopped at the sideboard, picked up three champagne flutes and a steak knife, loading it all onto a tray.

I put the glasses and the steak knife on the table, wincing a little as I put the knife in front of Cadwallader. If he'd really slit his brother's throat, I hated handing him a weapon. "Here you go," I said. Then I wrapped a napkin around the champagne bottle and lifted it out of the bucket.

Cadwallader put his hand out to block my move. "We'll have the champagne with our appetizers. Are they coming soon? Imogen needs to eat."

"Right away."

"Good. We'll have it to toast our engagement. And your mom's stupendous hospitality. She's invited me to stay for Christmas."

"What?" The image of personalized Linens and Pantries stockings labeled IMOGEN and WADE sprung into my head.

"Julia!" My mother didn't tolerate rudeness. "You've already invited Imogen. Of course Wade will stay. They're affianced."

I put the champagne bottle back in the bucket, ran to the kitchen, shucked the oysters, plated the salad, and ladled out the clam chowder for my mother. On the way back to their table, tray laden, I stopped beside Flynn at the bar.

"I have to know if that man is Wade or Wayne, and I have to know it now."

"Julia." Flynn's voice contained a warning.

"Please. Call your expert and beg him to look at the fingerprints tonight."

Flynn sighed. "Just hang in a little longer."

"I can't. He's Wayne and I'm going to prove it." I stomped off into the dining room. At the booth, I served the salad, soup, and oysters. Then I reached into the bucket for the champagne bottle. I'd had a lot of experience opening champagne because of the number of engagements, anniversaries, and special birthdays that were celebrated at the Snowden Family Clambake. I looked behind me to make sure Flynn was watching from the bar. Then I lowered the bottle, loosened the cork, and let it fly — straight at Cadwallader.

His hand shot out to protect himself from the hurtling missile. Proving quick reflexes, he caught it.

In his right hand.

I whirled around, my back to the booth, and shouted to Flynn, "Did you see? This is Wayne. Right-handed Wayne Cadwallader."

Out of the corner of my eye, I caught the blur of something hurtling toward me from behind.

"You bitch!" Imogen shrieked. "I told you to stay out of it!"

She leapt across the table and landed on my back with a terrific whack that took my breath away. I gyrated from side to side, trying to shake her off, but she clung to me like a spider monkey. I put my hands back to push her off and felt a slashing pain across my right fingers. The steak knife. "Eee-yow! Imogen! Get off! Get off!"

"I told you to stay out of it. I love him!"

The knife seared the side of my neck. Flynn and Chris ran toward us. Would one of them make it before she found an artery? I wasn't willing to find out.

I swung the bottle of champagne forward and then back over my head with every bit of strength I could muster.

"Ooof!" Imogen's grip loosened and she slid off my back. Chris dashed around me and held her on the ground.

Wayne jumped from his seat and dashed for the door. As he ran by, my mother stuck her size-five foot into the aisle and tripped him. He went down like he'd been shot.

Flynn jumped on top of him. "Don't move," he ordered. "You're both under arrest. No, not you," he reassured the astonished couple at the table next to him. "This guy. And his girlfriend."

"Fiancée," came Imogen's muffled correction from her position on the floor.

Chapter Fifteen

"I told you he was Wayne," I said to Flynn. We were at the police station, the next day, Christmas Eve, and I was reviewing my statement against Imogen for an assault charge.

"You did."

"And I told you he could be identified by right- versus left-handedness."

"You did." Flynn rose and picked my statement about Imogen's assault off the printer and brought it to me to sign. "Though I don't think the evidence of putting his right hand up to shield himself from a flying champagne cork will hold up in court." He paused. "But don't worry, there will be mountains more evidence."

"So *now* you have mountains of evidence."

He ignored me. "Neither of them is talking, but here's what we know from examining voice mails, texts, and e-mails, and talking to witnesses. You know, from doing

463

actual police work." He smiled, then continued. "I had a most interesting conversation with Imogen's mother when I spoke to her in Georgia. I called to confirm that Wade had come to Atlanta to court their daughter and enticed her to move to New York. That appeared to be true, but when I explored the state of Imogen's relationship with her parents, things got interesting. It seems they've been sending her money to pay the rent on your apartment, as you'd guessed, but not as a way to keep her tied to them. They sent her the money on the condition that she stay away."

He let me absorb that before continuing. "Imogen was always different from other girls her age, different from the Geinkes' other children. She stole without remorse, lied reflexively, and constantly chipped away at any sense of well-being or safety the other members of the family had. She frequently told her sister she was ugly and no one could ever love her, and her brother he was so stupid he'd never live on his own. Not in the way normal siblings do, but with a goal of crippling them emotionally. There was trouble at school. Bullying, cheating. Once, rather than study for a test, she repeatedly ran into a wall in her room and then showed her teacher the bruises and said she did poorly on the test because her parents had beaten her the night before. A guidance counselor called the police, but fortunately a medical expert said the bruises couldn't have occurred the way Imogen claimed they did."

"Wow," I said.

"She finished high school at an institution for troubled youth. It's only because her parents had means that she was able to get through college. Then her father got her that internship where she worked when she contacted you about the apartment."

"Wow," I repeated. "But how did she get mixed up with Wade or Wayne, or whoever it was at first?"

"In addition to his involvement with the Russian mob, Wayne had a sideline scamming women he met on online dating sites. Because 'successful employee of a big financial company' sounded a lot better than 'mid-level mob guy,' he always impersonated his twin brother when he ran these scams. He set up dates with women who had money, or whose parents did, and then got them to buy him things, pay for trips, and so on.

"When Wayne, posing as Wade, arrived in Atlanta to meet Imogen, it was a case of like meets like. Each one recognized a self in the other and they fell instantly in love, at least as in love as either of them was capable of being. Once he got her to New York, Wayne kept up the charade of being Wade for a while, meeting Imogen outside Wade's office building for dates, but eventually he either confessed or she guessed. The point is, she didn't care. The bad twin was more attractive to her."

"So she was always dating Wayne." This thought had never occurred to me. "Then how does Wade come into it? And why kill him?"

"Wade stumbled on his own profile on the dating Web site and figured out what Wayne was doing. Wade asked his brother to stop, repeatedly. He found out about Imogen and was concerned about her. He imagined her as his brother's innocent victim. He tracked the two of them to Yankee Stadium via an Instagram posting of Imogen's. Once he arrived there, Wade called his brother on his cell and threatened to have him arrested for identity theft. Wayne slunk off, and Wade went back to his seat, determined to tell Imogen the truth. He must have been shocked to find out Imogen already knew her boyfriend was an impostor. After that, Wade would show up from time to time to urge Imogen to break it off. He thought he was dealing with a naïve young woman, not someone just like his brother.

"Imogen and Wayne decided to marry. She hoped for reconciliation and a large wedding from her parents. But for that to happen, she had to return home with a respectable fiancé. Wayne had to become Wade permanently. Just as you theorized, it solved multiple problems for them, including getting Wayne out of the mob.

"Any threat that Wade would show up and ruin the charade had to be removed permanently. Your arrival in the city and subsequent trip back to Maine became the perfect ruse to lure Wade away from the places where he was known and kill him."

"So who followed the rental truck in the white Toyota?"

"That was Wayne. While you were at the rest stop, Imogen called Wade and said Wayne was threatening and extorting her. Nice guy that he was, Wade rushed to the rescue. When he arrived outside your house in the blue Audi at five in the morning, Imogen went outside to meet him. Wayne knocked him out. Then Imogen and Wayne loaded Wade in the truck. Wayne drove it out to the dumpsite, killed Wade, and left him in the back. Wayne hid the truck at the end of the lane to buy them a little time.

Imogen met him there and drove him back to town in the white Toyota. Wayne took Wade's cell phone and the Audi and drove to Portland to wait.

"He knew from his extensive dealings with law enforcement, that sooner or later, one of the agencies involved would find Wade's cell number and call it. As it happened, it was the New York City cops who did. Wayne acted shocked, told them he was Wade and said he'd drive up to identify the body right away. By the time the message got communicated to me, all I heard was the victim's brother was on the way. I was as surprised as you were that the brother was an identical twin claiming the victim was really his brother. Of course, at the time, Imogen acted the most surprised of all. But now we know, that's what it was. An act."

I sat back in the folding chair, astonished by the breadth of it all. "But why? Why steal the truck? Why not kill Wade and quietly take his place?"

"So that someone was looking for it. It did Wayne no good to leave his brother's body in the Maine woods to be covered by snow and quite possibly never found. Wayne needed his associates in the mob to believe he was dead. Wade's body had to be found for the switch to be successful."

"So that's why they emptied out the truck, to make the discovery as dramatic as possible."

Flynn nodded. "That's what we think. Though I still don't get why your furniture was arranged so carefully in the clearing."

"Imogen told me she loved that furniture, and she was careful about the things she loved," I answered. "What about the eggnog?"

Flynn relaxed his military posture and mirrored mine, leaning against the back of his chair. "She probably tainted it herself with eye drop fluid."

"Eye drop fluid?"

"Old fraternity prank. Dumping bottles of over-the-counter eye drops in the punch bowl. Results in severe stomach pains, vomiting, and diarrhea."

"So not a funny prank, then. Why would she do it?"

"I'm told by our consulting psychologist that people like Imogen have a constant need for attention. They don't care if it's good or bad, as long as it's attention."

I thought about the dunking the poor Coast Guardsman Santa took, the calamity of the Christmas trees. In both cases, all eyes were on Imogen. The kind of attention she basked in. "So she's not really a jinx?"

"She is. But not to herself. Just to everyone she comes in contact with." We were silent for a moment. Then Flynn said, "So, you were right. There was a psychopath staying at your mother's house. Two, in fact, including the one you invited."

Flynn saw the look on my face and took pity on me. "I'm surprised she took you in so thoroughly. You're normally a good judge of character."

That backhanded compliment was the first one he'd ever given me.

Our kitchen was filled with the delicious smells of Christmas Eve dinner. Chris had arrived with the first course, lobster stew, in a big pot that simmered on the stove. Livvie had covered flaky, white codfish with breadcrumbs and readied it for the oven. Page and I moved back and forth from the kitchen to the dining room, setting the table, putting out the candlesticks, and placing Mom's new Christmas centerpieces on the table.

"How did you know?" I asked Livvie when we were alone in the kitchen.

"Know what?"

"That Imogen was a bad person." I was embarrassed by how easily Imogen had manipulated me into doing so many things that were uncharacteristic, including inviting her home for Christmas.

"I didn't see that she was manipulating you, but I could tell she was doing it to Mom. Honestly, Julia, do you think it would ever be our mother's idea to decorate the house without us? Or to initiate the cookie baking? I saw a version of Mom I didn't recognize. I asked myself, why? What's different this Christmas? There was only one answer."

"Why didn't I see it?" I had seen Imogen as young, spoiled, even bratty, but I hadn't imagined she would conspire to murder anyone, much less a nice man she barely knew.

My sister gave me a hug, an act not easily accomplished around her belly. "Because you are a good person, Julia. You don't expect to be lied to, or cheated, or deceived by the people you come in contact with. I hope you always stay that way."

I hugged her back. I wasn't as naïve as she seemed to think I was. My job in venture capital had involved thoroughly vetting the entrepreneurs my firm considered investing in. Most were completely legit, but once in a while our research unearthed someone who was a total fraud. But I did try to give people the benefit of the doubt. I was glad my sister could see that.

Everyone gathered at the table: Mom at the head, then me and Chris, Livvie, Sonny, and Page, whose enthusiasm for the holiday no longer seemed like pretense. Our friends and honorary great-aunts, the Snugg sisters, came from their bed and breakfast across the street with a salad of spinach, goat cheese, and pears. As soon as he got off his shift, Jamie arrived bearing four bottles of wine. Gus and Mrs. Gus entered with her famous pies, apple, mince, and pumpkin, for the holiday.

The conversation was lively, the food delicious. I felt so grateful to be there, with the man I loved, the family I loved, the friends and neighbors I loved. And who loved me in return.

When the meal was done, we sat groaning, the last flakes of pie crust on our dessert plates.

"This was the best meal ever," Page sighed. "The only thing missing is, can we make some eggnog?"

"No!" everyone shouted at once.

But Mom smiled. "Maybe next year."

RECIPES

HAZELNUT WREATHS

In Nogged Off, *I attribute both recipes included here to Julia and Livvie's Grandma Snowden, someone we haven't yet seen in the Maine Clambake Mystery series, though I am sure her story will be told at some point. In reality, these recipes are from one of my most precious possessions, a handwritten book of recipes given to me by my grandmother before she died. She made these cookies, as did my mother, and as have I for more than thirty years — on a "cookie day" much like the one described in the story.*

Ingredients
1/2 pound butter, softened
1 cup sugar
2 eggs
2 1/2 cups flour
4 ounces chopped hazelnuts

Directions

Cream butter and sugar and set aside.

Beat the eggs well.

Add flour, nuts, and the creamed butter and sugar to the eggs and mix until blended. (I use a food processor for this.)

Form the dough into flat circles about the size of a saucer. You will get four to six of these.

Wrap well in wax paper and place in the refrigerator for four hours or overnight.

Remove one dough circle from the refrigerator and roll it out flat on a floured surface.

Cut into rings, using a cookie or doughnut cutter. Place rings on a parchment-covered cookie sheet.

When you have cut as many rings as you can, reroll the remaining dough and cut again until you have used all the dough. Then remove the next batch from the refrigerator and repeat.

Prior to baking, decorate as you wish. We use candied pineapple to form little bows on the wreaths with a red center and green at either side. However you choose to decorate, do it lightly. The flavor of the cookie is delicate and you don't want to overwhelm it.

Bake at 350 degrees for ten to twelve

minutes. The cookies should be lightly brown.

Pecan Puffs

The key to these delicious cookies is the dough is not all that sweet. It's the confectioners' sugar they are rolled in at the end that adds the sweetness.

Ingredients

2 cups pecans, broken
1/2 pound butter, softened
4 tablespoons granulated white sugar
2 cups flour
2 teaspoons vanilla
2 cups confectioners' sugar

Directions

Put the pecans in a food processor to break them up. Leave some pieces. Do not turn them all to dust.

Add the rest of the ingredients and mix until blended.

Put the dough in a bowl, cover it with plastic wrap, and place it in the refrigerator for one to two hours.

The dough will be stiff. Roll it into small balls (smaller than a walnut) and place on parchment paper on a cookie sheet.

Bake at 350 degrees for thirty to forty minutes. The bottoms will be light brown.

Take pecan puffs off the cookie sheets as soon as you can touch them and roll them in the confectioners' sugar. Place them on a cloth-covered surface to cool.

Dear Readers,

I hope you enjoyed "Nogged Off," the latest installment in the Maine Clambake Mystery series. I loved incorporating the traditions of my own little town on the Maine coast, where there really is a Men's Night and a Saturday morning when everyone shops in their pajamas. I also enjoyed writing about the rituals of the Snowden's Christmas cookie baking, which I took entirely from my own family. I am sorry to tell you that on cookie day, I normally occupy the dictatorial role of Livvie, though she is thwarted in this story.

If this is your first time meeting Julia Snowden, she made her debut in *Clammed Up*, when she answers a panicked call from her sister, Livvie, to return to Busman's Harbor, Maine, to save her family's failing clambake business. Her plans are nearly derailed when the best man at a wedding, the first event of the season, is found hanging from the grand staircase in the deserted mansion on the island where the clambakes are held.

Boiled Over takes place at the height of the summer season, when a foot rolls out of the clambake fire. Julia's newest employee is the primary suspect, but convinced of his innocence, Julia searches for the truth. *Mus-*

seled Out brings us to the fall when the Snowden Family Clambake is shutting down for the year. Will Julia return to her job in Manhattan, or stay in Busman's Harbor with the man she loves? The decision is complicated when a competitor is found drowned, trapped in the lines under a lobster boat, and Julia's brother-in-law, Sonny, becomes the focus of the police investigation. *Fogged Inn* takes place in the week after Thanksgiving. As Julia tries to build a life in Busman's Harbor, she discovers the corpse of a stranger in her landlord's walk-in refrigerator. Who is this stranger, and how is he tied to a mysterious group of diners who ate in the restaurant the night before?

That brings us to "Nogged Off." Julia's cutting ties to her old life and cleaning out her New York apartment, and . . . well, now you know how that goes. The next book in the series is *Iced Under,* coming in January 2017. In it, we learn how Julia's mother's family made their money, how they lost it, and how it all ties to a mysterious package Julia's mom receives on a snowy winter day.

I love writing about Julia, the Snowden family, their friends and neighbors, and the deep traditions and wonderful eccentricities of coastal Mainers (along with the occasional murder). I am always thrilled to hear from

480

readers. You can write to me at barbaraross@
maineclambakemysteries.com or find me via
my Web site at www.maineclambakemysteries
.com, or on Facebook at www.facebook.com/
barbaraannross, on Twitter @barbross, or
on Pinterest at www.pinterest.com/
barbaraannross.

If you read "Nogged Off" during the holidays,
I hope it contributed in some little way to your
enjoyment of the season. And if you read it at
any other time, I hope it transported you to
the warm glow of that time of year. I would
wish for you a plate of delicious cookies and
a nice cup of eggnog, but given the stories in
this volume, maybe you want to skip the eggnog.